U0454049

美国经典文学作品选读

主　编：姜晓瑜　　陈红锐　　邓纯旭

副主编：董妍妍　　赵子然　　宋　茜　　于　菲

知识产权出版社

全国百佳图书出版单位

图书在版编目（CIP）数据

美国经典文学作品选读/姜晓瑜,陈红锐,邓纯旭主编.—北京：
知识产权出版社，2019.5

ISBN 978 - 7 - 5130 - 3796 - 9

Ⅰ.①美… Ⅱ.①姜…②陈…③邓… Ⅲ.①文学—作品综合集—
美国—高等学校—教材 Ⅳ.①I712.11

中国版本图书馆 CIP 数据核字（2015）第 223821 号

内容提要

本教材是专门为在校大学生学习美国文学而编写的。教材内容贯穿整个美国文学
史，结集了美国文学史上重要作家的作品，再现了美国文学的多元性，读者可以了解
这些作家的社会背景、文学流派以及作品特点，在领略作家文学魅力的同时，也能够
关注作家的人格特征。本教材不仅可以作为美国文学普通学习者的培训教材，也可以
供英美文学专业的学生学习使用。

责任编辑：兰　涛　　　　　　　　责任校对：谷　洋
装帧设计：邵建文　　　　　　　　责任印制：刘译文

美国经典文学作品选读

主　　编：姜晓瑜　陈红锐　邓纯旭
副主编：董妍妍　赵子然　宋　茜　于　菲

出版发行：知识产权出版社有限责任公司	网　　址：http://www.ipph.cn		
社　　址：北京市海淀区气象路 50 号院	邮　　编：100081		
责编电话：010 - 82000860 转 8325	责编邮箱：lantao@cinpr.com		
发行电话：010 - 82000860 转 8101/8102	发行传真：010 - 82000893/82005070/82000270		
印　　刷：北京九州迅驰传媒文化有限公司	经　　销：各大网上书店、新华书店及相关专业书店		
开　　本：787mm×1092mm　1/16	印　　张：22.5		
版　　次：2019 年 5 月第 1 版	印　　次：2019 年 5 月第 1 次印刷		
字　　数：289 千字	定　　价：78.00 元		

ISBN 978-7-5130-3796-9

出版权专有　侵权必究

如有印装质量问题，本社负责调换。

American literature mainly refers to the literature produced by people living in the United States. During its early history, America was a series of British colonies on the eastern coast of the present-day United States. Therefore, its literary tradition begins as linked to the broader tradition of English literature. However, unique American characteristics and the breadth of its production usually now cause it to be considered a separate path and tradition.

The New England colonies were the center of early American literature. The revolutionary period contained political writings by Samuel Adams, Benjamin Franklin and Thomas Paine. In the post-war period, Thomas Jefferson's *United States Declaration of Independence* solidified his status as a key American writer. It was in the late 18th and early 19th centuries that the nation's first novels were published. With the War of 1812 and an increasing desire to produce uniquely American literature and culture, a number of key new literary figures emerged, perhaps most prominently Washington Irving and Edgar Allan Poe. In 1836, Ralph Waldo Emerson (1803 – 1882) started a movement known as Transcendentalism. Henry David Thoreau (1817 – 1862) wrote *Walden*, which urges resistance to the dictates of organized society. The political conflict surrounding abolitionism inspired the writings of William Lloyd Garrison and Harriet Beecher Stowe in her world-famous *Uncle Tom's Cabin*. These efforts were supported by the continuation of the slave narrative autobiography, of which the best known example from this period was

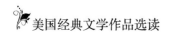

Frederick Douglass's Narrative of the Life of Frederick Douglass, an American Slave.

Nathaniel Hawthorne (1804 – 1864) is notable for his masterpiece *The Scarlet Letter*——a novel about adultery. Hawthorne influenced Herman Melville (1819 – 1891) who is notable for the books *Moby-Dick and Billy Budd*. America's two greatest 19th century poets were Walt Whitman (1819 – 1892) and Emily Dickinson (1830 – 1886). American poetry reached its peak in the early-to-mid-20th century, with such noted writers as Wallace Stevens, T. S. Eliot, Robert Frost, Ezra Pound, and E. E. Cummings. Mark Twain (the pen name used by Samuel Langhorne Clemens, 1835 – 1910) was the first major American writer to be born away from the East Coast. Henry James (1843 – 1916) was notable for novels like *The Turn of the Screw*. At the beginning of the 20th century, American novelists included Edith Wharton (1862 – 1937), Stephen Crane (1871 – 1900), and Theodore Dreiser (1871 – 1945). Experimentation in style and form is seen in the works of Gertrude Stein (1874 – 1946).

American writers expressed disillusionment following WWI. The stories and novels of F. Scott Fitzgerald (1896 – 1940) capture the mood of the 1920s, and John Dos Passos wrote about the war. Ernest Hemingway (1899 – 1961) became notable for *The Sun Also Rises* and *A Farewell to Arms*; in 1954, he won the Nobel Prize in Literature. William Faulkner (1897 – 1962) is notable for novels like *The Sound and the Fury*. American drama attained international status only in the 1920s and 1930s, with the works of *Eugene O'Neill*, who won four Pulitzer Prizes and the Nobel Prize. In the middle of the 20th century, American drama was dominated by the work of playwrights Tennessee Williams and Arthur Miller, as well as by the maturation of the American musical.

Depression era writers included John Steinbeck (1902 – 1968), notable for his novel *The Grapes of Wrath*. Henry Miller assumed a unique place in American Literature in the 1930s when his semi-autobiographical novels were banned from the US. From the end of World War II up until, roughly, the late 1960s and early 1970s saw the publication of some of the most popular works in American history such as *To Kill a Mockingbird* by Harper Lee. America's involvement in World War II influenced the creation of works such as Norman Mailer's *The Naked and the Dead* (1948), Joseph Heller's *Catch-22* (1961) and Kurt Vonnegut Jr.'s *Slaughterhouse-Five* (1969). John Updike was notable for his novel *Rabbit, Run* (1960). Philip Roth explores Jewish identity in American society. From the early 1970s to the present day the most important literary movement has been postmodernism and the flowering of literature by ethnic minority writers.

This book, with vivid illustration of pictures and detailed explanation and Chinese version presents you the best works of American literature and will help you have a profound understanding of the classics. I hope that this book will be helpful for your English learning.

Jiang Xiaoyu

June 2015

CONTENTS >>

I

Unit 1
Benjamin Franklin(1706 – 1790)

🌿 Bibliography

Benjamin Franklin (1706 – 1790) was one of the Founding Fathers of the United States and in many ways was "the First American". A renowned polymath, Franklin was a leading author, printer, political theorist, politician, postmaster, scientist, inventor, civic activist, statesman, and diplomat. As a scientist, he was a major figure in the American Enlightenment and the history of physics for his discoveries and theories regarding electricity. As an inventor, he is known for the lightning rod, bifocals, and the Franklin stove, among other inventions. He facilitated many civic organizations, including Philadelphia's fire department and a university.

Franklin earned the title of "The First American" for his early and indefatigable campaigning for colonial unity; as an author and spokesman in London for several colonies, then as the first United States Ambassador to France, he exemplified the emerging American nation. Franklin was foundational in defining the American ethos as a marriage of the practical values of thrift, hard work, education, community spirit, self-governing institutions, and opposition to authoritarianism both political and religious, with the scientific and tolerant values of the Enlightenment. In the words of historian Henry Steele Commager, "In a Franklin could be merged the virtues of Puritanism without its defects, the illumination of the Enlightenment without its heat. " To Walter Isaacson, this makes Franklin "the most accomplished American of his age and the most influential in inventing the type of society America would become. "

Franklin, always proud of his working class roots, became a successful newspaper editor and printer in Philadelphia, the leading city in the colonies. With two partners he published *the Pennsylvania Chronicle*, a newspaper that was known for its revolutionary sentiments and criticisms of the British policies. He became wealthy publishing *Poor Richard's Almanack* and *The Pennsylvania Gazette*. Franklin was also the printer of books for *the Moravians of Bethlehem*, *Pennsylvania* (1742 on). Franklin's printed Moravian books are preserved, and can be viewed, at the Moravian Archives located in Bethlehem. Franklin visited Bethlehem many times and stayed at the Moravian Sun Inn.

He played a major role in establishing the University of Pennsylvania and was elected the first president of the American Philosophical Society. Franklin became a national hero in America when as agent for several colonies he spearheaded the effort to have Parliament in London repeal the unpopular Stamp Act. An accomplished diplomat, he was widely admired among the French as American minister to Paris and was a major figure in the development of positive Franco-American relations. His efforts to secure support for the American Revolution by shipments of crucial munitions proved vital for the American war effort.

For many years he was the British postmaster for the colonies, which enabled him to set up the first national communications network. He was active in community affairs, colonial and state politics, as well as national and international affairs. From 1785 to 1788, he served as governor of Pennsylvania. Toward the end of his life, he freed his own slaves and became one of the most prominent abolitionists.

His colorful life and legacy of scientific and political achievement, and status as one of America's the most influential Founding Fathers, have seen Franklin honored on coinage and the MYM100 bill; warships; the names of many towns; counties; educational institutions; corporations; and, more than two centuries after his death, countless cultural references.

🎋 *Autobiography*

The Autobiography of Benjamin Franklin is the traditional name for the unfinished record of his own life written by Benjamin Franklin from 1771 to 1790; however, Franklin himself appears to have called the work his Memoirs. Although it had a tortuous publication history after Franklin's death, this work has become one of the most famous and influential examples of an autobiography ever written.

Franklin's account of his life is divided into four parts, reflecting the different periods at which he wrote them. There are actual breaks in the narrative between the first three parts, but Part Three's narrative continues into Part Four without an authorial break (only an editorial one).

Characters in the *Autobiography*

1. Benjamin Franklin—The author and protagonist of the Autobiography; The Autobiography tells of the major events of his life and many of his important scientific and political ideas, but the work does not discuss the American Revolution, in which Franklin was a major participant.

2. William Franklin—Benjamin's son and royal governor of New Jersey in 1771 when Ben begins writing the work. Ben begins the Autobiography as a letter to William with the intent of telling him about his life.

3. James Franklin—Franklin's elder brother who owns a printing house in Boston. Ben is apprenticed to James when Ben is 12, and while

3

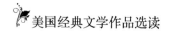

they do not always get along very well, Ben learns much from James and proves to be quite helpful. When James is arrested for holding subversive political ideas, Ben takes over the paper until James' release. When Ben breaks his contract and leaves for Philadelphia, James grows angry and spiteful.

4. Andrew Bradford—A printer in Philadelphia, he is unable to hire Franklin but he does allow Franklin to stay in his house. Later on, when Franklin runs his own paper, the two are competitors until Bradford leaves the printing industry.

5 Samuel Keimer—The printer in Philadelphia for whom Franklin works. Their relationship deteriorates over time, and eventually they have a falling out. Keimer, however, tries to make amends when he realizes that Ben can supply him with important printing tools.

6. John Read—A resident of Philadelphia, he houses Franklin shortly after Franklin arrives in Philadelphia.

7. Deborah Read—The daughter of John Read, she eventually marries Franklin even though their courtship is interrupted by his 18-month trip to England, during which time she marries another man who disappears thus allowing her marriage to Franklin.

Summary

Part One

Part One of the Autobiography is addressed to Franklin's son William, at that time (1771) Royal Governor of New Jersey. While in England at the estate of the Bishop of St. Asaph in Twyford, Franklin, now 65 years old, begins by saying that it may be agreeable to his son to know some of the incidents of his father's life; so with a week's uninterrupted leisure, he is beginning to write them down for William. He starts with some anecdotes of his grandfather, uncles, father and mother. He deals with his childhood, his fondness for reading, and his service as an apprentice to his brother James Franklin, a Boston printer and the publisher of the New England Courant. After improving his writing skills through study of the Spectator by Joseph Addison and Sir Richard Steele, he writes an anonymous paper and slips it under the door of the printing house by night.

Part Two

The second part begins with two letters Franklin received in the early 1780s while in Paris, encouraging him to continue the Autobiography, of which both correspondents have read Part One. (Although Franklin does not say so, there had been a breach with his son William after the writing of Part One, since the father had sided with the Revolutionaries and the son had remained loyal to the British Crown.)

At Passy, a suburb of Paris, Franklin begins Part Two in 1784, giving a more detailed account of his public library plan. He then discusses his "bold and arduous Project of arriving at moral Perfection", listing thirteen virtues he wishes to perfect in himself. He creates a book with columns for each day of the week, in which he marks with black spots his offenses against each virtue. Of these virtues, he notices that Order is the hardest for him to keep. He eventually realizes that perfection is not to be attained, but feels himself better and happier because of his attempt.

Part Three

Beginning in August 1788 when Franklin had returned to Philadelphia, the author says he will not be able to utilize his papers as much as he had expected, since many were lost in the recent Revolutionary War. He has, however, found and quotes a couple of his writings from the 1730s that survived. One is the "Substance of an intended Creed" consisting of what he then considered to be the "essentials" of all religions. He had intended this as a basis for a projected sect but, Franklin says, did not pursue the project.

In 1732, Franklin first publishes his Poor Richard's Almanac, which becomes very successful. He also continues his profitable newspaper. In 1734, a preacher named Rev. Samuel Hemphill arrives from County Tyrone Ireland; Franklin supports him and writes pamphlets on his behalf. However, someone finds out that Hemphill has been plagia-rizing portions of his sermons from others, although Franklin rationalizes this by saying he would rather hear good sermons taken from others than poor sermons of the man's own composition.

Franklin studies languages, reconciles with his brother James, and loses a four-year-old son to smallpox. Franklin's club, the Junto, grows and breaks up into subordinate clubs. Franklin becomes Clerk of the General Assembly in 1736, and the following year becomes Comptroller to the Postmaster General, which makes it easier to get reports and fulfill subscriptions for his newspaper. He proposes improvements to the city's watch and fire prevention regulations.

In 1740 he invents the Franklin stove, refusing a patent on the de-vice because it was for "the good of the people". He proposes an acade-my, which opens after money is raised by subscription for it and it ex-pands so much that a new building has to be constructed for it. Franklin obtains other governmental positions (city councilman, alderman, bur-gess, justice of the peace) and helps negotiate a treaty with the Indians. After helping Dr. Thomas Bond establish a hospital, he helps pave the streets of Philadelphia and draws up a proposal for Dr. John Fothergill about doing the same in London. In 1753 Franklin becomes Deputy Postmaster General.

The next year, as war with the French is expected, representatives of the several colonies, including Franklin, meet with the Indians to dis-cuss defense; Franklin at this time draws up a proposal for the union of the colonies, but it is not adopted. General Braddock arrives with two regiments, and Franklin helps him secure wagons and horses, but the general refuses to take Ben's warning about danger from hostile Indians during Braddock's planned march to Frontenac (now Kingston, Ontario). When Braddock's troops are subsequently attacked, the general is mor-tally wounded and his forces abandon their supplies and flee.

A militia is formed on the basis of a proposal by Benjamin Frank-lin, and the governor asks him to take command of the northwestern frontier. With his son as aide de camp, Franklin heads for Gnadenhut, raising men for the militia and building forts. Returning to Philadelphia, he is chosen colonel of the regiment; his officers honor him by personally escorting him out of town. This attention offends the proprietor of the colony (Thomas Penn, son of William Penn) when someone writes an account of it in a letter to him, whereupon the proprietor complains to the government in England about Franklin.

Now the Autobiography discusses "the Rise and Progress of [Franklin's] Philosophical Reputation". He starts experiments with electricity and writes letters about them that are published in England as a book. Franklin's description of his experiments is translated into French, and Abbé Nollet, who is offended because this work calls into question his own theory of electricity, publishes his own book of letters attacking Franklin. Declining to respond on the grounds that anyone could duplicate and thus verify his experiments, Franklin sees another French author refute Nollet, and as Franklin's book is translated into other languages, its views are gradually accepted and Nollet's are discarded. Franklin is also voted an honorary member of the Royal Society.

Part Four

Written sometime between November 1789 and Franklin's death on April 17, 1790, this section is very brief. After Franklin and his son arrive in London, the former is counselled by Dr. Fothergill on the best way to advocate his cause on behalf of the colonies. Franklin visits Lord Granville, president of the King's Privy Council, who asserts that the king is the legislator of the colonies. Franklin then meets the proprietaries (the switch to the plural is Franklin's, so apparently others besides Thomas Penn are involved). But the respective sides are far from any kind of agreement. The proprietaries ask Franklin to write a summary of the colonists' complaints; when he does so, their solicitor for reasons of personal enmity delays a response. Over a year later, the proprietaries finally respond to the assembly, regarding the summary to be a "flimsy Justification of their Conduct". During this delay the assembly has pre-

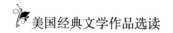

vailed on the governor to pass a taxation act, and Franklin defends the act in English court so that it can receive royal assent. While the assembly thanks Franklin, the proprietaries, enraged at the governor, turn him out and threaten legal action against him; in the last sentence, Franklin tells us the governor "despised the Threats, and they were never put in Execution".

Comments on *Autobiography*

It is regarded as one of the most important works of American literature produced during the 18th century. It is a record of a man rising to wealth and fame from a state of poverty and obscurity, an account of the colorful career of America's first self-made man. It is perhaps the first real post-revolutionary American writing as well as the first real autobiography in English. First of all, it is a puritan document. The most famous section describes his scientific scheme of self-examination and self-improvement.

Its style shows the pattern of Puritan simplicity, directness, and concision. The narrative is lucid, the structure is simple, the imagery is homely. It is an exemplary illustration of the American style of writing.

"Firsts" associated with the Autobiography

1. It is considered the first popular self-help book ever published.

2. It was the first and only work written in American before the 19th century that has retained bestseller popularity since its release.

3. It was the first major secular American autobiography.

4. It is also the first real account of the American Dream in action as told from a man who experienced it firsthand.

Introduction to Part One

The Autobiography opens with a salutation to Ben Franklin's son, William Franklin who at the time was the royal governor of New Jersey. Franklin is writing in the summer of 1771 on vacation in a small town about 50 miles south of London. Franklin says that because his son may wish to know about his life, he is taking his one week's vacation in the English countryside to record his past. Franklin says that he has enjoyed his life and would like to repeat it, although he would like to correct some small errors if the opportunity arose. But since Franklin cannot repeat life, he can instead recollect it. He thanks God for allowing him to live a good life. Ben, at the age of 12, signed a contract to work for James for the next eight years.

From   *Autobiography*
Part One

I have ever had pleasure in obtaining any little anecdotes of my ancestors. You may remember the inquiries I made among the remains of my relations when you were with me in England, and the journey I undertook for that purpose. Imagining it may be equally agreeable to you to know the circumstances of my life, many of which you are yet unacquainted with, and expecting the enjoyment of a week's uninterrupted leisure in my present country retirement, I sit down to write them for you. To which I have besides some other inducements[1]. Having emerged from the poverty and obscurity in which I was born and bred, to a state of affluence and some degree of reputation in the world, and having gone so far through life with a considerable share of felicity[2], the conducing means I made use of, which with the blessing of God so well succeeded, my posterity[3] may like to know, as they may find some of them suitable to their own situations, and therefore fit to be imitated.

That felicity, when I reflected on it, has induced me sometimes to say, that were it offered to my choice, I should have no objection to a repetition of the same life from its beginning, only asking the advantages authors have in a second edition to correct some faults of the first. So I might, besides correcting the faults, change some sinister accidents and events of it for others more favorable. But though this was denied, I should still accept the offer. Since such a repetition is not to be expected, the next thing most like living one's life over again seems to be a recollection of that life, and to make that recollection as durable as possible by putting it down in writing. Hereby, too, I shall indulge the inclination so natural in old men, to be talking of themselves and their own past actions; and I shall indulge it without being tiresome to others, who, through respect to age, might conceive themselves obliged to give me a hearing, since this may be read or not as any one pleases. And, lastly (I may as well confess it, since my denial of it will be believed by nobody), perhaps I shall a good deal gratify my own vanity. Indeed, I scarce ever heard or saw the introductory words, "Without vanity I may say," but some vain thing immediately followed. Most people dislike vanity in others, whatever share they have of it themselves; but I give it fair quarter wherever I meet with it, being persuaded that it is often productive of good to the possessor, and to others that are within his sphere of action; and therefore, in many cases, it would not be altogether absurd if a man were to thank God for his vanity among the other comforts of life.

And now I speak of thanking God, I desire with all humility to acknowledge that I owe the mentioned happiness of my past life to His kind providence, which lead me to the means I used and gave them success. My belief of this induces me to hope, though I must not presume, that the same goodness will still be exercised toward me, in continuing that happiness, or enabling me to bear a fatal reverse, which I may experience as others have done: the complexion of my future fortune being known to Him only in whose power it is to bless to us even our afflictions[4].

The notes one of my uncles (who had the same kind of curiosity in collecting family anecdotes) once put into my hands, furnished me with several particulars relating to our ancestors. From these notes I learned that the family had lived in the same village, Ecton, in Northamptonshire, for three hundred years, and how much longer he knew not (perhaps from the time when the name of Franklin, that before was the name of an order of people, was assumed by them as a surname when others took surnames all over the kingdom), on a freehold of about thirty acres, aided by the smith's business, which had continued in the family till his time, the eldest son being always bred to that business; a custom which he and my father followed as to their eldest sons. When I searched the registers at Ecton, I found an account of their births, marriages and burials from the year 1555 only, there being no registers kept in that parish[5] at any time preceding. By that register I perceived that I was the youngest son of the youngest son for five generations back. My grandfather Thomas, who was born in 1598, lived at Ecton till he grew too old to follow business longer, when he went to live with his son John, a dyer at Banbury, in Oxfordshire, with whom my father served an apprenticeship. There my grandfather died and lies buried. We saw his gravestone in 1758. His eldest son Thomas lived in the house at Ecton, and left it with the land to his only child, a daughter, who, with her husband, one Fisher, of Wellingborough, sold it to Mr. Isted, now lord of the manor there. My grandfather had four sons that grew up, viz. : Thomas, John, Benjamin and Josiah. I will give you what account I can of them, at this distance from my papers, and if these are not lost in my absence, you will among them find many more particulars.

Thomas was bred a smith under his father; but, being ingenious, and encouraged in learning (as all my brothers were) by an Esquire Palmer, then the principal gentleman in that parish, he qualified himself for the business of scrivener[6]; became a considerable man in the county; was a chief mover of all public-spirited undertakings for the county or town of Northampton shire, and his own village, of which many instances were related of him; and much taken notice of and patronized by the then Lord Halifax. He died in 1702, January 6, old style, just four years to a day before I was born. The account we received of his life and character from some old people at Ecton, I remember, struck you as something extraordinary, from its similarity to what you knew of mine. "Had he died on the same day," you said, "one might have supposed a transmigration. "

John was bred a dyer, I believe of woolens. Benjamin was bred a silk dyer, serving an apprenticeship at London. He was an ingenious man. I remember him well, for when I was a boy he came over to my father in Boston, and lived in the house with us some years. He lived to a great age. His grandson, Samuel Franklin, now lives in Boston. He left behind him two quarto volumes, MS., of his own poetry, consisting of little occasional pieces addressed to his friends and relations, of which the following, sent to me, is a specimen. He had formed a short-hand of his own, which he taught me, but, never practising it, I have now forgot it. I was named after this uncle, there being a particular affection between him and my father. He was very pious, a great attender of sermons of the best preachers, which he took down in his short-hand, and had with him many volumes of them. He was also much of a politician; too much, perhaps, for his station. There fell lately into my hands, in London, a collection he had made of all the principal pamphlets, relating to public affairs, from 1641 to 1717; many of the volumes are wanting as appears by the numbering, but there still remain eight volumes in folio, and twenty-four in quarto and in octavo[7]. A dealer in old books met with them, and knowing me by my sometimes buying of him, he brought them to me. It seems my uncle must have left them here, when he went to America, which was about fifty years since. There are many of his notes in the margins. But the poetry is not given. Mr. Sparks informs us that these volumes had been preserved, and were in possession of Mrs. Emmons, of Boston, great-granddaughter of their author.

This obscure family of ours was early in the Reformation, and continued Protestants through the reign of Queen Mary, when they were sometimes in danger of trouble on account of their zeal against popery. They had got an English Bible, and to conceal and secure it, it was fastened open with tapes under and within the cover of a joint-stool. When my great-great-grandfather read it to his family, he turned up the joint-stool upon his knees, turning over the leaves then under the tapes. One of the children stood at the door to give notice if he saw the apparitor coming, who was an officer of the spiritual court. In that case the stool was turned down again upon its feet, when the Bible remained concealed under it as before. This anecdote I had from my uncle Benjamin. The family continued all of the Church of England till about the end of Charles the Second's reign, when some of the ministers that had been outed for nonconformity holding conventicles in Northamptonshire, Benjamin and Josiah adhered to them, and so continued all their lives: the rest of the family remained with the Episcopal Church.

Josiah, my father, married young, and carried his wife with three children into New England, about 1682. The conventicles having been forbidden by law, and frequently disturbed, induced some considerable men of his acquaintance to remove to that country, and he was prevailed with to accompany them thither, where they expected to enjoy their mode of religion with freedom. By the same wife he had four children more born there, and by a second wife ten more, in all seventeen; of which I remember thirteen sitting at one time at his table, who all grew up to be men and women, and married; I was the youngest son, and the youngest child but two, and was born in Boston, New England. My mother, the second wife, was Abiah Folger, daughter of Peter Folger, one of the first settlers of New England, of whom honorable mention is made by Cotton Mather in his church history of that country, entitled Magnalia Christi Americana, as "a godly, learned Englishman", if I remember the words rightly. I have heard that he wrote sundry small occasional pieces, but only one of them was printed, which I saw now many years since. It was written in 1675, in the home-spun verse of that time and people, and addressed to those then concerned in the government there. It was in favor of liberty of conscience, and on behalf of the Baptists, Quakers, and other sectaries that had been under persecution, ascribing the Indian wars, and other distresses that had befallen the country, to that persecution, as so many judgments of God to punish so heinous an offense, and exhorting a repeal of those uncharitable laws. The whole appeared to me as written with a good deal of decent plainness and manly freedom. The six concluding lines I remember, though I have forgotten the two first of the stanza; but the purport of them was, that his censures proceeded from good-will, and, therefore, he would be known to be the author. "Because to be a libeller (says he) I hate it with my heart; From Sherburne town, where now I dwell My name I do put here; Without offense your real friend, It is Peter Folgier."

My elder brothers were all put apprentices to different trades. I was put to the grammar-school at eight years of age, my father intending to devote me, as the tithe of his sons, to the service of the Church. My early readiness in learning to read (which must have been very early, as I do not remember when I could not read), and the opinion of all his friends, that I should certainly make a good scholar, encouraged him in this purpose of his. My uncle Benjamin, too, approved of it, and proposed to give me all his short-hand volumes of sermons, I suppose as a stock to set up with, if I would learn his character. I continued, however, at the grammar-school not quite one year, though in that time I had risen gradually from the middle of the class of that year to be the head of it, and farther was removed into the next class above it, in order to go with that into the third at the end of the year. But my father, in the meantime, from a view of the expense of a college education, which having so large a family he could not well afford, and the mean living many so educated were afterwards able to obtain-reasons that be gave to his friends in my hearing—altered his first intention, took me from the grammar-school, and sent me to a school for writing and arithmetic, kept by a then famous man, Mr. George Brownell, very successful in his profession generally, and that by mild, encouraging methods. Under him I acquired fair writing pretty soon, but I failed in the arithmetic, and made no progress in it. At ten years old I was taken home to assist my father in his business, which was that of a tallow-chandler and sope-boiler; a business he was not bred to, but had assumed on his arrival in New England, and on finding his dying trade would not maintain his family, being in little request. Accordingly, I was employed in cutting wick for the candles, filling the dipping mold and the molds for cast candles, attending the shop, going of errands[8], etc. I disliked the trade, and had a strong inclination for the sea, but my father declared against it; however, living near the water, I was much in and about it, learnt early to swim well, and to manage boats; and when in a boat or canoe with other boys, I was commonly allowed to govern, especially in any case of difficulty; and upon other occasions I was generally a leader among the boys, and sometimes led them into scrapes, of which I will mention one instance, as it shows an early projecting public spirit, tho' not then justly conducted.

There was a salt-marsh that bounded part of the mill-pond, on the edge of which, at high water, we used to stand to fish for minnows. By much trampling, we had made it a mere quagmire[9]. My proposal was to build a wharf there fit for us to stand upon, and I showed my comrades a large heap of stones, which were intended for a new house near the marsh, and which would very well suit our purpose. Accordingly, in the evening, when the workmen were gone, I assembled a number of my play-fellows, and working with them diligently like so many emmets, sometimes two or three to a stone, we brought them all away and built our little wharf. The next morning the workmen were surprised at missing the stones, which were found in our wharf. Inquiry was made after the removers; we were discovered and complained of; several of us were corrected by our fathers; and though I pleaded the usefulness of the work, mine convinced me that nothing was useful which was not honest.

I think you may like to know something of his person and character. He had an excellent constitution of body, was of middle stature, but well set, and very strong; he was ingenious, could draw prettily, was skilled a little in music, and had a clear pleasing voice, so that when he played psalm tunes on his violin and sung withal, as he sometimes did in an evening after the business of the day was over, it was extremely agreeable to hear. He had a mechanical genius too, and, on occasion, was very handy in the use of other tradesmen's tools; but his great excellence lay in a sound understanding and solid judgment in prudential matters, both in private and public affairs. In the latter, indeed, he was never employed, the numerous family he had to educate and the straitness of his circumstances keeping him close to his trade; but I remember well his being frequently visited by leading people, who consulted him for his opinion in affairs of the town or of the church he belonged to, and showed a good deal of respect for his judgment and advice: he was also much consulted by private persons about their affairs when any difficulty occurred, and frequently chosen an arbitrator between contending parties. At his table he liked to have, as often as he could, some sensible friend or neighbor to converse with, and always took care to start some ingenious or useful topic for discourse, which might tend to improve the minds of his children. By this means he turned our attention to what was good, just, and prudent in the conduct of life; and little or no notice was ever taken of what related to the victuals on the table, whether it was well or ill dressed, in or out of season, of good or bad flavor, preferable or inferior to this or that other thing of the kind, so that I was brot up in such a perfect inattention to those matters as to be quite indifferent what kind of food was set before me, and so unobservant of it, that to this day if I am asked I can scarce tell a few hours after dinner what I dined upon. This has been a convenience to me in travelling, where my companions have been sometimes very unhappy for want of a suitable gratification of their more delicate, because better instructed, tastes and appetites.

My mother had likewise an excellent constitution: she suckled all her ten children. I never knew either my father or mother to have any sickness but that of which they died, he at 89, and she at 85 years of age. They lie buried together at Boston, where I some years since placed a marble over their grave, with this inscription:

JOSIAH FRANKLIN, and ABIAH his Wife, lie here interred. They lived lovingly together in wedlock fifty-five years. Without an estate, or any gainful employment, By constant labor and industry, with

God's blessing, They maintained a large family comfortably, and brought up thirteen children and seven grandchildren reputably. From this instance, reader, Be encouraged to diligence in thy calling, And distrust not Providence. He was a pious and prudent man; She, a discreet and virtuous woman.

Their youngest son, In filial regard to their memory, Places this stone.

J. F. born 1655, died 1744, — 89. A. F. born 1667, died 1752,—85.

By my rambling[10] digressions I perceive myself to be grown old. I used to write more methodically. But one does not dress for private company as for a public ball. Tis perhaps only negligence.

To return: I continued thus employed in my father's business for two years, that is, till I was twelve years old; and my brother John, who was bred to that business, having left my father, married, and set up for himself at Rhode Island, there was all appearance that I was destined to supply his place, and become a tallow-chandler. But my dislike to the trade continuing, my father was under apprehensions that if he did not find one for me more agreeable, I should break away and get to sea, as his son Josiah had done, to his great vexation. He therefore sometimes took me to walk with him, and see joiners, bricklayers, turners, braziers, etc. , at their work, that he might observe my inclination, and endeavor to fix it on some trade or other on land. It has ever since been a pleasure to me to see good workmen handle their tools; and it has been useful to me, having learnt so much by it as to be able to do little jobs myself in my house when a workman could not readily be got, and to construct little machines for my experiments, while the intention of making the experiment was fresh and warm in my mind. My father at last fixed upon the cutler's trade, and my uncle Benjamin's son Samuel, who was bred to that business in London, being about that time established in Boston, I was sent to be with him some time on liking. But his expectations of a fee with me displeasing my father, I was taken home again.

From a child I was fond of reading, and all the little money that came into my hands was ever laid out in books. Pleased with the *Pilgrim's Progress*, my first collection was of John Bunyan's works in separate little volumes. I afterward sold them to enable me to buy R. Burton's *Historical Collections*; they were small chapmen's books, and cheap, 40 or 50 in all. My father's little library consisted chiefly of books in polemic divinity, most of which I read, and have since often regretted that, at a time when I had such a thirst for knowledge, more proper books had not fallen in my way since it was now resolved I should not be a clergyman. Plutarch's *Lives* there was in which I read abundantly, and I still think that time spent to great advantage. There was also a book of De Foe's, called *an Essay on Projects*, and another of Dr. Mather's, called *Essays to do Good*, which perhaps gave me a turn of thinking that had an influence on some of the principal future events of my life.

This bookish inclination at length determined my father to make me a printer, though he had already one son (James) of that profession. In 1717 my brother James returned from England with a press and letters to set up his business in Boston. I liked it much better than that of my father, but still had a hankering for the sea. To prevent the apprehended effect of such an inclination, my father was impatient to have me bound to my brother. I stood out some time, but at last was persuaded, and signed the indentures when I was yet but twelve years old. I was to serve as an apprentice till I was twenty-one years of age, only I was to be allowed journeyman's wages during the last year. In a little time I made great proficiency in the business, and became a useful hand to my brother. I now had access to better books. An acquaintance with the apprentices of booksellers enabled me sometimes to borrow a small one, which I was careful to return soon and clean. Often I sat up in my room reading the greatest part of the night, when the book was borrowed in the evening and to be returned early in the morning, lest it should be missed or wanted.

And after some time an ingenious tradesman, Mr. Matthew Adams, who had a pretty collection of books, and who frequented our printing-house, took notice of me, invited me to his library, and very kindly lent me such books as I chose to read. I now took a fancy to poetry, and made some little pieces; my brother, thinking it might turn to account, encouraged me, and put me on composing occasional ballads. One was called *The Lighthouse Tragedy*, and contained an account of the drowning of Captain Worthilake, with his two daughters: the other was a sailor's song, on the taking of Teach (or Blackbeard) the pirate. They were wretched stuff, in the Grub-street-ballad style; and when they were printed he sent me about the town to sell them. The first sold wonderfully, the event being recent, having made a great noise. This flattered my vanity; but my father discouraged me by ridiculing my performances, and telling me verse-makers were generally beggars. So I escaped being a poet, most probably a very bad one; but as prose writing bad been of great use to me in the course of my life, and was a principal means of my advancement, I shall tell you how, in such a situation, I acquired what little ability I have in that way.

Notes:

1. inducement *n.* 诱导，劝诱；诱因，动机；

    E. g. They offer every inducement to foreign businesses to invest in their states.

    He hasn't much inducement to study English.

2. felicity *n.* 幸福；恰当，妥帖

    E. g. Have you anything to propose for my domestic felicity?

3. posterity *n.* 后代，后世；子孙；后裔；儿孙

    E. g. A photographer recorded the scene on video for posterity.

    Their music has been preserved for posterity.

4. afflictions *n.* 苦恼（affliction 的名词复数）；灾难；苦恼的原因

E. g. Afflictions are sometimes blessings in disguise.

In Britain, we have so far escaped, in large measure, either of these afflictions.

5. parish *n.* 教区以下的地方行政区;(英国)郡以下的行政区

6. scrivener *n.* 公证人,代笔人

E. g. He was a simple-looking lawyer's clerk, elevated to the extraordinary dignity of a provincial scrivener.

7. octavo *n.* 八开的纸,八开本的书

8. errands *n.* errand 的复数;差使(errand 的名词复数);差事

E. g. Frank ran dodgy errands for a seedy local villain.

She was forever running errands for her housebound grandmother.

9. quagmire *n.* 沼泽地;泥潭;无法脱身的困境

E. g. His people had fallen further and further into a quagmire of confusion.

We have no intention of being drawn into a political quagmire.

10. ramble *vi.* 漫游;漫步;漫谈;蔓延 n. 漫步;漫游;漫谈

E. g. This is the best season for a ramble in the suburbs.

It would have been best written in a more concise way as it does tend to ramble.

Questions:

1. Why did Franklin write his Autobiography?

2. What made Franklin decide to leave the brother to whom he had been apprenticed?

3. How would you describe Franklin's writing style?

4. What does the Autobiography tell us about the 18th century?

5. What is the purpose of the Autobiography, and how does that purpose change throughout the work?

Analysis of Part 1

The opening part of the Autobiography addresses some themes that will come up later on in the book, namely, self-betterment and religion. Franklin's tone at the beginning of the book is humble. He claims to write only so that his own life may be an example for his son of how one can live well and how one can get through hardships. Franklin's book, a story of self-betterment, is written so as to be a model for the betterment of others. This general motive for writing, as well as Franklin's mention of correcting some errors were he to relive his life, both indicate Franklin's constant interest in self-improvement. This is perhaps the largest theme in the Autobiography; it dominates Part Two and recurs often in Part One. Also notice that Franklin thanks God for helping him to lead a good life. Franklin does not often show a religious side, and he will explain in greater depth later on that he is a Deist(自然神论信仰者)without ascribing to any particular religious denomination(教派). Franklin is often seen as the prototypical American and the first real example of the classic American Dream in action. Notice how Franklin carefully draws out throughout the book how he rose up with help primarily from hard work and skills. This part of the Autobiography is interesting from a literary standpoint because Ben Franklin is essentially creating the legend of the American Dream.

中文译文：

　　我一向爱好搜集有关祖上的一切珍闻逸事。你也许还记得当你跟我同住在英国的时候我曾经为了那个缘故跋涉旅途，遍访家族中的老人。目前我正在乡间休假，预料有整整一个星期的空闲，我想你也许同样地喜欢知道我一生的事迹（其中有许多你还没有听过），因此我就坐了下来替你把这些事迹写出来。除此以外，我还有一些别的动机。我出身贫寒，幼年生长在穷苦卑贱的家庭中，后来居然生活优裕，在世界上稍有声誉，迄今为止我一生一帆风顺，遇事顺利，我的立身之道，得蒙上帝的祝福，获得巨大的成就，我的子孙或许愿意知道这些处世之道，其中一部分或许与他们的情况适合，因此他们可以仿效。

　　我回顾我一生中幸运的时候，我有时候不禁这样说：如果有人提议我重新做人的话，我倒乐意把我的一生再从头重演一遍，我仅仅要求像作家那样，在再版时有改正初版某些缺陷的机会。如若可能，除了改正错误以外，我也同样地要把某些不幸的遭遇变得更顺利些。但是即使无法避免这些厄运，我还是愿意接受这个建议。但是由于这种重演是不可能的，那么最接近重演的似乎就是回忆了。为了使回忆尽可能地保持久远，似乎就需要把它记下来。

因此我将顺从一种老人中常有的癖好来谈论自己和自己过去的作为。但是我这样做，将不使听者感到厌倦，他们或是因为敬老，觉得非听我的话不可，但是一经写下来，听与不听就可以悉听尊便了。最后(我还是自己承认了好，因为即使我否认，别人也不会相信)，写自传，或许还会大大地满足我的自负心。说句老实话，我时常听见或在书上读到别人在刚说完了像"我可以毫不自夸地说……"这种开场白以后，接着就是一大篇自吹自擂的话。大多数人不喜欢别人的虚夸，不管他们自己是多么自负。但是无论在什么地方，我对这种自负心总是宽宥的。因为我相信这种心理对自己和他周围的人都有好处。所以，在许多情况下，一个人如果把自负心当作生命的慰藉而感谢上帝，这也不能算是怪诞悖理的。

自传中既然我提到了感谢上帝，我愿意十分谦恭地承认，上面提到的我过去一生中的幸福当归功于上帝仁慈的旨意，上帝使我找到了处世之道，并且使这些方法获得成功。这种信仰使我希望，上帝在将来会像以前一样地祝福我，不论是使我继续享受幸福，或是使我忍受命中注定的逆运(像其他人一样，我也可能有这样的遭遇)，虽然我不应该臆断，因为我未来命运的轮廓只有上帝知道，上帝甚至能够通过苦难来祝福我们。

我有一位伯父，他也同样爱好搜集家族中的奇闻逸事，有一次他交给我一些笔记，其中讲到关于我们祖先的一些事情。从这些笔记我知道我们的家族在诺桑普顿郡的爱克顿教区至少已经住了三百年，究竟在这以前还有多少年，他就不知道了。(也许从他们采用"富兰克林"为姓的那时候起。"富兰克林"在这以前是一个人民阶层[1]的名称，当时英国各地人们都在采用姓氏。)他们享有三十

---

① 此处原文是 an order of people。按 franklin 一词原指英国十四、十五世纪的非贵族的小土地所有者或自由农。——译者

英亩的自由领地,以打铁为副业。直到我伯父的时候为止,打铁这一行业一直保持在我们家族中。家中的长子总是学打铁的,我伯父和我父亲都按照这个传统叫他们的长子学铁匠。我查考了爱克顿教区的户籍册,我只找到了一五五五年以后的出生、嫁娶和丧葬的记录,那时以前的户籍册在那个教区里已经没有了,从这个户籍册里我发现我是五世以来小儿子的小儿子。我祖父汤麦斯生于一五九八年,住在爱克顿直到他年迈不能从事生产的时候为止,然后他住到他儿子约翰的地方去,他儿子是牛津郡班布雷村的一个染匠,我父亲就是跟着他当学徒的。我的祖父就死在那里,葬在那里。我们在一七五八年看到了他的墓碑。他的长子汤麦斯住在爱克顿的住宅里,后来把住宅和田产遗留给他的独生女儿。他女儿和她的丈夫(是威灵堡的一个叫作费雪的人)又把房产卖给伊斯德先生,他现在就是那里的庄园领主。我祖父养大了四个儿子,名叫汤麦斯、约翰、本杰明和约瑟。我手边没有材料,但是我将把我记得的给你写出来。如果我的记录在我离家以后未曾遗失的话,你可以从记录里找到更详细的材料。

汤麦斯跟他父亲学了打铁,但是他秉性颖悟,当地教区的大绅士伯麦老爷鼓励他求学上进(他的弟弟们也得到同样的鼓励),他获得了充当书记官的资格,成为地方上有声望的人,也是当地(无论是他的本村,诺桑普顿的城镇或是他所在的州)一切公益事业的主要推动者,我们听到了许多关于这一类的事例。在爱克顿教区他颇受到当时的哈利法克斯勋爵的赏识和奖励。他死在旧历一七〇二年一月六日,恰巧是我出生以前的四年整。我记得当我们从爱克顿教区的一些老人口中听到关于他的生平和性格的时候,你觉得很像你所知道的我的一生和个性,颇为惊异,你说:"他如果死在您出世的那一天,人家也许认为是灵魂转生呢!"

约翰学了染匠,我相信是染毛织品的。本杰明是丝绸染匠,在伦敦拜师受业。他秉性聪颖。我很清楚地记得他,因为当我还是一个孩子的时候,他渡海到波士顿来,住在我父亲那里,跟我们同住了几年之久。他一直活到高龄,他的孙子撒木耳·富兰克林现在还住在波士顿。他死后留下了两本四开本的诗稿,里面是一些写赠给他亲友的即兴短诗。下面寄给我的一首诗就是一个实例。①
他自己制订了一套速写术，并且教会了我，但是因为我从来不练，
所以现在忘光了。我是跟这位伯父命名的，因为我父亲跟他感情
特别融洽。他笃信宗教，经常去听著名传教师的布道，并且把他们
的布道用他的速记术记下来，他身边有许多这样的笔记本。他也
是一个很好的政治家，或许从他的地位来讲，他过分地关心政治
了。最近在伦敦我获得了他搜集的从 1641 年到 1717 年间重要的
政论手册，从书本上的卷号看来，有许多册已经遗失了，但是还留
下了对开本八本，四开本和八开本二十四本。一个旧书商人获得
了这些书籍，因为我有时候从他这里买书，他认识我，所以就把它
们送到我这里来。看样子是我伯父在去美洲之前留在伦敦的，这
已经是五十多年以前的事了。在书边上他还加了许多注解。斯派
克斯先生告诉我们这些书曾经被保存并属于作者的曾孙女埃蒙斯
夫人。

我们这一卑微的家族很早就参加了宗教改革运动，在玛丽女
王统治时期他们一直坚信新教，当时由于他们激烈地反对教皇，时
有遭受迫害的危险。他们有一本英语版的《圣经》②，为了隐藏和保
管这本《圣经》，他们把它打开用带子绑在一个折凳的凳面底部。
当我的高祖对着全家宣读经文时，他把折凳翻过来放在膝盖上，翻
动带子下面的书页。他的一个孩子站在门口，假如他瞧见教会法
庭的官吏走过来，他就预先通风报信。这时候板凳又重新翻过来
四脚落地，《圣经》就像原先一样藏匿起来了。这是我从本杰明伯
父那里听来的，直到大约查理二世统治的末期，全家还是一致地信
奉国教。但是那时候，有一些牧师因为不信奉国教教义而被开除
教籍，在诺桑普顿举行会议，本杰明和约瑟追随他们，一生信守不
渝，家里其他人仍然继续信奉国教。

我父亲约瑟早年就成了家，大约在 1682 年带着妻子和三个孩
子迁到新英格兰来。非国教的宗教集会受到法律的禁止，而且时
常受到干扰，因此我父亲的好友中有一些有声望的人就想移居到

---

① 富兰克林在括弧中加了一个注："嵌在这儿"，但是未附实例。
② 天主教的《圣经》是拉丁文的，他们信奉新教，所以采用英语版的《圣经》。

新大陆去，我父亲答应陪同他们前往美洲。他们希望在新大陆可以享有宗教信仰的自由，在新英格兰这位太太又生了四个孩子，后来他的第二任妻子又生了十个，共十七个孩子。我还记得有一个时期他的餐桌旁围坐着十三个孩子，这十三个孩子都长大成人，各自婚嫁。我是幼子，比我小的只有两个妹妹。我生在新英格兰的波士顿。我母亲是我父亲的继室，名叫阿拜亚·福求，是彼得·福求的女儿。我的外祖父是新英格兰的最初移民之一。可顿·马太在他的美洲教会史中曾经加以表扬，称他为"一个虔诚而有学问的英国人"，如果我没有记错的话。我听说他曾经写过各样的即兴短诗，但是只有一篇付印，我在好多年以前曾经读过。这首诗写于一六七五年，是用当时民间流行的诗歌体裁写成的，写给当时当地的执政当局。它拥护信仰自由，声援受迫害的浸礼会、教友会和其他教派，认为殖民地遭受到的印第安人战争和其他灾祸是迫害教徒的后果，是上帝对这种重大罪行的判决和惩罚，奉劝当局废止那些残暴不仁的立法。整首诗在我看来写得简单平易、落落大方。我还记得这首诗的最后六行，但是最初的两行我已经记不清了，不过这两行的大意是说他的批评出于善意，因此他并不隐匿他的真姓实名：由于从心底里我憎恶做一个匿名诽谤的人；我的姓名我定要写出，我现在是住在舍本城；毫无恶意，你的真实朋友，是彼得·福求。

　　我的哥哥们都拜师学了各种不同的行业。我父亲打算把我当作儿子中的什一捐奉献给教会，所以在八岁时就把我送到语法学校去念书。我早年读书颖悟（我一定很早就识字，因为我记不起我曾经有过不识字的时期），他的朋友们又都说我将来读书一定很有成就，这一切都鼓励了我父亲把我送到学校去念书。我伯父本杰明也赞成我念书，并且提议把他全部布道的速记本赠送给我（我想大概是作为开业的资本吧），如果我肯学习他的速记术的话。但是我在语法学校里念了不到一年，虽然在这一年中我逐步地从该班的中等生升到全班的优等生，接着就升入了二年级，好让我在那年年终随班升入三年级。但是这时候我父亲因为家庭人口多，负担不起大学求学的费用，同时他看到许多受过大学教育的人日后穷困潦倒（这是他在我面前对他的朋友们讲的），他改变了他原先的主张，叫我离开语法学校，把我送到一所书算学校去。这所学校是当时著名的乔治·布朗纳先生主持的，一般说来他办学很有成绩，并且能够循循善诱、春风化雨。在他的教导之下，我很快地学会了一手清晰的书法，但是算术我考不及格，并且毫无进步。在十岁时我父亲把我接回家来，帮助他营业。他经营的是油烛和肥皂制造业。这原不是他的本行，但是到了新英格兰，他发现染色业生意清淡，不能维持一家的生活，所以改了皂烛业。因此我父亲就叫我做剪烛芯、灌烛模、管店铺、出差等工作。

我厌恶这个行业，同时我非常想去航海，但是我父亲不赞成。可是因为住在沿海，我常到水中和海边去。我很早就擅长游泳，也学会了划船。当我和其他小孩在小舟或独木船上的时候，他们平常总是听我的命令，特别是在处境困难的时候。在其他场合我一般也是孩子们的头儿，有时候我使他们陷入窘境。我想举其中的一个例子，因为这件事显示了我早年突出的热心公益的精神，虽然当时这件事是做得不对的。

在水车贮水池的一边有一个盐泽，在涨潮的时候，我们时常站在盐泽的边上钓鲦鱼。由于践踏得多了，我们把盐泽的边沿弄成一个泥沼了。我提议在那里修筑一个我们可以站立的码头，我把一大堆石块指点给我的同伴们看，这些石块原是为了在盐泽边上建筑一所新屋预备的，它们却很符合我们的需要。因此在晚上当工人们已经离开的时候，我召集了几个同伴，我们像一群蚂蚁似的不辞劳苦地工作着，有时候两三个人搬一块石头，我们终于把石块全搬来了，修好了我们的小码头。第二天早晨工人们不见了石块大为惊异，后来才在我们的码头上找到了。他们查究这是谁干的。接着他们发现了这是我们的把戏，就向我们的家长告状。我们中有几个就因此受到了父亲的责备。虽然我辩解说这桩事是有益的，但是我父亲使我深信：不诚实的事是不会有益的。

我想你或许想知道一点我父亲的外貌和性格吧。他体格健全，身材中等，但长得很结实，十分强壮。他生性颖悟，善画，稍懂音乐。他的嗓子发出的声音清脆悦耳，所以，有时候在晚间工作完毕后，当他在提琴上拉着赞美歌的调子，一面唱着歌的时候，听上去是怪好听的。他对于机械工作也很有才能，有时候碰到其他行业的工具，他也能运用自如。但是他最大的长处是在处理公私重大问题时表现出的深刻见解和正确判断。后来，他也确实从来没有参加工作，家里孩子众多，需要他去教育，家境又困难，使他无法离开他的行业。但是我清楚地记得常常有地方上的领导人来请教他关于镇上或他所属教会的问题，他们很重视他的判断和忠告，同时当人们在个人生活中遇到了困难问题的时候，他们也常常来向他讨教，他常常被人们选定为争执双方的仲裁人。他喜欢尽可能地时常请一些通达的友人或邻居来进餐叙谈，在这种时候他总是设法提出一些明智或有益的讨论题，好增进孩子们的智慧。这样他使我们注意到立身处世中善良、正直和审慎的种种美德，对于餐桌上的食物很少留意或完全不注意，不管菜肴烹调的优劣，当令或落令，滋味的好坏，以及与同类中其他菜肴的比较。结果当我长大时我对这些事物完全不加注意，对我面前的菜肴漠不关心，粗心大意到这样一个程度：甚至在饭后几小时内人们若问我饭餐的内容我会瞠目结舌不知所对。在旅途中，当我的旅伴们因为缺乏可口的食物，不能满足他们比较高贵精致的口味和食欲而感到痛苦的时候，我这种习惯倒是一种方便。

同样我母亲也有一个健壮的体格：她替她所有的十个孩子哺乳。除了我父母死前患病以外，我从未听说过我父亲或母亲患过病。父亲活到八十九岁，母亲活到八十五岁，他们的遗体同葬在波士顿。几年前我在他们的墓前立了一块大理石墓碑，上面铭刻着如下的碑文：

约赛亚·富兰克林和他的妻子阿拜亚共葬于此。在婚后的五十五年中他们相亲相爱地生活着。他们既无田产，又无高俸厚禄，靠着不断的劳动和勤勉，蒙上帝的祝福，他们维持了一个人口众多的家庭，安乐度日。并且抚养了十三个孩子和七个孙儿孙女，声誉良好。读者，从这个实例中，你应当勉励自己，在你的职业中勤奋从事，切勿不信上帝。约赛亚是一个虔诚谨慎的男子，阿拜亚是一个细心贞洁的妇女。

他们的幼子　立此碑铭　聊表孝意和纪念。

约赛亚·富兰克林生于一六五五年，死于一七四四年，享年八十九岁。

阿拜亚·富兰克林生于一六六七年，死于一七五二年，享年八十五岁。

我唠唠叨叨地讲了许多离题的话，从这里我看出我已在逐渐衰老了，过去我写文章比现在条理清楚，但是在私人的团聚中，人们的衣着远不同于在公共的舞会。可能这只不过是疏懒罢了。

闲话休提，言归正传：我在我父亲的铺子里这样继续工作了两年，就是说，直到我十二岁的时候为止。我哥哥约翰本来是学皂烛制造业的，这时已经离开了我父亲，成了家，在罗特岛独自做起生意来，很明显我注定要接替他的位置，成为一个蜡烛制造匠了。但是由于这时候我仍然不喜欢这个行业，我父亲害怕假如他不替我找一个更合适的职业的话，我会像他的儿子约赛亚一样地私自脱逃去航海，使他十分恼怒。因此他有时带我去散步，去观看细木匠、砖匠、旋工、铜匠等工作，以便观察我的志趣，力图把我的兴趣固定在陆地上的某种行业上。从那时起我一直爱好留心观察手艺高明的工人运用他们的工具。这种细心观察对我一直很有用：由于从观察中我学到了很多东西，所以当一时找不到工人的时候，我自己能够做我家里的小修理工作，当做实验的兴致在我心里还是很新鲜强烈的时候，我能够替我自己的实验制造小小的机器。我父亲最后决定让我从事制刀业。由于大约在那时我伯父本杰明的儿子撒木耳在伦敦学了制刀业，在波士顿开了业，我就被送到他那里去，试试这个行业。但是因为他希望从我身上获得一些报酬，触怒了我父亲，所以他又把我带回了家。

我从小就爱好读书，我一直把我手上的全部零用钱都花在书上。因为我喜爱《天路历程》，所以我一开始就收集了约翰·班扬文集单独发行的小册子。以后我把它们卖了，用这笔钱我买了柏顿的《历史文集》。这些是开本很小的由小贩们贩卖的书籍，价格便宜，全集共有四五十册，我父亲的小图书馆收藏的主要是一些有关神学论辩的书籍，其中大多数我都读了，但是既然当时业已决定我不做牧师了，正当我的求知欲那样旺盛的时候，我没有机会阅读更适当的书籍，迄今常使我感到遗憾。在那里有一本普鲁泰克的《英雄传》，我读了不少，我还认为读这本书所花的时间是非常值得的。那里也有笛福的一本名为《论计划》的书，另一本是马太博士的书,名为《论行善》。这本书可能在我思想上形成了一种对于我以后一生中的某些重大事件都有影响的倾向。

这种对书籍的爱好最后使我父亲决定让我学印刷业,虽然他已经有一个儿子(詹姆士)学了这种行业。一七一七年我哥哥詹姆士从英国回来,带来了一台印刷机和铅字,准备在波士顿开业。我对印刷业的爱好远胜过我父亲的行业,但是尽管如此,我对于航海仍不能忘怀。为了预防这种渴望产生忧惧的后果,我父亲急欲让我跟我哥哥当学徒。我反对了一段时间,但是最后我同意了,签订了师徒合同,当时我只有十二岁。按照合同,我将充当学徒直到我二十一岁时为止,但在最后一年中我将按照合同获得出师职工的工资。在很短的时期内,我熟悉了印刷业,成为我哥哥的得力助手。这时我有机会阅读较好的书籍了。我跟一些书铺的学徒们打交道,这种相识有时使我能够从他们那里借到一本小书,但是我很小心,很快地交还给他们,并且保持书本的整洁。有时候在晚间借到一本书,为了怕被人发现缺书或是怕有人要买这本书,第二天一清早即须归还,因此我常常坐在房间阅读到深夜。

过了一些时候,有一个很聪明的商人,名叫马太·亚当先生,经常到我们的印刷铺里来。他家藏书颇多,他注意到了我,邀我到他的藏书室里去,欣然借给我一些我要读的书籍,这时我爱上了诗歌,写了几首小诗。我哥哥认为写诗可能以后有用,所以鼓励我并且命我编写两首应时故事诗。一首叫作《灯塔悲剧》,叙述华萨雷船长和他的两个女儿溺毙的故事。另一首是水手歌,叙述捉拿海盗铁契(或叫作"黑胡子")的经过。这两首都是毫无价值的东西,是用低级小调的格式写成的。印好了以后,我哥哥让我到镇上各处去叫卖。第一首销路很好,因为它所叙述的是新近发生的、曾经轰动一时的事件。这事使我沾沾自喜;但是我父亲却反对,他嘲笑我的诗歌,他说诗人一般都是穷光蛋。这使我幸免成为一个诗人,很可能成为一个十分低劣的诗人,但是由于在我一生中散文的写作对我十分有用,而且是我发迹的一种主要手段,因此我将告诉你,在这种情况下,我是如何在这方面获得我现有的一点小小才能的。

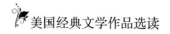

🌿 Answers for questions

1. Franklin says that because his son may wish to know about his life, he is taking his one week vacation in the English countryside to record his past. He also says that he has enjoyed his life and would like to repeat it.

2. His brother was passionate, and had often beaten him. The aversion to arbitrary power that has stuck to him through his whole life. After a brush with the law, Franklin left his brother.

3. A good answer would comment on Franklin's use of humor and his attempts to poke fun at himself so as to not seem arrogant. Moreover, Franklin's style is terse and witty; he usually makes his points using as few words as possible, which in part leads to his tendency to create aphorisms. Franklin's style is predominantly didactic as the Autobiography is intended to be read partly as a self-help manual. Franklin contributed to the development of journalism as type of writing that presents the facts in the order of most important to least important, using as few words as are necessary.

4. There are many answers to this question, some of which are mentioned here. First, Franklin shows from a sociological standpoint the possibilities for economic mobility in colonial America. After all, Franklin himself arrived in Philadelphia at 17 years old without a penny to his name, and from those beginnings he worked his way up to being a successful printer, a talented inventor and a Founding Father of America. Second, Franklin's idealism and faith in the betterment of mankind, as well as his Deism and utilitarianism, places him intellectually in the Age of Reason, a time when people often believed optimistically that the world and man could be perfected through science. Religion was also questioned during this age, and that questioning manifests itself in Franklin's philosophy. Franklin's creation of the Junto is a testament to his interest in the importance of debate, another 18th century intellectual ideal. Third, Franklin shows us how people went about their day to

day lives in the 1700s. While this isn't a major thrust of the book, we learn about the way apprenticeships worked and how the government operated in the colonies, among a variety of other glimpses into 18th century life.

5. The Autobiography never has one clearly defined audience. Its opening is addressed to William Franklin, Benjamin's son. After approximately eight pages, however, the work becomes a more general account of Franklin's early memories and experiences. Franklin's tone reflects the purpose of accounting for the major events of history as Franklin witnessed them and took part in them.

References

[1] http://image. baidu. com/i? tn = baiduimage&ps = 1&ct = 201326592&lm = − 1&cl = 2&nc = 1&ie = utf − 8&word = benjamin%20franklin （图片来源）

[2] http://en. wikipedia. org/wiki/Ben_Franklin

[3] http://www. en8848. com. cn/soft/

[4] 胡荫桐, 刘树森. 美国文学教程[C]. 南开大学出版社, 1995.

Unit 2
Thomas Jefferson (1743 – 1826)

✿ Bibliography

Thomas Jefferson (1743 – 1826) was an American Founding Father, the principal author of *the Declaration of Independence* (1776), and the third President of the United States (1801 – 1809). He was a spokesman for democracy, and embraced the principles of republicanism and the rights of the individual with worldwide influence. At the beginning of the American Revolution, he served in the Continental Congress, representing Virginia, and then served as a wartime Governor of Virginia (1779 – 1781). In May 1785, he became the United States Minister to France and later the first United States Secretary of State (1790 – 1793) serving under President George Washington. In opposition to Alexander Hamilton's Federalism, Jefferson and his close friend, James Madison, organized the Democratic—Republican Party, and later resigned from Washington's cabinet. Elected Vice President in 1796 in the administration of John Adams, Jefferson opposed Adams, and with Madison secretly wrote the Kentucky and Virginia Resolutions, which attempted to nullify the Alien and Sedition Acts.

Elected president in what Jefferson called the "Revolution of 1800", he oversaw acquisition of the vast Louisiana Territory from France (1803), and sent out the Lewis and Clark Expedition (1804 – 1806), and later three others, to explore the new west. Jefferson doubled the size of the United States during his presidency. His second term was beset with troubles at home, such as the failed treason trial of his former Vice President Aaron Burr. When Britain threatened American shipping challenging U. S. neutrality during its war with Napoleon, he tried economic warfare with his embargo laws, which only impeded American foreign trade. In 1803, President Jefferson initiated a process of Indian tribal removal to the Louisiana Territory west of the Mississippi River, having opened lands for eventual American settlers. In 1807 Jefferson drafted and signed into law a bill that banned slave importation into the United States.

A leader in the Enlightenment, Jefferson was a polymath in the arts, sciences and politics. Considered an important architect in the classical tradition, he designed his home Monticello and other notable buildings. Jefferson was keenly interested in science, invention, architecture, religion, and philosophy; he was an active member and eventual president of the American Philosophical Society. He was conversant in French, Greek, Italian, Latin and Spanish, and studied other languages and linguistics, interests which led him to found the University of Virginia after his presidency. Although not a notable orator, Jefferson was a skilled writer and corresponded with many influential people in America and Europe throughout his adult life.

As long as he lived, Jefferson expressed opposition to slavery, yet he owned hundreds of slaves and freed only a few of them. Historians generally believe that after the death of his wife Jefferson had a long-term relationship with his slave, Sally Hemings, and fathered some or all of her children. Although criticized by many present-day scholars over the issues of racism and slavery, Jefferson is consistently rated as one of the greatest U. S. presidents.

❧ *The Declaration of Independence*

The Declaration of Independence is the usual name of a statement adopted by the Continental Congress on July 4, 1776, which announced that the thirteen American colonies, then at war with Great Britain, regarded themselves as thirteen newly independent sovereign states, and no longer a part of the British Empire. Instead they formed a new nation—the United States of America. John Adams was a leader in pushing for independence, which was unanimously approved on July 2. A committee of five had already drafted the formal declaration, to be ready when Congress voted on independence. The term "Declaration of Independence" is not used in the document itself.

Adams persuaded the committee to select Thomas Jefferson to compose the original draft of the document, which Congress would edit to produce the final version. The Declaration was ultimately a formal explanation of why Congress had voted on July 2 to declare independence from Great Britain, more than a year after the outbreak of the American Revolutionary War. The national birthday, Independence Day, is celebrated on July 4, although Adams wanted July 2.

After ratifying the text on July 4, Congress issued the Declaration of Independence in several forms. It was initially published as the printed Dunlap broadside that was widely distributed and read to the public. The source copy used for this printing has been lost, and may have been a copy in Thomas Jefferson's hand. Jefferson's original draft, complete with changes made by John Adams and Benjamin Franklin, and Jefferson's notes of changes made by Congress, are preserved at the Library of Congress. The most famous version of the Declaration, a signed copy that is popularly regarded as the official document, is displayed at the National Archives in Washington, D. C. This engrossed copy was ordered by Congress on July 19, and signed primarily on August 2.

The sources and interpretation of the Declaration have been the subject of much scholarly inquiry. The Declaration justified the independence of the United States by listing colonial grievances against King George III, and by asserting certain natural and legal rights, including a right of revolution. Having served its original purpose in announcing independence, references to the text of the Declaration were few for the next four score years. Abraham Lincoln made it the center piece of his rhetoric (as in *the Gettysburg Address* of 1863), and his policies. Since then, it has become a well-known statement on human rights, particularly its second sentence:

> We hold these truths to be self-evident, that all men are created equal, that they are endowed by their Creator with certain unalienable Rights, that among these are Life, Liberty and the pursuit of Happiness.

This has been called "one of the best-known sentences in the English language", containing "the most potent and consequential words in American history". The passage came to represent a moral standard to which the United States should strive. This view was notably promoted by Abraham Lincoln, who considered the Declaration to be the foundation of his political philosophy, and argued that the Declaration is a statement of principles through which the United States Constitution should be interpreted.

It provided inspiration to numerous national declarations of independence throughout the world. Historian David Armitage, after examining the influence of the American "Declaration" on over 100 other declarations of independence, says:

> The American Revolution was the first outbreak of the contagion of sovereignty that has swept the world in the centuries since 1776. Its influence spread first to the Low Countries and then to the Caribbean, Spanish America, the Balkans, West Africa, and Central Europe in the decades up to 1848... *Declarations of independence* were among the primary symptoms of this contagion of sovereignty.

Summary

1. The first sentence of the Declaration asserts as a matter of Natural law the ability of a people to assume political independence, and acknowledges that the grounds for such independence must be reasonable, and therefore explicable, and ought to be explained.

One of the most famous quotes of the Declaration is: "We hold this truth to be self-evident that all men are created equal, that they are endowed by their creator with certain unalienable rights, that among this are life, liberty and the pursuit of happiness. To secure this right governments are instituted among men, deriving their just power from the consent of the governed. "

When in the Course of human events, it becomes necessary for one people to dissolve the political bands which have connected them with another, and to assume among the powers of the earth, the separate and equal station to which the Laws of Nature and of Nature's God entitle them, a decent respect to the opinions of mankind requires that they should declare the causes which impel them to the separation.

2. The next section, the famous preamble, includes the ideas and ideals that were principles of the Declaration. It is also an assertion of what is known as the "right of revolution", that is, people have certain rights, and when a government violates these rights, the people have the right to "alter or abolish" that government.

We hold these truths to be self-evident, that all men are created equal, that they are endowed by their Creator with certain unalienable Rights, that among these are Life, Liberty and the pursuit of Happiness. That to secure these rights, Governments are instituted among Men, deriving their just powers from the consent of the governed. That whenever any Form of Government becomes destructive of these ends, it is the Right of the People to alter or to abolish it, and to institute new Government, laying its foundation on such principles and organizing its powers in such form, as to them shall seem most likely to effect their

Safety and Happiness. Prudence, indeed, will dictate that Governments long established should not be changed for light and transient causes, and accordingly all experience hath shewn, that mankind are more disposed to suffer, while evils are sufferable, than to right themselves by abolishing the forms to which they are accustomed. But when a long train of abuses and usurpations, pursuing invariably the same object evinces a design to reduce them under absolute Despotism, it is their right, it is their duty, to throw off such Government, and to provide new Guards for their future security.

3. The next section is a list of charges against King George which aim to demonstrate that he has violated the colonists' rights and is therefore unfit to be their ruler:

Such has been the patient sufferance of these Colonies, and such is now the necessity which constrains them to alter their former Systems of Government. The history of the present King of Great Britain is a history of repeated injuries and usurpations, all having in direct object the establishment of an absolute Tyranny over these States. To prove this, let Facts be submitted to a candid world.

In every stage of these Oppressions, we have Petitioned for Redress in the most humble terms: our repeated Petitions have been answered only by repeated injury. A Prince whose character is thus marked by every act which may define a Tyrant, is unfit to be the ruler of a free people.

4. Many Americans still felt a kinship with the people of Great Britain, and had appealed in vain to the prominent among them, as well as to Parliament, to convince the King to relax his more objectionable policies toward the colonies. The next section represents disappointment that these attempts had been unsuccessful.

Nor have We been wanting in attentions to our British brethren. We have warned them from time to time of attempts by their legislature to extend an unwarrantable jurisdiction over us. We have reminded them of the circumstances of our emigration and settlement here. We have appealed to their native justice and magnanimity, and we have conjured them by the ties of our common kindred to disavow these usurpations, which, would inevitably interrupt our connections and correspondence. They too have been deaf to the voice of justice and of consanguinity. We must, therefore, acquiesce in the necessity, which denounces our Separation, and hold them, as we hold the rest of mankind, Enemies in War, in Peace Friends.

5. In the final section, the signers assert that there exist conditions under which people must change their government, that the British have produced such conditions, and by necessity the colonies must throw off political ties with the British Crown and become independent states. The conclusion incorporates language from Lee's resolution of independence that had been passed on July 2.

Comments

1. Having served its original purpose in announcing the independence of the United States, the Declaration was initially neglected following the American Revolution Early celebrations of Independence Day, like early histories of the Revolution, largely ignored the Declaration. Although the act of declaring independence was considered important, the text announcing that act attracted little attention. The Declaration was rarely mentioned during the debates about the United States Constitution, and its language was not incorporated into that document. George Mason's draft of the Virginia Declaration of Rights was more influential, and its language was echoed in state constitutions and state bills of rights more often than Jefferson's words. "In none of these documents", wrote Pauline Maier, "is there any evidence whatsoever that the Declaration of Independence lived in men's minds as a classic statement of American political principles."

2. Although some leaders of the French Revolution admired the Declaration of Independence, they were more interested in the new American state constitutions. The French Declaration of the Rights of Man and Citizen (1789) borrowed language from George Mason and not

Jefferson's Declaration, although Jefferson was in Paris at the time and was consulted during the drafting process. According to historian David Armitage, the United States Declaration of Independence did prove to be internationally influential, but not as a statement of human rights. Armitage argued that the Declaration was the first in a new genre of declarations of independence that announced the creation of new states.

3. In the United States, interest in the Declaration was revived in the 1790s with the emergence of America's first political parties. Throughout the 1780s, few Americans knew, or cared, who wrote the Declaration. But in the next decade, Jeffersonian Republicans sought political advantage over their rival Federalists by promoting both the importance of the Declaration and Jefferson as its author. Federalists responded by casting doubt on Jefferson's authorship or originality, and by emphasizing that independence was declared by the whole Congress, with Jefferson as just one member of the drafting committee. Federalists insisted that Congress's act of declaring independence, in which Federalist John Adams had played a major role, was more important than the document announcing that act. But this view, like the Federalist Party, would fade away, and before long the act of declaring independence would become synonymous with the document.

4. A less partisan appreciation for the Declaration emerged in the years following the War of 1812, thanks to a growing American nationalism and a renewed interest in the history of the Revolution. In 1817, Congress commissioned John Trumbull's famous painting of the signers, which was exhibited to large crowds before being installed in the Capital. The earliest commemorative printings of the Declaration also appeared at this time, offering many Americans their first view of the signed document. Collective biographies of the signers were first published in the 1820s, giving birth to what Garry Wills called the "cult of the signers". In the years that followed, many stories about the writing and signing of the document would be published for the first time.

5. When interest in the Declaration was revived, the sections that

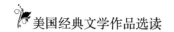

were most important in 1776—the announcement of the independence of the United States and the grievances against King George—were no longer relevant. But the second paragraph, with its talk of self-evident truths and unalienable rights, had lost none of its relevance. Because the Constitution and the Bill of Rights lacked sweeping statements about rights and equality, advocates of marginalized groups turned to the Declaration for support. Starting in the 1820s, variations of the Declaration were issued to proclaim the rights of workers, farmers, women, and others. In 1848, for example, the Seneca Falls Convention, a meeting of women's rights advocates, declared that "all men and women are created equal". But the Declaration would have its most prominent influence on the debate over slavery.

The Declaration of Independence
IN CONGRESS, JULY 4, 1776

THE UNANIMOUS DECLARATION OF THE THIRTEEN UNITED STATES OF AMERAICA

When in the course of human events, it becomes necessary for one people to dissolve[1] the political bands which have connected them with another, and to assume among the powers of the earth, the separate and equal station to which the laws Nature and Nature's God entitle them, a decent respect to the opinions of mankind requires that they should declare the causes which impel them to the separation.

We hold these truths to be self-evident, that all men are created equal, that they are endowed by their creator with certain unalienable rights, that they are among these are life, liberty and the pursuit of happiness.

That to secure these rights, governments are instituted among them, deriving their just power from the consent of the governed. That whenever any form of government becomes destructive of these ends, it is the right of the people to alter or to abolish[2] it, and to institute new government, laying its foundation on such principles and organizing its powers in such form, as to them shall seem most likely to effect their safety and happiness.

Prudence[3], indeed, will dictate that governments long established should not be changed for light and transient[4] causes; and accordingly all experience hath shown that mankind are more disposed to suffer, while evils are sufferable, than to right themselves by abolishing the forms to which they are accustomed.

But when a long train of abuses and usurpations[5], pursuing invariably the same object evinces a design to reduce them under absolute despotism[6], it is their right, it is their duty, to throw off such government, and to provide new guards for their future security.

Such has been the patient sufferance of these colonies; and such is now the necessity, which constrains them to alter their former systems of government. The history of the present King of Great Britain is usurpations, all having in direct object tyranny over these States. To prove this, let facts be submitted to a candid world.

He has refused his assent to laws, the most wholesome and necessary for the public good.

He has forbidden his Governors to pass laws of immediate and pressing importance, unless suspended in their operation till his assent should be obtained; and when so suspended, he has utterly neglected to attend them.

He has refused to pass other laws for the accommodation of large districts of people, unless those people would relinquish[7] the right of representation in the Legislature, a right inestimable to them and formidable to tyrants only.

He has called together legislative bodies at places unusual, uncomfortable, and distant from the depository of their public records, for the sole purpose of fatiguing them into compliance with his measures.

He has dissolved representative houses repeatedly, for opposing with manly firmness his invasion on the rights of the people.

He has refused for a long time, after such dissolution, to cause others to be elected; whereby the legislative powers, incapable of annihilation[8], have returned to the people at large for their exercise; the State remaining in the meantime exposed to all the dangers of invasion from without and convulsion within.

He has endeavored to prevent the population of these states; for that purpose obstructing the laws of naturalizing of foreigners; refusing to pass others to encourage their migration hither, and raising the condition of new appropriations of lands.

He has obstructed the administration of justice, by refusing his assent of laws for establishing judiciary powers.

He has made judges dependent on his will alone, for the tenure[9] of their office, and the amount and payment of their salary.

He has erected a multitude of new officers, and sent hither swarms of officers to harass[10] our people, and eat out our substances.

He has kept among us, in times of peace, standing armies without the consent of our legislatures.

He has affected to render the military independent of and superior to the civil power.

He has combined with others to subject us to a jurisdiction[11] foreign to our constitution, and unacknowledged by our laws, giving his assent to their acts of pretended legislation.

For quartering large bodies of armed troops among us;

For protecting them, by a mock trial, from punishment for any murder which they should commit on the inhabitants of these States.

For cutting off our trade with all parts of the world;

For imposing taxes on us without our consent;

For depriving us in many cases, of the benefits of trial by jury;

For transporting us beyond seas to be tried for pretended offenses;

For abolishing the free systems of English laws in a neighboring Province, establishing therein an arbitrary government, and enlarging its boundaries so as to render it at once an example and fit instrument for introducing the same absolute rule these Colonies;

For taking away our charters, abolishing our most valuable laws, and altering fundamentally the forms of our governments;

For suspending our own legislatures, and declaring themselves invested with power to legislate for us in all cases whatsoever.

He has abdicated[12] government here, by declaring us out of his protection and waging war against us.

He has plundered our seas, ravaged our coasts, burnt our towns, and destroyed the lives of our people.

He is at this time transporting large armies of foreign mercenaries to complete the works of death, desolation and tyranny, already begun with circumstances of cruelty and perfidy[13] scarcely parallel in the most barbarous ages, and totally unworthy the head of a civilized nation.

He has constrained our fellow citizens taken captive on the high seas to bear arms against their country, to become the executioners of their friends and brethren[14], or to fall themselves by their hands.

He has excited domestic insurrection[15] amongst us, and has endeavored to bring on the inhabitants of our frontiers, the merciless Indian savages, whose known rule of warfare, is an undistinguished destruction of all ages, sexes, and conditions.

In every stage of these oppressions, we have petitioned[16] for redress in the most humble terms: our repeated petition have been answered only by repeated injury. A prince whose character is thus marked by every act which may define a tyrant is unfit to be the ruler of a free people.

Nor have we been wanting in attention to our British brethren. We have warned them from time to time of attempts by their legislature to extend an unwarrantable jurisdiction over us. We have reminded them of the circumstances of our emigration and settlement here. We have appealed to their native justice and magnanimity[17], and we have conjured them by the ties of our common kindred to disavow these usurpation, which would inevitably interrupt our connections and correspondence. They too have been deaf to the voice of justice and of consanguinity[18].

We must, therefore, acquiesce[19] in the necessity, which denounces our separation, and hold them, as we hold the rest of mankind, enemies in war, in peace friends.

We, therefore, the Representatives of the United States of America, in General Congress assembled, appealing to the supreme Judge of the world for the rectitude[20] of our intentions, do, in the name, and by authority of the good people of these Colonies, solemnly publish and declare, That these United States Colonies and Independent States; that they are absolved by from all allegiance to the British Crown, and that all political connection between them and the State, they have full power to levy war, conclude peace, contract alliances, establish commerce, and to do all other acts and things which Independent States may of right do. And for the support of this declaration, with a firm reliance on the protection of Divine Providence, we mutually pledge to each other our lives, our fortunes, and our sacred honor.

Notes:

1. dissolve *v.* 解散, 散去

   E. g. Kaifu threatened to dissolve the Parliament and call an election.

   The King agreed to dissolve the present commission.

2. abolish *v.* 废除, 废止

   E. g. The following year Parliament voted to abolish the death penalty for murder.

   The government consider it imprudent to abolish the death penalty.

3. prudence *n.* 谨慎, 节俭, 精明

   E. g. Western businessmen are showing remarkable prudence in investing in the region.

   A lack of prudence may lead to financial problems.

4. transient *adj.* 短暂的，临时的

    E. g. Her feeling of depression was transient.

    In most cases, pain is transient.

5. usurpation *n.* 篡夺

    E. g. And by that measure, China's usurpation indeed ushers in a new order.

6. despotism *n.* 专制、专制统治

    E. g. Their starting point is bourgeois despotism, which in culture becomes the cultural despotism of the bourgeoisie.

    Diem, a profound traditionlist, ran a family despotism in the oriental manner.

7. relinquish *v.* 放弃，松手

    E. g. They will never voluntarily relinquish their independence.

    He was forced to relinquish control of the company.

8. annihilation *n.* 歼灭，灭绝

    E. g. They were to surrender immediately or face total annihilation.

    We favour the well-being and progress, not the annihilation, of mankind.

9. tenure *n.* 占有，占有期

    E. g. He remained popular throughout his tenure of the office of mayor.

    He has recently been refused tenure.

10. harass *v.* 骚扰，烦扰，折磨

    E. g. He has sent hither swarms of officers to harass our people.

11. jurisdiction *n.* 司法权，管辖权

    E. g. The court has no jurisdiction over foreign diplomats living in this country.

12. abdicate *v.* 放弃，退位

    E. g. Many parents simply abdicate all responsibility for their children.

13. perfidy *n.* 背信弃义

    E. g. As devotion unites lovers, so perfidy estranges friends.

    The knowledge of Hurstwood's perfidy wounded her like a knife.

14. brethren *n.* 兄弟，同胞

    E. g. Sri Lankans share a common ancestry with their Indian brethren.

    We must help our brethren, it is our duty.

15. insurrection *n.* 造反，暴乱

    E. g. They were plotting to stage an armed insurrection.

    We are not prepared for an armed insurrection.

16. petition *n.* 情愿，请求

    E. g. His lawyers filed a petition for all charges to be dropped.

    Public employees, teachers and liberals are circulating a petition for his recall.

17. magnanimity *n.* 宽宏大量

    E. g. Nothing pays richer dividends than magnanimity.

18. consanguinity *n.* 血亲，同族

    E. g. Aside from a thorough medical family history, there is no need to offer any genetic testing on the basis of consanguinity alone.

    They too have been deaf to the voice of justice and of consanguinity.

19. acquiesce *v.* 默许，默认

    E. g. Steve seemed to acquiesce in the decision.

    Her parents will never acquiesce in such an unsuitable marriage.

20. rectitude *n.* 操行端正，笔直

    E. g. She was indignant with his presumption and self-satisfaction and conscious rectitude.

    He exuded a rectitude so matter-of-fact that he never needed to appeal to it.

Questions：

1. According to *The Declaration of Independence*, what certain unalienable rights did colonial people have? Why were they "self-evident"?

2. How could the history of the present King of Great Britain be understood? How had it been proved?

3. What had been unanimously declared in *The Declaration of Independence*?

中文译文：

在有关人类事务的发展过程中，当一个民族必须解除其和另一个民族之间的政治联系并在世界各国之间依照自然法则和上帝的意旨，接受独立和平等的地位时，出于对人类舆论的尊重，必须把他们不得不独立的原因予以宣布。

我们认为下面这些真理是不证自明的：人人生而平等，造物者赋予他们若干不可剥夺的权利，其中包括生命权、自由权和追求幸福的权利。为了保障这些权利，人类才在他们之间建立政府，而政府之正当权力，是经被治理者的同意而产生的。当任何形式的政府对这些目标具破坏作用时，人民便有权力改变或废除它，以建立一个新的政府；其赖以奠基的原则，其组织权力的方式，务使人民认为唯有这样才最可能获得他们的安全和幸福。为了慎重起见，成立多年的政府，是不应当由于轻微和短暂的原因而予以变更的。过去的一切经验也都说明，任何苦难，只要是尚能忍受，人类都宁愿容忍，而无意为了本身的权益便废除他们久已习惯了的政府。但是，当追逐同一目标的一连串滥用职权和强取豪夺长期发生，证明政府企图把人民置于专制统治之下时，那么人民就有权利，也有义务推翻这个政府，并为他们未来的安全建立新的保障——这就是这些殖民地过去逆来顺受的情况，也是它们现在不得不改变以前政府制度的原因。当今大不列颠国王的历史，是接连不断的伤天害理和强取豪夺的历史，这些暴行的唯一目标，就是想在这些州建立专制的暴政。为了证明所言属实，现把下列事实向公正的世界宣布：

他拒绝批准那些对公共福利最有益、最必要的法律。

他禁止他的总督们批准那些紧急的、极其重要的法律，除非那些法律在经他同意之前暂停施行；而暂停施行期间，他又对那些法律完全置之不理。

他拒绝批准其他有关人民向广大地区迁居的法律，除非那些人民愿意放弃其在立法机关中的代表权；这种代表权对人民来说具有无可估量的意义，只有对暴君来说才是可怕的。

他把各州立法团体召集到特别的、极不方便的、远离政府档案库的地方去开会，其唯一的目的就是使他们疲于奔命，不得不顺从他的旨意。

他屡次解散各州的议会，因为这些议会曾坚定不移地反抗他对人民权利的侵犯。

他在解散各州议会之后，又长时期地不让人民另选新议会；不可抹杀的立法权力又归一般民众行使；而其时各州仍然处于内乱外患的危险之中。

他竭力抑制各州的人口增长；为此目的，他为《外国人归化法》设置障碍，拒绝批准其他鼓励外国人移居各州的法律，并提高了重新分配土地的条件。

他拒绝批准确立司法权力的法律，从而阻碍司法行政管理工作。

他使法官的任职年限、薪金数额及支付办法完全由他个人意志来决定。

他滥设新职，派遣大批官吏来钳制我们的人民，耗尽我们人民的财力。

他不经我们立法机关的同意，在和平时期就把常备军驻扎在我们各州。

他力图使军队独立于政权，并凌驾于政权之上。

他与某些人相互勾结，要我们屈服于一种与我们的体制格格不入、没有为我们法律所承认的管辖权之下；并且批准那些炮制的假冒法案。

在我们这里驻扎大量的武装部队，用欺骗性审讯来包庇那些杀害我们各州居民的人，使他们得以逍遥法外。

切断我们与世界各地的贸易。

未经我们的同意即向我们强行征税。

　　在许多案件中剥夺我们的陪审权力。以莫须有的罪名押送我们去海外受审。

　　在邻近的地区废除保障自由的英国法律体制，建立专制政府，并扩大其疆界，企图使它迅即成为一个样板和一件顺手的工具，以便进而把同样的专制统治引向我们这些殖民地。

　　取消我们的宪章，废除我们那些最宝贵的法令，并且从根本上改变我们的政府形式。

　　关闭我们自己的立法机关，有权就一切事宜为我们制定法律。

　　他宣布我们已不受其保护，并对我们开战。这样，表明了他已放弃在这里的政权。

　　他在我们的海域大肆掠夺，骚扰我们的沿海地区，焚毁我们的城镇，并残害我们人民的生命。

　　他此刻正在调运大量的外籍雇佣军，意在制造死亡、毁灭和专制暴虐。

　　他已经造成即使在人类历史上最野蛮的时代都罕见的残暴和背信弃义的气氛。

　　他完全不配做一个文明国家的元首。

　　他强迫在公海上被俘的我们的同胞武装起来反对自己的国家，充当残杀自己亲人和朋友的刽子手，或者死于自己亲人朋友之手。

　　他在我们之间煽动内乱，并竭力挑动我们的边疆居民、那些残酷无情的未开化的印第安人；而印第安人的著名的作战原则是不分男女老幼、不论何种情况，一概格杀勿论。

　　在这些高压政策的每一个阶段，我们都曾以最谦卑的言辞请求予以纠正；而每次的吁请所得到的答复都只是屡遭损害。

　　一个君主，当他的每个行为都已打上暴君的烙印时，是不配做自由人民的统治者。

　　我们并没有置我们的英国弟兄于不顾。我们时常提醒他们，他们的立法机构企图把不合理的管辖权横加到我们头上；我们曾提醒他们注意，我们移植来此和在这里定居的情况。我们曾经向他们天生的正义感和侠义精神呼吁，恳请他们念及同种同宗的情谊，抵制那些掠夺行为以免影响我们之间的联系和友谊。但是，他们对这种正义的、血肉之亲的呼吁置若罔闻。因此，我们不得不宣布与他们脱离，并且以对待世界上其他民族一样的态度对待他们：和我们作战，就是敌人；和我们和好，就是朋友。

因此，我们，集合在大会中的美利坚合众国的代表们，以这些殖民地的善良人民的名义，并经他们授权，向全世界最崇高的正义人士呼吁，说明我们的严正意向，同时庄严宣布：这些联合一致的殖民地从此成为，而且按其权利必须成为自由独立的国家；它们已经解除一切效忠于英王室的义务，从此完全断绝并必须断绝与大不列颠王国之间的一切政治联系。作为自由独立的国家；它们享有全权去宣战、缔和、同盟、通商或采取其他一切独立国家有权采取的行动。为了拥护此项宣言，我们怀着神明保佑的坚定信心，以我们的生命、我们的财产和我们神圣的荣誉，互相宣誓。

Answers for the questions

1. All men are created equal, that they are endowed by their creator with certain unalienable rights, that they are among these are life, liberty and the pursuit of happiness.

2. The history of the present King of Great Britain is usurpations, all having in direct object tyranny over these States. To prove this, let facts be submitted to a candid world.

3. That these United States Colonies and Independent States; that they are absolved by from all allegiance to the British Crown, and that all political connection between them and the State, they have full power to levy war, conclude peace, contract alliances, establish commerce, and to do all other acts and things which Independent States may of right do.

References

[1] http://pic. sogou. com/pics? ie = utf8&p = 40230504&interV = kKIOkrELjb-gQmLkEkrYTkKIMkbELjboJmLkEkL8TkKIMkLELjb8TkKIKmrELjbkImLkElb s = _ – 1655971149&query = thomas%20jefferson& （图片来源）

[2] http://www. u148. net/article/49478. html

[3] http://en. wikipedia. org/wiki/United_States_Declaration_of_Independence

[4] 吴伟仁. 美国文学史及选读[C]. 外语教学与研究出版社, 2000.

Unit 3
Edgar Allan Poe (1809 – 1849)

🎋 Bibliography

Edgar Allan Poe (January 19, 1809 – 1849) was an American author, poet, editor and literary critic, considered part of the American Romantic Movement. Best known for his tales of mystery and the macabre, Poe was one of the earliest American practitioners of the short story, and is generally considered the inventor of the detective fiction genre. He is further credited with contributing to 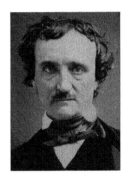 the emerging genre of science fiction. He was the first well-known American writer to try to earn a living through writing alone, resulting in a financially difficult life and career.

Born in Boston, Poe was the second child of two actors. His father abandoned the family in 1810, and his mother died the following year. Thus orphaned, the child was taken in by John and Frances Allan, of Richmond, Virginia. Although they never formally adopted him, Poe was with them well into young adulthood. Tension developed later as John Allan and Edgar repeatedly clashed over debts, including those incurred by gambling, and the cost of secondary education for the young man. Poe attended the University of Virginia for one semester but left due to lack of money. Poe quarreled with Allan over the funds for his education and enlisted in the Army in 1827 under an assumed name. It was at this time his publishing career began, albeit humbly, with an anonymous collection of poems, *Tamerlane and Other Poems* (1827), credited only to "a Bostonian". With the death of Frances Allan in 1829, Poe and Allan reached a temporary rapprochement. Later failing as an officer's cadet at West Point and declaring a firm wish to be a poet and writer, Poe parted ways with John Allan.

Poe switched his focus to prose and spent the next several years working for literary journals and periodicals, becoming known for his own style of literary criticism. His work forced him to move among several cities, including Baltimore, Philadelphia and New York City. In Baltimore in 1835, he married Virginia Clemm, his 13-year-old cousin. In January 1845 Poe published his poem, *The Raven*, to instant success. His wife died of tuberculosis two years after its publication. For years, he had been planning to produce his own journal, *The Penn* (later renamed *The Stylus*), though he died before it could be produced. On October 7, 1849, at age 40, Poe died in Baltimore. The cause of his death is unknown and has been variously attributed to alcohol, brain congestion, cholera, drugs, heart disease, rabies, suicide, tuberculosis, and other agents.

Poe and his works influenced literature in the United States and around the world, as well as in specialized fields, such as cosmology and cryptography. Poe and his work appear throughout popular culture in literature, music, films, and television. A number of his homes are dedicated museums today. The Mystery Writers of America present an annual award known as the Edgar Award for distinguished work in the mystery genre.

The Black Cat

The Black Cat is a short story by Edgar Allan Poe. It was first published on August 19, 1843, edition of *The Saturday Evening Post*. *The Black Cat* is one of Edgar Allan Poe's most memorable stories. The tale centers around a black cat and the subsequent deterioration of a man. It is a study of the psycho-logy of guilt, often paired in analysis with Poe's "The Tell-Tale Heart". In both, a murderer carefully conceals his crime and believes himself unassailable, but eventually breaks down and reveals himself, impelled by a nagging reminder of his guilt.

"The Black Cat" first appeared in *The Saturday Evening Post* on August 19, 1843. This first-person narrative falls into the realm of Horror/Gothic Literature, and has been examined in association with themes of insanity and alcoholism.

Characters in *The Black Cat*

1. The narrator—a murderer
2. Pluto—the black cat

Summary

The story is presented as a first-person narrative using an unreliable narrator. He is a condemned man at the outset of the story. The narrator tells us that from an early age he has loved animals. He and his wife have many pets, including a large, beautiful black cat (as described by the narrator) named Pluto. This cat is especially fond of the narrator and vice versa. Their mutual friendship lasts for several years, until the narrator becomes an alcoholic. One night, after coming home completely intoxicated, he believes the cat to be avoiding him. When he tries to seize it, the panicked cat bites the narrator, and in a fit of rage, he seizes the animal, pulls a pen-knife from his pocket, and deliberately gouges out the cat's eye.

From that moment onward, the cat flees in terror at his master's approach. At first, the narrator is remorseful and regrets his cruelty. "But this feeling soon gave place to irritation. And then came, as if to my final and irrevocable overthrow, the spirit of perverseness". He takes the cat out in the garden one morning and ties a noose around its neck, hanging it from a tree where it dies. That very night, his house mysteriously catches fire, forcing the narrator, his wife and their servant to flee the premises.

The next day, the narrator returns to the ruins of his home to find, imprinted on the single wall that survived the fire, the apparition of a gigantic cat, with a rope around the animal's neck.

At first, this image deeply disturbs the narrator, but gradually he determines a logical explanation for it, that someone outside had cut the cat from the tree and thrown the dead creature into the bedroom to wake him during the fire. The narrator begins to miss Pluto, feeling guilty. Some time later, he finds a similar cat in a tavern. It is the same size and color as the original and is even missing an eye. The only difference is a large white patch on the animal's chest. The narrator takes it home, but soon begins to loathe, even fear the creature. After a time, the white patch of fur begins to take shape and, to the narrator, forms the shape of the gallows. This terrifies and angers him more, and he avoids the cat whenever possible. Then, one day when the narrator and his wife are visiting the cellar in their new home, the cat gets under its master's feet and nearly trips him down the stairs. Enraged, the man grabs an axe and tries to kill the cat but is stopped by his wife, whom, out of fury, he kills instead. To conceal her body he removes bricks from a protrusion in the wall, places her body there, and repairs the hole. A few days later, when the police show up at the house to investigate the wife's disappearance, they find nothing and the narrator goes free. The cat, which he intended to kill as well, has also gone missing. This grants him the freedom to sleep, even with the burden of murder.

On the last day of the investigation, the narrator accompanies the police into the cellar. They still find nothing significant. Then, completely confident in his own safety, the narrator comments on the sturdiness of the building and raps upon the wall he had built around his wife's body. A loud, inhuman wailing sound fills the room. The alarmed police tear down the wall and find the wife's corpse, and on rotting head, to the utter horror of the narrator, is the screeching black cat. As he words it: "I had walled the monster up within the tomb!"

Comments on *The Black Cat*

Like the narrator in Poe's *The Tell-Tale Heart*, the narrator of *The Black Cat* has questionable sanity. Near the beginning of the tale, the narrator says he would be "mad indeed" if he should expect a reader to believe the story, implying that he has already been accused of madness.

The extent to which the narrator claims to have loved his animals suggests mental instability in the form of having "too much of a good thing". His partiality for animals substitutes "the paltry friendship and gossamer fidelity of mere Man". Since the narrator's wife shares his love of animals, he likely thinks of her as another pet, seeing as he distrusts and dislikes humans. Additionally, his failure to understand his excessive love of animals foreshadows his inability to explain his motives for his actions.

One of Poe's darkest tales, *The Black Cat* includes his strongest denunciation of alcohol. The narrator's perverse actions are brought on by his alcoholism, a "disease" and "fiend" which also destroys his personality. The use of the black cat evokes various superstitions, including the idea voiced by the narrator's wife that they are all witches in disguise. Poe owned a black cat. In his "Instinct *vs* Reason—A Black Cat" he stated: the writer of this article is the owner of one of the most remarkable black cats in the world—and this is saying much, for it will be remembered that black cats are all of them witches. In Scottish and Irish mythology, the Cat is described as being a black cat with a white spot on its chest, not unlike the cat the narrator finds in the tavern. The titular cat is named Pluto after the Roman god of the Underworld.

Although Pluto is a neutral character at the beginning of the story, he becomes antagonistic in the narrator's eyes once the narrator becomes an alcoholic. The alcohol pushes the narrator into fits of intemperance and violence, to the point at which everything angers him—Pluto in particular, who is always by his side, becomes the malevolent witch who haunts him even while avoiding his presence. When the narrator cuts Pluto's eye from its socket, this can be seen as symbolic of self-inflicted partial blindness to his own vision of moral goodness.

The fire that destroys the narrator's house symbolizes the narrator's "almost complete moral disintegration". The only remainder is the impression of Pluto upon the wall, which represents his unforgivable and incorrigible sin.

From   *The Black Cat*

For the most wild, yet most homely narrative which I am about to pen, I neither expect nor solicit belief. Mad indeed would I be to expect it, in a case where my very senses reject their own evidence. Yet, mad am I not—and very surely do I not dream. But tomorrow I die, and today I would unburthen my soul. My immediate purpose is to place before the world, plainly, succinctly[1], and without comment, a series of mere household events. In their consequences, these events have terrified—have tortured—have destroyed me. Yet I will not attempt to expound them. To me, they have presented little but Horror—to many they will seem less terrible than barroques[2]. Hereafter, perhaps, some intellect may be found which will reduce my phantasm[3] to the commonplace—some intellect more calm, more logical, and far less excitable than my own, which will perceive, in the circumstances I detail with awe, nothing more than an ordinary succession of very natural causes and effects.

From my infancy I was noted for the docility and humanity of my disposition. My tenderness of heart was even so conspicuous as to make me the jest of my companions. I was especially fond of animals, and was indulged by my parents with a great variety of pets. With these I spent most of my time, and never was so happy as when feeding and caressing them. This peculiarity of character grew with my growth, and in my manhood, I derived from it one of my principal sources of pleasure. To those who have cherished an affection for a faithful and sagacious[4] dog, I need hardly be at the trouble of explaining the nature or the intensity of the gratification thus derivable. There is something in the unselfish and self-sacrificing love of a brute, which goes directly to the heart of him who has had frequent occasion to test the paltry friendship and gossamer[5] fidelity of mere Man.

I married early, and was happy to find in my wife a disposition not uncongenial with my own. Observing my partiality for domestic pets, she lost no opportunity of procuring those of the most agreeable kind. We had birds, gold-fish, a fine dog, rabbits, a small monkey, and a cat.

This latter was a remarkably large and beautiful animal, entirely black, and sagacious to an astonishing degree. In speaking of his intelligence, my wife, who at heart was not a little tinctured[6] with superstition, made frequent allusion to the ancient popular notion, which regarded all black cats as witches in disguise. Not that she was ever serious upon this point—and I mention the matter at all for no better reason than that it happens, just now, to be remembered.

Pluto—this was the cat's name—was my favorite pet and playmate. I alone fed him, and he attended me wherever I went about the house. It was even with difficulty that I could prevent him from following me through the streets.

Our friendship lasted, in this manner, for several years, during which my general temperament and character—through the instrumenta lity of the Fiend Intemperance—had (I blush to confess it) experienced a radical alteration for the worse. I grew, day by day, more moody, more irritable, more regardless of the feelings of others. I suffered myself to use intemperate language to my wife. At length, I even offered her personal violence. My pets, of course, were made to feel the change in my disposition. I not only neglected, but ill-used them also. For Pluto, however, I still retained sufficient regard to restrain me from maltreating him, as I made no scruple[7] of maltreating the rabbits, the monkey, or even the dog, when by accident, or through affection, they came in my way. But my disease grew upon me—for what disease is like Alcohol! —and at length even Pluto, who was now becoming old, and consequently somewhat peevish[8]—even Pluto began to experience the effects of my ill temper.

One night, returning home, much intoxicated, from one of my haunts about town, I fancied that the cat avoided my presence. I seized him; when, in his fright at my violence, he inflicted a slight wound upon my hand with his teeth. The fury of a demon instantly possessed me. I knew myself no longer. My original soul seemed, at once, to take its flight from my body; and a more than fiendish malevolence, gin-nurtured, thrilled every fibre of my frame. I took from my waistcoat-pocket a pen-knife, opened it, grasped the poor beast by the throat, and deliberately cut one of its eyes from the socket[9]! I blush, I burn, I shudder, while I pen the damnable atrocity.

When reason returned with the morning—when I had slept off the fumes of the night's debauch[10]—I experienced a sentiment half of horror, half of remorse, for the crime of which I had been guilty; but it was, at best, a feeble and equivocal feeling, and the soul remained untouched. I again plunged into excess, and soon drowned in wine all memory of the deed.

In the meantime the cat slowly recovered. The socket of the lost eye presented, it is true, a frightful appearance, but he no longer appeared to suffer any pain. He went about the house as usual, but, as might be expected, fled in extreme terror at my approach. I had so much of my old heart left, as to be at first grieved by this evident dislike on the part of a creature which had once so loved me. But this feeling soon gave place to irritation. And then came, as if to my final and irrevocable overthrow, the spirit of PERVERSENESS. Of this spirit philosophy takes no account. Yet I am not more sure that my soul lives, than I am that perverseness is one of the primitive impulses of the human heart— one of the indivisible primary faculties, or sentiments, which give direction to the character of Man. Who has not, a hundred times, found himself committing a vile or a silly action, for no other reason than because he knows he should not? Have we not a perpetual inclination, in the teeth of our best judgment, to violate that which is Law, merely because we understand it to be such? This spirit of perverseness, I say, came to my final overthrow. It was this unfathomable longing of the soul to vex itself—to offer violence to its own nature—to do wrong for the wrong's sake only—that urged me to continue and finally to consummate the injury I had inflicted upon the unoffending brute. One morning, in cool blood, I slipped a noose about its neck and hung it to the limb of a tree—hung it with the tears streaming from my eyes, and with the bitterest remorse at my heart—hung it because I knew that it had loved me, and because I felt it had given me no reason of offence—hung it because I knew that in so doing I was committing a sin—a deadly sin that would so jeopardize my immortal soul as to place it—if such a thing were possible—even beyond the reach of the infinite mercy of the Most Merciful and Most Terrible God.

On the night of the day on which this cruel deed was done, I was aroused from sleep by the cry of fire. The curtains of my bed were in flames. The whole house was blazing. It was with great difficulty that my wife, a servant, and myself, made our escape from the conflagration[11]. The destruction was complete. My entire worldly wealth was swallowed up, and I resigned myself thenceforward to despair.

I am above the weakness of seeking to establish a sequence of cause and effect, between the disaster and the atrocity. But I am detailing a chain of facts—and wish not to leave even a possible link imperfect. On the day succeeding the fire, I visited the ruins. The walls, with one exception, had fallen in. This exception was found in a compartment wall, not very thick, which stood about the middle of the house, and against which had rested the head of my bed. The plastering had here, in great measure, resisted the action of the fire—a fact which I attributed to its having been recently spread. About this wall a dense crowd were collected, and many persons seemed to be examining a particular portion of it with very minute and eager attention. The words "strange!" "singular!" and other similar expressions, excited my curiosity. I approached and saw, as if graven[12] in bas relief upon the white surface, the figure of a gigantic cat. The impression was given with an accuracy truly marvellous. There was a rope about the animal's neck.

When I first beheld this apparition—for I could scarcely regard it as less—my wonder and my terror were extreme. But at length reflection came to my aid. The cat, I remembered, had been hung in a garden adjacent to the house. Upon the alarm of fire, this garden had been immediately filled by the crowd—by some one of whom the animal must have been cut from the tree and thrown, through an open window, into my chamber. This had probably been done with the view of arousing me from sleep. The falling of other walls had compressed the victim of my cruelty into the substance of the freshly-spread plaster; the lime of which, with the flames, and the ammonia from the carcass, had then accomplished the portraiture as I saw it.

Although I thus readily accounted to my reason, if not altogether to my conscience, for the startling fact just detailed, it did not the less fail to make a deep impression upon my fancy. For months I could not rid myself of the phantasm of the cat, and, during this period, there came back into my spirit a half-sentiment that seemed, but was not, remorse. I went so far as to regret the loss of the animal, and to look about me, among the vile haunts which I now habitually frequented, for another pet of the same species, and of somewhat similar appearance, with which to supply its place.

One night as I sat, half stupified, in a den of more than infamy, my attention was suddenly drawn to some black object, reposing upon the head of one of the immense hogsheads of Gin, or of Rum, which constituted the chief furniture of the apartment. I had been looking steadily at the top of this hogshead for some minutes, and what now caused me surprise was the fact that I had not sooner perceived the object thereupon. I approached it, and touched it with my hand. It was a black cat—a very large one—fully as large as Pluto, and closely resembling him in every respect but one. Pluto had not a white hair upon any portion of his body; but this cat had a large, although indefinite splotch[13] of white, covering nearly the whole region of the breast.

Upon my touching him, he immediately arose, purred loudly, rubbed against my hand, and appeared delighted with my notice. This, then, was the very creature of which I was in search. I at once offered to purchase it of the landlord, but this person made no claim to it—knew nothing of it—had never seen it before.

I continued my caresses, and, when I prepared to go home, the animal evinced[14] a disposition to accompany me. I permitted it to do so, occasionally stooping and patting it as I proceeded. When it reached the house it domesticated itself at once, and became immediately a great favorite with my wife.

For my own part, I soon found a dislike to it arising within me. This was just the reverse of what I had anticipated, but—I know not how or why it was—its evident fondness for myself rather disgusted and annoyed. By slow degrees, these feelings of disgust and annoyance rose into the bitterness of hatred. I avoided the creature, a certain sense of shame, and the remembrance of my former deed of cruelty, preventing me from physically abusing it. I did not, for some weeks, strike, or otherwise violently ill use it; but gradually—very gradually—I came to look upon it with unutterable loathing, and to flee silently from its odious presence, as from the breath of a pestilence[15].

What added, no doubt, to my hatred of the beast, was the discovery, on the morning after I brought it home, that, like Pluto, it also had been deprived of one of its eyes. This circumstance, however, only endeared it to my wife, who, as I have already said, possessed, in a high degree, that humanity of feeling which had once been my distinguishing trait, and the source of many of my simplest and purest pleasures.

With my aversion to this cat, however, its partiality for myself seemed to increase. It followed my footsteps with a pertinacity[16] which it would be difficult to make the reader comprehend. Whenever I sat, it would crouch beneath my chair, or spring upon my knees, covering me with its loathsome caresses. If I arose to walk it would get between my feet and thus nearly throw me down, or, fastening its long and sharp claws in my dress, clamber, in this manner, to my breast. At such times, although I longed to destroy it with a blow, I was yet withheld from so doing, partly by a memory of my former crime, but chiefly—let me confess it at once—by absolute dread of the beast.

This dread was not exactly a dread of physical evil—and yet I should be at a loss how otherwise to define it. I am almost ashamed to own—yes, even in this felon's cell, I am almost ashamed to own—that the terror and horror with which the animal inspired me, had been heightened by one of the merest chimeras it would be possible to conceive. My wife had called my attention, more than once, to the character of the mark of white hair, of which I have spoken, and which constituted the sole visible difference between the strange beast and the one I had destroyed. The reader will remember that this mark, although large, had been originally very indefinite; but, by slow degrees—degrees nearly imperceptible, and which for a long time my Reason struggled to reject as fanciful—it had, at length, assumed a rigorous distinctness of outline. It was now the representation of an object that I shudder to name—and for this, above all, I loathed, and dreaded, and would have rid myself of the monster had I dared—it was now, I say, the image of a hideous—of a ghastly thing—of the GALLOWS ! —oh, mournful and terrible engine of Horror and of Crime—of Agony and of Death !

And now was I indeed wretched beyond the wretchedness of mere Humanity. And a brute beast—whose fellow I had contemptuously destroyed—a brute beast to work out for me—for me a man, fashioned in the image of the High God—so much of insufferable wo! Alas! neither by day nor by night knew I the blessing of Rest any more! During the former the creature left me no moment alone; and, in the latter, I started, hourly, from dreams of unutterable fear, to find the hot breath of the thing upon my face, and its vast weight—an incarnate[17] Night-Mare that I had no power to shake off—incumbent eternally upon my heart !

Beneath the pressure of torments such as the feeble remnant of the good within me succumbed. Evil thoughts became my sole intimates— the darkest and most evil of thoughts. The moodiness of my usual temper increased to hatred of all things and of all mankind, while, from the sudden, frequent, and ungovernable outbursts of a fury to which I now blindly abandoned myself, my uncomplaining wife, alas! was the most usual and the most patient of sufferers.

One day she accompanied me, upon some household errand, into the cellar of the old building which our poverty compelled us to inhabit. The cat followed me down the steep stairs, and, nearly throwing me headlong, exasperated me to madness. Uplifting an axe, and forgetting, in my wrath, the childish dread which had hitherto stayed my hand, I aimed a blow at the animal which, of course, would have proved instantly fatal had it descended as I wished. But this blow was arrested by the hand of my wife. Goaded, by the interference, into a rage more than demoniacal, I withdrew my arm from her grasp and buried the axe in her brain. She fell dead upon the spot, without a groan.

This hideous murder accomplished, I set myself forthwith, and with entire deliberation, to the task of concealing the body. I knew that I could not remove it from the house, either by day or by night, without the risk of being observed by the neighbors. Many projects entered my mind. At one period I thought of cutting the corpse into minute fragments, and destroying them by fire. At another, I resolved to dig a grave for it in the floor of the cellar. Again, I deliberated about casting it in the well in the yard—about packing it in a box, as if merchandize, with the usual arrangements, and so getting a porter to take it from the house. Finally I hit upon what I considered a far better expedient than either of these. I determined to wall it up in the cellar—as the monks of the middle ages are recorded to have walled up their victims.

For a purpose such as this the cellar was well adapted. Its walls were loosely constructed, and had lately been plastered throughout with a rough plaster, which the dampness of the atmosphere had prevented from hardening. Moreover, in one of the walls was a projection, caused by a false chimney, or fireplace, that had been filled up, and made to resemble the rest of the cellar. I made no doubt that I could readily displace the bricks at this point, insert the corpse, and wall the whole up as before, so that no eye could detect any thing suspicious.

And in this calculation I was not deceived. By means of a crow-bar I easily dislodged the bricks, and, having carefully deposited the body against the inner wall, I propped it in that position, while, with little trouble, I relaid the whole structure as it originally stood. Having procured mortar, sand, and hair, with every possible precaution, I prepared a plaster which could not be distinguished from the old, and with this I very carefully went over the new brick-work. When I had finished, I felt satisfied that all was right. The wall did not present the slightest appearance of having been disturbed. The rubbish on the floor was picked up with the minutest care. I looked around triumphantly, and said to myself, "Here at least, then, my labor has not been in vain."

My next step was to look for the beast which had been the cause of so much wretchedness, for I had, at length, firmly resolved to put it to death. Had I been able to meet with it, at the moment, there could have been no doubt of its fate, but it appeared that the crafty animal had been alarmed at the violence of my previous anger, and forebore to present itself in my present mood. It is impossible to describe, or to imagine, the deep, the blissful sense of relief which the absence of the detested creature occasioned in my bosom. It did not make its appearance during the night—and thus for one night at least, since its introduction into the house, I soundly and tranquilly slept, aye, slept even with the burden of murder upon my soul!

The second and the third day passed, and still my tormentor came not. Once again I breathed as a freeman. The monster, in terror, had fled the premises forever! I should behold it no more! My happiness was supreme! The guilt of my dark deed disturbed me but little. Some few inquiries had been made, but these had been readily answered. Even a search had been instituted—but of course nothing was to be discovered. I looked upon my future felicity as secured.

Upon the fourth day of the assassination, a party of the police came, very unexpectedly, into the house, and proceeded again to make rigorous investigation of the premises. Secure, however, in the inscrutability of my place of concealment, I felt no embarrassment whatever. The officers bade me accompany them in their search. They left no nook or corner unexplored. At length, for the third or fourth time, they descended into the cellar. I quivered not in a muscle. My heart beat calmly as that of one who slumbers in innocence. I walked the cellar from end to end. I folded my arms upon my bosom, and roamed easily to and fro. The police were thoroughly satisfied and prepared to depart. The glee at my heart was too strong to be restrained. I burned to say if but one word, by way of triumph, and to render doubly sure their assurance of my guiltlessness.

"Gentlemen," I said at last, as the party ascended the steps, "I delight to have allayed your suspicions. I wish you all health, and a little more courtesy. By the way, gentlemen, this—this is a very well constructed house. " (In the rabid desire to say something easily, I scarcely knew what I uttered at all.)—"I may say an excellently well constructed house. These walls—are you going, gentlemen? —these walls are solidly put together;" and here, through the mere phrenzy of bravado[18], I rapped heavily, with a cane which I held in my hand, upon that very portion of the brick-work behind which stood the corpse of the wife of my bosom.

But may God shield and deliver me from the fangs of the Arch-

Fiend! No sooner had the reverberation of my blows sunk into silence, than I was answered by a voice from within the tomb! —by a cry, at first muffled and broken, like the sobbing of a child, and then quickly swelling into one long, loud, and continuous scream, utterly anomalous and inhuman—a howl—a wailing shriek, half of horror and half of triumph, such as might have arisen only out of hell, conjointly from the throats of the dammed in their agony and of the demons that exult in the damnation.

Of my own thoughts it is folly to speak. Swooning, I staggered to the opposite wall. For one instant the party upon the stairs remained motionless, through extremity of terror and of awe. In the next, a dozen stout arms were toiling at the wall. It fell bodily. The corpse, already greatly decayed and clotted with gore, stood erect before the eyes of the spectators. Upon its head, with red extended mouth and solitary eye of fire, sat the hideous beast whose craft had seduced me into murder, and whose informing voice had consigned me to the hangman. I had walled the monster up within the tomb!

Notes:

1. succinct *adj.* 简明的, 简洁的

   E. g. Simon's book provides a succinct outline of artificial intelligence and its application to robotics.

   The book gives an admirably succinct account of the technology and its history.

2. baroque *adj.* /*n.* 巴洛克(的), 怪异(的)

   E. g. The baroque church of San Leonardo is worth a quick look.

   A more widespread interest in baroque music developed only slowly in the Sixties and Seventies.

3. phantasm *n.* 幻觉; 幻象

4. sagacious *adj.* 精明的, 有判断力的

   E. g. The sagacious minister offered what he considered a rather clever explanation.

The Prince Prospero was happy and dauntless and sagacious.

5. gossamer *adj.* 轻而薄的；虚无缥缈的；如蛛丝的

E. g. The prince helped the princess, who was still in her delightful gossamer gown.

Binding wire yarn gossamer threads, flaxen thread, retrieve and etc.

6. tincture *n.* 酊剂

E. g. I'd say he is a man who has the least tincture of learning.

He has not a tincture of evil in his nature.

7. scruple *n.* /*v.* 于心不安，顾忌

E. g. The villain made no scruple of committing murder.

She didn't scruple to take Tom from his wife.

8. peevish *adj.* 脾气坏的，易动怒的

E. g. She glared down at me with a peevish expression on her face.

A peevish child is unhappy and makes others unhappy.

9. socket *n.* ［解］眼窝，孔窝

E. g. Her eyes were sunk deep into their sockets.

10. debauch *vt.* 使堕落，败坏

E. g. Printing money would worsen inflation, debauch the currency and bring a balance-of-payments crisis.

11. conflagration *n.* 大火，火灾

E. g. A conflagration in 1947 reduced 90 percent of the houses to ashes.

The light of that conflagration will fade away.

12. graven *adj.* 雕刻的，不可磨灭的 *v.* 坟墓(grave 的过去分词)；死亡

E. g. His advice was firmly graven on my heart.

Thou shalt not make unto thee any graven image.

13. splotch *n.* 斑点

E. g The kitten was black with white front paws and a white splotch on her chest.

There was still the rayed splotch in the upper right-hand corner where a tear had fallen.

14. evince *vt.* 表明, 标示

E. g. She at last condescended to evince awareness of his proximity.

Thirdly, Live life without fear, confront all obstacles and evince that you can overcome them.

15. pestilence *n.* 瘟疫

E. g. They were crazed by the famine and pestilence of that bitter winter.

16. pertinacity *n.* 执拗, 顽固

17. incarnate *adj.* 人体化的; 拟人化的; 肉色的, 粉红色的

E. g. The pharaoh is Osiris, the moon bull incarnate.

18. bravado *n.* 虚张声势; 故作勇敢; 冒险

E. g. His stories about his sexual experimentation were more bravado than fact.

Questions:

1. How does the narrator become the monster? What does it mean?

2. What is the symbolic meaning of the black cat?

3. What are the literary styles of themes of Edgar Allan Poe's novels?

Analysis of *The Black Cat*

This short story easily achieved the effect that Poe was looking for through the use of description of setting, symbolism, plot development, diverse word choice, and detailed character development. In most cases, the setting is usually indelible to a story, but "The Black Cat" relies little on this element. This tale could have occurred anywhere and can be placed in any era. This makes the setting the weakest element of "The Black Cat".

Poe's plot development added much of the effect of shocking insanity to "The Black Cat". To dream up such an intricate plot of perverseness, alcoholism, murders, fire, revival, and punishment is quite amazing. This story has almost any plot element you can imagine a horror story containing. Who could have guessed, at the beginning of the story, that narrator had killed his wife? The course of events in *The Black Cat's* plot is shockingly insane by itself! Moreover, the words in "The Black Cat" were precisely chosen to contribute to Poe's effect of shocking insanity. As the narrator pens these he creates a splendidly morbid picture of the plot. Perfectly selected, sometimes rare, and often dark, his words create just the atmosphere that he desired in the story. Expressions such as "apparition" "vile haunts", and "fiendish malevolence" were added for atmosphere. Another way that Poe used word choice was with synonyms. The cat was not only the "black cat", it was the "playmate", the "beast", the "brute", the "apparition", and the "monster".

Finally, character development was most important to Poe's effect of shocking insanity in "The Black Cat". Without the perversely insane narrator this story can't exist, let alone put across an effect. It is mentioned many times that he loves animals and that he is an alcoholic. In fact many of his rages were caused more by alcohol rather than the black cat. The cat(s) was also vividly developed. At one point early in "The Black Cat", the narrator spends two paragraphs describing his then delightful pet. But as the story progresses both characters change dramatically. The cat is dynamic in that it is hung, reappears with a white splotch on its chest, and has a different disposition than before. The narrator spirals out of control into fits of rage and numerous hideous, unthinkable actions, commencing with the walling up of his own wife in the cellar.

Obviously, the setting, symbolism, plot, word choice, and character development contributed greatly to the effect of shocking insanity in Edgar Allan Poe's masterpiece "The Black Cat". Without these, there would be no story at all. Poe's skillful use of all of these elements, the least of these being setting and the greatest of these being character development, creates a shocking tale, which leaves the mind to ponder in all its horror.

中文译文：

黑　猫

　　我要开讲的这个故事极其荒唐，而又极其平凡，我并不企求各位相信，就连我的心里都不相信这些亲身经历的事，若是指望人家相信，岂不是发疯了吗？但是我眼下并没有发疯，而且确实不是在做梦。不过明天我就死到临头了，我要趁今天把这事说出来好让灵魂安生。我迫切打算把这些纯粹的家常琐事一五一十、简洁明了、不加评语地公之于世。由于这些事的缘故，我饱尝惊慌，受尽折磨，终于毁了一生。但是我不想详细解释。这些事对我来说，只有恐怖，可对大多数人来说，这无非是奇谈，没有什么可怕。也许，后世一些有识之士会把这种无稽之谈看作寻常小事。某些有识之士头脑比我更加冷静，更加条理分明，不像我这样遇事慌张。我这样诚惶诚恐、细细叙述的事情，在他们看来一定是一串有其因必有其果的普通事罢了。

　　我从小就以心地善良温顺出名。我心肠软的初期，一时竟成为小朋友的笑柄。我特别喜欢动物，父母就百般纵容，给了我各种各样玩赏的小动物。我大半时间都泡在同这些小动物玩上面，每当我喂食和抚弄它们的时候，就感到无比高兴。我长大了，这个癖性也随之而发展，一直到我成人，这点还是我的主要乐趣。有人疼爱忠实伶俐的狗，对于他们来说，根本用不着多费口舌来说明个中乐趣无穷了吧。你若经常尝到人类那种薄情寡义的滋味，那么对于兽类那种自我牺牲的无私之爱，准会感到刻骨铭心。

　　我很早就结了婚，幸喜妻子跟我意气相投，她看到我偏爱饲养家禽，只要有机会物色到中意的玩物总不放过。我们养了小鸟、金鱼、良种狗、小兔子，一只小猴和一只猫。

　　这只猫个头特大，非常好看，浑身乌黑，而且伶俐绝顶。我妻子生来就好迷信，她一说到这猫的灵性，往往就要扯上古老传说，认为凡是黑猫都是巫婆变化的。我倒不是说我妻子对这点极为认真，我这里提到这事只是顺便想到而已。

这猫名叫普路托，原是我心爱的东西和玩伴。我亲自喂养它，我在屋里走到哪儿，它跟到哪儿。连我上街去，它都要跟，想尽法儿也赶不掉它。

我和猫的交情就这样维持了好几年。在这几年工夫中，说来不好意思，由于我喝酒上了瘾，脾气习性都彻底变坏了。我一天比一天喜怒无常，动不动就使性子，不顾人家受得了受不了。我竟任性恶言秽语地辱骂起妻子来了。最后，还对她拳打脚踢。我饲养的那些小动物当然也感到我脾气的变坏。我不仅不照顾它们，反而虐待它们。那些兔子，那小猴，甚至那只狗，出于亲热，或是碰巧跑到我跟前来，我总是肆无忌惮地糟蹋它们。只有对待普路托，我还有所怜惜，未忍下手。不料我的病情日益严重——你想世上哪有比酗酒更厉害的病啊——这时普路托老了，脾气也倔了，于是我索性把普路托也当作出气筒了。

有一天晚上，我在城里一个常去的酒吧喝得酩酊大醉而归，我以为这猫躲着我，就一把抓住它，它看见我凶相毕露吓坏了，不由在我手上轻轻咬了一口，留下牙印。我顿时像恶魔附身，怒不可遏。我一时忘乎所以。原来那个善良的灵魂一下子飞出了我的躯壳，酒性大发，变得赛过凶神恶煞，浑身不知哪来的一股狠劲。我从背心口袋里掏出一把小刀，打开刀子，攥住那可怜畜生的喉咙，居心不良地把它眼珠剜了出来！写到这幕该死的暴行，我不禁面红耳赤，不寒而栗。

睡了一夜，宿醉方醒。到第二天早上起来，神智恢复过来了，对自己犯下这个罪孽才悔惧莫及。但这至多不过是一种淡泊而模糊的感觉而已。我的灵魂还是毫无触动。我狂饮滥喝起来，一旦沉湎醉乡，自己所作所为早已统统忘光。

这时那猫伤势渐渐好转，眼珠剜掉的那只眼窝果真是十分可怕，看来它再也不感到痛了。它照常在屋里走动，只是一见我走近，就不出所料地吓得拼命逃走。我毕竟天良未泯，因此最初看见过去如此热爱我的畜生竟这样嫌恶我，不免感到伤心。但是这股伤心之感一下子就变为恼怒了。到后来，那股邪念又上升了，终于

71

害得我一发不可收拾。关于这种邪念，哲学上并没有重视。不过我深信不疑，这种邪念是人心本能的一股冲动，是一种微乎其微的原始功能，或者说是情绪，人类性格就由它来决定。谁没有在无意中多次干下坏事或蠢事呢？而且这样干时无缘无故，心里明知干不得而偏要干。哪怕我们明知这样干犯法，我们不是还会无视自己看到的后果，有股拼命想去以身试法的邪念吗？唉，就是这股邪念终于断送了我的一生。正是出于内心这股深奥难测的渴望，渴望自找烦恼，违背本性，为作恶而作恶，我竟然对那只无辜的畜生继续下起毒手来，最后害它送了命。有一天早晨，我心狠手辣，用根套索勒住猫脖子，把它吊在树枝上，眼泪汪汪，心里痛悔不已，就此把猫吊死了。我出此下策，就因为我知道这猫爱过我，就因为我觉得这猫没冒犯过我，就因为我知道这样干是在犯罪——犯下该下地狱的大罪，罪大之极，足以害得我那永生的灵魂永世不得超生，如若有此可能，就连慈悲为怀、可敬可畏的上帝都无法赦免我的罪过。

就在我干下这个伤天害理的勾当的当天晚上，我在睡梦中忽听得喊叫失火，马上惊醒。床上的帐子已经着了火。整栋屋子都烧着了。我们夫妇和一个佣人好不容易才在这场火灾中保住性命。这场火灾烧得真彻底。我的一切财物统统化为乌有，从此以后，我索性万念俱灰了。

我倒也不至于那么懦弱，会在自己所犯罪孽和这场火灾之间找因果关系。不过我要把事实的来龙去脉详细说一说，但愿别把任何环节拉下。失火的第二天，我去凭吊这堆废墟。墙壁都倒塌了，只有一道还没塌下来。一看原来是一堵墙壁，厚倒不厚，正巧在屋子中间，我的床头就靠近这堵墙。墙上的灰泥大大挡住了火势，我把这件事看成是新近粉刷的缘故。墙根前密密麻麻聚集了一堆人，看来有不少人非常仔细和专心地在查看这堵墙，只听得大家连声喊着"奇怪"以及诸如此类的话，我不由感到好奇，就走近一看，但见白壁上赫然有个浅浮雕，原来是只偌大的猫。这猫刻得惟妙惟肖，一丝不差，猫脖子还有一根绞索。

我一看到这个怪物，简直以为自己活见鬼了，不由惊恐万分。但是转念一想终于放了心。我记得，这猫明明吊在宅边花园里。

火警一起，花园里就挤满了人，准是哪一个把猫从树上放下来，从开着的窗口扔进我的卧室。他这样做可能是打算唤醒我。另外几堵墙倒下来，正巧把受我残害而送命的猫压在新刷的泥灰壁上，壁间的石灰加上烈火和尸骸发出的氨气，三者起了某种作用，墙上才会出现我刚看到的浮雕像。

对于刚刚细细道来的这一令人惊心动魄的事实，即使良心上不能自圆其说，于理说来倒也稀松平常，但是在我心灵上，总留下一个深刻的印象。有好几个月我摆脱不了那猫幻象的纠缠。这时节，我心里又滋生一股说是悔恨又不是悔恨的模糊情绪。我甚至后悔害死这猫，因此就在经常出入的下等场所中，到处物色一只外貌多少相似的黑猫权作填补。

有一天晚上，我醉醺醺地坐在一个下等酒寮里，忽然间我注意到一只盛放金酒或朗姆酒的大酒桶，这是屋里一件主要家什，桶上有个黑乎乎的东西。我刚才一直目不转睛地盯着大酒桶好一会儿，奇怪的是竟然没有及早看出上面那东西。我走近它，用手摸摸。原来是只黑猫，长得偌大，个头跟普路托完全一样，除了一处之外，其他处处都极相像。普路托全身没有一根白毛，而这只猫几乎整个胸前都长满一片白斑，只是模糊不清而已。

我刚摸着它，它就有所表示，立即跳了起来，咕噜咕噜直叫，身子在我手上一味蹭着，表示承蒙我注意而很高兴。这猫正是我梦寐以求的，我当场向店东要求买下，谁知店东一点都不晓得这猫的来历，而且也从没见到过，所以也没有开价。

我继续撸着这猫，正准备动身回家，这猫却流露出要跟我走的样子。我就让它跟着，一面走一面常常弯下身子去摸摸它。这猫一到我家马上很乖，一下子就博得我妻子的欢心。

至于我嘛，不久就对这猫厌恶起来了。这正出乎我的意料，我也不知道这是怎么回事，也不知道是什么道理。它对我的眷恋如此明显，我见了反而又讨厌又生气。渐渐地，这些情绪竟变为深恶痛绝了。我尽量避开这猫，正因心里感到羞愧，再加之回想起早先犯下的残暴行为，我才不敢动手欺凌它。我有好几个星期一直没有去打它，也没粗暴虐待它。但是久而久之，我就渐渐对这猫有说不出的厌恶了，一见到它那副丑相，我就像躲避瘟疫一样，悄悄溜之大吉。

不消说，使我更加痛恨这畜生的原因，就是我把它带回家的第二天早晨，看到它竟同普路托一个样儿，眼珠也被剜掉一个。可是，我妻子见此情形，反而格外喜欢它了。我在上面说过，我妻子是个富有同情心的人。我原先身上也具有这种出色的美德，它曾使我感受到无比纯正的乐趣。

尽管我对这猫这般嫌恶，它对我反而越来越亲热。它跟我寸步不离，这鼓拧劲儿读者一定难以理解。只要我一坐下，它就会蹲在我椅子脚边，或是跳到我膝上，在我身上到处撒娇，实在讨厌。我一站起来走路，它就缠在我脚边，差点把我绊倒；再不，就用又长又尖的爪子钩住我衣服，顺势爬上我胸口。我虽然恨不得一拳把它揍死，可是这时候，我还是不敢动手，一则是因为我想起自己早先犯下的罪过，而主要的原因还在于——索性让我说明吧——我对这畜生害怕极了。

这层害怕倒不是生怕皮肉受苦，可是要想说个清楚倒也为难。我简直羞于承认——唉，即使如今身在死牢，我也简直羞于承认，这猫引起我的恐惧竟由于可以想象到的纯粹幻觉而更加厉害了。我妻子不止一次要我留神看这片白毛的斑迹。想必各位还记得，我上面提过，这只怪猫跟我杀掉的那只猫唯一明显的不同地方就是这片斑迹。想必各位还记得，我说过这斑迹大虽大，原来倒是很模糊的，可是逐渐逐渐的、不知不觉的竟明显了，终于现出一个一清二楚的轮廓来了。好久以来我的理智一直不肯承认，竭力把这当成幻觉。这时那斑迹竟成了一样东西，我一提起这东西的名称就不由得浑身发毛。正因如此，我对这怪物特别厌恶和惧怕，要是我有胆量的话，早把它干掉了。我说呀，原来这东西是个吓人的幻象，是个恐怖东西的幻象——一个绞刑台！哎呀，这是多么可悲、多么可怕的刑具啊！这是恐怖的刑具、正法的刑具！这是叫人受罪的刑具、送人死命的刑具呀！

这时我真落到要多倒霉有多倒霉的地步了。我行若无事地杀害了一只没有理性的畜生。它的同类，一只没有理性的畜生竟对我——一个按照上帝形象创造出来的人，带来那么多不堪忍受的灾祸！哎呀！无论白天，还是黑夜，我再也不得安宁了！在白天里，这畜生片刻都不让我单独太太平平的；到了黑夜，我时时刻刻都从说不出有多可怕的噩梦中惊醒，一看见这东西在我脸上喷着热气，我心头永远压着这东西的千钧棒，丝毫也摆脱不了这具体的梦魇！

我身受这般痛苦的煎熬，心里仅剩的一点善性也丧失了。邪念竟成了我唯一的内心活动，转来转去都是极为卑鄙龌龊的邪恶念头。我脾气向来就喜怒无常，如今发展到痛恨一切事，痛恨一切人了。我盲目地放任自己，往往动不动就突然发火，管也管不住。哎呀！经常遭殃、逆来顺受的就数我那毫无怨言的妻子了。

由于家里穷，我们只好住在一栋老房子里。有一天，为了点家务事，她陪着我到这栋老房子的地窖里去。这猫也跟着我走下那陡峭的阶梯，差点儿害得我摔了个倒栽葱，气得我直发疯。我抡起斧头，盛怒中忘了自己对这猫还怀有幼稚的恐惧，对准这猫一斧砍下去，要是当时真按我心意砍下去，不消说，这猫当场就完蛋了。谁知，我妻子伸出手来一把攥住我。我正在火头上，给她这一拦，格外暴跳如雷，趁势挣脱胳膊，对准她脑壳就砍了一斧。可怜她哼也没哼一声就当场送了命。

干完了这件伤天害理的杀人勾当，我就索性细细盘算藏匿尸首的事了。我知道无论白天还是黑夜，要把尸首搬出去，难免要给左邻右舍撞见，我心里想起了不少计划。一会儿我想把尸首剁成小块烧掉，来个毁尸灭迹；一会儿我到院子中的井里去。还打算把尸首当作货物装箱，按照常规，雇个脚夫把它搬出去。末了，我忽然想出一条自忖的万全良策。我打定主意把尸首砌进地窖的墙里，据传说，中世纪的僧侣就是这样把殉道者砌进墙里的。

这个地窖派这个用场真是再合适也没有了。墙壁结构很松，新近刚用粗灰泥全部刷新过，因为地窖里潮湿，灰泥至今还没有干燥。而且有堵墙因为有个假壁炉而矗出一块，已经填没了，做得跟地窖其他的部分一模一样。我可以不费什么手脚地把这地方的墙砖挖开，将尸首塞进去，再照旧把墙完全砌上，这样包管什么人都看不出破绽来。

这个主意果然不错。我用了一根铁锹，一下子就撬掉砖墙，再仔仔细细把尸首贴着里边的夹墙放好，让它撑着不掉下来，然后没费半点事就把墙照原样砌上。我弄来了石灰、黄沙和乱发，做好一切准备，我就调配了一种跟旧灰泥分别不出的新灰泥，小心翼翼地把它涂抹在新砌的砖墙上。等我完了事，看到一切顺当才放了心。这堵墙居然一点都看不出动过土的痕迹来。地上落下的垃圾也仔仔细细地收拾干净了。我得意扬扬地朝四下看看，不由暗自说，"这下子到底没有白忙啊！"

接下来我就要寻找替我招来那么些灾害的祸根，我终于横下一条心来。不料我刚才大发雷霆的时候，那个鬼精灵见势不妙就溜了，眼下见着我这股火性，自然不敢露脸。这只讨厌的畜生终于不在了。我心头压着的这块大石头也终于放下了，这股深深的乐劲儿实在无法形容，也无法想象。到了夜里，这猫还没露脸，这样，自从这猫上我家以来，我至少终于太太平平地酣睡了一夜。哎呀，尽管我心灵上压着杀人害命的重担，我还是睡着了。

过了第二天，又过了第三天，这只折磨人的猫还没来。我才重新像个自由人那样呼吸。这只鬼猫吓得从屋里逃走了，一去不回了！眼不见为净，这份乐趣就甭提有多大了！尽管我犯下滔天大罪，但心里竟没有什么不安。官府来调查过几次，我三言两语就把他们搪塞过去了。甚至还来抄过一次家，可当然查不出半点线索来。我就此认为前途安然无忧了。

到了我杀妻的第四天，不料屋里突然闯来了一帮警察，又动手严密地搜查了一番。不过，我自恃藏尸地方隐蔽，他们绝对料不到，所以一点也不感到慌张。那些警察命我陪同他们搜查。他们连一个角落也不放过。搜到第三遍第四遍，他们终于走下地窖。我泰然自若、毫不动容。平生不做亏心事，半夜敲门心不惊，我一颗心如此平静。我在地窖里从这头走到那头。胸前抱着双臂，若无其事地走来走去。警察完全放了心，正准备要走。我心花怒放、乐不可支。为了表示得意，我恨不得开口说话，哪怕说一句也好，这样就更可以叫他们放心地相信我无罪了。

这些人刚走上阶梯，我终于开了口。"诸位先生，承蒙你们脱了我的嫌疑，我感激不尽。谨向你们请安了，还望多多关照。诸位先生，顺便说一句，这屋子结构很牢固。"我一时头脑发昏、随心所欲地信口胡说，简直连自己都不知道说了些什么。"这栋屋子可以说结构好得不得了。这几堵墙——诸位先生，想走了吗？——这几堵墙砌得很牢固。"说到这里，我一时昏了头，故作姿态，竟然拿起手里一根棒，使劲敲着竖放我爱妻遗骸的那堵砖墙。

哎哟，求主保佑，把我从恶魔的虎口中拯救出来吧！我敲墙的回响余音未寂，就听得墓冢里发出一下声音！——一下哭声，开头瓮声瓮气、断断续续，像个小孩在抽泣，随即一下子变成连续不断的高声长啸，声音异常，惨绝人寰——这是一声哀号——一声悲鸣，半似恐怖，半似得意，只有堕入地狱的受罪冤魂痛苦的惨叫，和魔鬼见了冤魂遭受天罚的欢呼打成一片，才跟这声音差不离。

要说我当时的想法未免荒唐可笑。我昏头昏脑、跟跟跄跄地走到那堵墙边。阶梯上那些警察大惊失色，吓得要命，一时呆若木鸡。过了一会儿，就见十来条粗壮的胳膊忙着拆墙。那堵墙整个倒下来。那具尸体已经腐烂不堪、凝满血块，赫然直立在大家眼前。尸体头部上就坐着那只可怕的畜生，张开血盆大口，独眼里冒着火。它捣了鬼，诱使我杀了妻子，如今又用唤声报了警，把我送到刽子手的手里。原来我把这怪物砌进墓墙里去了！

✤ Answers for questions

1. On the surface, it is the alcohol that makes the narrator become a monster. But when deep read it, we will find that the narrator is a man who is influenced by various things from inside and outside. On the inside, plenty of negative emotions such as jealousy, violence, irritation make the man be jealous to the black cat who was loved by his wife and be violent and irritable to the cat in that the cat was so close to the man that the man felt troublesome. On the outside, the man was always haunting in the bar and was alcoholic, which shows that his life is aimless and disordered. Both inside reasons and outside reasons lead the man to the depth of sin. And the black cat is a victim and witness. In addition, the black cat's singular-eye like a beacon light that makes all evils exposed. So justice exists and has long arms.

2. The cat's name has a special meaning—Pluto. This is the Roman god of the underworld. Pluto contributes to a strong sense of hell

and may even symbolize the devil himself. Another immensely symbolic part of "The Black Cat" is the title itself, since onyx cats have long connoted bad luck and misfortune.

3. Poe's best known fiction works are Gothic, a genre he followed to appease the public taste. Poe's works featured accounts of terrifying experiences in ancient castles—experienced with subterranean dungeons, secret passageways, flickering lamps, screams, moans, bloody hands, ghosts, graveyards, and the rest. In "The Black Cat", the protagonist was living in a typical Gothic building. The cellar in which he hid his wife's body was pervaded a sense of horror, because it was well adapt for his vicious purpose, that is, walling his wife's body. Also in many of Poe's works, setting is used to paint a dark and gloomy picture in our minds. His most recurring themes deal with questions of death, including its physical signs, the effects of decomposition, concerns of premature burial, the reanimation of the dead, and mourning. In his novel, he uses the symbolism a lot to achieve its special effect.

References

[1] http://image. baidu. com/i? tn = baiduimage&ipn = r&ct = 201326592&cl = 2&lm = -1&st = -1&fm = result&fr = &sf = 1&fmq = 1429499100453_R&pv = &ic =0&nc = 1&z = &se = 1&showtab = 0&fb = 0&width = &height = &face = 0&istype =2&ie = utf -8&word = allen + Poe

[2] http://en. wikipedia. org/wiki/Edgar_Allan_Poe

[3] http://en. wikipedia. org/wiki/The_Black_Cat_(short_story)

[4] http://blog. sina. com. cn/s/blog_61c844cb0100idez. html

[5] http://www. 123helpme. com/view. asp? id =5639

Unit 4
Ralph Waldo Emerson (1803 – 1882)

🌿 Bibliography

Ralph Waldo Emerson (1803 – 1882) was an American essayist, lecturer and poet, who led the Transcendentalist movement of the mid-19th century. He was seen as a champion of individualism and a prescient critic of the countervailing pressures of society, and he disseminated his thoughts through dozens of published essays and more than 1,500 public lectures across the United States.

Emerson gradually moved away from the religious and social beliefs of his contemporaries, formulating and expressing the philosophy of Transcendentalism in his 1836 essay, *Nature*. Following this ground-breaking work, he gave a speech entitled *The American Scholar* in 1837, which Oliver Wendell Holmes, Sr. considered to be America's "Intellectual Declaration of Independence".

Emerson wrote most of his important essays as lectures first, then revised them for print. His first two collections of essays—*Essays: First Series and Essays: Second Series*, published respectively in 1841 and 1844—represent the core of his thinking, and include such well-known essays as *Self-Reliance*, *The Over-Soul*, *Circles*, *The Poet and Experience*. Together with *Nature*, these essays made the decade from the mid-1830s to the mid-1840s Emerson's most fertile period.

Emerson wrote on a number of subjects, never espousing fixed philosophical tenets, but developing certain ideas such as individuality, freedom, the ability for humankind to realize almost anything, and the relationship between the soul and the surrounding world. Emerson's *Nature* was more philosophical than naturalistic: "Philosophically considered, the universe is composed of Nature and the Soul." Emerson is one of several figures who "took a more pantheist or pandeist approach by rejecting views of God as separate from the world".

He remains among the linchpins of the American romantic movement, and his work has greatly influenced the thinkers, writers and poets that have followed him. When asked to sum up his work, he said his central doctrine was "the infinitude of the private man". Emerson is also well known as a mentor and friend of fellow Transcendentalist Henry David Thoreau.

🌼 *Nature*

Nature is an essay written by Ralph Waldo Emerson, and published by James Munroe and Company in 1836. In this essay Emerson put forth the foundation of Transcendentalism, a belief system that espouses a non-traditional appreciation of nature. Transcendentalism suggests that the divine, or God, suffuses nature, and suggests that reality can be understood by studying nature. Emerson's visit to  the Muséum National d'Histoire Naturelle in Paris inspired a set of lectures he later delivered in Boston which were then published.

Within the essay, Emerson divides nature into four usages: Commodity, Beauty, Language and Discipline. These distinctions define the ways by which humans use nature for their basic needs, their desire for delight, their communication with one another and their understanding of the world. Emerson followed the success of *Nature* with a speech, *The American Scholar*, which together with his previous lectures laid the foundation for Transcendentalism and his literary career.

Summary

In *Nature*, Emerson lays out and attempts to solve an abstract problem: that humans do not fully accept nature's beauty. He writes that people are distracted by the demands of the world, whereas nature gives but humans fail to reciprocate. The essay consists of eight sections: Nature, Commodity, Beauty, Language, Discipline, Idealism, Spirit and Prospects. Each section takes a different perspective on the relationship between humans and nature.

In the essay Emerson explains that to experience the "wholeness" with nature for which we are naturally suited, we must be separate from the flaws and distractions imposed on us by society. Emerson believed that solitude is the single mechanism through which we can be fully engaged in the world of nature, writing "To go into solitude, a man needs to retire as much from his chamber as from society. I am not solitary whilst I read and write, though nobody is with me. But if a man would be alone, let him look at the stars".

When a person experiences true solitude, in nature, it "take(s)him away". Society, he says, destroys wholeness, whereas "Nature, in its ministry to man, is not only the material, but is also the process and the result. All the parts incessantly work into each other's hands for the profit of man. The wind sows the seed; the sun evaporates the sea; the wind blows the vapor to the field; the ice, on the other side of the planet, condenses rain on this; the rain feeds the plant; the plant feeds the animal; and thus the endless circulations of the divine charity nourish man".

Emerson defines a spiritual relationship. In nature a person finds its spirit and accepts it as the Universal Being. He writes: "Nature is not fixed but fluid; to a pure spirit, nature is everything."

Comments on *Nature*

The Harmonious Relationship between Human and Nature

Nature depicts the harmonious relationship between human and na-

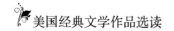

ture, the inter-relation between human and nature is delicately shown. This harmonious relationship needs our human being's maintenance and care. Striking the balance between human and nature depends on handling relationships, for instance, in our current point of views, those between population growth, the use of natural resources and natural protection. As what has mentioned above, eco-criticism is a term which has in some way stated the relation between human and nature, our human should not be satisfied only in basic living conditions but following the objective principle of the harmonious development of humankind and nature. The goal of building a harmonious relationship between human and nature is a substantial part of protecting our human's long lasting existence and human culture. Nature is existing in an abstract form, but it can be felt by our human being. By direct communication with nature, we should communicate it with our whole-heart and with a kind of passion. One obtains spiritual and material wealth by following the objective principle of the harmonious relationship development of human and nature. The harmonious existence between human and nature is a circulated circle which can maintain the order of our universe.

Nature is a common link to the whole, the corresponding Heaven. Universe is not an isolated existence, and in which human and nature are mutual influenced, interactive, interrelated and interdependent with each other. A harmonious society needs a peaceful relation between the human beings and the nature.

Change and Continuity in the Human-Nature Relationship

To maintain the harmonious human-nature relationship is a long term and arduous task. Go back to early ages, we can see that our ancestor try their utmost to overcome difficulties while living without settled places or in wilderness, and they have a sense of respect towards nature. With time going, men perceive the human and nature relations quite differently. Take Emerson's Nature for example, it stresses a balance between humans and nature in order to promote unity between heaven and the earth. In 1836 back in America, Emerson published his masterpiece Nature, from his description about nature, we could perceive the relationship between human and nature in a different perspective. And we may better understand how Emerson's conception of nature.

"The western clouds divided and subdivided themselves into pink flakes modulated with tints of unspeakable softness; and the air had so much life and sweetness, that it was a pain to come within doors. " (Ralph Waldo Emerson, 1836: 33)

It shows the poet's love of nature. Nature here has the function of comforting one's feelings and refreshing one's soul. Emerson means that the universe is composed of matter and spirit, and with the latter as the only origin. Nature includes both the common nature and man's body. And Nature is brought by the over-soul. However, Emerson never denied or excluded the common nature. He had said in the introduction of Nature that "I shall use the word (nature) in both senses; —in its common and in its philosophical import. " So apart from the philosophical Nature, Emerson's conception of the common nature also plays an essential part, which should never be omitted or neglected. Emerson perceives that nature is symbolic of man's mind, or in his own words "nature always wears the colors of the spirit". (Ralph Waldo Emerson, 1836: 16) *Nature* in Emerson's opinion, "is the least part" which he continues that "the shows of day, the dewy morning, the rainbow, mountains, orchards in blossoms, stars, moonlight, shadows in still water, and the like, if too eagerly hunted, become shows merely, and mock us with their unreality. "(Ralph Waldo Emerson, 1836: 35) And a high and divine beauty lies in "the combination with the human will". In Chapter IV Language of *Nature*, Emerson stated clearly that, "Every natural fact is a symbol of some spiritual fact. Every appearance in nature corresponds to some state of the mind, and that state of mind can only be described by presenting that natural appearance as its picture. " In Chapter VII Spirit of *Nature*, Emerson stated that, "It (nature) is the organ through which the universal spirit speaks to individual, and strives to lead back the individual to it. " It means only by combining nature with man's mind can nature has some significance, and if without, nature is lifeless and valueless. Therefore, the beauty of nature derives from the beauty of the mind, which transcends people's limits of senses but rely on instinct to realize. And the reason why man owns such an instinct is that within every man exists the over-soul, that every man is divine, and can converse with God directly. So the over-soul functions as a ministry through which man can recognize the beauty of nature. Stating this point, Emerson also used the device of metaphor:

"that spirit, that is, the Supreme Being, does not build up nature around us, but puts it forth through us, as the life of the tree puts forth new branches and leaves through the pores of the old. " (Ralph Waldo Emerson, 1836: 59)

The universe is a whole one, with matter and spirit both from the same spiritual origin. Then it is rational for us to infer that the common nature and human being also should be in a harmonious one, namely, his idealist monism calls for a unity of man and nature.

The human-nature relationship in Nature spiritualized the wilderness. The principles inherent in human and nature relations corresponded with harmony to ensure internal stability in an unpredictable world. Human's conception of natural surroundings emerged from the people's fears of natural disasters and their sense of superiority over nature stemmed from their efforts to control an unpredictable wilderness. The change and continuity of human-nature relationship is subtly shown in Emerson's Nature, and the current conception of human-nature relationship is different from Emerson's. No matter it is in an abstract way of conception in Nature or in our modern human's conception of human-nature relations. It does undergo great change and will bond together forever.

Reaction against the Industrialization

The Transcendentalists stressed the importance of the individual, the new notion of the individual and his importance represented, obviously, a new way of looking at man. It was a reaction against the

process of dehumanization which came in the wake of developing capitalism. The industrialization of New England was turning men into nonhuman. People were losing their individuality and were becoming uniform.
And it was also a reaction Calvinist concept that man is totally depraved, he is sinful and perseveres in sinhood, and can not hope to be
saved except through the grace of God.

It was feared that the rising industrialization would result in a loss
of individuality and creativity, so Emerson was against capitalism and
industrialization. His thought was shown in his masterpiece Nature, in
which he stated that nature should be the place where our thoughts rested and no matter what it is like, our men should keep a clear view upon
our own thought. Men were all powerful if they had held his individuality and his own features. Through nature, men would transcend, would
turn into a transparent eyeball and saw what they want to.

Emphasis on the Significance of the Individual

Nature has been called the manifesto of Transcendentalism. And
the Transcendentalists stressed the importance of the individual, in
Emerson's Nature, the individual was the most important element in society. As the regeneration of society could only come about through the
regeneration of the individual, his perception, his self-culture and self-
improvement, and not the wildly excited or frantic effort to get rich,
should become the first concern of his life. The ideal type of man was
the self-reliant individual whom Emerson never stopped talking about all
his life. In Nature, Emerson was telling people to depend on themselves
for spiritual perfection if they cared the effort, because in Emerson's o-
pinion, the individual soul communed with the Oversoul and therefore
divine. Now this new notion of the individual and his importance represented, obviously, a new way of looking at man. It was a reaction a-
gainst Calvinist concept that man is totally depraved, he is sinful and
perseveres in sinhood, and cannot hope to be saved except through the
grace of God. It was also a reaction against the process of dehumanization which came in the wake of developing capitalism. The industrializa-

tion of New England was turning men into nonhuman. People were losing their individuality and were becoming uniform. In Nature, by trying to reassure the importance of the individual, Emerson emphasized the significance of men regaining their lost personality.

Introduction to Chapter 1

Chapter 1 introduces Emerson's view of nature. In this chapter, Emerson expresses the idea that one should try and see life as a child does. Also human beings should look at life each day with fresh eyes and constantly learn from nature. He also shows the importance of unity and harmony between mankind nature and God.

From   *Nature*

Chapter 1

To go into solitude, a man needs to retire as much from his chamber as from society. I am not solitary whilst I read and write, though nobody is with me. But if a man would be alone, let him look at the stars. The rays that come from those heavenly worlds, will separate between him and what he touches. One might think the atmosphere was made transparent with this design, to give man, in the heavenly bodies, the perpetual presence of the sublime[1]. Seen in the streets of cities, how great they are! If the stars should appear one night in a thousand years, how would men believe and adore; and preserve for many generations the remembrance of the city of God which had been shown! But every night come out these envoys of beauty, and light the universe with their admonishing smile.

The stars awaken a certain reverence, because though always present, they are inaccessible; but all natural objects make a kindred impression, when the mind is open to their influence. Nature never wears a mean appearance. Neither does the wisest man extort[2] her secret, and lose his curiosity by finding out all her perfection. Nature never became a toy to a wise spirit. The flowers, the animals, the mountains, reflected the wisdom of his best hour, as much as they had delighted the simplicity of his childhood.

When we speak of nature in this manner, we have a distinct but most poetical sense in the mind. We mean the integrity of impression made by manifold natural objects. It is this which distinguishes the stick of timber[3] of the wood-cutter, from the tree of the poet. The charming landscape which I saw this morning, is indubitably[4] made up of some twenty or thirty farms. Miller owns this field, Locke that, and Manning the woodland beyond. But none of them owns the landscape. There is a property in the horizon which no man has but he whose eye can integrate all the parts, that is, the poet. This is the best part of these men's farms, yet to this their warranty-deeds give no title.

To speak truly, few adult persons can see nature. Most persons do not see the sun. At least they have a very superficial seeing. The sun illuminates only the eye of the man, but shines into the eye and the heart of the child. The lover of nature is he whose inward and outward senses are still truly adjusted to each other; who has retained the spirit of infancy even into the era of manhood. His intercourse with heaven and earth, becomes part of his daily food. In the presence of nature, a wild delight runs through the man, in spite of real sorrows. *Nature* says — he is my creature, and maugre all his impertinent griefs, he shall be glad with me. Not the sun or the summer alone, but every hour and season yields its tribute of delight; for every hour and change corresponds to and authorizes a different state of the mind, from breathless noon to grimmest midnight. *Nature* is a setting that fits equally well a comic or a mourning piece. In good health, the air is a cordial[5] of incredible virtue. Crossing a bare common, in snow puddles, at twilight, under a clouded sky, without having in my thoughts any occurrence of special good fortune, I have enjoyed a perfect exhilaration. In the woods too, a man casts off his years, as the snake his slough, and at what period soever of life, is always a child. In the woods, is perpetual youth. Within these plantations of God, a decorum[6] and sanctity reign, a perennial[7] festival is dressed, and the guest sees not how he should tire of them in a thousand years. In the woods, we return to reason and faith. There I feel that nothing can befall me in life — no disgrace, no calamity, (leaving me my eyes,) which nature cannot repair. Standing on the bare ground — my head bathed by the blithe air, and uplifted into infinite space — all mean egotism vanishes. I become a transparent eye-ball; I am nothing; I see all; the currents of the Universal Being circulate through me; I am part or particle of God. The name of the nearest friend sounds then foreign and accidental: to be brothers, to be acquaintances — master or servant, is then a trifle and a disturbance. I am the lover of uncontained and immortal beauty. In the wilderness, I find something more dear and connate[8] than in streets or villages. In the tranquil landscape, and especially in the distant line of the horizon, man beholds somewhat as beautiful as his own nature.

The greatest delight which the fields and woods minister, is the suggestion of an occult[9] relation between man and the vegetable. I am not alone and unacknowledged. They nod to me, and I to them. The waving of the boughs in the storm, is new to me and old. It takes me by surprise, and yet is not unknown. Its effect is like that of a higher thought or a better emotion coming over me, when I deemed I was thinking justly or doing right.

Yet it is certain that the power to produce this delight, does not reside in nature, but in man, or in a harmony of both. It is necessary to use these pleasures with great temperance. For, nature is not always tricked in holiday attire, but the same scene which yesterday breathed perfume and glittered as for the frolic of the nymphs[10], is overspread with melancholy today. To a man laboring under calamity, the heat of his own fire hath sadness in it. Then, there is a kind of contempt of the landscape felt by him who has just lost by death a dear friend. The sky is less grand as it shuts down over less worth in the population.

Notes:

1. sublime *adj.* 庄严的

   E. g. At times the show veered from the sublime to the ridiculous.

2. extort *vt.* 敲诈；曲解

   E. g. Some magistrates have abused their powers of arrest to extort confessions.

   The police used torture to extort a confession from him.

3. timber *n.* 木材，木料

   E. g. These Severn Valley woods have been exploited for timber since Saxon times.

   A natural timber deck leads into the main room of the home.

4. indubitable *adj.* 不容置疑的，明确无疑的；无可置疑

   E. g. The indubitable evidence we produced bore down our opponents in the debate.

5. cordial *adj.* 热诚的；诚恳的；兴奋的

   E. g. The conversation was carried on in a cordial and friendly atmosphere.

   The meeting of the old classmates was extremely cordial.

6. decorum *n.* 端庄得体；体统

   E. g. The new King seemed to be carrying out his duties with grace and due decorum.

7. perennial *adj.* 终年的，长久的；多年生的；

   E. g. I wonder at her perennial youthfulness.

   There's a perennial shortage of teachers with science qualifications.

8. connate *adj.* 天生的，先天的，同族的

   E. g. The term connate implies born, produced or originated together.

   In the wilderness, I find something more dear and connate than in streets or villages.

9. occult *adj.* 超自然的；神秘的；隐藏的

    E. g. He's interested in witchcraft and the occult.

          Were not all things charged with occult virtues?

10. nymph *n.* 仙女；幼虫

    E. g. She fled as if she were a startled nymph.

Questions：

1. What is Emerson's view of nature?

2. What does Emerson want to express through the sentence "To go into solitude, a man needs to retire as much from his chamber as from society"？（para 1）

3. Explain "Standing on the bare ground, my head bathed by the blithe air and uplifted into infinite space, all mean egotism vanishes. I become a transparent eyeball; I am nothing; I see all; the currents of the Universal Bing circulate through me; I am part of God".（para 2 line 45）

中文译文：

走入孤独，远离书斋，如同远离社会一样重要。纵然无人在我身旁，当我读书或写作时，并非独处一隅。如果一个人渴望独处，就请他注目于星辰吧。那从天界下行的光芒，使人们得以出离可触摸的现世。可以这样说，我们假想，大气之所以透明，就是为了让人们看到天国的灿烂光芒。从普通城市的街道向上看，它们是如此深邃伟岸。假如星辰千年一现，人类关于上帝之城的记忆，必将世代相传，为人们长久地信仰着，珍存着，崇拜着。然而，每一晚，这些美的使者都会降临，以它们无可置疑的微笑照亮宇宙。

星辰唤醒心中的景仰，即使它们常在，也遥远而不可触摸；而当思想敞开心门，自然景物总会留下熟稔而亲切的印迹。自然永无恶意可憎的容颜。如同大智慧者不会因穷尽自然的和谐底蕴而失去对她的好奇之心。自然之于智慧的心灵绝非玩具。花朵、动物、群山，它们折射着智者思维的灵光，如同它们娱乐了他纯真的童年。当我们这样谈论自然时，我们的心灵感觉清晰独特、诗意盎然。我们在感觉着多面的自然客体和谐完整的映象。正是这映象区分了伐木工手中的圆木与诗人心中的树木。

今晨我看到那令人愉悦的风景，它们无疑是由二十个到三十个农场组成。米勒拥有这片地，洛克拥有那片，而曼宁是那片树林的主人。但是他们都不能占有这片风景。只有诗人的双眼可以拥有这地平线，这是他们农场中最可贵的，却无人能凭产权而据为己有。说实话，成年人难得看到自然本身。多数人看不到太阳，至少，他们所见只是浮光掠影。阳光只照亮了成人的双眼所见，却照进儿童的眼睛和心灵深处。自然的热爱者，内向和外向的感觉尚能和谐的相应，他尚能在成年时保有婴儿的心灵。与天地的交汇成为必需，就如每日的食物一样。自然当前时，奔腾的喜悦传遍他全身，尽管可能他正身处现实的苦境。他是我的造物，泯灭他无关紧要的悲伤，与我同在他应欢悦，自然向他如是说。不仅阳光和夏天带来欢跃，四季的每一时分都奉献出愉悦；自然变化的每一时辰无不如是。从闷热的午后到漆黑的子夜，四季早晚的嬗变对应并验证着人们不同的精神状态。自然既可是悲剧的，也可以是喜剧的背景。身体康健时，空气就是让人难以置信的补剂甜酿。越过空旷的公地，停留深雪潭边，注目晨昏曦微光芒，在满布乌云的天空下，并非出于特别的当头好运，我享受了完美无缺的欣喜。我欣喜以至有些胆怯。在树林里也是一样，人们抖落岁月如蛇脱旧皮，无论身处生命的哪一阶段，都会心如孩童。在森林中，有永恒的青春。在上帝的庄园里，气派和圣洁是主宰，四季的庆典准备就绪，客人们居此千年也不会厌倦。在森林里，我们回归理性和信仰，在那里，任何不幸不会降临于我的生命，没有任何屈辱和灾病—请留下我的双眼—是自然无法平复的。站在空旷大地之上，我的头脑沐浴于欢欣大气并升腾于无限空间，一切卑劣的自高自大和自我中心消失无踪。我变成一个透明的眼球，我化为乌有，我却遍览一切；宇宙精神的湍流环绕激荡着我。我成为上帝的一部分，我是他的微粒。密友的名字听起来陌生而无足轻重，兄弟、朋友、主人或仆从，这一切变得细碎而搅扰。我是不受拘束永恒不朽自然之美的情人。与街市和村庄相比，在旷野里，我体味到更亲切更可贵的实在。在静谧的风景里，尤其是在那遥远的地平线，我们看到自然

91

美丽有如我们美丽自身和本性。

田野和树林带给我们心灵的巨大欢悦，指说着人类和植物的隐秘关联。我并非独在而不受关注，植物向我颔首，我向它们点头。风雨中树枝摇动对我是既新鲜又熟稔。它令我惊异又让我安然。它们对于我的影响，就如同我确信自我思维妥帖所为正当时，全身涌起的超越而高尚的感情。

然而，可以肯定地说，这欢悦的力量不仅源于自然本身，它存在于人，或者说，存在于自然和人的和谐中。要谨慎节制地享有这种欢悦，这很重要。自然并不总悦人以节日盛装，昨日氤氲芬芳晶亮悦目—如为林仙嬉乐而设的同一景致，今天就可能蒙上悲伤的面纱。自然总是折射着观者的精神状态。对于在病痛中挣扎的人，他自身散发的焦虑挣扎就涵容着悲伤。当爱友逝去时，人们会对那风景感到些许漠然。当蓝天落幕于社会底层者眼前，它的壮丽也会减色。

🌿 Answers for questions

1. Emerson loves nature. His nature is the garment of the over-soul, symbolic and moral bound. Nature is not something purely of the matter, but alive with God's presence. It exercises a healthy and restorative influence on human beings. Children can see nature better than adult.

2. He set up a claim to support self-cultivation and thought only when human beings were alone and stayed in solitude that their inherent talents could be brought to full play. Nature is the embodiment of human's mind. Joyful nature represents happiness, while sad nature shows sorrow.

3. This was a famous sentence which illustrated the harmony between nature and human beings. This thought was the main part of romanticism and the key point of the book nature. Nature always wore the colors of the spirit. Moreover, nature was the symbol of spirit. Emerson stresses that men are in harmony with the nature.

References

[1] http://en. wikipedia. org/wiki/Ralph_Waldo_Emerson

[2] http://en. wikipedia. org/wiki/Nature_(essay)

[3] http://blog. sina. com. cn/s/blog_3fdc7d7401014hg4. html

[4] http://www. tde. net. cn/wx/2012/1125/23079. html

Unit 5
Henry David Thoreau (1817 – 1862)

Bibliography

Henry David Thoreau (1817 – 1862) was an American author, poet, philosopher, abolitionist, naturalist, tax resister, development critic, surveyor, and historian. A leading transcendentalist, Thoreau is best known for his book *Walden*, a reflection upon simple living in natural surroundings, and his essay *Resistance to Civil Government* (also known as *Civil Disobedience*) , an argument for disobedience to an unjust state.

Thoreau's books, articles, essays, journals, and poetry total over 20 volumes. Among his lasting contributions are his writings on natural history and philosophy, where he anticipated the methods and findings of ecology and environmental history, two sources of modern-day environmentalism. His literary style interweaves close natural observation, personal experience, pointed rhetoric, symbolic meanings, and historical lore, while displaying a poetic sensibility, philosophical austerity, and "Yankee" love of practical detail. He was also deeply interested in the idea of survival in the face of hostile elements, historical change, and natural decay, at the same time he advocated abandoning waste and illusion in order to discover life's true essential needs.

He was a lifelong abolitionist, delivering lectures that attacked the Fugitive Slave Law while praising the writings of Wendell Phillips and

defending abolitionist John Brown. Thoreau's philosophy of civil disobedience later influenced the political thoughts and actions of such notable
figures as Leo Tolstoy, Mohandas Gandhi, and Martin Luther King, Jr.

Thoreau is sometimes cited as an anarchist. Though Civil Disobedience seems to call for improving rather than abolishing government —
"I ask for, not at once no government, but at once a better government"— the direction of this improvement points toward anarchism:
"'That government is best which governs not at all', and when men are
prepared for it, that will be the kind of government which they will
have. " Richard Drinnon partly blames Thoreau for the ambiguity, noting that Thoreau's "sly satire, his liking for wide margins for his writing, and his fondness for paradox provided ammunition for widely diver-
gent interpretations of' Civil Disobedience'. "

🌿 Walden

Walden, by noted transcendentalist Henry
David Thoreau, is a reflection upon simple living in natural surroundings. The work is part
personal declaration of independence, social experiment, voyage of spiritual discovery, satire,
and manual for self-reliance. First published in
1854, it details Thoreau's experiences over the
course of two years, two months, and two days
in a cabin he built near Walden Pond, amidst
woodland owned by his friend and mentor Ralph
Waldo Emerson, near Concord, Massachusetts.

The book compresses the time into a single calendar year and uses passages of four seasons to symbolize human development.

By immersing himself in nature, Thoreau hoped to gain a more objective understanding of society through personal introspection. Simple
living and self-sufficiency were Thoreau's other goals, and the whole
project was inspired by transcendentalist philosophy, a central theme of

the American Romantic Period. As Thoreau made clear in his book, his cabin was not in wilderness but at the edge of town, about two miles (3 km) from his family home.

Summary

Thoreau spent two years at Walden Pond living a simple life without support of any kind. Readers are reminded that at the time of publication, Thoreau is back to living among the civilized again. The book is separated into specific chapters that each focus on specific themes.

Economy: In this first and longest chapter, Thoreau outlines his project: a two-year, two-month, and two-day stay at a cozy, "tightly shingled and plastered", English-style 10 × 15 cottage in the woods near Walden Pond. He does this, he says, to illustrate the spiritual benefits of a simplified lifestyle. He easily supplies the four necessities of life (food, shelter, clothing, and fuel) with the help of family and friends, particularly his mother, his best friend, and Mr. and Mrs. Ralph Waldo Emerson. The latter provided Thoreau with a work exchange-he could build a small house and plant a garden if he cleared some land on the woodlot and did other chores while there. Thoreau meticulously records his expenditures and earnings, demonstrating his understanding of "economy", as he builds his house and buys and grows food. At the end of this chapter, Thoreau inserts a poem, "The Pretensions of Poverty", by seventeenth-century English poet Thomas Carew. The poem criticizes those who think that their poverty gives them unearned moral and intellectual superiority. The chapter is filled with figures of practical advice, facts, big ideas about individualism versus social exis tence …manifesto of social thought and meditations on domestic management. Much attention is devoted to the skepticism and wonderment with which townspeople greeted both him and his project as he tries to protect his views from those of the townspeople who seem to view society as the only place to live. He recounts the reasons for his move to Walden Pond along with detailed steps back to the construction of his new home (methods, support, etc.).

Where I Lived, and What I Lived For: Thoreau recollects thoughts of places he stayed at before selecting Walden Pond. Quotes Roman Philosopher Cato's advice "consider buying a farm very carefully before signing the papers". His possibilities included a nearby Hollowell farm. Thoreau takes to the woods dreaming of an existence free of obligations and full of leisure. He announces that he resides far from social relationships that mail represents (post office) and the majority of the chapter focuses on his thoughts while constructing and living in his new home.

Reading: Thoreau discusses the benefits of classical literature, preferably in the original Greek or Latin, and bemoans the lack of sophistication in Concord evident in the popularity of unsophisticated literature. He also loved to read books by world travelers. He yearns for a time when each New England village supports "wise men" to educate and thereby ennoble the population.

Sounds: Thoreau encourages the reader to be "forever on the alert" and "looking always at what is to be seen. " Although truth can be found in literature, it can equally be found in nature. In addition to self-development, an advantage of developing one's perceptiveness is its tendency to alleviate boredom. Rather than "look abroad for amusement, to society and the theatre," Thoreau's own life, including supposedly dull pastimes like housework, becomes a source of amusement that "never ceases to be novel. " Likewise, he obtains pleasure in the sounds that ring around his cabin: church bells ringing, carriages rattling and rumbling, cows lowing, whip-poor-wills singing, owls hooting, frogs croaking, and cockerels crowing. "All sound heard at the greatest possible distance," he contends, "produces one and the same effect. " Likening the train's cloud of steam to a comet tail and its commotion to "the scream of a hawk," the train becomes homologous with nature and Thoreau praises its associated commerce for its enterprise, bravery, and cosmopolitanism, proclaiming: "I watch the passage of the morning cars with the same feeling that I do the rising of the sun. "

Solitude: Thoreau reflects on the feeling of solitude. He explains how loneliness can occur even amid companions if one's heart is not open to them. Thoreau meditates on the pleasures of escaping society and the petty things that society entails (gossip, fights, etc.). He also reflects on his new companion, an old settler who arrives nearby and an old woman with great memory. Thoreau repeatedly reflects on the benefits of nature and of his deep communion with it and states that the only "medicine he needs is a draught of morning air".

Visitors: Thoreau talks about how he enjoys companionship (despite his love for solitude) and always leaves three chairs ready for visitors. The entire chapter focuses on the coming and going of visitors, and how he has more comers in Walden than he did in the city. He receives visits from those living or working nearby and gives special attention to a French Canadian born woodsman named Alec Thérien. Unlike Thoreau, Thérien cannot read or write and is described as leading an "animal life". He compares Thérien to Walden Pond itself. Thoreau then reflects on the women and children who seem to enjoy the pond more than men...and how men are limited because their lives are taken up.

The Bean-Field: Reflection on Thoreau's planting and his enjoyment of this new job/hobby. He touches upon the joys of his environment, the sights and sounds of nature, but also on the military sounds nearby. The rest of the chapter focuses on his earnings and his cultivation of crops (including how he spends just under fifteen dollars on this).

The Village: The chapter focuses on Thoreau's second bath and on his reflections on the journeys he takes several times a week to Concord, where he gathers the latest gossip and meets with townsmen. On one of his journeys into Concord, Thoreau is detained and jailed for his refusal to pay a poll tax to the "state that buys and sells men, women, and children, like cattle at the door of its senate-house".

The Ponds: In autumn, Thoreau discusses the countryside and writes down his observations about the geography of Walden Pond and its neighbors: Flint's Pond (or Sandy Pond), White Pond, and Goose Pond. Although Flint's is the largest, Thoreau's favorites are Walden and White ponds, which he describes as lovelier than diamonds.

Baker Farm: While on an afternoon ramble in the woods, Thoreau gets caught in a rainstorm and takes shelter in the dirty, dismal hut of John Field, a penniless but hard-working Irish farmhand, and his wife and children. Thoreau urges Field to live a simple but independent and fulfilling life in the woods, thereby freeing himself of employers and creditors. But the Irishman won't give up his aspirations of luxury and the quest for the American dream.

Higher Laws: Thoreau discusses whether hunting wild animals and eating meat is necessary. He concludes that the primitive, carnal sensuality of humans drives them to kill and eat animals, and that a person who transcends this propensity is superior to those who cannot. (Thoreau eats fish and occasionally salt pork and woodchuck.) In addition to vegetarianism, he lauds chastity, work, and teetotalism. He also recognizes that Native Americans need to hunt and kill moose for survival in "The Maine Woods", and ate moose on a trip to Maine while he was living at Walden.

Brute Neighbors: is a simplified version of one of Thoreau's conversations with William Ellery Channing, who sometimes accompanied Thoreau on fishing trips when Channing had come up from Concord. The conversation is about a hermit (himself) and a poet (Channing) and how the poet is absorbed in the clouds while the hermit is occupied with the more practical task of getting fish for dinner and how in the end, the poet regrets his failure to catch fish. The chapter also mentions Thoreau's interaction with a mouse that he lives with, the scene in which an ant battles a smaller ant, and his frequent encounters with cats.

House-Warming: After picking November berries in the woods, Thoreau adds a chimney, and finally plasters the walls of his sturdy house to stave off the cold of the oncoming winter. He also lays in a good supply of firewood, and expresses affection for wood and fire.

Former Inhabitants; and Winter Visitors: Thoreau relates the stories of people who formerly lived in the vicinity of Walden Pond. Then he talks about a few of the visitors he receives during the winter: a farmer, a woodchopper, and his best friend, the poet Ellery Channing.

Winter Animals: Thoreau amuses himself by watching wildlife during the winter. He relates his observations of owls, hares, red squirrels, mice, and various birds as they hunt, sing, and eat the scraps and corn he put out for them. He also describes a fox hunt that passes by.

The Pond in Winter: Thoreau describes Walden Pond as it appears during the winter. He claims to have sounded its depths and located an underground outlet. Then he recounts how 100 laborers came to cut great blocks of ice from the pond, the ice to be shipped to the Carolinas.

Spring: As spring arrives, Walden and the other ponds melt with powerful thundering and rumbling. Thoreau enjoys watching the thaw, and grows ecstatic as he witnesses the green rebirth of nature. He watches the geese winging their way north, and a hawk playing by itself in the sky. As nature is reborn, the narrator implies, so is he. He departs Walden on September 6, 1847.

Conclusion: This final chapter is more passionate and urgent than its predecessors. In it, he criticizes conformity: "If a man does not keep pace with his companions, perhaps it is because he hears a different drummer. Let him step to the music which he hears, however measured or far away". By doing so, men may find happiness and self-fulfillment.

Comments on *Walden*

The book is not only a dairy of living near the pond but a record of his embodied philosophy. Thoreau looked deeply into the essential of "life" and gave out his unique remarks on the relationship between man and nature as well as his opinions about environmental conservation.

Thoreau led a peaceful, smooth, quiet and simple life near the lake and so was his writing style. He had an ironic attitude to the modern civilization and highlighted the intrinsic value of nature and, what is more important, human nature. The railway construction, at that time, was rapidly promoted due to the Westward Movement, which could be seen as a reckless invasion to the nature world and had another name, Trail of Tears. Thoreau had realized that civilization could construct various luxuries but richness itself couldn't tell people how life should be and which kind of life is worth living. He said, "Most of the luxuries, and many of the so called comforts of life, are not only not indispensable, but positive hindrances to the elevation of mankind. "

What's more, he takes advantage of his writing talent to make his words in the book polysemantic and thought-provoking. For example, "It is the luxurious and dissipated who set the fashions which the herd so diligently follow" or "It (refers to civilization) has created palaces, but it was not so easy to create noblemen and kings. "

What's actually the content of the book? It's difficult to say. The book is roughly a description of a natural and harmonious life by the lake, but certainly more than that. It's better to take it as a philosophical work rather than a travel notes. He actually reflects everything in the modern life such as government, tax, farms, citizens, children, human spirit and environment of course. The peaceful lake enables him to be far away from the society and then he could have an objective sight into the life and the relationship between human civilization and the world they dwell. He finds out that we are actually misled by the development of the idea of industrialization and consumerism where everyone is told to go after their desires and to chase a so called comfortable life which is actually somewhat luxurious and mediocre. Thoreau did not advocate the social regression. Instead, he tried his best to appeal to his fellows to cultivate decent individual morality. He said, "As I have said, I do not propose to write an ode to dejection, but to brag as lustily as chanticleer in the morning, standing on his roost, if only to wake my neighbors up. " On one hand, he rejects the access of industrialization, which gives rise to seriously destroy not only to the environment but also tradi-tional and social morality. On the other, he highlights the great impor-tance of poetry and art, which would lead people to sublime and nobili-ty. Besides all of his philosophical thinking, Thoreau also writes about the joys in his daily life, such as bread baking, bean cultivating and house building. He also talks about Sounds, Solitude and Reading, all of which are really deep-going.

Criticism about the book is mainly on his idealism. Thoreau is cer-tainly a rebel to the modern industrial production and the ideas related to consumerism, and therefore, draws some criticism from the industry. Even one of his supporters, A. P. Peabody, admitted that the author's life in the woods was on too narrow a scale to find imitators. But Peabody pointed out, "he says so many pithy and brilliant things, and offers so many piquant, and, we may add, so many just, comments on society as it is, that this book is well worth the reading, both for its actual contents and its suggestive capacity." As a matter of fact, Walden is so success-ful a book that it has profoundly changed the world. Events and move-ments influenced by the this masterpiece include The National Park sys-tem, the British Labor Movement, the Creation of India, the Civil Rights Movement, the Hippie revolution, the environmental Movement and the wilderness Movement. Furthermore, the book is well-known in China. The famous poet Haizi, formerly known as Richard Haisheng, committed suicide in 1989, carrying three books with him. One of the three is Walden. He said that Walden could help him to rethink his life and save his spirit and soul.

In conclusion, Walden is such a book with profound thinking and wisdom. It tells people what life is and how to achieve simplicity and sublime.

Introduction to *The Ponds*

In Walden, Thoreau wrote a lot of beautiful scenery, the woods, the birds, the hills, Walden Pond and so on. However, the most attractive thing to him was Walden Pond. The Ponds and The Pond in winter, using a lot of graceful and vivid words to make them attractive to readers. For example, he told readers the details about the ponds such as the water, the shore, the trees around or in it, and the waterfowls, which changed with seasons. Walden Pond was a small world which can give Thoreau enough space to ramble in his own world of thought. He gave symbolization to it of everything spiritual, philosophical, and personal. The pond was a self-reliance ecosystem which remind readers Thoreau's transcendental ideas. He wanted to show us that man can know nature and get close to it. People can know nature and get higher truth from it.

From   *Walden*
The Ponds

The scenery of Walden is on a humble scale[1], and, though very beautiful, does not approach to grandeur, nor can it much concern one who has not long frequented it or lived by its shore; yet this pond is so remarkable for its depth and purity as to merit a particular description. It is a clear and deep green well, half a mile long and a mile and three quarters in circumference, and contains about sixty-one and a half acres; a perennial[2] spring in the midst of pine and oak woods, without any visible inlet or outlet except by the clouds and evaporation. The surrounding hills rise abruptly from the water to the height of forty to eighty feet, though on the southeast and east they attain to about one hundred and one hundred and fifty feet respectively, within a quarter and a third of a mile. They are exclusively woodland. All our Concord waters have two colors at least; one when viewed at a distance, and another, more proper, close at hand. The first depends more on the light, and follows the sky. In clear weather, in summer, they appear blue at a little distance, especially if agitated, and at a great distance all appear alike. In stormy weather they are sometimes of a dark slate-color. The sea, however, is said to be blue one day and green another without any perceptible change in the atmosphere. I have seen our river, when, the landscape being covered with snow, both water and ice were almost as green as grass. Some consider blue "to be the color of pure water, whether liquid or solid. " But, looking directly down into our waters from a boat, they are seen to be of very different colors. Walden is blue at one time and green at another, even from the same point of view. Lying between the earth and the heavens, it partakes[3] of the color of both. Viewed from a hilltop it reflects the color of the sky; but near at hand it is of a yellowish tint next the shore where you can see the sand, then a light green, which gradually deepens to a uniform dark green in the body of the pond. In some lights, viewed even from a hilltop, it is of a vivid green next the shore. Some have referred this to the reflection of the verdure[4]; but it is equally green there against the railroad sandbank, and in the spring, before the leaves are expanded, and it may be simply the result of the prevailing blue mixed with the yellow of the sand. Such is the color of its iris. This is that portion, also, where in the spring, the ice being warmed by the heat of the sun reflected from the bottom, and also transmitted through the earth, melts first and forms a narrow canal about the still frozen middle. Like the rest of our waters, when much agitated, in clear weather, so that the surface of the waves may reflect the sky at the right angle, or because there is more light mixed with it, it appears at a little distance of a darker blue than the sky itself; and at such a time, being on its surface, and looking with divided vision, so as to see the reflection, I have discerned a matchless and indescribable light blue, such as watered or changeable silks and sword blades suggest, more cerulean[5] than the sky itself, alternating with the original dark green on the opposite sides of the waves, which last appeared but muddy in comparison. It is a vitreous greenish blue, as I remember it, like those patches of the winter sky seen through cloud vistas in the west before sundown. Yet a single glass of its water held up to the light is as colorless as an equal quantity of air. It is well known that a large plate of glass will have a green tint, owing, as the makers say, to its "body," but a small piece of the same will be colorless. How large a body of Walden water would be required to reflect a green tint I have never proved. The water of our river is black or a very dark brown to one loo-king directly down on it, and, like that of most ponds, imparts to the body of one bathing in it a yellowish tinge; but this water is of such crystalline purity that the body of the bather appears of an alabaster whiteness, still more unnatural, which, as the limbs are magnified and distorted withal, produces a monstrous effect, making fit studies for a Michael Angelo[6].

The water is so transparent that the bottom can easily be discerned at the depth of twenty-five or thirty feet. Paddling over it, you may see, many feet beneath the surface, the schools of perch and shiners, per-haps only an inch long, yet the former easily distinguished by their transverse bars, and you think that they must be ascetic fish that find a subsistence there. Once, in the winter, many years ago, when I had been cutting holes through the ice in order to catch pickerel, as I stepped ashore I tossed my axe back on to the ice, but, as if some evil genius had directed it, it slid four or five rods directly into one of the holes, where the water was twenty-five feet deep. Out of curiosity, I lay down on the ice and looked through the hole, until I saw the axe a little on one side, standing on its head, with its helve erect and gently swa-ying to and fro with the pulse of the pond; and there it might have stood erect and swaying till in the course of time the handle rotted off, if I had not disturbed it. Making another hole directly over it with an ice chisel which I had, and cutting down the longest birch which I could find in the neighborhood with my knife, I made a slip-noose, which I attached to its end, and, letting it down carefully, passed it over the knob of the handle, and drew it by a line along the birch, and so pulled the axe out again.

The shore is composed of a belt of smooth rounded white stones like paving-stones, excepting one or two short sand beaches, and is so steep that in many places a single leap will carry you into water over your head; and were it not for its remarkable transparency, that would be the last to be seen of its bottom till it rose on the opposite side. Some think it is bottomless. It is nowhere muddy, and a casual observer would say that there were no weeds at all in it; and of noticeable plants, except in the little meadows recently overflowed, which do not properly belong to it, a closer scrutiny does not detect a flag nor a bulrush, nor even a lily, yellow or white, but only a few small heart-leaves and potamogetons, and perhaps a water-target or two; all which however a bather might not perceive; and these plants are clean and bright like the element they grow in. The stones extend a rod or two into the water, and then the bottom is pure sand, except in the deepest parts, where there is usually a little sediment, probably from the decay of the leaves which have been wafted[8] on to it so many successive falls, and a bright green weed is brought up on anchors even in midwinter.

We have one other pond just like this, White Pond, in Nine Acre Corner, about two and a half miles westerly; but, though I am acquainted with most of the ponds within a dozen miles of this centre I do not know a third of this pure and well-like character. Successive nations perchance have drank at, admired, and fathomed it, and passed away, and still its water is green and pellucid [9]as ever. Not an intermitting spring! Perhaps on that spring morning when Adam and Eve were driven out of Eden Walden Pond was already in existence, and even then breaking up in a gentle spring rain accompanied with mist and a southerly wind, and covered with myriads of ducks and geese, which had not heard of the fall, when still such pure lakes sufficed them. Even then it had commenced to rise and fall, and had clarified its waters and colored them of the hue they now wear, and obtained a patent of Heaven to be the only Walden Pond in the world and distiller of celestial dews. Who knows in how many unremembered nations' literatures this has been the Castalian Fountain? Or what nymphs presided over it in the Golden Age? It is a gem of the first water which Concord wears in her coronet.

Yet perchance the first who came to this well have left some trace of their footsteps. I have been surprised to detect encircling the pond, even where a thick wood has just been cut down on the shore, a narrow shelf-like path in the steep hillside, alternately rising and falling, approaching and receding from the water's edge, as old probably as the race of man here, worn by the feet of aboriginal hunters, and still from time to time unwittingly trodden by the present occupants of the land. This is particularly distinct to one standing on the middle of the pond in winter, just after a light snow has fallen, appearing as a clear undulating white line, unobscured by weeds and twigs, and very obvious a quarter of a mile off in many places where in summer it is hardly distinguishable close at hand. The snow reprints it, as it were, in clear white type alto-relievo[10]. The ornamented grounds of villas which will one day be built here may still preserve some trace of this.

Notes:

1. on a scale: 在一定范围内

   E. g. On a world scale the earthquake was a tiddler.

   She was accused of corruption, of vote rigging on a massive scale.

2. perennial *a.* 终年的, 长久的;

   E. g. I wonder at her perennial youthfulness.

3. partake *vi.* 参加; 参与; 吃 n. 参与者, 分担者

   E. g. Would you care to partake of some refreshment?

   Will you partake of our simple meal?

4. verdure *n.* 〈文〉青翠的草木; 新鲜; 繁盛; 朝气

   E. g. The hills are covered with verdure.

   The rugged surface of the Palatine was muffled with tender verdure。

5. cerulean *a.* 蔚蓝的, 天蓝的; 天蓝色

   E. g. And then I think it was St. Laurent, wasn't it, who showed cerulean military jackets?

6. Michel Angelo: commonly known as Michelangelo, was an Italian sculptor, painter, architect, poet, and engineer of the High Renaissance who exerted an unparalleled influence on the development of Western art. Considered the greatest living artist in his lifetime, he has since been held as one of the greatest artists of all time. Despite making few forays beyond the arts, his versatility in the disciplines he took up was of such a high order that he is often considered a contender for the title of the archetypal Renaissance man, along with his fellow Italian Leonardo da Vinci.

7. sediment *n.* [地]沉淀物; 沉积物, 沉渣

E. g. Many organisms that die in the sea are soon buried by sediment.

8. waft *vt. & vi.* 吹送, 飘送; *n.* 一股; 一阵微风

E. g. A waft of perfume drifted into Ingrid's nostrils.

A good year, which this is, of course, will waft.

9. pellucid *a.* 透明的, 清澈的

E. g. After reading these stodgy philosophers, I find his pellucid style very enjoyable.

10. altorelievo *n.* 高凸浮雕

Questions:

1. What does Thoreau emphasize in describing the pond?

2. The scenery of Walden is on a humble scale, and, though very beautiful, does not approach to grandeur, nor can it much concern one who has not long frequented it or lived by its shore; yet this pond is so remarkable for its depth and purity as to merit a particular description. What's the function of the sentence?

3. How does the author describe the purity of the pond?

Analysis of *The Ponds*

The author vividly described the pond in autumn and winter. When the water was flowing, the pond looked like a huge blue mirror. Everything it was frozen and everywhere your eyesight reached was white and holy. Just like the pure green water, the ice was always green and looked like precious diamond. In Thoreau' eyes, Walden Pond was the vitality and tranquility of nature and it can purify people's soul. People those who came here would be happier than in any other places.

In spring, trucks took the ice-cutters to Walden Pond, leading the pond melting in an earlier period. The ice-cutters broke the ice and took it to big cities to serve people. According to them, the ice in Walden was the greenest they had ever seen and it could be kept for a long time. Walden Pond was not only self-reliance, but also can provide human beings what they wanted. It was both natural and societal. Thoreau advocated to live a simple life and opposed the high speed industrial society. However, he did not mean to live alone, departing from the society. Human beings infested to get basic sense of safety. They could live a simple life without those complicated modern things which seemed useful and necessary but actually not. For Thoreau, the pond was the connection between the nature and the human society. As he can fish and have fun in it. When other people came to the pond, they would always bring many interesting thing for him, for instance, old fish man's unexpected stories, some curious people's humorous activities and questions.

In Walden, the pond was the connection of the whole book. The author lived near it for two years and two months, enjoyed the true essence of nature. The pond was not only a pond. It symbolized the vitality and tranquility of nature, all pure things that human beings have been pursued all the time. To some extent, the pond was the representative of God. People can get close to the pond and know it well, which implied that human beings can know the higher truth of nature otherwise. The ponds in Walden were beautiful and divine, and the author gave a lot of meanings to it. In Walden, Thoreau wanted to show us such a fact that people can live a simple life and get happier emotions from nature than the industrial world.

中文译文：

瓦尔登的风景是卑微的，虽然很美，却并不是宏伟的，不常去游玩的人，不住在它岸边的人未必能被它吸引住：但是这是一个以深邃和清澈著称的湖，值得给予突出的描写。这是一个明亮的深绿色的湖，半英里长，圆周约一又四分之三英里，面积约六十一英亩半；它是松树和橡树林中央的岁月悠久的老湖，除了雨和蒸发之外，还没有别的来龙去脉可寻。四周的山峰突然地从水上升起到四十至八十英尺的高度，但在东南面高到一百英尺，而东边更高到一百五十英尺，其距离湖岸，不过四分之一英里及三分之一英里。山上全部都是森林。所有我们康科德地方的水波，至少有两种颜色，一种是站在远处望见的，另一种，更接近本来的颜色，是站在近处看见的。第一种更多地靠的是光，根据天色变化。在天气好的夏季里，从稍远的地方望去，它呈现了蔚蓝颜色，特别在水波荡漾的时候，但从很远的地方望去，却是一片深蓝。在风暴的天气下，有时它呈现出深石板色。海水的颜色则不然，据说它这天是蓝色的，另一天却又是绿色了，尽管天气连些微的可感知的变化也没有。我们这里的水系中，我看到当白雪覆盖这一片风景时，水和冰几乎都是草绿色的。有人认为，蓝色"乃是纯洁的水的颜色，无论那是流动的水，或凝结的水"。可是，直接从一条船上俯看近处湖水，它又有着非常之不同的色彩。甚至从同一个观察点，看瓦尔登是这会儿蓝，那忽儿绿。置身于天地之间，它分担了这两者的色素。从山顶上看，它反映天空的颜色，可是走近了看，在你能看到近岸的细沙的地方，水色先是黄澄澄的，然后是淡绿色的了，然后逐渐地加深起来，直到水波一律地呈现了全湖一致的深绿色。却在有些时候的光线下，便是从一个山顶望去，靠近湖岸的水色也是碧绿得异常生动的。有人说，这是绿原的反映；可是在铁路轨道这儿的黄沙地带的衬托下，也同样是碧绿的，而且，在春天，树叶还没有长大，这也许是太空中的蔚蓝，调和了黄沙以后形成的一个单纯的效果。这是它的虹色彩圈的色素。也是在这一个地方，春天一来，冰块给水底反射上来的太阳的热量，也给土地中传播的太阳的热量溶解了，这里首先溶解成一条狭窄的运河的样子，而中间还是冻冰。在晴朗的气候中，像我们其余的水波，激湍地流动时，波平面是在九十度的直角度里反映了天空的，或者因为太光亮了，从较远处望去，它比天空更蓝些；而在这种时候，泛舟湖上，四处眺望倒影，我发现了一种无可比拟、不能描述的淡蓝色，像浸水的或变色的丝绸，还像青锋宝剑，比之天空还更接近天蓝色，它和那波光的另一面原来的深绿色轮番地闪现，那深绿色与之相比便似乎很混浊了。这是一个玻璃似的带绿色的蓝色，照我所能记忆的，它仿佛是冬天里，日落以前，西方乌云中露出的一角晴天。可是你举起一玻璃杯水，放在空中看，它却毫无颜色，如同装了同样数量的一杯空气一样。众所周知，一大块厚玻璃板便呈现了微绿的颜色，据制造玻璃的人说，那是"体积"的关系，同样的玻璃，少了就不会有颜色了。瓦尔登湖应该有多少的水量才能泛出这样的绿色呢，我从来都无法证明。一个直接朝下望着我们的水色的人所见到的是黑的，或深棕色的，一个到河水中游泳的人，河水像所有的湖一样，会给他染上一种黄颜色；但是这个湖水却是这样的纯洁，游泳者会白得像大理石一样，而更奇怪的是，在这水中四肢给放大了，并且给扭曲了，形态非常夸张，值得让米开朗琪罗来做一番研究。

　　水是这样的透明，二十五至三十英尺下面的水底都可以很清楚地看到。赤脚踏水时，你看到在水面下许多英尺的地方有成群的鲈鱼和银鱼，大约只一英寸长，连前者的横行的花纹也能看得清清楚楚，你会觉得这种鱼也是不愿意沾染红尘，才到这里来生存的。有一次，在冬天里，好几年前了，为了钓梭鱼，我在冰上挖了几个洞，上岸之后，我把一柄斧头扔在冰上，可是好像有什么恶鬼故意要开玩笑似的，斧头在冰上滑过了四五杆远，刚好从一个窟窿中滑了下去，那里的水深二十五英尺，为了好奇，我躺在冰上，从那窟窿里望，我看到了那柄斧头，它偏在一边头向下直立着，那斧柄笔直向上，顺着湖水的脉动摇摇摆摆，要不是我后来又把它吊了起来，它可能就会这样直立下去，直到木柄烂掉为止。就在它的上面，用我带来的凿冰的凿子，我又凿了一个洞，又用我的刀，割下了我看到的附近最长的一条赤杨树枝，我做了一个活结的绳圈，放在树枝的一头，小心地放下去，用它套住了斧柄突出的地方，然后用赤杨枝旁边的绳子一拉，这样就把那柄斧头吊了起来。

　　湖岸是由一长溜像铺路石那样的光滑的圆圆的白石组成的；

除一两处小小的沙滩之外，它陡立着，纵身一跃便可以跳到一个人深的水中；要不是水波明净得出奇，你绝不可能看到这个湖的底部，除非是它又在对岸升起。有人认为它深得没有底。它没有一处是泥泞的，偶尔观察的过客或许还会说，它里面连水草也没有一根；至于可以见到的水草，除了最近给上涨了的水淹没的，并不属于这个湖的草地以外，便是细心地查看也确实是看不到菖蒲和芦苇的，甚至没有水莲花，无论是黄色的或是白色的，最多只有一些心形叶子和河蓼草，也许还有一两张眼子菜；然而，游泳者也看不到它们；便是这些水草，也像它们生长在里面的水一样的明亮而无垢。岸石伸展入水，只一二杆远，水底已是纯粹的细沙，除了最深的部分，那里总不免有一点沉积物，也许是腐朽了的叶子，多少个秋天来，落叶被刮到湖上，另外还有一些光亮的绿色水苔，甚至在深冬时令拔起铁锚来的时候，它们也会跟着被拔上来的。

我们还有另一个这样的湖，在九亩角那里的白湖，在偏西两英里半之处；可是以这里为中心的十二英里半径的圆周之内，虽然还有许多的湖沼是我熟悉的，我却找不出第三个湖有这样的纯洁得如同井水的特性。大约历来的民族都饮用过这湖水，艳羡过它并测量过它的深度，而后他们一个个消逝了，湖水却依然澄清，发出绿色。一个春天也没有变化过！也许远在亚当和夏娃被逐出伊甸乐园时，那个春晨之前，瓦尔登湖已经存在了，甚至在那个时候，随着轻雾和一阵阵的南风，飘下了一阵柔和的春雨，湖面不再平静了，成群的野鸭和天鹅在湖上游着，它们一点都没有知道逐出乐园这一回事，能有这样纯粹的湖水真够满足啦。就是在那时候，它已经又涨，又落，纯清了它的水，还染上了现在它所有的色泽，还专有了这一片天空，成了世界上唯一的一个瓦尔登湖，它是天上露珠的蒸馏器。谁知道，在多少篇再没人记得的民族诗篇中，这个湖曾被誉为喀斯泰里亚之泉？在黄金时代里，有多少山林水泽的精灵曾在这里居住？这是在康科德的冠冕上的第一滴水明珠。

第一个到这个湖边来的人们可能留下过他们的足迹。我曾经很惊异地发现，就在沿湖被砍伐了的一个浓密的森林那儿，峻峭的山崖中，有一条绕湖一匝的狭窄的高架的小径，一会儿上，一忽儿下，一会儿接近湖，一忽儿又离远了一些，它或许和人类同年，土著的猎者，用脚步走出了这条路来，以后世世代代都有这片土地上的居住者不知不觉地用脚走过去。冬天，站在湖中央，看起来这就更加清楚，特别在下了一阵小雪之后，它就成了连绵起伏的一条白线，败草和枯枝都不能够掩蔽它，许多地点，在四分之一英里以外看起来还格外清楚，但是夏天里，便是走近去看，也还是看不出来。可以说，雪花用清楚的白色的浮雕又把它印刷出来了。但愿到了将来，人们在这里建造一些别墅的装饰庭园时，还能保留这一残迹。

❧ Answers for the questions

1. It emphasizes the importance of self-reliance, solitude, contemplation, and closeness to nature in transcending the crass existence that is supposedly the lot of most humans. The book is neither a novel nor a true autobiography, but combines these genres with a social critique of contemporary Western culture's consumerist and materialist attitudes and its distance from and destruction of nature.

2. The sentence here is to pave the way for the description of the colors and purity of the pond. It also shows the author's attitude toward the pond.

3. Combining far-distance and near-distance description, he also employs several methods to describe the purity of pond from many different angles.

References

[1] http://wenku. baidu. com/view/286ec67ba5e9856a561260a8. html

[2] http://wenku. baidu. com/view/5ec0e91752d380eb62946db5. html

[3] http://blog. sina. com. cn/s/blog_50c61beb0102drv9. html

[4] http://wenku. baidu. com/view/c85fdefd910ef12d2af9e7e4. html? re = view

Unit 6
Nathaniel Hawthorne（1804－1864）

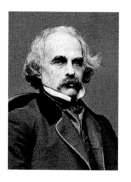 Biography

Nathaniel Hawthorne was born on July 4, 1804, in Salem, Massachusetts, a descendant of a long line of Puritan ancestors including John Hathorne, a presiding magistrate in the Salem witch trials. In order to distance himself from his family's shameful involvement in the witch trials, Hawthorne added the "w" to his last name while in his early 20s. Also among his ancestors was William Hathorne, one of the first Puritan settlers who arrived in New England in 1630.

After his father, a ship captain, died of yellow fever at sea when Nathaniel was only four, his mother became overly protective and pushed him toward relatively isolated pursuits. Hawthorne's childhood left him shy and bookish, which molded his life as a writer.

Hawthorne turned to writing after his graduation from Bowdoin College. His first novel, *Fanshawe*, was unsuccessful and Hawthorne himself later disavowed the work as amateurish. He wrote several successful short stories, however, including "*My Kinsman, Major Molineux*", "*Roger Malvin's Burial*", and "*Young Goodman Brown*" — arguably Hawthorne's most famous short story. Despite the critical acclaim it has received since, Hawthorne twice rejected this work when asked to select a compilation of short stories for publication.

His insufficient earnings as a writer forced Hawthorne to enter a career as a Boston Custom House measurer in 1839. After three years Hawthorne was dismissed from his job with the Salem Custom House. By 1842, his writing finally provided him income sufficient enough to marry Sophia Peabody and move to The Manse in Concord, which was the center of the transcendental movement.

Hawthorne returned to Salem in 1845, where he was appointed surveyor of the Boston Custom House by President James Polk, but he was dismissed from this post when Zachary Taylor became president. Hawthorne then devoted himself to his most famous novel, *The Scarlet Letter*. He zealously worked on the novel with a determination he had not known before. His intense suffering infused the novel with imaginative energy, leading him to describe it as a " hell-fired story ". On February 3, 1850, Hawthorne read the final pages to his wife. He wrote, " It broke her heart and sent her to bed with a grievous headache, which I look upon as a triumphant success. "

The Scarlet Letter was an immediate success that allowed Hawthorne to devote himself completely to his writing. He left Salem for a temporary residence in Lenox, a small town in the Berkshires, where he completed the romance *The House of the Seven Gables* in 1851. While in Lenox, Hawthorne met with Herman Melville and became a major proponent of Melville's work, but their friendship later became strained. Hawthorne's subsequent novels, *The Blithedale Romance* based on his years of communal living at Brook Farm and the romance *The Marble Faun* were both considered disappointments. Hawthorne supported himself through another political post, the consulship in Liverpool, which he was given for writing a campaign biography for Franklin Pierce.

In 1852, after the publication of *The Blithedale Romance*, Hawthorne returned to Concord and bought a house called Hillside, owned by Louisa May Alcott's family. Hawthorne renamed it The Wayside. He went on to travel and live in France and Italy for a spell, but he returned to The Wayside just before the Civil War began. He published an article entitled "*Chiefly About War Matters*" for the *Atlantic Monthly* just before he fell ill, detailing the account of his travels to the Virginia battlefields of Manassas and Harpers Ferry and to the White House.

Hawthorne passed away on May 19, 1864, in Plymouth, New Hampshire, after a long period of illness during which he suffered severe bouts of dementia. By this time, he had completed several chapters of what was to be a romance, and this work was published posthumously as *The Dolliver Romance*.

Hawthorne was buried in Sleepy Hollow Cemetery in Concord, Massachusetts. Transcendentalist poet and essayist Ralph Waldo Emerson, a neighbor of Hawthorne's, described the life of his acquaintance as one of "painful solitude. " Hawthorne had maintained a strong friendship with Franklin Pierce, but otherwise he had had few intimates and little engagement with any sort of social life.

A number of his unfinished works were published posthumously. His works remain notable for their treatment of New England Puritanism, personal guilt, and the complexities of moral choices. Though Hawthorne was perpetually dissatisfied with his body of work throughout his life, he remains lauded as one of the greatest American writers.

The Scarlet Letter

The Scarlet Letter is an 1850 romantic work of fiction in a historical setting, and is considered to be his magnum opus. Set in 17th-century Puritan Boston, Massachusetts during the years 1642 to 1649, it tells the story of Hester Prynne, who conceives a daughter through an affair and struggles to create a new life of repentance and dignity. Throughout the book, Hawthorne explores themes of legalism, sin, and guilt.

Major characters in *The Scarlet Letter*

1. Hester Prynne—Hester is the book's protagonist and the wearer of the scarlet letter that gives the book its title. The letter, a patch of fabric in the shape of an " A ", signifies that Hester is an "adulterer. " As a young woman, Hester married an elderly scholar, Chillingworth, who sent her ahead to America to live but never followed her. While waiting for him, she had an affair with a Puritan minister named Dimmesdale, after which she gave birth to Pearl. Hester is passionate but also strong—she endures years of shame and scorn. She equals both her husband and her lover in her intelligence and thoughtfulness. Her alienation puts her in the position to make acute observations about her community, particularly about its treatment of women.

2. Arthur Dimmesdale—Dimmesdale is a young man who achieved fame in England as a theologian and then emigrated to America. In a moment of weakness, he and Hester became lovers. Although he will not confess it publicly, he is the father of her child. He deals with his guilt by tormenting himself physically and psychologically, developing a heart condition as a result. Dimmesdale is an intelligent and emotional man, and his sermons are thus masterpieces of eloquence and persuasiveness. His commitments to his congregation are in constant conflict with his feelings of sinfulness and need to confess.

3. Roger Chillingworth—Roger Chillingworth is actually Hester's husband in disguise. He is much older than she is and had sent her to America while he settled his affairs in Europe. Because he is captured by Native Americans, he arrives in Boston belatedly and finds Hester and her illegitimate child being displayed on the scaffold. He lusts for revenge, and thus decides to stay in Boston despite his wife's betrayal and disgrace. He is a scholar and uses his knowledge to disguise himself as a doctor, intent on discovering and tormenting Hester's anonymous lover. Chillingworth is self-absorbed and both physically and psychologically monstrous. His single-minded pursuit

of retribution reveals him to be the most malevolent character in the novel.

4. Pearl—Hester's illegitimate daughter Pearl is a young girl with a moody, mischievous spirit and an ability to perceive things that others do not. For example, she quickly discerns the truth about her mother and Dimmesdale. The townspeople say that she barely seems human and spread rumors that her unknown father is actually the Devil. She is wise far beyond her years, frequently engaging in ironic play having to do with her mother's scarlet letter.

Summary

The story begins in seventeenth-century Boston, then a Puritan settlement. A young woman, Hester Prynne, is led from the town prison with her infant daughter, Pearl, in her arms and the scarlet letter "A" on her breast. A man in the crowd tells an elderly onlooker that Hester is being punished for adultery. Hester's husband, a scholar much older than she is, sent her ahead to America, but he never arrived in Boston. The consensus is that he has been lost at sea. While waiting for her husband, Hester has apparently had an affair, as she has given birth to a child. She will not reveal her lover's identity, however, and the scarlet letter, along with her public shaming, is her punishment for her sin and her secrecy. On this day Hester is led to the town scaffold and harangued by the town fathers, but she again refuses to identify her child's father.

The elderly onlooker is Hester's missing husband, who is now practicing medicine and calling himself Roger Chillingworth. He settles in Boston, intent on revenge. He reveals his true identity to no one but Hester, whom he has sworn to secrecy. Several years pass. Hester supports herself by working as a seamstress, and Pearl grows into a willful, impish child. Shunned by the community, they live in a small cottage on the outskirts of Boston. Community officials attempt to take Pearl away from Hester, but, with the help of Arthur Dimmesdale, a young and eloquent minister, the mother and daughter manage to stay together. Dimmesdale, however, appears to be wasting away and suffers from mysterious heart trouble, seemingly caused by psychological distress. Chillingworth attaches himself to the ailing minister and eventually moves in with him so that he can provide his patient with round-the-clock care. Chillingworth also suspects that there may be a connection between the minister's torments and Hester's secret, and he begins to test Dimmesdale to see what he can learn. One afternoon, while the minister sleeps, Chillingworth discovers a mark on the man's breast (the details of which are kept from the reader), which convinces him that his suspicions are correct.

Dimmesdale's psychological anguish deepens, and he invents new tortures for himself. In the meantime, Hester's charitable deeds and quiet humility have earned her a reprieve from the scorn of the community. One night, when Pearl is about seven years old, she and her mother are returning home from a visit to a deathbed when they encounter Dimmesdale atop the town scaffold, trying to punish himself for his sins. Hester and Pearl join him, and the three link hands. Dimmesdale refuses Pearl's request that he acknowledge her publicly the next day, and a meteor marks a dull red "A" in the night sky. Hester can see that the minister's condition is worsening, and she resolves to intervene. She goes to Chillingworth and asks him to stop adding to Dimmesdale's self-torment. Chillingworth refuses.

Hester arranges an encounter with Dimmesdale in the forest because she is aware that Chillingworth has probably guessed that she plans to reveal his identity to Dimmesdale. The former lovers decide to flee to Europe, where they can live with Pearl as a family. They will take a ship sailing from Boston in four days. Both feel a sense of release and Hester removes her scarlet letter and lets down her hair. Pearl, playing nearby, does not recognize her mother without the letter. The day before the ship is to sail, the townspeople gather for a holiday and Dimmesdale preaches his most eloquent sermon ever. Meanwhile, Hester

美国经典文学作品选读

has learned that Chillingworth knows of their plan and has booked passage on the same ship. Dimmesdale, leaving the church after his sermon, sees Hester and Pearl standing before the town scaffold. He impulsively mounts the scaffold with his lover and his daughter, and confesses publicly, exposing a scarlet letter seared into the flesh of his chest. He falls dead, as Pearl kisses him.

Frustrated in his revenge, Chillingworth dies a year later. Hester and Pearl leave Boston, and no one knows what has happened to them. Many years later, Hester returns alone, still wearing the scarlet letter, to live in her old cottage and resume her charitable work. She receives occasional letters from Pearl, who has married a European aristocrat and established a family of her own. When Hester dies, she is buried next to Dimmesdale. The two share a single tombstone, which bears a scarlet "A".

Comments on *The Scarlet Letter*

Nathaniel Hawthorne was an influential American romantic novelist. Many of his works are inspired by Puritan New England, combining historical romance loaded with symbolism and deep psychological themes, bordering on surrealism. *The Scarlet Letter* is a foundational work of American literature. It is considered a historical romance written in the midst of the American literary movement called transcendentalism. Transcendentalism stressed the romantic tenets of mysticism, idealism, and individualism. This work represents the height of Hawthorne's literary genius, dense with terse descriptions. It remains relevant for its philosophical and psychological depth, and continues to be read as a classic tale on a universal theme. Many American critics have given high credit to him. Critic Evert Augustus Duyckinck, a friend of Hawthorne's, said he preferred the author's Washington Irving-like tales. Another friend, critic Edwin Percy Whipple, objected to the novel's "morbid intensity" with dense psychological details, writing that the book "is therefore apt to become, like Hawthorne, too painfully anatomical in his exhibition of them". Most literary critics praised the book but religious leaders took issue with the novel's subject matter. *The Scarlet Letter* was also one of the first mass-produced books in America. The first mechanized printing of The Scarlet Letter, 2,500 volumes, sold out within ten days.

Introduction to Chapter Two

As the crowd watches, Hester Prynne, a young woman holding an infant, emerges from the prison door and makes her way to a scaffold (a raised platform), where she is to be publicly condemned. The women in the crowd make disparaging comments about Hester; they particularly criticize her for the ornaments of the embroidered badge on her chest—a letter "A" stitched in gold and scarlet. From the women's conversation and Hester's reminiscences as she walks through the crowd, we can deduce that she has committed adultery and has borne an illegitimate child, and that the "A" on her dress stands for "Adulterer. "

The beadle calls Hester forth. Children taunt her and adults stare. Scenes from Hester's earlier life flash through her mind: she sees her parents standing before their home in rural England, and then she sees a "misshapen" scholar, much older than herself, whom she married and followed to continental Europe. But now the present floods in upon her, and she inadvertently squeezes the infant in her arms, causing it to cry out. She regards her current fate with disbelief.

From   *The Scarlet Letter*
Chapter Two The Market-place

The grass-plot before the jail, in Prison Lane, on a certain summer morning, not less than two centuries ago, was occupied by a pretty large number of the inhabitants of Boston; all with their eyes intently fastened on the iron-clamped oaken door. Amongst any other population, or at a later period in the history of New England, the grim rigidity that petrified the bearded physiognomies[1] of these good people would have augured some awful business in hand. It could have betokened[2] nothing short of the anticipated execution of some rioted culprit, on whom the sentence of a legal tribunal had but confirmed the verdict of public sentiment. But, in that early severity of the Puritan[3] character, an inference of this kind could not so indubitably be drawn. It might be that a sluggish bond-servant, or an undutiful child, whom his parents had given over to the civil authority, was to be corrected at the whipping-post. It might be, that an Antinomian, a Quaker, or other heterodox religionist, was to be scourged out of the town, or an idle and vagrant Indian, whom the white man's firewater had made riotous about the streets, was to be driven with stripes into the shadow of the forest. It might be, too, that a witch, like old Mistress Hibbins, the bitter-tempered widow of the magistrate, was to die upon the gallows. In either case, there was very much the same solemnity of demeanour on the part of the spectators; as befitted a people amongst whom religion and law were almost identical, and in whose character both were so thoroughly interfused, that the mildest and the severest acts of public discipline were alike made venerable and awful. Meager, indeed, and cold, was the sympathy that a transgressor might look for, from such bystanders, at the scaffold[4]. On the other hand, a penalty which, in our days, would infer a degree of mocking infamy and ridicule might then be invested with almost as stern a dignity as the punishment of death itself.

The door of the jail being flung open from within there appeared, in the first place, like a black shadow emerging into sunshine, the grim and grisly presence of the town-beadle, with a sword by his side, and his staff of office in his hand. This personage prefigured and represented in his aspect the whole dismal severity of the Puritanic code of law, which it was his business to administer in its final and closest application to the offender. Stretching forth the official staff in his left hand, he laid his right upon the shoulder of a young woman, whom he thus drew forward; until, on the threshold of the prison-door, she repelled him, by an action marked with natural dignity and force of character, and stepped into the open air, as if by her own free will. She bore in her arms a child, a baby of some three months old, who winked and turned aside its little face from the too vivid light of day; because its existence, heretofore[5], had brought it acquaintance only with the grey twilight of a dungeon, or other darksome apartment of the prison.

When the young woman— the mother of this child—stood fully revealed before the crowd, it seemed to be her first impulse to clasp the infant closely to her bosom; not so much by an impulse of motherly affection, as that she might thereby conceal a certain token, which was wrought or fastened into her dress. In a moment, however, wisely judging that one token of her shame would but poorly serve to hide another, she took the baby on her arm, and, with a burning blush, and yet a haughty[6] smile, and a glance that would not be abashed, looked around at her townspeople and neighbours. On the breast of her gown, in fine red cloth, surrounded with an elaborate embroidery and fantastic flourishes of gold thread, appeared the letter A. It was so artistically done, and with so much fertility and gorgeous luxuriance of fancy, that it had all the effect of a last and fitting decoration to the apparel which she wore; and which was of a splendour in accordance with the taste of the age, but greatly beyond what was allowed by the sumptuary regulations of the colony.

The young woman was tall, with a figure of perfect elegance on a large scale. She had dark and abundant hair, so glossy that it threw off the sunshine with a gleam, and a face which, besides being beautiful from regularity of feature and richness of complexion, had the impressiveness belonging to a marked brow and deep black eyes. She was ladylike, too, after the manner of the feminine gentility of those days; characterised by a certain state and dignity, rather than by the delicate, evanescent[7], and indescribable grace, which is now recognised as its indication. And never had Hester Prynne appeared more ladylike, in the antique interpretation of the term, than as she issued from the prison. Those who had before known her, and had expected to behold her dimmed and obscured by a disastrous cloud, were astonished, and even startled, to perceive how her beauty shone out, and made a halo of the misfortune and ignominy in which she was enveloped. It may be true, that, to a sensitive observer, there was something exquisitely painful in it. Her attire, which, indeed, she had wrought for the occasion, in prison, and had modelled much after her own fancy, seemed to express the attitude of her spirit, the desperate recklessness of her mood, by its wild and picturesque peculiarity. But the point which drew all eyes, and, as it were, transfigured the wearer — so that both men and women, who had been familiarly acquainted with Hester Prynne, were now impressed as if they beheld her for the first time — was that scarlet letter, so fantastically embroidered and illuminated upon her bosom. It had the effect of a spell, taking her out of the ordinary relations with humanity, and enclosing her in a sphere by herself.

Had there been a Papist among the crowd of Puritans, he might have seen in this beautiful woman, so picturesque in her attire and mien, and with the infant at her bosom, an object to remind him of the image of Divine Maternity, which so many illustrious painters have vied with one another to represent; something which should remind him, indeed, but only by contrast, of that sacred image of sinless motherhood, whose infant was to redeem[8] the world. Here, there was the taint of deepest sin in the most sacred quality of human life, working such effect, that the world was only the darker for this woman's beauty, and the more lost for the infant that she had borne.

The scene was not without a mixture of awe, such as must always invest the spectacle of guilt and shame in a fellow-creature, before society shall have grown corrupt enough to smile, instead of shuddering, at it. The witnesses of Hester Prynne's disgrace had not yet passed beyond their simplicity. They were stern enough to look upon her death, had that been the sentence, without a murmur at its severity, but had none of the heartlessness of another social state, which would find only a theme for jest in an exhibition like the present. Even if there had been a disposition to turn the matter into ridicule, it must have been repressed and overpowered by the solemn presence of men no less dignified than the governor, and several of his counselors, a judge, a general, and the ministers of the town; all of whom sat or stood in a balcony of the meetinghouse, looking down upon the platform. When such personages could constitute a part of the spectacle, without risking the majesty or reverence of rank and office, it was safely to be inferred that the infliction of a legal sentence would have an earnest and effectual meaning. Accordingly, the crowd was somber and grave. The unhappy culprit sustained herself as best a woman might, under the heavy weight of a thousand unrelenting eyes, all fastened upon her and concentrated at her bosom. It was almost intolerable to be borne. Of an impulsive and passionate nature, she had fortified herself to encounter the stings and venomous stabs of public contumely, wreaking itself in every variety of insult; but there was a quality so much more terrible in the solemn mood of the popular mind, that she longed rather to behold all those rigid countenances contorted with scornful merriment, and herself the object. Had a roar of laughter burst from the multitude — each man, each woman, each little shrill-voiced child, contributing their individual parts — Hester Prynne might have repaid them all with a bitter and disdainful smile. But, under the leaden infliction which it was her doom to endure, she felt, at moments, as if she must needs shriek out with the full power of her lungs, and cast herself from the scaffold down upon the ground, or else go mad at once.

Yet there were intervals when the whole scene, in which she was the most conspicuous object, seemed to vanish from her eyes, or at least, glimmered indistinctly before them, like a mass of imperfectly shaped and spectral images. Her mind and especially her memory was preternaturally active, and kept bringing up other scenes than this roughly hewn street of a little town, on the edge of the Western wilderness; other faces than were lowering upon her from beneath the brims of those steeple-crowned hats. Reminiscences, the most trifling and immaterial, passages of infancy and school-days, sports, childish quarrels, and the little domestic traits of her maiden years, came swarming back upon her, intermingled with recollections of whatever was gravest in her subsequent life; one picture precisely as vivid as another; as if all were of similar importance, or all alike a play. Possibly, it was an instinctive device of her spirit, to relieve itself, by the exhibition of these phantas-magoric forms, from the cruel weight and hardness of the reality.

Be that as it might, the scaffold of the pillory was a point of view that revealed to Hester Prynne the entire track along which she had been treading, since her happy infancy. Standing on that miserable emi-nence, she saw her native village, in old England, and her paternal home; a decayed house of grey stone, with a poverty-stricken aspect, but retaining a half obliterated shield of arms over the portal, in token of antique gentility. She saw her father's face, with its bald brow, and rev-erend white beard, that flowed over the old-fashioned Elizabethan ruff; her mother's, too, with the look of heedful and anxious love which it al-ways wore in her remembrance, and which, even since her death, had so often laid the impediment of a gentle remonstrance in her daughter's pathway. She saw her own face, glowing with girlish beauty, and illumi-nating all the interior of the dusky mirror in which she had been won't to gaze at it. There she beheld another countenance, of a man well strick-en in years, a pale, thin, scholar-like visage, with eyes dim and bleared by the lamplight that had served them to pore over many ponder-ous[9] books. Yet those same bleared optics had a strange, penetrating power, when it was their owner's purpose to read the human soul. This figure of the study and the cloister, as Hester Prynne's womanly fancy failed not to recall, was slightly deformed, with the left shoulder a trifle higher than the right. Next rose before her, in memory's picture-gallery, the intricate and narrow thoroughfares, the tall grey houses, the huge cathedrals, and the public edifices, ancient in date and quaint in archi-tecture, of a Continental city; where a new life had awaited her, still in connection with the misshapen scholar; a new life, but feeding itself on

time-worn materials, like a tuft[10] of green moss on a crumbling wall. Lastly, in lieu of these shifting scenes, came back the rude market-place of
the Puritan settlement, with all the townspeople assembled and leveling
their stern regards at Hester Prynne — yes, at herself — who stood on the
scaffold of the pillory, an infant on her arm, and the letter A, in scarlet,
fantastically embroidered with gold thread, upon her bosom!

Could it be true? She clutched the child so fiercely to her breast,
that it sent forth a cry; she turned her eyes downward at the scarlet letter, and even touched it with her finger, to assure herself that the infant
and the shame were real. Yes, these were her realities all else had vanished!

Notes:

1. physiognomy *n.* 相貌，面相，相面术

   E. g. I blended a multitude of human physiognomies to create
      this plausible simulation

2. betoken *vt.* 预示，表示

   E. g. The soviet union's space-faring triumph did not betoken
      much of an economic threat.

3. Puritan *n.* 清教徒

   E. g. They all eat at the canteen and are all ridiculously puri-
      tan.

4. scaffold *n.* 脚手架，断头台

   E. g. This was true of the Tudor politicians who knew their last
      speech might be on the scaffold.

5. heretofore *n.* 以前，迄今为止

   E. g. We will continue to hold meetings on Thursdays, as here-
      tofore.

6. haughty *a.* 傲慢的，目中无人的，自大的

   E. g. His haughty response prompted Mr Dahal's action.

7. evanescent *a.* 迅速消失遗忘的，短暂的

E. g. A tiny few have accumulated vast wealth but even that has an evanescent, almost ghostly quality.

8. redeem *n.* 赎回，挽回；履行；偿还；兑现

E. g. If an issuer does not redeem then, they must pay a higher penalty coupon rate.

9. ponderous *a.* 沉重的；笨重的；呆板的

E. g. The fat woman's movements were ponderous

10. tuft *vi.* 丛生；*n.* 一簇；丛生植物

E. g. Give him a tuft of hair and furry eyebrows.

Questions:

1. What is the historical context of *The Scarlet Letter*?

2. What is Puritanism and what do the Puritans promote and advocate?

3. How would you describe Hawthorne's writing style?

4. What does the scarlet letter "A" that Hester wears symbolize?

5. What is the most difficult thing for Hester as she stands before the crowd?

Analysis of Chapter Two

This chapter introduces the reader to Hester Prynne and begins to explore the theme of sin, along with its connection to knowledge and social order. The chapter' use of symbols, as well as their depiction of the political reality of Hester Prynne's world, testifies to the contradictions inherent in Puritan society. This is a world that has already "fallen," that already knows sin: the colonists are quick to establish a prison and a cemetery in their "Utopia," for they know that misbehavior, evil, and death are unavoidable. This belief fits into the larger Puritan doctrine, which puts heavy emphasis on the idea of original sin—the notion that all people are born sinners because of the initial transgressions of Adam and Eve in the Garden of Eden.

But the images of the chapter—the public gatherings at the prison and at the scaffold, both of which are located in central common spaces—also speak to another Puritan belief: the belief that sin not only permeates our world but that it should be actively sought out and exposed so that it can be punished publicly. The beadle reinforces this belief when he calls for a "blessing on the righteous Colony of the Massachusetts, where iniquity is dragged out into the sunshine. " His smug self-righteousness suggests that Hester's persecution is fueled by more than the villagers' quest for virtue. While exposing sin is meant to help the sinner and provide an example for others, such exposure does more than merely protect the community. Indeed, Hester becomes a scapegoat, and the public nature of her punishment makes her an object for voyeuristic contemplation; it also gives the townspeople, particularly the women, a chance to demonstrate—or convince themselves of—their own piety by condemning her as loudly as possible. Rather than seeing their own potential sinfulness in Hester, the townspeople see her as someone whose transgressions outweigh and obliterate their own errors.

中文译文：

第二章　市场

二百多年前一个夏日的上午，狱前街上牢房门前的草地上，满满地站着好大一群波士顿的居民，他们一个个都紧盯着布满铁钉的橡木牢门。如若换成其他百姓，或是推迟到新英格兰后来的历史阶段，这些蓄着胡须的好心肠的居民们板着的冷冰冰的面孔，可能是面临凶险的征兆，至少也预示着某个臭名昭著的罪犯即将受到人们期待已久的制裁，因为在那时，法庭的判决无非是认可公众舆论的裁处。但是，由于早年清教徒性格严峻，这种推测未免过于武断。也许，是一个慷倾的奴隶或是被家长送交给当局的一名逆子要在这笞刑柱上受到管教。也许，是一位唯信仰论者、一位教友派的教友或信仰其他异端的教徒被鞭挞出城，或是一个闲散的印第安游民，因为喝了白人的烈酒满街胡闹，要挨着鞭子给赶进树林。也许，那是地方官的遗孀西宾斯老夫人那样生性恶毒的巫婆，将要给吊死在绞架上。无论属于哪种情况，围观者总是摆出分毫不爽的庄严姿态；这倒十分符合早期移民的身份，因为他们将宗教和法律视同一体，二者在他们的品性中融溶为一，凡涉及公共纪律的条款，不管是最轻微的还是最严重的都同样令他们肃然起敬和望而生畏，确实，一个站在刑台上的罪人能够从这样一些旁观者身上谋得的同情是少而又少、冷而又冷的。另外，如今只意味着某种令人冷嘲热讽的惩罚，在当时却可能被赋予同死刑一样严厉的色彩。

牢门从里面给一下子打开了，最先露面的是狱吏，他腰侧挎着剑，手中握着权杖，那副阴森可怖的模样像个暗影似的出现在日光之中。这个角色的尊容便是清教徒法典全部冷酷无情的象征和代表，对触犯法律的人最终和最直接执法则是他的差事。此时他伸出左手举着权杖，右手抓着一个年轻妇女的肩头，挽着她向前走；到了牢门口，她用了一个颇能说明她个性的力量和天生的尊严的动作，推开狱吏，像是出于她自主的意志一般走进露天地。她怀里抱着一个三个月左右的婴儿，那孩子眨着眼睛，转动她的小脸躲避着过分耀眼的阳光——自从她降生以来，还只习惯于监狱中的土牢或其他暗室那种昏晦的光线呢。

当那年轻的妇女——就是婴儿的母亲——全身伫立在人群面前时，她的第一个冲动似乎就是把孩子抱在胸前；她这么做与其说是出于母爱的激情，不如说可以借此掩盖钉在她衣裙上的标记。然而，她很快就醒悟过来了，用她的耻辱的一个标记来掩盖另一个标记是无济于事的，于是，索性用一条胳膊架着孩子，她虽然面孔红得发烧，却露出高傲的微笑，用毫无愧色的目光环视着她的同镇居民和街坊邻里。她的裙袍的前胸上露出了一个用红色细布做就、周围用金丝线精心绣成奇巧花边的一个字母 A。这个字母制作别致，体现了丰富华美的匠心，佩在衣服上构成尽美尽善的装饰，而她的衣服把她那年月的情趣衬托得恰到好处，只是其艳丽程度大大超出了殖民地俭仆标准的规定。

那年轻妇女身材颀长，体态优美之极。她头上乌黑的浓发光彩夺目，在阳光下熠熠生辉。她的面孔不仅皮肤滋润、五官端正、容貌秀丽，而且还有一对鲜明的眉毛和一双漆黑的深目，十分楚楚动人。就那个时代女性举止优雅的风范而论，她也属贵妇之列；她自有一种端庄的风韵，并不同于如今人们心目中的那种纤巧、轻盈和不可言喻的优雅。即使以当年的概念而言，海丝特·白兰也从来没有像步出监狱的此时此刻这样更像贵妇。那些本来就认识她的人，原先满以为她经历过这一磨难，会黯然失色，结果却惊得都发呆了，因为他们所看到的，是她焕发的美丽，竟把笼罩着她的不幸和耻辱凝成一轮光环。不过，目光敏锐的旁观者无疑能从中觉察出一种微妙的痛楚。她在狱中按照自己的想象，专门为这场合制作的服饰，以其特有的任性和别致，似乎表达了她的精神境界和由绝望而无所顾忌的心情。但是，吸引了所有的人的目光而且事实上使海丝特·白兰焕然一新的，则是在她胸前频频闪光的绣得妙不可言的那个红字，以致那些与她熟识的男男女女简直感到是第一次与她谋面。这个红字具有一种震慑的力量，竟然把她从普通的人际关系中超脱出来，紧裹在自身的氛围里。

若在这一群清教徒之中有一个罗马天主教徒的话，他就会从这个服饰和神采如画、怀中紧抱婴儿的美妇身上，联想起众多杰出画家所竞先描绘的圣母的形象，诚然，他的这种联想只能在对比中才能产生，因为圣像中那圣洁清白的母性怀中的婴儿是献给世人来赎罪的。然而在她身上，世俗生活中最神圣的品德，却被最深重的罪孽所玷污了，其结果，只能使世界由于这妇人的美丽而更加晦默，由于她生下的婴儿而益发沉沦。

在人类社会尚未腐败到极点之前，目睹这种罪恶与羞辱的场面，人们还不会以淡然一笑代替不寒而栗，总会给留人下一种敬畏心理。亲眼看到海丝特·白兰示众的人们尚未失去他们的纯真。如果她被判死刑，他们会冷冷地看着她死去，而不会咕哝一句什么过于严苛；但他们谁也不会像另一种社会形态中的人那样，把眼前的这种示众只当作笑柄。即使有人心里觉得这事有点可笑，也会因为几位至尊至贵的大人物的郑重出席，而吓得不敢放肆。总督、他的几位参议、一名法官、一名将军和镇上的牧师们就在议事厅的阳台上或坐或立，俯视着刑台。能有这样一些人物到场，而不失他们地位的显赫和职务的威严，我们可以有把握地推断，所做的法律判决肯定具有真挚而有效的含义。因之，人群也显出相应的阴郁和庄重。这个不幸的罪人，在数百双无情的目光紧盯着她、集中在她前胸的重压之下，尽一个妇人的最大可能支撑着自己。这实在是难以忍受的。她本是一个充满热情、容易冲动的人，此时她已使自己坚强起来，以面对用形形色色的侮辱来发泄的公愤的毒刺和利刃；但是，人们那种庄重的情绪反倒隐含着一种可怕得多的气氛，使她宁可看到那一张张僵硬的面孔露出轻蔑的嬉笑来嘲弄她。如果从构成这一群人中的每一个男人、每一个女人和每一个尖嗓门的孩子的口中爆发出哄笑，海丝特·白兰或许可以对他们所有的人报以倨傲的冷笑。可是，在她注定要忍受的这种沉闷的打击之下，她时时感到要鼓足胸腔中的全部力量来尖声呼号，并从刑台上翻到地面，否则，她会立刻发疯的。

然而，在她充当众目所瞩的目标的全部期间，她不时感到眼前茫茫一片，至少，人群像一大堆支离破碎、光怪陆离的幻象般地朦胧模糊。她的思绪，尤其是她的记忆，却不可思议地活跃，越出这蛮荒的大洋西岸边缘上的小镇的祖创的街道，不断带回来别的景色与场面；她想到的，不是那些尖顶高帽藐视她的面孔。她回忆起那些最琐碎零散、最无关紧要的事情；孩提时期和学校生活，儿时的游戏和争斗，以及婚前在娘家的种种琐事蜂拥回到她的脑海，其中还混杂着她后来生活中最重大的事件的种种片断，一切全都历历如在目前；似乎全都同等重要，或者全都像一出戏。可能，这是她心理上的一种本能反应：通过展现这些各色各样、变幻莫测的画面，把自己的精神从眼前这残酷现实的无情重压下解脱出来。

无论如何，这座示众刑台成了一个瞭望点，在海丝特·白兰面前展现出自从她幸福的童年以来的全部轨迹。她痛苦地高高站在那里，再次看见了她在老英格兰故乡的村落和她父母的家园：那是一座破败的灰色石屋，虽说外表是一派衰微的景象，但在门廊上方还残存着半明半暗的盾形家族纹章，标志着远祖的世系。她看到她父亲的面容：光秃秃的额头和飘洒在伊丽莎白时代老式环状皱领上的威风凛凛的白须；她也看到了她母亲的面容，那种无微不至和牵肠挂肚的爱的表情，时时在她脑海中萦绕，即使在母亲去世之后，仍在女儿的人生道路上经常留下温馨忆念的告诫。她看到了自己少女时代的光彩动人的美貌，把她惯于映照的那面昏暗的镜子的整个镜心都照亮了。她还看到了另一副面孔，那是一个年老力衰的男人的面孔，苍白而瘦削，看上去一副学者模样，由于在灯光下研读一册册长篇巨著而老眼昏花。然而正是这同一双昏花的烂眼，在一心窥测他人的灵魂时，又具有那么奇特的洞察力。尽管海丝特·白兰那女性的想象力竭力想摆脱他的形象，但那学者和隐士的身影还是出现了：他略带畸形，左肩比右肩稍高。在她回忆的画廊中接下来升到她眼前的，是欧洲大陆一座城市里的纵横交错又显得狭窄的街道，以及年深日久、古色古香的公共建筑物，宏伟的天主教堂和高大的灰色住宅；一种崭新的生活在那里等待着她，不过仍和那个畸形的学者密切相关；那种生活像是附在颓垣上的一簇青苔，只能靠腐败的营养滋补自己。最终，这些接踵而至的场景烟消云散，海丝特·白兰又回到这片清教徒殖民地的简陋的市场上，全镇的人都聚集在这里，一双双严厉的眼睛紧紧盯着她——是的，盯着她本人——她站在示众刑台上，怀中抱着婴儿，胸前钉着那个用金丝线绝妙地绣着花边的鲜红的字母 Λ！

这一切会是真的吗？她把孩子往胸前猛地用力一抱，孩子哇的一声哭了；她垂下眼睛注视着那鲜红的字母，甚至还用指头触摸了一下，以便使自己确信婴儿和耻辱都是实实在在的。是啊——这些便是她的现实，其余的一切全都消失了！

❧ Answers for questions

1. The Scarlet Letter, which takes as its principal subject colonial seventeenth-century New England, was written in the middle of the nineteenth century. The novel is considered a historical romance written in the midst of the American literary movement called transcendentalism. The principle writers of transcendentalism included Ralph Waldo Emerson, Henry David Thoreau, Margaret Fuller, and W. H. Channing. Transcendentalism was, broadly speaking, a reaction against the rationalism of the previous century and the religious orthodoxy of Calvinist New England. Transcendentalism stressed the romantic tenets of mysticism, idealism, and individualism. In religious terms it saw God not as a distant and harsh authority, but as an essential aspect of the individual and the natural world, which were themselves considered inseparable. Because of this profound unity of all matter, human and natural,

knowledge of the world and its laws could be obtained through a kind of mystical rapture with the world.

2. Puritanism is one of the Protestant factions. It starts in the sixteenth century as a movement to reform the Church of England. Because of the dissatisfaction with the reform of church, Puritans required punishing the corruption, but they failed and fled to the American continent. At that time, the Puritans constituted the main part of the North American immigrants and Puritanism became the common value of people. They promote the concept of piety, humility, seriousness, honesty, diligence and frugality. Inspired by these values, the Puritans overcame difficulties, and soon harvested prosperity and wealth. Puritan are the most devout and holy protestants. They believed that human beings were predestined by God before they were born. Some were God's chosen people. The success of one's work or the prosperity in his calling is given by the God. Therefore, everyone must work hard. Working hard and living a moral life were their ethics. To the Puritans, a person by nature was wholly sinful, so they also advocated self-discipline and introspection. They regarded Bible to be the authority of their doctrine. To be able to read the Bible and understand God's will, education was essential for Puritans.

3. Nathaniel Hawthorne was a prominent early American Author who contributed greatly to the evolution of modern American literature. Hawthorne developed a style of romance fiction representative of his own beliefs. Although Nathaniel Hawthorne's writing style was often viewed as outdated when compared to modern literature, Hawthorne conveyed modern themes of psychology and human nature through his crafty use of allegory and symbolism.

4. Hester has committed adultery and has borne an illegitimate child, and that the letter "A" on her dress stands for "Adulterer." The writer uses the scarlet letters to symbolize the harshness of Puritan society, showing how they brand sinners for life

5. As a married woman, Hester should be honest, loyal, and re-

sponsible for her family. She had lost herself, and forgotten her responsibility. On one hand, she should be punished, especially in the Puritan society. On the other hand, she was brave enough to peruse true love. It is very difficult for her to face the cruel punishment with a mind of courage.

References

［1］http://en. wikipedia. org/wiki/Nathaniel_Hawthorne（图片来源）

［2］http://img3. douban. com/lpic/s10840115. jpg（图片来源）

［3］http:// www. gradesaver. com/author/hawthorne

［4］http://novel. tingroom. com/html/book/show/67/

［5］王松年. 美国文学作品选读［M］. 上海. 上海交通大学出版社, 1998.

［6］吴定柏. 美国文学大纲［M］. 上海. 上海外语教育出版社, 2003.

［7］胡荫桐, 刘树森. 美国文学教程［C］. 天津. 南开大学出版社, 1995.

Unit 7
Herman Melville (1819 – 1891)

✿ Biography

Herman Melville(1819 – 1891) was an American novelist, writer of short stories, and poet from
the American Renaissance period. Most of his writings were published between 1846 and 1857. Best
known for his sea adventure *Typee* (1846) and his
whaling novel *Moby Dick* (or *The Whale*) (1851),
he was almost forgotten during the last thirty years
of his life. Melville's writing draws on his experience at sea as a common sailor, exploration of literature and philosophy, and engagement in
the contradictions of American society in a period of rapid change. The
main characteristic of his style is probably its heavy allusiveness, a reflection of his use of written sources. Melville's way of adapting what he
read for his own new purposes, scholar Stanley T. Williams wrote, "was
a transforming power comparable to Shakespeare's. "

Born in New York City as the third child of a merchant in French
dry-goods who went bankrupt, his formal education stopped abruptly after the death of his father in 1832, shortly after bankruptcy. Melville
briefly became a schoolteacher before he first took to sea in 1839, as a
common sailor on a merchant voyage to Liverpool, the basis for his
fourth book, *Redburn* (1849). In late December 1840 he signed up for
his first whaling voyage aboard the whaler Acushnet, but jumped ship
eighteen months later in the Marquesas Islands. He lived among the n-

atives for up to a month, of which his first book, *Typee* (1846), is a fictionalized account that became such a success that he worked up a sequel, *Omoo* (1847). The same year Melville married Elizabeth Knapp Shaw; their four children were born between 1849 and 1855.

In August 1850, Melville moved to a farm near Pittsfield, Massachusetts, where he established a profound but short-lived friendship with Nathaniel Hawthorne and wrote *Moby Dick*, which, published in 1851, made Melville's public disappointed. One newspaper called the book "so much" trash. Nor was there much appreciation for his next work, *Pierre* (1852), which is psychologically complex and elaborate. The next years he turned to writing short fiction for magazines, of which "Bartleby, the Scrivener" was the first. After the serialized novel *Israel Potter* was published as a book in 1855, the short stories were collected in 1856 as *The Piazza Tales*. In 1857, Melville voyaged to England and the Near East: twenty years later, he worked his experience in Egypt and Palestine into an epic poem, *Clarel: A Poem and Pilgrimage in the Holy Land* (1876). In 1857 *The Confidence-Man* appeared, the last prose work published during his lifetime. Having secured a position of Customs Inspector in New York, he now turned to poetry, the first example of which is his poetic reflection on the Civil War, *Battle-Pieces and Aspects of the War* (1866).

In 1867 his oldest child Malcolm died at home from a self-inflicted gunshot. In 1886 he retired as Customs Inspector and privately published two volumes of poetry. During the last years of his life, he returned to prose once again and worked on *Billy Budd, Sailor*, left unfinished at his death, and eventually published in 1924. His death in 1891 from cardiovascular disease subdued the reviving interest in him, but the centennial of his birth marked the starting point of the "Melville Revival", and Melville's rise through the canon to the eventual appreciation of his writings as world classics.

🌸 *Moby Dick*

Melville started to write *Moby Dick* in February 1850. Published in 1851, *Moby Dick* tells the story of obsessed Captain Ahab's quest for revenge on the White Whale as observed by a common seaman who identifies himself only as Ishmael. To get to know the 19th century American mind and American itself, one has to read this book. It is an encyclopedia of everything, history, philosophy, religion, etc. in addition to a detailed account of the operations of the whaling industry.

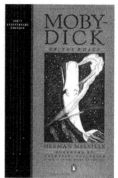

Major characters in *Moby Dick*

1. Ishmael—Ishmael, the only surviving crewmember of the *Pequod*, is the narrator of the book. As a character he is a few years younger than as a narrator. His importance relies on his role as narrator; as a character, he is only a minor participant in the action. The name has come to symbolize orphans, exiles, and social outcasts.

2. Ahab—He may have been Melville's portrait of an Emersonian self-reliant individual. Ahab, the Pequod's obsessed captain, represents both an ancient and a modern type of hero. His tremendous overconfidence, leads him to defy common sense and believe that, like a god, he can enact his will and remain immune to the forces of nature. He considers Moby Dick the embodiment of evil in the world, and he pursues the White Whale monomaniacally because he believes it his inescapable fate to destroy this evil.

3. Moby Dick—A white whale which on a previous voyage destroyed Ahab's ship and severed his leg at the knee. Moby Dick is an impersonal force, one that many critics have interpreted as an allegorical representation of God, an inscrutable and all-powerful being that humankind can neither understand nor defy. The novel claimed that

Moby Dick is possibly the largest sperm whale that ever lived. At the end of the novel Moby Dick destroys the *Pequod*. Ahab and the crew are drowned, with the exception of Ishmael.

4. Starbuck—He is one of the Pequod's three mates used primarily to provide philosophical contrasts with Ahab. Starbuck, the first mate, is a religious man. Sober and conservative, he relies on his Christian faith to determine his actions and interpretations of events. In Starbuck's view, the Moby Dick is just an animal in nature, which is God's management agent. Therefore, to find the Moby Dick for revenge is against God, which also is a sign of disrespect for the God.

5. Stubb—Stubb is the second mate, is jolly and cool in moments of crisis. He has worked in the dangerous occupation of whaling for so long that the possibility of death has ceased to concern him. Unlike Ahab, who believes that he can alter his world, he is a fatalist, believing that things happen as they are meant to and that there is little that he can do about it.

6. Flask—Flask is another perspective used to accentuate Ahab's monomania. Flask simply enjoys the thrill of the hunt and takes pride in killing whales. Unlike Ahab, who thinks and interprets, he doesn't stop to consider consequences at all and is "utterly lost...to all sense of reverence" for the whale. He is fearless, but careless and mindless.

Summary

Ishmael, the narrator, announces his intent to ship aboard a whaling vessel. He has made several voyages as a sailor but none as a whaler. He travels to New Bedford, Massachusetts, where he met Queequeg. The two decide to seek work on a whaling vessel together. They take a ferry to Nantucket, the traditional capital of the whaling industry. There they secure berths on the Pequod, a savage-looking ship adorned with the bones and teeth of sperm whales. Peleg and Bildad, the Pequod's Quaker owners, drive a hard bargain in terms of salary. They also mention the ship's mysterious captain, Ahab, who is still recovering from losing his leg in an encounter with a sperm whale on his last voyage.

The Pequod leaves Nantucket on a cold Christmas Day with a crew made up of men from many different countries and races. Soon the ship is in warmer waters, and Ahab makes his first appearance on deck, balancing gingerly on his false leg, which is made from a sperm whale's jaw. He announces his desire to pursue and kill Moby Dick, the legendary great white whale who took his leg, because he sees this whale as the embodiment of evil. Ahab nails a gold doubloon to the mast and declares that it will be the prize for the first man to sight the whale. As the Pequod sails toward the southern tip of Africa, whales are sighted and unsuccessfully hunted.

During another whale hunt, Pip, the Pequod's black cabin boy, jumps from a whaleboat and is left behind in the middle of the ocean. He goes insane as the result of the experience and becomes a crazy but prophetic jester for the ship. Soon after, the Pequod meets the Samuel Enderby, whaling ship whose skipper, Captain Boomer, has lost an arm in an encounter with Moby Dick. The two captains discuss the whale; Boomer, happy simply to have survived his encounter, cannot understand Ahab's lust for vengeance. Not long after, Queequeg falls ill and has the ship's carpenter make him a coffin in anticipation of his death. He recovers, however, and the coffin eventually becomes the Pequod's replacement life buoy.

Ahab orders a harpoon forged in the expectation that he will soon encounter Moby Dick. He baptizes the harpoon with the blood of the Pequod's three harpooners. The Pequod kills several more whales. Issuing a prophecy about Ahab's death, Fedallah declares that Ahab will first see two hearses, the second of which will be made only from American wood, and that he will be killed by hemp rope. Ahab interprets these words to mean that he will not die at sea, where there are no hearses and no hangings. A typhoon hits the Pequod, illuminating it with electrical fire. Ahab takes this occurrence as a sign of imminent confrontation and success, but Starbuck, the ship's first mate, takes it as a bad omen and considers killing Ahab to end the mad quest. After the storm ends, one of the sailors falls from the ship's masthead and drowns—a grim foreshadowing of what lies ahead.

The next day, Moby Dick is sighted again, and the boats are lowered once more. The whale is harpooned, but Moby Dick again attacks Ahab's boat. Fedallah, trapped in the harpoon line, is dragged overboard to his death. Starbuck must maneuver the Pequod between Ahab and the angry whale.

On the third day, the boats are once again sent after Moby Dick, who once again attacks them. The men can see Fedallah's corpse lashed to the whale by the harpoon line. Moby Dick rams the Pequod and sinks it. Ahab is then caught in a harpoon line and hurled out of his harpoon boat to his death. All of the remaining whaleboats and men are caught in the vortex created by the sinking Pequod and pulled under to their deaths. Only Ishmael escapes. He was thrown from a boat at the beginning of the chase, was far enough away to escape the whirlpool, and he alone survives. He floats atop Queequeg's coffin, which popped back up from the wreck, until he is picked up by the Rachel, which is still searching for the crewmen lost in her earlier encounter with Moby Dick.

Comments on *Moby Dick*

Moby Dick is an American book of wonders. It may be read on several levels. It is, basically, a thrilling adventure story, "the world's greatest sea novel," compounded of search, pursuit, conflict, and catastrophe. It is the plot of unceasing search for revenge, the "Americanized Gothic" of mystery and terror, crowded with omens and forebodings from the cracked Eligah's warning's to the prophecies of Fedallah, which are reminiscent of the witch's croaking in *Macbeth*. Clear throughout is a mastery of suspense and horror, of both subtle and broad humor, of exciting narrative in vigorous prose. Readers for the story's sake are dismayed by the numerous chapters on whales and whaling, but they provide truths. The chapters on whaling prepare the reader for the unfamiliar events, skillfully retard the swift action, and present an authentic, full way of life.

The more important levels are these of characterization and meaning. A gallery of unique portraits emerges. Peter Coffin, Captains Bildad and Peleg, and the officers of passing vessels are vividly described. Melville most convincingly individualizes Starbuck, Stubb, and Flask. The characterizations of the semi-autobiographical Ishmael and of Ahab are the most important and they are inextricably tied up with the book's meaning.

Moby Dick has a richness which has had enduring value for generations. Its symbolism is vast. Major symbols:

1. The Pequod: Named after a Native American tribe in Massachusetts that did not long survive the arrival of white men and thus memorializing the extinction, the Pequod is a symbol of doom. It is painted a gloomy black and covered in whale teeth and bones, literally bristling with the mementos of violent death. It is, in fact, marked for death. Adorned like a primitive coffin, the Pequod becomes one.

2. Moby Dick: Moby Dick possesses various symbolic meanings for various individuals. To the Pequod's crew, the legendary White Whale is a concept onto which they can displace their anxieties about their dangerous and often very frightening jobs. Because they have no delusions about Moby Dick acting malevolently toward men or literally embodying evil, tales about the whale allow them to confront their fear, manage it, and continue to function. Ahab, on the other hand, believes that Moby Dick is a manifestation of all that is wrong with the world, and he feels that it is his destiny to eradicate this symbolic evil.

3. Queequeg's Coffin: Queequeg's coffin alternately symbolizes life and death. Queequeg has it built when he is seriously ill, but when he recovers; it becomes a chest to hold his belongings and an emblem of his will to live. He perpetuates the knowledge tattooed on his body by carving it onto the coffin's lid. The coffin further comes to symbolize life, in

a morbid way, when it replaces the Pequod's life buoy. When the Pequod sinks, the coffin becomes Ishmael's buoy, saving not only his life
but the life of the narrative that he will pass on.

Introduction to Chapter I

The narrative of Moby-Dick begins with the famous brief sentence,
"Call me Ishmael. " Ishmael, a sailor, describes a typical scene in New
York City, with large groups of men gathering on their days off to contemplate the ocean and dream of a life at sea. He explains that he himself went to sea because, like these men, he was feeling a "damp, drizzly November in his soul" and craved adventure. Shunning anything too
"respectable" (or expensive), he always ships as a common sailor rather than as a passenger.

From   *Moby Dick*

Chapter I Loomings

Call me Ishmael.

Some years ago—never mind how long precisely—having little or
no money in my purse, and nothing particular to interest me on shore, I
thought I would sail about a little and see the watery part of the world. It
is a way I have of driving off the spleen[1] and regulating the circulation.
Whenever I find myself growing grim about the mouth; whenever it is a
damp, drizzly November in my soul; whenever I find myself involuntari-
ly pausing before coffin warehouses, and bringing up the rear of every
funeral I meet; and especially whenever my hypos get such an upper
hand of me, that it requires a strong moral principle to prevent me from
deliberately stepping into the street, and methodically knocking people's
hats off—then, I account it high time to get to sea as soon as I can. This
is my substitute for pistol and ball. With a philosophical flourish Cato
throws himself upon his sword; I quietly take to the ship. There is nothing surprising in this. If they but knew it, almost all men in their degree, some time or other, cherish very nearly the same feelings towards

the ocean with me.

There now is your insular city of the Manhattoes, belted round by wharves as Indian isles by coral reefs—commerce surrounds it with her surf. Right and left, the streets take you waterward. Its extreme downtown is the battery, where that noble mole is washed by waves, and cooled by breezes, which a few hours previous were out of sight of land. Look at the crowds of water-gazers there.

Circumambulate[2] the city of a dreamy Sabbath afternoon. Go from Corlears Hook to Coenties Slip, and from thence, by Whitehall, northward. What do you see? —Posted like silent sentinels all around the town, stand thousands upon thousands of mortal men fixed in ocean reveries. Some leaning against the spiels; some seated upon the pierheads; some looking over the bulwarks of ships from China; some high aloft in the rigging, as if striving to get a still better seaward peep.

But these are all landsmen; of week days pent up in lath and plaster—tied to counters, nailed to benches, clinched to desks. How then is this? Are the green fields gone? What do they here?

But look! Here come more crowds, pacing straight for the water, and seemingly bound for a dive. Strange! Nothing will content them but the extremest limit of the land; loitering[3] under the shady lee[4] of yonder warehouses will not suffice. No. They must get just as nigh[5] the water as they possibly can without falling in. And there they stand—miles of them—leagues. Inlanders all, they come from lanes and alleys, streets and avenues, — north, east, south, and west. Yet here they all unite. Tell me, does the magnetic virtue of the needles of the compasses of all those ships attract them thither?

Once more. Say you are in the country; in some high land of lakes. Take almost any path you please, and ten to one it carries you down in a dale, and leaves you there by a pool in the stream. There is magic in it. Let the most absent-minded of men be plunged in his deepest reveries—stand that man on his legs, set his feet a-going, and he will infallibly lead you to water, if water there be in all that region. Should you ever be athirst in the great American desert, try this experiment, if your caravan happen to be supplied with a metaphysical professor. Yes, as every one knows, meditation and water are wedded for ever.

But here is an artist. He desires to paint you the dreamiest, shadiest, quietest, most enchanting bit of romantic landscape in all the valley of the Saco. What is the chief element he employs? There stand his trees, each with a hollow trunk, as if a hermit and a crucifix were within; and here sleeps his meadow, and there sleep his cattle; and up from yonder cottage goes a sleepy smoke. Deep into distant woodlands winds a mazy way, reaching to overlapping spurs of mountains bathed in their hill-side blue. But though the picture lies thus tranced, and though this pine-tree shakes down its sighs like leaves upon this shepherd's head, yet all were vain, unless the shepherd's eye were fixed upon the magic stream before him. Go visit the Prairies in June, when for scores on scores of miles you wade knee-deep among Tiger-lilies—what is the one charm wanting? —Water—there is not a drop of water there! Were Niagara but a cataract of sand, would you travel your thousand miles to see it? Why did the poor poet of Tennessee, upon suddenly receiving two handfuls of silver, deliberate whether to buy him a coat, which he sadly needed, or invest his money in a pedestrian trip to Rockaway Beach? Why is almost every robust healthy boy with a robust healthy soul in him, at some time or other crazy to go to sea? Why upon your first voyage as a passenger, did you yourself feel such a mystical vibration, when first told that you and your ship were now out of sight of land? Why did the old Persians hold the sea holy? Why did the Greeks give it a separate deity[6], and own brother of Jove? Surely all this is not without meaning. And still deeper the meaning of that story of Narcissus, who because he could not grasp the tormenting, mild image he saw in the fountain, plunged into it and was drowned. But that same image, we ourselves see in all rivers and oceans. It is the image of the ungraspable phantom of life; and this is the key to it all.

Now, when I say that I am in the habit of going to sea whenever I begin to grow hazy about the eyes, and begin to be over conscious of my lungs, I do not mean to have it inferred that I ever go to sea as a passenger. For to go as a passenger you must needs have a purse, and a purse is but a rag unless you have something in it. Besides, passengers get sea-sick—grow quarrelsome—don't sleep of nights—do not enjoy themselves much, as a general thing;—no, I never go as a passenger; nor, though I am something of a salt, do I ever go to sea as a Commodore, or a Captain, or a Cook. I abandon the glory and distinction of such offices to those who like them. For my part, I abominate all honorable respectable toils, trials, and tribulations of every kind whatsoever. It is quite as much as I can do to take care of myself, without taking care of ships, barques, brigs, schooners, and what not. And as for going as cook,— though I confess there is considerable glory in that, a cook being a sort of officer on ship-board—yet, somehow, I never fancied broiling fowls;—though once broiled, judiciously buttered, and judgmatically salted and peppered, there is no one who will speak more respectfully, not to say reverentially, of a broiled fowl than I will. It is out of the idolatrous[7] dotings of the old Egyptians upon broiled ibis and roasted river horse, that you see the mummies of those creatures in their huge bake-houses the pyramids.

No, when I go to sea, I go as a simple sailor, right before the mast, plumb down into the fore-castle, aloft there to the royal mast-head. True, they rather order me about some, and make me jump from spar to spar, like a grasshopper in a May meadow. And at first, this sort of thing is unpleasant enough. It touches one's sense of honor, particularly if you come of an old established family in the land, the Van Rensselaers, or Randolphs, or Hardicanutes. And more than all, if just previous to putting your hand into the tar-pot, you have been lording it as a country schoolmaster, making the tallest boys stand in awe of you. The transition is a keen one, I assure you, from a schoolmaster to a sailor, and requires a strong decoction of Seneca and the Stoics to enable you to grin and bear it. But even this wears off in time.

What of it, if some old hunks of a sea-captain orders me to get a broom and sweep down the decks? What does that indignity amount to, weighed, I mean, in the scales of the New Testament? Do you think the archangel Gabriel thinks anything the less of me, because I promptly and respectfully obey that old hunks in that particular instance? Who ain't a slave? Tell me that. Well, then, however the old sea-captains may order me about—however they may thump and punch me about, I have the satisfaction of knowing that it is all right; that everybody else is one way or other served in much the same way— either in a physical or metaphysical point of view, that is; and so the universal thump is passed round, and all hands should rub each other's shoulder-blades, and be content.

Again, I always go to sea as a sailor, because they make a point of paying me for my trouble, whereas they never pay passengers a single penny that I ever heard of. On the contrary, passengers themselves must pay. And there is all the difference in the world between paying and being paid. The act of paying is perhaps the most uncomfortable infliction that the two orchard thieves entailed upon us. But being paid,—what will compare with it? The urbane activity with which a man receives money is really marvellous, considering that we so earnestly believe money to be the root of all earthly ills, and that on no account can a monied man enter heaven. Ah! How cheerfully we consign ourselves to perdition[8]!

Finally, I always go to sea as a sailor, because of the wholesome exercise and pure air of the fore-castle deck. For as in this world, head winds are far more prevalent than winds from astern(that is, if you never violate the Pythagorean maxim) , so for the most part the Commodore on the quarter-deck gets his atmosphere at second hand from the sailors on the forecastle. He thinks he breathes it first; but not so. In much the same way do the commonalty lead their leaders in many other things, at the same time that the leaders little suspect it. But wherefore it was that after having repeatedly smelt the sea as a merchant sailor, I should now take it into my head to go on a whaling voyage; this the invisible police officer of the Fates, who has the constant surveillance of me, and secretly dogs me, and influences me in some unaccountable way—he can better answer than any one else. And, doubtless, my going on this whaling voyage, formed part of the grand programme of Providence that was drawn up a long time ago. It came in as a sort of brief interlude and solo between more extensive performances. I take it that this part of the bill must have run something like this:

> "Grand Contested Election for the Presidency of the United States."
> "*WHALING VOYAGE BY ONE ISHMAEL.*"
> "BLOODY BATTLE IN AFFGHANISTAN."

Though I cannot tell why it was exactly that those stage managers, the Fates, put me down for this shabby part of a whaling voyage, when others were set down for magnificent parts in high tragedies, and short and easy parts in genteel comedies, and jolly parts in farces—though I cannot tell why this was exactly; yet, now that I recall all the circumstances, I think I can see a little into the springs and motives which being cunningly presented to me under various disguises, induced me to set about performing the part I did, besides cajoling me into the delusion that it was a choice resulting from my own unbiased freewill and discriminating judgment.

Chief among these motives was the overwhelming idea of the great whale himself. Such a portentous and mysterious monster roused all my curiosity. Then the wild and distant seas where he rolled his island bulk; the undeliverable[9], nameless perils of the whale; these, with all the attending marvels of a thousand Patagonian sights and sounds, helped to sway me to my wish. With other men, perhaps, such things would not have been inducements; but as for me, I am tormented with an everlasting itch for things remote. I love to sail forbidden seas, and land on barbarous coasts. Not ignoring what is good, I am quick to perceive a horror, and could still be social with it—would they let me—

since it is but well to be on friendly terms with all the inmates of the place one lodges in.

By reason of these things, then, the whaling voyage was welcome; the great flood-gates of the wonder-world swung open, and in the wild conceits[10] that swayed me to my purpose, two and two there floated into my inmost soul, endless processions of the whale, and, mid most of them all, one grand hooded phantom, like a snow hill in the air.

Notes:

1. spleen *n.* 坏脾气

   E. g. Paul Fussell's latest book vents his spleen against every-thing he hates about his country.

2. circumambulate *vt.* 巡行；绕行

   E. g. We circumamlated the city on a dreamy Sabbath afternoon.

3. loiter *vi.* 虚度；闲荡；徘徊

   E. g. Unemployed young men loiter at the entrance of the factory.

4. lee *n.* 保护；背风处

   E. g. The sea started to ease as we came under Cuba's lee.

5. nigh *prep.* (near)靠近；近似于 *adv.* 几乎

   E. g. They've lived in that house for nigh on 30 years.

6. deity *n.* 神；神性

   E. g. Polytheism refers to the worship of many deities.

7. idolatrous *adj.* 盲目崇拜的；崇拜偶像的

   E. g. An idolatrous love of material wealth will lead to self-de-struction.

8. perdition *n.* 毁灭，破灭；地狱

   E. g. It was their remarkable spirit that had prevented them from perdition.

9. undeliverable *adj.* 无法投递的；无法送达的

   E. g. Undeliverable postal materials shall be returned to the senders.

10. conceit *n.* 自负；狂妄

E. g. No one admires a man who is full of conceit.

Questions：

1. Why does the book begin with "Call me Ishmael"?

2. What does the whaling voyage mean to Ishmael?

3. Ishmael asks, "Who ain't a slave? Tell me that. " What do you know about Ishmael?

4. How is paying different from being paid according to Ishmael?

5. What may "loomings" mean?

Analysis of Chapter I：

The novel begins with the famous statement by the book's narrator："Call me Ishmael. " He has the habit of going to sea whenever he begins to grow "hazy about the eyes. " He goes to sea as a laborer, not as a Commodore, a Captain or a Cook, but as a simple sailor. He does so because he may be paid and because it affords him wholesome exercise and pure sea air.

Ishmael's name connotes the wanderer and outcast. He shares the illness and restlessness of the romantic hero, but he rises above them. He is no mere escapist.

中文译文：

第一章　若即若离的诱惑

管我叫以实玛丽吧。数年前——也别管它究竟是多少年——我的钱袋里只有一点点钱，或者说是没有钱，岸上呢，也没有什么使我特别感兴趣的事情，我觉得我还是出去航行一番，去认识一下这个世界的水上部分。这就是我用来驱除肝火、调节血液循环的一种方式。每当我发现我说话变得尖酸苛刻；每当我的心情像十一月的天气那样灰蒙蒙的；每当我发现自己不由自主地止步于棺材店门前，每逢葬礼便尾随而去；尤其是每当我的忧郁症占据了上风，需要一种强有力的道德准则来规范我的行为，以免我跑到街上，故意把人们的帽子一顶顶有条不紊地掀掉——我认为，这就是我该出海的时候了。这是我的手枪和子弹的替代品。和哲学繁荣时期的伽图拔剑自刎相比；我呢，却静静地上了船。在这个问题上没有什么好惊奇的。几乎所有的人，只要了解其中的奥秘，都会在一定程度上，在某个时候，对大海怀有和我同样的感情。

唔，这就是曼哈托斯岛城。码头众多，环绕四周，宛如珊瑚礁环绕的西门印度群岛；商业浪潮汹涌，将其团团围住。左右的街道会把你引向水边。曼哈托斯最远的商业区在炮台。几个小时前还望不见大陆，而现在你却能看到，微风送爽，海浪拍打着那宏伟壮观的防波堤。瞧，那还有一群在驻足眺望的人。

不妨在一个轻松的休息日下午，去城里兜上一圈。从科利亚斯·胡克出发到科恩蒂斯·斯利普，再从那儿经过怀特豪尔向北走。你看到些什么呢？——那城镇的周围像布满了无声的哨兵一般，成千上万的人站在那里，望着大海出神。有的靠着树桩；有的坐在凸式码头的尽头；有的望着中国船的舷墙；有的爬上高高的索具，仿佛要把那片海尽收眼底。但是，这些都是从未出过海的人，他们终日都被禁锢在木架泥糊的屋子里——拴在柜台边，钉在木凳上，扎在写字台上。那么，这又是怎么一回事呢？绿色的田野消失了吗？他们来这里干什么呢？

瞧啊！又有一群人来喽，他们径直奔向海边，好像是要去跳水似的。怪事！没有任何东西可以使他们满意，只有陆地的尽头才称他们的心。在仓库那边的庇荫处闲逛一番也不够味。不够的。只要不掉进海里，他们是一定要尽可能贴近大海的。他们站在那里——连绵几英里，连绵几十英里都是。所有这些内地人，他们来自大街小巷，东西南北。然而，他们却汇集于大海的岸边。请告诉我，是不是所有那些船的罗盘指针的磁力把他们吸引到这儿的？

再说呀，比如你身处乡下，生活在湖泊密布的高原。那么，随便你走哪条路，十有九条会把你引向山谷，而后把你引到溪流的水池边。这里可真有一种魔力。不妨找个最为心不在焉的人，让他醉于沉思之中——这个人站起来，迈开双脚。如果那一带有水的话，他会准确无误地把你引向水边。想象你身处美洲大漠，并感到口干舌燥，而且你的商队里又恰巧有个形而上学的教授，请做一做这个实验。不错，正如大家所知道的那样，沉思和水永远是联系在一起的。

　　这里有位画家，他想为你画一幅萨科河谷中最令人心宁神静、绿树成荫、幽静迷人的田园风景。在这幅画中他利用的主要元素是什么呢？那边画的是树林，而树干却是空的，仿佛那里面有位隐士和耶稣受难像；他的牧场在这里入睡，他的牛群在那里休息；那边的小屋升起了带有睡意的炊烟。一条迷津小径，弯弯曲曲地拐入远处的树林，向着那沐浴在绿色中的重峦叠嶂延伸而去。可是，尽管这幅画面美如仙境，尽管这株松树将它的叹息声像落叶似的撒在牧羊人的头上，然而，除非那牧羊人的眼睛注视着他面前的那条富有魔力的溪流，否则，这一切均为枉然。六月里，光顾一下大草原吧。在没过膝盖的卷丹草中艰难跋涉几十英里——这里缺少哪种有诱惑力的东西呢？——水——你不可能找到一滴水。如果尼亚加拉只是一帘黄沙瀑布，那你还会不会不远千里前来欣赏它？为什么田纳西州的那个穷诗人，在突然得到两大把银子时，会突然心生这种念头：究竟是买一件他急需的大衣，还是把钱花在去洛克韦海滩的远足上？为什么几乎所有的身心健康、精力充沛的小伙子有时会发疯似的闹着出海呢？为什么你初次航海旅行，第一次听人说你和你的船已经望不到陆地了，你心中会感到一种神秘的震颤呢？为什么古波斯人把大海奉为神圣呢？为什么希腊人赋予海以独立的神性，并把他视为约芙的手足兄弟呢？当然，所有这一切不都是没有意义的。还有那那西萨斯的故事，其意义就更为深刻了。他因抓不到水中那折磨人但又柔美的影子而跳进水中被淹死了。那个影像也正是我们自己在江河海洋里所看到的影像。它是那抓不住的生命中的幻影，这就是所有问题的答案所在。

　　每当我的眼睛变得蒙昽，肺部开始敏感的时候，我就有到海上去的习惯。我并不想让人得出我是以船客的身份到海上去的结论。因为去做船客，就得有钱袋，可那钱袋也只不过是一块破布而已，除非钱袋里有钱。还有，船客还会晕船——变得爱吵爱闹——夜里不睡觉——一般来说，这不会有什么乐趣可言——不，我从来没有以一名船客的身份出去过，也从来没有做过船队总指挥、船长或厨师，虽然我还可说是一位老水手。我愿意把这些让给那些喜欢荣耀和殊勋的人。就我而言，我讨厌各种各样的、尊贵的、叫人敬重的劳动、考验和折磨。我能够照顾好自己就很不错了，更管不了什么大船、三桅船、两桅方帆船、纵帆式小桅船等。至于做厨师——虽然我承认做厨师相当光荣，而且在船上，厨师也算得上是个头目——可是，不知怎的，我从来没有烤鸡的雅兴——鸡一旦烤好，黄油涂得很有水平，盐巴和胡椒也加得恰到好处，那我会比任何人都更加起劲地称赞它，虽不至于五体投地，也可说是心悦诚服的。古埃及人当初就是出于对烤朱鹭、烧河马有种崇拜偶像似的偏爱，所以到今天你还能在那些金字塔中，也就是他们那些巨大的烧烤房里看见这些动物的木乃伊。

　　不，我到海上去，总是当一名普通的水手，站在船桅前，钻进前甲板的船头楼，爬上更上方高大的桅顶。不错，他们还会把我呼来唤去，叫我从一根圆木跳到另一根圆木，就像五月草地里的蚱蜢一样。最初，这种事情确实不太令人愉快。它触动一个人的自尊，特别是如果你出身于陆地上的名门望族，比如什么凡·伦塞勒家族，伦道夫家族，哈狄卡纽特家族等。还不止这些，如果你的手伸入柏油罐子之前，你一直在逞一位乡村学校校长的威风，甚至让个子最高的男孩子也畏惧地站在你面前，那你就更能没面子了。我向你保证，从校长到水手这一过程是痛苦的。需要具有赛内加和那些苦行学派的坚强道行，才能使你做到含笑而忍。不过，就是这一点也会随着时间的逝去而慢慢消失。

　　如果某一位大块头的船长命令我去拿把扫帚打扫甲板，那又有什么关系呢？我的意思是，要是把这件事拿到《新约》的天平上称一称的话，这种羞辱这又算得了什么呢？难道你认为，因为我迅速而尊敬地服从了那大块头船长的命令，迦百列天使长就会瞧不起我吗？谁不是奴隶呢？请告诉我。唔，那么，不管船长们如何使唤我——不管他们怎么对我拳打脚踢，如果我清楚这算不了什么，其他人也这样或那样被奴役着——也就是说，从形而下或形而上的观点来看，每个人都是受奴役的——我便感到心满意足了。因此，重重的击打在我们中间轮过一番之后，大家应该互相按摩一下对方的肩胛骨，感到心安理得。

　　再说，我之所以出海做水手，是因为他们总是付钱给我以酬劳我的辛苦，可我从来就没听说过他们付给船客一个子儿。相反，船客们必须自己付钱。而且，在这个世界上，付钱给别人和别人给你付钱是截然不同的。付钱给别人这种行为也许就是那两个偷果园的贼带给我们的令人不舒服的苦痛。但是，别人帮我们付钱又会怎么样呢？考虑到我们都诚挚地相信钱是尘世间一切罪恶的根源，有钱的人是绝对不能进入天堂的，一个人接受钱时的那种温文尔雅的举止倒是妙不可言的。啊！我们是多么高兴地把自己沦于万劫不复的境地呀！

最后，我之所以总是出海做水手，是因为那有益于健康的操劳和船头楼甲板上的纯净空气。由于这个世界上顶风要比顺风来得多（那就是说，如果你从没有违背毕达哥拉斯的格言），因此，在极大程度上，后甲板的总指挥呼吸的只是船头楼的水手呼吸过的空气。然而，他却以为他先呼吸到新鲜空气。可事实并非如此。在许多别的事情上，老百姓也是这样领导他们的领袖的，而那些领袖却对此毫无察觉。可是，我以前出海一直是做商船水手，现在我怎么会异想天开，要去进行一次捕鲸的航行呢？司命运之神那位隐形警官一直在监视着我，秘密跟踪着我，还难以解释的左右着我。他对这一点会做出比别人更好的解释。而且，毫无疑问，我这次捕鲸之旅是上天很久以前就已经拟定好伟大的节目单的一部分。它是穿插在两个大型节目中间的一个小小的插曲和独唱，我想节目单上的这部分肯定是这样写的：

美国总统大选
以实玛利的捕鲸之行
阿富汗血战记

虽然我不能确切地知道为什么那些舞台经理、司命运之神，派我担任捕鲸航行中这一寒酸的角色，而别人却被派去扮演崇高悲剧中的华贵角色，扮演附庸风雅的喜剧中的轻松角色，扮演讽刺剧里的丑角——虽然我不能确切地说出为什么，不过，既然回想起了这种种情形，我对那些以各种伪装狡黠地呈现在我面前的目的和动机也略有端倪。这种目的和动机除了哄骗我去幻想这是我自己的公正、自愿的意志和敏锐的判断的抉择，还诱使我开始扮演起我扮演的角色。

　　这些动机之首是有关那条大鲸本身压倒一切的想法。就是这样一个预兆不详而又神秘可怕的怪物激起了我所有的猎奇心。还有那任大鲸随意滚动它那岛屿般躯体的遥远而蛮荒的大海，与大鲸有关的不可言表和难以名状的惊险以及在巴塔哥尼亚一带听到和见到的那些数不清的声色俱全的传奇，都影响了我的抉择。在另一些人的眼里，这类事情也许不可能成为诱惑；但是，就我而言，一切遥远的东西永远折磨得我痛痒难熬，苦恼不已。我就喜欢航行在烟波浩渺的重洋，涉足蛮野的海岸。我并不是分不清好歹，我是长于认识恐怖，并与之结交为伴——只要人们允许我——因为一个人投宿于一地，并能与此地的居民友好相处，才是恰当可取的。

　　由于上述种种原因，捕鲸之旅被我欣然接受，通往那神奇境地的大闸门豁然洞开。在那影响我做出抉择的狂想里，无尽的大鲸列阵而来，成双成对地游弋入我灵魂的深处。其中有一庞大的、面门突出的幻影，犹如雪山一般，耸立在云霄。

Answers for questions

　　1. "Call me Ishmael," chapter I begins: The borrowed name lets us know that he will tell us only what he wants to, and that he is a man apart from his fellows. The Ishmael we hear at the beginning is in some ways the book's most illusive character because, just as the biblical name suggests an outsider, a wanderer of sorts, he wanders in and out of the novel's narrative voice as it moves along. In the early chapters he is fully present as a character as he leads us toward the Pequod. But once on board he soon melds into the crew as his storytelling duties are taken over by the much more knowledgeable narrator whose arrival is not announced, but whose presence is clear as early as chapter XXIX when we overhear an exchange between Ahab and Stubb, the second mate. The Epilogue brings him back in full, first-person voice, and it is set in italics in a good print version, which sets it visually apart from all other paragraphs of prose in the book. That leaves us an impression that it seems to set apart a new Ishmael, united as one mind again but as a

markedly different person than he was in the Loomings of Chapter 1.

2. To Ishmael, this voyage has become a journey in quest of happiness, knowledge and values.

3. His vision of obedience, power relationships, and the "universal thump".

4. The act of paying is perhaps the most uncomfortable infliction, while being paid is really marvellous, considering that we so earnestly believe money to be the root of all earthly ills, and that on no account can a monied man enter heaven.

5. "Loomings" has several implications. It may refer to the white whale and foreshadowings of his presence.

References

[1] http://en. wikipedia. org/wiki/Herman_Melville（图片来源）

[2] http://en. wikipedia. org/wiki/Herman_Melville（图片来源）

[3] http://book. douban. com/subject/1547198/

[4] http://www. sparknotes. com/lit/mobydick/canalysis. html

[5] http://www. sparknotes. com/lit/mobydick/summary. html

[6] http://www. sparknotes. com/lit/mobydick/themes. html

[7] 常耀信. 美国文学简史[M]. 天津: 南开大学出版社, 1990.

[8]【美】麦尔维尔. 容新芳, 温荣耀, 译. 白鲸[M]. 北京: 中国致公出版社, 2003.

Unit 8
Mark Twain (1835 – 1910)

🌿 Bibliography

Samuel Langhorne Clemens (1835 – 1910), better known by his pen name Mark Twain, was an American author and humorist. He wrote *The Adventures of Tom Sawyer* (1876) and its sequel—*Adventures of Huckleberry Finn* (1885), the latter often called "The Great American Novel".

Twain grew up in Hannibal, Missouri, which provided the setting for Huckleberry Finn and Tom Sawyer. After an apprenticeship with a printer, he worked as a typesetter and contributed articles to the newspaper of his older brother, Orion Clemens. He later became a riverboat pilot on the Mississippi River before heading west to join Orion in Nevada. He referred humorously to his singular lack of success at mining, turning to journalism for the Virginia City Territorial Enterprise. In 1865, his humorous story "The Celebrated Jumping Frog of Calaveras County" was published, based on a story he heard at Angels Hotel in Angels Camp, California, where he had spent some time as a miner. The short story brought international attention, and was even translated into classic Greek. His wit and satire, in prose and in speech, earned praise from critics and peers, and he was a friend to presidents, artists, industrialists and European royalty.

Though Twain earned a great deal of money from his writings and lectures, he invested in ventures that lost a great deal of money, notably the Paige Compositor, a mechanical typesetter, which failed because of its complexity and imprecision. In the wake of these financial setbacks, he filed for protection from his creditors via bankruptcy, and with the help of Henry Huttleston Rogers eventually overcame his financial troubles. Twain chose to pay all his pre-bankruptcy creditors in full, though he had no legal responsibility to do so.

Twain was born shortly after a visit by Halley's Comet, and he predicted that he would "go out with it", too. He died the day after the comet returned. He was lauded as the "greatest American humorist of his age", and William Faulkner called Twain "the father of American literature".

The Adventures of Tom Sawyer

The Adventures of Tom Sawyer, first published in 1876, is a child's adventure story; it is also, however, the story of a young boy's transition into a young man. In some ways, it is a bildungsroman, a novel whose principle subject is the moral, psychological, and intellectual development of a youthful main character. It is not a true bildungsroman, however, because Twain did not take Tom into full manhood.

One of America's best-loved tales, Tom Sawyer has a double appeal. First, it appeals to the young adolescent as the exciting adventures of a typical boy during the mid-nineteenth century, adventures that are still intriguing and delightful because they appeal to the basic instincts of nearly all young people, regardless of time or culture. Second, the novel appeals to the adult reader who looks back on his or her own childhood with fond reminiscences. In fact, in his preface to the first edition, Twain wrote, "Although my book is intended mainly for the entertainment of boys and girls el part of my plan has been to pleasantly remind adults of what they once were themselves, and what they felt and thought". Thus, the novel is a combination of the past and the present, of the well-remembered events from childhood told in such a way as to e-voke remembrances in the adult mind.

Whether or not one has read the novel, many of the scenes are familiar and have become a part of our cultural heritage: Consider for example, the scene in which Tom manipulates others to paint a fence he himself was to have painted, the scene with Tom and Becky lost in the cave, and the scene of the boys in the graveyard. Twain captures the essence of childhood, with all its excitement, fear, and mischievousness. Likewise, the characters—Tom himself, Becky Thatcher, Huck Finn, Injun Joe, and Aunt Polly—have become part of our American heritage.

Although Tom Sawyer is set in a small town along the western frontier on the banks of the legendary Mississippi River sometime during the 1840s, readers from all parts of the world respond to the various adventures experienced by Tom and his band of friends. The appeal of the novel lies mostly in Twain's ability to capture—or recapture—universal experiences and dreams and fears of childhood.

Characters in *The Adventures of Tom Sawyer*

1. Tom Sawyer—The novel's protagonist. Tom is a mischievous boy with an active imagination who spends most of the novel getting himself and often his friends into and out of trouble. Despite his mischief, Tom has a good heart and a strong moral conscience. As the novel progresses, he begins to take more seriously the responsibilities of his role as a leader among his schoolfellows.

2. Aunt Polly—Tom's aunt and guardian. Aunt Polly is a simple, kind-hearted woman who struggles to balance her love for her nephew with her duty to discipline him. She generally fails in her attempts to keep Tom under control because, although she worries about Tom's safety, she seems to fear constraining him too much.

3. Huckleberry Finn—The son of the town drunk. Huck is a juvenile outcast who is shunned by respectable society and adored by the local

boys. Like Tom, Huck is highly superstitious, and both boys are always ready for an adventure. Huck gradually replaces Tom's friend Joe Harper as Tom's sidekick in his escapades.

4. Becky Thatcher—Judge Thatcher's pretty, yellow-haired daughter. From almost the minute she moves to town, Becky is the "Adored Unknown" who stirs Tom's lively romantic sensibility. Na? ve at first, Becky soon matches Tom as a romantic strategist, and the two go to great lengths to make each other jealous.

5. Joe Harpe—Tom's "bosom friend" and frequent playmate. Joe is a typical best friend, a convention Twain parodies when he refers to Joe and Tom as "two souls with but a single thought". As the novel progresses, Huck begins to assume Joe's place as Tom's companion.

6. Sid—Tom's half-brother. Sid is a goody-goody who enjoys getting Tom into trouble. He is mean-spirited but presents a superficial show of model behavior. He is thus the opposite of Tom.

7. Injun Joe—A violent, villainous man who commits murder, becomes a robber, and plans to mutilate the Widow Douglas. Injun Joe's predominant motivation is revenge. Half Native American and half Caucasian, he has suffered social exclusion, probably because of his race.

Summary

Tom Sawyer is a troublemaker. After Tom gets in trouble, he is ordered by Aunt Polly, with whom he lives, to whitewash their fence. When his friends see him painting the fence, Tom pretends like he loves the chore to make his friends jealous. They beg him to let them help. This is a prime example of the type of trouble Tom Sawyer is always getting up to.

Part of the novel is devoted to Tom's romance with Becky Thatcher, a new girl in town. They like each other, but Becky is hurt when she finds out that Tom liked someone else before her. Eventually, he takes the blame for a book she ruined, making her like him again.

Tom is always getting into trouble, usually with his friend, Huckleberry Finn. Together they sneak out to a graveyard at night, where they witness Injun Joe murder Dr. Robinson.

Tom, Huck, and their friend, Joe Harper, run away for a little while, making the town think they are dead. Eventually they come back, though, and Tom testifies against Injun Joe in court.

Afterward, Injun Joe runs away and Tom is terrified for his life. His terror does not stop him from making trouble, though. While he and Huck are hunting for treasure one night, they discover that Injun Joe, who is disguised as a deaf-mute Spaniard, has treasure of his own to bury.

Huck agrees to spy on Injun Joe to see where he buries the treasure, while Tom goes on a picnic with his class to McDougal's Cave. During the picnic, Tom and Becky wander off and get lost.

Huck figures out that Injun Joe plans on hurting Widow Douglas. He reports the crime and Injun Joe runs away to McDougal's Cave. Meanwhile, Tom and Becky are lost for several days in the cave. Eventually they stumble across Injun Joe, but hide before he sees them. Shortly after, Tom figures out how to get out of the cave with Becky. He tells Judge Thatcher about Injun Joe being inside and the town decides to seal Injun Joe inside the cave.

Later, Tom returns to the cave, where he discovers Injun Joe's starved corpse. Shortly thereafter, he and Huck discover where Injun Joe hid his gold. The Widow Douglas adopts Huck, who is unhappy about this development. Tom convinces him to give it a try, promising that it won't stop them from getting up to the occasional mischief.

Comments on *The Adventures of Tom Sawyer*

Concerned with Tom's personal growth and quest for identity, *The Adventures of Tom Sawyer* incorporates several different genres. It resembles a bildungsroman, a novel that follows the development of a hero from childhood through adolescence and into adulthood. The novel also

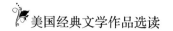

resembles novels of the picaresque genre, in that Tom moves from one adventurous episode to another. *The Adventures of Tom Sawyer* also fits the genres of satire, frontier literature, folk narrative, and comedy.

Introduction to Chapter 2

Aunt Polly finds Tom in the pantry where he has been eating forbidden jam. As she gets a switch, Tom convinces her that something is behind her. As she turns, he escapes, leaving her to contemplate how he constantly plays tricks on her. She is concerned whether or not she is "doing her duty by him", but because he is her dead sister's child, she cannot bring herself to be harsh with him.

That afternoon, Tom plays hooky from school, and at supper that night, Aunt Polly tries to trap him into revealing that he skipped school. Tom is able to avert her questioning, until Sid, Tom's brother, squelches on him. Before Aunt Polly can say more, Tom escapes.

Heading into town, Tom meets a stranger, "a boy larger than himself" and dressed up like a "city slicker." He and Tom get into a fight. Tom gets the better of the other boy and follows him home. The boy's mother appears and calls Tom a "bad vicious, vulgar child" and orders him away. When Tom returns home with his clothes dirty and torn, Aunt Polly decides that, as punishment, he will lose his freedom on Saturday and will have to whitewash the fence.

From *The Adventures of Tom Sawyer*
Chapter 2

Saturday morning was come, and all the summer world was bright and fresh, and brimming[1] with life. There was a song in every heart; and if the heart was young the music issued at the lips. There was cheer in every face and a spring in every step. The locust-trees were in bloom[2] and the fragrance of the blossoms filled the air. Cardiff Hill, beyond the village and above it, was green with vegetation and it lay just far enough away to seem a Delectable Land, dreamy, reposeful[3], and inviting.

Tom appeared on the sidewalk with a bucket[4] of whitewash and a long-handled brush. He surveyed the fence, and all gladness left him and a deep melancholy[5] settled down upon his spirit. Thirty yards of board fence nine feet high. Life to him seemed hollow, and existence but a burden. Sighing, he dipped his brush and passed it along the top-most plank[6]; repeated the operation; did it again; compared the insignificant whitewashed streak with the far-reaching continent of unwhitewashed fence, and sat down on a tree-box discouraged. Jim came skipping out at the gate with a tin pail, and singing Buffalo Gals. Bringing water from the town pump[7] had always been hateful work in Tom's eyes, before, but now it did not strike him so. He remembered that there was company at the pump. White, mulatto[8], and negro boys and girls were always there waiting their turns, resting, trading playthings, quarrelling, fighting, skylarking.

And he remembered that although the pump was only a hundred and fifty yards off, Jim never got back with a bucket of water under an hour — and even then somebody generally had to go after him. Tom said:

"Say, Jim, I'll fetch the water if you'll whitewash some. "

Jim shook his head and said:

"Can't, Mars Tom. Ole missis, she tole me I got to go an' git dis water an' not stop foolin' roun' wid anybody. She say she spec' Mars Tom gwine to ax me to whitewash, an' so she tole me go' long an' ' ' tend to my own business — she' lowed she'd' tend to de white wash in'. "

"Oh, never you mind what she said, Jim. That's the way she always talks. Gimme the bucket — I won't be gone only a minute. She won't ever know. "

"Oh, I dosn't, Mars Tom. Ole missis she'd take an' tar de head off'n me. ' Deed she would. "

"She! She never licks[10] anybody — whacks'em over the head with her thimble — and who cares for that, I'd like to know. She talks awful, but talk don't hurt — anyways it don't if she don't cry. Jim, I'll give you a marvel[11]. I'll give you a white alley[12]!"

Jim began to waver.

"White alley, Jim! And it's a bully taw. "

"My! Dat's a mighty gay marvel, I tell you! But Mars Tom I's powerful' fraid ole missis —"

"And besides, if you will I'll show you my sore toe. "

Jim was only human — this attraction was too much for him. He put down his pail[13], took the white alley, and bent over the toe with absorbing interest while the bandage was being unwound. In another moment he was flying down the street with his pail and a tingling rear, Tom was whitewashing with vigor, and Aunt Polly was retiring from the field with a slipper in her hand and triumph in her eye.

But Tom's energy did not last. He began to think of the fun he had planned for this day, and his sorrows multiplied. Soon the free boys would come tripping along on all sorts of delicious expeditions[14], and they would make a world of fun of him for having to work — the very thought of it burnt him like fire. He got out his worldly wealth and examined it — bits of toys, marbles, and trash; enough to buy an exchange of work, maybe, but not half enough to buy so much as half an hour of pure freedom. So he returned his straitened means to his pocket, and gave up the idea of trying to buy the boys. At this dark and hopeless moment an inspiration burst upon him! Nothing less than a great, magnificent inspiration.

He took up his brush and went tranquilly[15] to work. Ben Rogers hove[16] in sight presently — the very boy, of all boys, whose ridicule he had been dreading. Ben's gait[17] was the hop-skip-and-jump — proof enough that his heart was light and his anticipations high. He was eating an apple, and giving a long, melodious[18] whoop[19], at intervals, followed by a deep-toned ding-dong-dong, ding-dong-dong, for he was personating a steamboat.

As he drew near, he slackened[20] speed, took the middle of the street, leaned far over to starboard and rounded to ponderously[21] and with laborious pomp[22] and circumstance—for he was personating the Big Missouri, and considered himself to be drawing nine feet of water. He was boat and captain and engine-bells combined, so he had to imagine himself standing on his own hurricane-deck giving the orders and executing them:

"Stop her, sir! Ting-a-ling-ling!" The headway ran almost out, and he drew up slowly toward the sidewalk.

"Ship up to back! Ting-a-ling-ling!" His arms straightened and stiffened down his sides.

"Set her back on the starboard[23]! Ting-a-ling-ling! Chow! ch-chow-wow! Chow!"

His right hand, meantime, describing stately[24] circles — for it was representing a forty-foot wheel.

"Let her go back on the labboard[25]! Ting-a-ling-ling! Chow-ch-chowchow!"

The left hand began to describe circles.

"Stop the starboard! Ting-a-ling-ling! Stop the labboard! Come a-head on the starboard! Stop her! Let your outside turn over slow! Ting-a-lingling!

Chow-ow-ow! Get out that head-line! Lively now! Come — out with your spring-line — what're you about there! Take a turn round that stump[26] with the bight of it! Stand by that stage, now — let her go! Done with the engines, sir! Ting-a-ling-ling! Sh't! S'h't! Sh't!" (trying the gaugecocks[27]).

Tom went on whitewashing — paid no attention to the steamboat. Ben stared a moment and then said: "Hi-yi! You're up a stump, ain't you!"

No answer. Tom surveyed his last touch with the eye of an artist, then he gave his brush another gentle sweep and surveyed the result, as before.

Ben ranged up alongside of him. Tom's mouth watered for the apple, but he stuck to his work. Ben said:

"Hello, old chap, you got to work, hey?"

Tom wheeled suddenly and said: "Why, it's you, Ben! I warn't noticing. "

"Say — I'm going in a-swimming, I am. Don't you wish you could? But of course you'd druther work — wouldn't you? Course you would!"

Tom contemplated the boy a bit, and said: "What do you call work?"

"Why, ain't that work?"

Tom resumed his whitewashing, and answered carelessly: "Well, maybe it is, and maybe it ain't. All I know, is, it suits Tom Sawyer. "

"Oh come, now, you don't mean to let on that you like it?" The brush continued to move.

"Like it? Well, I don't see why I oughtn't to like it. Does a boy get a chance to whitewash a fence every day?"

That put the thing in a new light. Ben stopped nibbling[28] his apple. Tom swept his brush daintily[29] back and forth — stepped back to note the effect — added a touch here and there — criticised the effect again — Ben watching every move and getting more and more interested, more and more absorbed. Presently he said: "Say, Tom, let me whitewash a little. "

Tom considered, was about to consent; but he altered his mind: "No — no — I reckon it wouldn't hardly do, Ben. You see, Aunt Polly's awful particular about this fence — right here on the street, you know — but if it was the back fence I wouldn't mind and she wouldn't. Yes, she's awful particular about this fence; it's got to be done very careful; I reckon there ain't one boy in a thousand, maybe two thousand, that can do it the way it's got to be done. "

"No — is that so? Oh come, now — lemme just try. Only just a little — I'd let you, if you was me, Tom. "

"Ben, I'd like to, honest injun; but Aunt Polly — well, Jim wanted to do it, but she wouldn't let him; Sid wanted to do it, and she wouldn't let Sid.

Now don't you see how I'm fixed? If you was to tackle this fence and anything was to happen to it —"

"Oh, shucks, I'll be just as careful. Now lemme try. Say — I'll give you the core of my apple. "

"Well, here — No, Ben, now don't. I'm afeard —"

"I'll give you all of it!"

Tom gave up the brush with reluctance in his face, but alacrity[30] in his heart. And while the late steamer Big Missouri worked and sweated in the sun, the retired artist sat on a barrel in the shade close by, dangled his legs, munched his apple, and planned the slaughter[31] of more innocents.

There was no lack of material; boys happened along every little while; they came to jeer, but remained to whitewash. By the time Ben was fagged out, Tom had traded the next chance to Billy Fisher for a kite, in good repair; and when he played out, Johnny Miller bought in for a dead rat and a string to swing it with — and so on, and so on, hour after hour. And when the middle of the afternoon came, from being a poor poverty-stricken boy in the morning, Tom was literally rolling in wealth.

He had besides the things before mentioned, twelve marbles, part of a jews-harp[32], a piece of blue bottle-glass to look through, a spool cannon[33], a key that wouldn't unlock anything, a fragment of chalk, a glass stopper of a decanter[34], a tin soldier, a couple of tadpoles[35], six firecrackers, a kitten with only one eye, a brass doorknob, a dog-collar — but no dog — the handle of a knife, four pieces of orange-peel, and a dilapidated[36] old window sash[37].

He had had a nice, good, idle time all the while — plenty of company — and the fence had three coats of whitewash on it! If he hadn't run out of whitewash he would have bankrupted every boy in the village.

Tom said to himself that it was not such a hollow world, after all. He had discovered a great law of human action, without knowing it —

namely, that in order to make a man or a boy covet[38] a thing, it is only necessary to make the thing difficult to attain. If he had been a great and wise philosopher, like the writer of this book, he would now have comprehended that Work consists of whatever a body is obliged to do, and that Play consists of whatever a body is not obliged to do. And this would help him to understand why constructing artificial flowers or performing on a tread-mill is work, while rolling ten-pins or climbing Mont Blanc is only amusement. There are wealthy gentlemen in England who drive four-horse passenger-coaches twenty or thirty miles on a daily line, in the summer, because the privilege costs them considerable money; but if they were offered wages for the service, that would turn it into work and then they would resign. The boy mused[39] awhile over the substantial change which had taken place in his worldly circumstances, and then wended[40] toward headquarters to report.

Notes:

1. brimming *adj.* 满溢的;横溢的

   E. g. Michael looked at him imploringly, eyes brimming with tears.

   I noticed Dorabella was brimming over with excitement.

2. bloom *n.* 开花期;最盛期

   E. g. Our educational work is like a hundred flowers in bloom.

   The almonds were in bloom

3. reposeful *adj.* 平稳的,沉着的

   E. g. If she could quiet down and keep still a couple of minutes at a time, it would be a reposeful spectacle.

4. bucket *n.* 水桶;一桶的量

5. melancholy *n.* 忧郁;悲哀

   E. g. A profound melancholy seized her.

   All at once he fell into a state of profound melancholy.

6. plank *n.* (厚)木板;支持物

7. pump *n.* 泵；打气筒

8. mulatto *adj.* 白黑混血儿的，黄褐色的

9. lick *vt. & vi.* 轻轻拍打；战胜

10. marvel *n.* 奇迹；令人惊奇的事物(或事例)

    E. g. Ade is going to lick his wound.

        He licked the dust and got faint.

11. alley *n.* 胡同，小巷；小径；球道

12. pail *n.* 桶，提桶；一桶的量

13. expedition *n.* 考察；远征军

14. tranquilly *adv.* 安静地，平静地

15. hove (heave 的过去式及过去分词) vt. 举起；投掷

16. gait *n.* 步态，步法

17. melodious *adj.* 有旋律的；悦耳的

18. whoop *n.* 大叫；呐喊；喘息声；哮喘声

19. slacken *vt. & vi.* (使)放慢；(使)放松

    E. g. Redouble your efforts and not slacken off.

        We cannot afford to slacken our efforts in the slightest.

20. ponderously *adv.* 沉重地，生硬地

    E. g. He turns and marches away ponderously to the right.

        The play was staged with ponderously realistic sets.

21. laborious pomp 艰苦的盛况

22. starboard *n.* (船舶、飞机的)右舷，右侧

23. stately *adj.* 庄严的；高贵的；雄伟的；富丽堂皇的

    E. g. Instead of moving at his usual stately pace, he was almost running.

        The building rose before him, tall and stately.

24. labboard *n.* (船舶、飞机的)右舷，右侧

25. stump *n.* (被砍下的树的)树桩

26. gaugecock *n.* 试水位旋塞

27. nibble *v.* 啃，一点一点地咬(吃)

28. daintily *adv.* 优美地；讲究地

    E. g. She nibbled daintily at her cake.

Some people wear casu-ally and some people are dressed daintily.

29. alacrity *n.* 敏捷；活泼；欣然；乐意

E. g. They fell on the sandwiches with alacrity.

They accepted the offer with alacrity.

30. slaughter *n.* 屠宰(动物)；强烈谴责

E. g. Hundreds of innocent civilians were cruelly slaughtered.

That wasn't war, it was simply slaughter.

31. jews-harp *n.* 破口琴

32. spool cannon *n.* 线轴大炮

33. decanter *n.* 玻璃水瓶

34. tadpole *n.* 蝌蚪

35. dilapidated *adj.* 残破的，失修的；荒废的

E. g. The house is very dilapidated but it has possibilities

The walls of the dilapidated shed lean outward.

36. sash *n.* 腰带，肩带

37. covet *vt. & vi.* 贪求，觊觎

E. g. I do not covet goods not mine.

What are people who covet these things saying about themselves?

38. muse *vi.* 沉思；冥想

E. g. Many of the papers muse on the fate of the President

He once mused that he would have voted Labour in 1964 had he been old enough.

39. wend *v.* 行；走

E. g He wended his way to the riverside.

The trail wends its way through leafy woodland and sunny meadows.

Questions：

1. What kind of strategy did Tom employ to get other kids to do his work？

2. What's the relationship between Tom and his friends？

3. According to MT, what is the difference between work and play?

4. Name three things that Tom got the kids to give him.

5. Analyze the character of Aunt Polly and her relationship to Tom.

Analysis of Chapter Two

In this chapter, Tom reveals his basic knowledge of human psychology; that is, that a person most desires what cannot be easily attained. Tom is also a fine actor, and he cleverly uses this ability in handling his friends. Thus, Tom is able to use this basic understanding of human nature to get others to do his work for him and to pay for the privilege of doing it. Instead of being able to join the others at the town center, he brings the center of the town to him, has others do his work for him, and he ends up with all sorts of treasures. In this way, Twain reveals Tom as a natural leader. Throughout the novel, we will see that Tom is the leader; it will always be "Tom Sawyer's gang"; it is always Tom's ideas of what game to play; and Tom is always the winner in games as well as in fights with his peers. He is also usually the winner in his conflicts with the adult world.

The reader is constantly reminded that this is a child's world. Tom tries to make a game out of everything; Aunt Polly's slave, Jim, is fascinated with Tom's sore toe; and Ben Rogers arrives pretending that he is a steamboat on the Missouri River. The wealth or loot the boys offer to Tom is ludicrous and silly and of no worth except to boys of their age.

Note that the occasional and brief appearances of Jim—and other slaves throughout the work—serve to remind the reader that this is slave territory. Slavery never becomes a significant theme in this work—Twain, of course, saved that for Adventures of Huckleberry Finn—however the awareness of the slave environment is important.

中文译文:

星期六的早晨到了。夏天的世界，阳光明媚，空气新鲜，充满了生机。每个人的心中都荡漾着一首歌，有些年轻人情不自禁地唱出了这首歌。每个人脸上都洋溢着欢乐，每个人的脚步都是那么轻盈。洋槐树正开着花，空气里弥漫着芬芳的花香。村庄外面高高的卡第夫山上覆盖着绿色的植被，这山离村子不远不近，就像一块"乐土"，宁静安详，充满梦幻，令人向往。

　　汤姆出现在人行道上，一只手拎着一桶灰浆，另一只手拿着一把长柄刷子。他环顾栅栏，所有的快乐烟消云散，心中充满了惆怅。栅栏可是三十码长，九英尺高啊。生活对他来说太乏味空洞了，活着仅是一种负担。他叹了一口气，用刷子蘸上灰浆，沿着最顶上一层木板刷起来。接着又刷了一下，二下。看看刚刷过的不起眼的那块，再和那远不着边际的栅栏相比，汤姆灰心丧气地在一块木箱子上坐下来。这时，吉姆手里提着一个锡皮桶，嘴中唱着"布法罗的女娃们"蹦蹦跳跳地从大门口跑出来。在汤姆眼中，到镇上从抽水机里拎水，一向是件令人厌烦的差事，现在他可不这样看了。他记得在那里有很多伴儿。有白人孩子、黑人孩子，还有混血孩子，男男女女都在那排队等着提水。大家在那儿休息，交换各自玩的东西，吵吵闹闹，争斗嬉戏。而且他还记得尽管他们家离拎水处只有一百五十码左右，可是吉姆从没有在一个小时里拎回一桶水来——有时甚至还得别人去催才行。汤姆说：

　　"喂，吉姆，如果你来刷点墙，我就去提水。"

　　吉姆摇摇头，说：

　　"不行，汤姆少爷。老太太，她叫我去提水，不准在路上停下来和人家玩。她说她猜到汤姆少爷你会让我刷墙，所以她吩咐我只管干自己的活，莫管他人闲事——她说她要亲自来看看你刷墙。"

　　"咳，吉姆，你别管她对你说的那一套。她总是这样说的。把水桶给我——我很快就回来。她不会知道的。"

　　"哦，不，我可不敢，汤姆少爷。老太太会把我的头给拧下来的，她真的会的！"

　　"她吗？她从来没搡过任何人——她不过是用顶针在头上敲敲罢了——谁还在乎这个，我倒是想问问你。她不过是嘴上说得凶，可是说说又伤害不了你——只要她不大叫大嚷就没事。吉姆，我给你一个好玩意儿，给你一个白石头子儿！"

　　吉姆开始动摇了。

　　"白石头子，吉姆！这可是真正好玩的石头子啊。"

　　"嘿，老实说，那是个挺不错的好玩意。可是汤姆少爷，我害怕老太太……"

　　"还有，吉姆，只要你答应了的话，我还给你看我那只脚趾头，那只肿痛的脚趾头。"

　　吉姆到底是个凡人，不是神仙——这诱惑对他太大了。他放下水桶，接过白石头子儿，还饶有兴趣地弯着腰看汤姆解开缠在脚上的布带子，看那只肿痛的脚趾。可是，一会儿之后，吉姆的屁股直痛，拎着水桶飞快地沿着街道跑掉了；汤姆继续用劲地刷墙，因为波莉姨妈此时从田地干活回来了。她手里提着一只拖鞋，眼里流露出满意的神色。

　　不过，汤姆这股劲没持续多久。他开始想起原先为这个休息日所作的一些玩耍的安排，心里越想越不是滋味。再过一会儿，那些自由自在的孩子们就会蹦跳着跑过来，做各种各样开心好玩的游戏，他们看到他不得不刷墙干活，会大肆嘲笑挖苦他的——一想到这，汤姆心里就像火烧似的难受。他拿出他全部的家当宝贝，仔细地看了一阵——有残缺不全的玩具、一些石头子、还有一些没有什么用处的东西。这些玩意足够用来换取别的孩子为自己干活，不过，要想换来半个小时的绝对自由，也许还差得远呢。于是他又把这几件可怜的宝贝玩意装进口袋，打消了用这些来收买那些男孩子的念头。正在这灰心绝望的时刻，他忽然灵机一动，计上心来。这主意实在是聪明绝伦，妙不可言。

　　他拿起刷子，一声不响地干了起来。不一会儿，本·罗杰斯出现了——在所有的孩子们当中，正是这个男孩叫汤姆最害怕。汤姆最怕他的讥讽。本走路好像是做三级跳——这证明他此时的心情轻松愉快，而且还打算干点痛快高兴的事。他正在吃苹果，不时地发出长长的、好听的"呜——"的叫声，隔会儿还"叮当当、叮当当"地学铃声响，他这是在扮演一只蒸汽轮船。他越来越近，于是他减慢速度，走到街中心，身体倾向右舷，吃力、做作地转了船头使船逆风停下——他在扮演"大密苏里号"，好像已吃水九英尺深。他既当船，又当船长还要当轮机铃。因此他就想象着自己站在轮船的顶层甲板上发着命令，同时还执行着这些命令。

"停船，伙计！叮——啊铃！"船几乎停稳了，然后他又慢慢地向人行道靠过来。

"调转船头！叮——啊铃——铃！"他两臂伸直，用力往两边垂着。

"右舷后退，叮——啊铃——铃！嚓呜——嚓——嚓呜！嚓呜！"

他一边喊着，一边用右手比画着画个大圈——这代表着一个四十英尺大转轮。

"左舷后退！叮——啊铃——铃！嚓呜——嚓——嚓呜——嚓呜！"左手开始画圈。

"右舷停！叮——啊铃——铃！左舷停！右舷前进！停！外面慢慢转过来！叮——啊铃——铃！嚓——呜——呜！把船头的绳索拿过来！快点！喂——再把船边的绳索递过来——你在发什么呆！把绳头靠船桩绕住好，就这么拉紧——放手吧！发动机停住，伙计！叮——啊铃——铃！希特——希特——希特！"（模仿着汽门排气的声音。）

汤姆继续刷栅栏，——不去理睬那只蒸汽轮船，本瞪着眼睛看了一会儿，说：

"哎呀，你日子好过了，是不是？"

汤姆没有回答。只是用艺术家的眼光审视他最后刷的那一块，接着轻轻地刷了一下。又像刚才那样打量着栅栏。本走过来站在他身旁。看见那苹果，汤姆馋得直流口水，可是他还是继续刷他的墙。本说：

"嘿，老伙计，你还得干活呀，咦？"

汤姆猛然地转过身来说道："咳！是你呀，本。我还没注意到你呢。"

"哈，告诉你吧，我可是要去游泳了。难道你不想去吗？当然啦，你宁愿在这干活，对不对？当然你情愿！"

汤姆打量了一下那男孩，说：

"你说什么？这叫干活？"

"这还不叫干活，叫干什么？"

汤姆重新又开始刷墙，漫不经心地说："这也许是干活，也许不是。我只知道这对汤姆·索亚来说倒是很得劲。"

"哦，得了吧！难道你的意思是说你喜欢干这事?"刷子还在不停地刷着。

"喜欢干? 哎，我真搞不懂为什么我要不喜欢干，哪个男孩子能天天有机会刷墙?"

这倒是件新鲜事。于是，本停止了啃苹果。汤姆灵巧地用刷子来回刷着——不时地停下来退后几步看看效果——在这儿补一刷，在那儿补一刷——然后再打量一下效果——本仔细地观看着汤姆的一举一动，越看越有兴趣，越看越被吸引住了。后来他说：

"喂，汤姆，让我来刷点儿看看。"

汤姆想了一下，正打算答应他;可是他立刻又改变了主意：

"不——不行，本——我想这恐怕不行。要知道，波莉姨妈对这面墙是很讲究的——这可是当街的一面呀——不过要是后面的，你刷刷倒也无妨，姨妈也不会在乎的。是呀，她对这道墙是非常讲究的。刷这墙一定得非常精心。我想在一千，也许在两千个孩子里，也找不出一个能按波莉姨妈的要求刷好这道墙的。""哦，是吗? 哎，就让我试一试吧。我只刷一点儿——汤姆，如果我是你的话，我会让你试试的。"

"本，我倒是愿意，说真的。可是，波莉姨妈——唉，吉姆想刷，可她不叫他刷，希德也想干，她也不让希德干。现在，你知道我该有多么为难? 要是你来摆弄这墙，万一出了什么毛病……"

"啊，没事，我会小心仔细的。还是让我来试试吧。嘿——我把苹果核给你。"

"唉，那就……不行，本，算了吧。我就怕……"

"我把这苹果全给你!"

汤姆把刷子让给本，脸上显示出不情愿，可心里却美滋滋的。

当刚才那只"大密苏里号"在阳光下干活，累得大汗淋漓的时候，这位离了职的艺术家却在附近的阴凉下，坐在一只木桶上，跷着二郎腿，一边大口大口地吃着苹果，一边暗暗盘算如何再宰更多的傻瓜。这样的小傻瓜会有许多。每过一会儿，就有些男孩子从这经过;起先他们都想来开开玩笑，可是结果都被留下来刷墙。在本累得筋疲力尽时，汤姆早已经和比利·费施做好了交易。比利用一个修得很好的风筝换来接替本的机会。等到比利也玩得差不多的时候，詹尼·米勒用一只死老鼠和拴着它的小绳子购买了这个特权——一个又一个的傻小子受骗上了当，接连几个钟头都没有间断。下午快过了一半的时候，汤姆早上还是个贫困潦倒的穷小子，现在一下子就变成了腰包鼓鼓的阔佬了。除了以上提到的那些玩意以外，还有十二颗石头子；一只破口琴；一块可以透视的蓝玻璃片；一门线轴做的大炮；一把什么锁也不开的钥匙；一截粉笔；一个大酒瓶塞子；一个锡皮做的小兵；一对蝌蚪；六个鞭炮；一只独眼小猫；一个门上的铜把手；一根拴狗的颈圈——却没有狗——一个刀把；四片橘子皮；还有一个破旧的窗框。

他一直过得舒舒服服，悠闲自在——同伴很多——而且墙整整被刷了三遍。要不是他的灰浆用光了的话，他会让村里的每个孩子都掏空腰包破产的。

汤姆自言自语道，这世界原来并不是那么空洞乏味啊。他已经不知不觉地发现了人类行为的一大法则——那就是为了让一个大人或一个小孩渴望干什么事，只需设法将这事变得难以到手就行了。如果他是位伟大而明智的哲学家，就像这本书的作者，他就会懂得所谓"工作就是一个人被迫要干的事情"，至于"玩"就是一个人没有义务要干的事。这个道理使他明白了为什么做假花和蹬车轮就算是工作，而玩十柱戏和爬勃朗峰就算是娱乐。英国有钱的绅士在夏季每天驾着四轮马拉客车沿着同样的路线走上二三十里，他们为这种特权竟花了很多钱。可是如果因此付钱给他们的话，那就把这桩事情变成了工作，他们就会撒手不干了。汤姆思考了一会那天发生在他身边的实质性变化，然后就到司令部报告去了。

❧ Answers for questions

1. Tom understands the basic knowledge of psychology; that is, that a person most desires what cannot be easily attained. Tom is a fine actor, and he cleverly uses this ability in handling his friends. Thus, Tom is able to use this basic understanding of human nature to get others to do his work for him and to pay for the privilege of doing it.

2. Tom seems to be a natural leader. It will always be "Tom

Sawyer's gang"; it is always Tom's ideas of what game to play; and Tom is always the winner in games as well as in fights with his peers. He is also usually the winner in his conflicts with the adult world.

3. Work consists of whatever a body is obliged to do, and that play consists of whatever a body is not obliged to do.

4. Sucker, kite, sandwich.

5. Though Tom and Aunt Polly position themselves as foes within the family, they are actually similar in many ways. Aunt Polly has a humorous appreciation for Tom's cleverness and his antics that often prevents her from disciplining him as severely as she should. But, despite their superficially adversarial relationship, there is a real bond of loyalty and love between Tom and Aunt Polly. Aunt Polly embodies a more positive kind of authority than the rest of adult society because her strictness is balanced with real love and concern. Like Tom, she exhibits the truly positive elements of social relations, without all the hypocrisy and insincerity.

References

［1］ http://en. wikipedia. org/wiki/Mark_Twain（图片来源）

［2］ http://en. wikipedia. org/wiki/The_Adventures_of_Tom_Sawyer（图片来源）

［3］ http://www. sparknotes. com/lit/tomsawyer/characters. html

［4］ http://www. sparknotes. com/lit/tomsawyer/study. html

［5］ http://www. literaturepage. com/read/tomsawyer – 11. html

［6］ http://www. ncut. edu. cn/yyzx/novel/tom/ctom02. htm

Unit 9
Henry James (1843 – 1916)

🎋 Bibliography

Henry James, OM (15 April 1843— 28, February 1916) was an American-English writer who
spent most of his writing career in Britain. He is regarded as one of the key figures of 19th-century literary realism. He was the son of Henry James, Sr.
and the brother of philosopher and psychologist William James and diarist Alice James.

James alternated between America and Europe for the first 20 years
of his life, eventually he settled in England, becoming a British subject
in 1915, one year before his death. He is best known for a number of
novels showing Americans encountering Europe and Europeans. His
method of writing from the point of view of a character within a tale allows him to explore issues related to consciousness and perception, and
his style in later works has been compared to impressionist painting.

James contributed significantly to literary criticism, particularly in
his insistence that writers be allowed the greatest possible freedom in
presenting their view of the world. James claimed that a text must first
and foremost be realistic and contain a representation of life that is re-
cognizable to its readers. Good novels, to James, show life in action and
are, most importantly, interesting. His imaginative use of point of view,
interior monologue and unreliable narrators in his own novels and tales
brought a new depth and interest to narrative fiction. An extraordinarily

productive writer, in addition to his voluminous works of fiction he published articles and books of travel, biography, autobiography, and criticism, and wrote plays, some of which were performed during his lifetime, though with limited success when compared to the success of his
novels. James was nominated for the Nobel Prize in Literature in 1911,
1912 and 1916.

🌸 *Daisy Miller*

Exploring the conflict between concepts at the
heart of the American dream—personal freedom
and the social limitation others want to place on
that freedom—*Daisy Miller* was a smashing success
when originally published in 1878. It remains one
of the most popular books written by author Henry
James. The short novel established James's reputation as an author on both sides of the Atlantic.

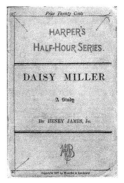

James had two significant inspirations for the tale he told in *Daisy
Miller*. In the fall of 1877, he heard a story in Rome about a somewhat
ignorant, unknowing American mother new to the ways of Europe. The
mother allowed her daughter to befriend a Roman man, whom she introduced to new friends they met in the city. Because of their poor social
choice, the mother and daughter suffered social outfall and were ostracized by other Americans living in the city. James also had a free-spiri-
ted cousin, Minny Temple, who, though dead for several years, was an
inspiration for Daisy and many of his early female heroines.

Characters in the *Daisy Miller*
1. Daisy Miller—A rich, pretty, American girl traveling through Europe
   with her mother and younger brother. Daisy wants to be exposed to
   European high society but refuses to conform to old-world notions of
   propriety laid down by the expatriate community there. In Rome, she
   becomes involved with an Italian man named Giovanelli, and she e-

ventually dies from malaria as a result of being outside with him at night. Along with Winterbourne, Daisy is the novel's other possible protagonist.

2. Winterbourne—A young American who has lived most of his life in Geneva. Winterbourne is the novel's central narrative consciousness and possibly the protagonist. He is initially intrigued by Daisy because of her frivolity and independence, but he eventually loses respect for her. After she dies, however, he regrets his harsh judgment and wonders if he made a mistake in dismissing her so quickly.

3. Randolph Miller—Daisy's younger brother. Randolph is a loud, ill-mannered, ungovernable little boy of about nine or ten.

4. Mrs. Miller—Daisy and Randolph's vague, weak, ineffectual mother. Mrs. Miller seems obsessed with her health and is utterly incapable of governing the behavior of her children. She is silly and clueless, but when Daisy falls ill, she proves "a most judicious and efficient nurse".

5. Mrs. Costello—Winterbourne's aunt, a shallow, self-important woman who seems genuinely fond of Winterbourne. Mrs. Costello is the voice of snobbish high society. She also fulfills the role of "confidante", a frequent figure in Henry James's novels.

6. Eugenio—The Millers' supercilious interpreter/guide, often referred to as "the courier". Eugenio has better judgment and a greater sense of propriety than either Daisy or Mrs. Miller and often treats them with thinly veiled contempt.

7. Mrs. Walker—A wealthy, well-connected American widow who lives in Rome, knows Winterbourne from Geneva, and has befriended Daisy. Mrs. Walker shares the values of the rest of the American expatriate community, but she genuinely seems to care what happens to Daisy and tries to save her.

8. Mr. Giovanelli—An Italian of unknown background and origins. Mr. Giovanelli's indiscreet friendship with Daisy is misinterpreted by the American expatriate community and leads, directly or indirectly, to Daisy's ostracism and death.

Summary

At a hotel in the resort town of Vevey, Switzerland, a young American named Winterbourne meets a rich, pretty American girl named Daisy Miller, who is traveling around Europe with her mother and her younger brother, Randolph. Winterbourne, who has lived in Geneva most of his life, is both charmed and mystified by Daisy, who is less proper than the European girls he has encountered. She seems wonderfully spontaneous, if a little crass and "uncultivated". Despite the fact that Mrs. Costello, his aunt, strongly disapproves of the Millers and flatly refuses to be introduced to Daisy, Winterbourne spends time with Daisy at Vevey and even accompanies her, unchaperoned, to Chillon Castle, a famous local tourist attraction.

The following winter, Winterbourne goes to Rome, knowing Daisy will be there, and is distressed to learn from his aunt that she has taken up with a number of well-known fortune hunters and become the talk of the town. She has one suitor in particular; a handsome Italian named Mr. Giovanelli, of uncertain background, whose conduct with Daisy mystifies Winterbourne and scandalizes the American community in Rome. Among those scandalized is Mrs. Walker, who is at the center of Rome's fashionable society.

Both Mrs. Walker and Winterbourne attempt to warn Daisy about the effect her behavior is having on her reputation, but she refuses to listen. As Daisy spends increasingly more time with Mr. Giovanelli, Winterbourne begins to have doubts about her character and how to interpret her behavior. He also becomes uncertain about the nature of Daisy's relationship with Mr. Giovanelli. Sometimes Daisy tells him they are engaged, and other times she tells him they are not.

One night, on his way home from a dinner party, Winterbourne passes the Coliseum and decides to look at it by moonlight, braving the bad night air that is known to cause "Roman fever", which is malaria. He finds Daisy and Mr. Giovanelli there and immediately comes to the conclusion that she is too lacking in self-respect to bother about. Winterbourne is still concerned for Daisy's health, however, and he reproaches Giovanelli and urges him to get her safely home.

A few days later, Daisy becomes gravely ill, and she dies soon after. Before dying, she gives her mother a message to pass on to Winterbourne that indicates that she cared what he thought about her after all. At the time, he does not understand it, but a year later, still thinking about Daisy, he tells his aunt that he made a great mistake and has lived in Europe too long. Nevertheless, he returns to Geneva and his former life.

Comments on *Daisy Miller*

Daisy Miller serves as both a psychological description of the mind of a young woman, and an analysis of the traditional views of a society where she is a clear outsider. Henry James uses Daisy's story to discuss what he thinks Europeans and Americans believe about each other, and more generally the prejudices common in any culture. In a letter James said that Daisy is the victim of a " social rumpus " that goes on either over her head or beneath her notice.

Daisy Miller was an immediate and widespread popular success for James, despite some criticism that the story was " an outrage on American girlhood ". The story continues to be one of James' most popular works, along with *The Turn of the Screw* and *The Portrait of a Lady*. Critics have generally praised the freshness and vigor of the storytelling.

In 1909 James revised *Daisy Miller* extensively for the New York Edition. He altered the tone of the story but some feel he robbed the original version of its color and immediacy.

Introduction to Part 1

Exploring the conflict between concepts at the heart of the American dream—personal freedom and the social limitation others want to place on that freedom—*Daisy Miller* was a smashing success when originally published in 1878. It remains one of the most popular books writ-

ten by author Henry James. The short novel established James's reputation as an author on both sides of the Atlantic.

James had two significant inspirations for the tale he told in *Daisy
Miller*. In the fall of 1877, he heard a story in Rome about a somewhat
ignorant, unknowing American mother new to the ways of Europe. The
mother allowed her daughter to befriend a Roman man, whom she introduced to new friends they met in the city. Because of their poor social
choice, the mother and daughter suffered social outfall and were ostracized by other Americans living in the city. James also had a free-spiri
ted cousin, Minny Temple, who, though dead for several years, was an
inspiration for Daisy and many of his early female heroines.

From   *Daisy Miller*
Part 1

At the little town of Vevey, in Switzerland, there is a particularly
comfortable hotel. There are, indeed, many hotels, for the entertainment of tourists is the business of the place, which, as many travelers
will remember, is seated upon the edge of a remarkably blue lake—a
lake that it behooves[1] every tourist to visit. The shore of the lake presents an unbroken array of establishments of this order, of every catego-
ry, from the "grand hotel" of the newest fashion, with a chalk-white
front, a hundred balconies, and a dozen flags flying from its roof, to the
little Swiss pension[2] of an elder day, with its name inscribed in German-
looking lettering upon a pink or yellow wall and an awkward summer-
house in the angle of the garden. One of the hotels at Vevey, however,
is famous, even classical, being distinguished from many of its upstart[3]
neighbors by an air both of luxury and of maturity. In this region, in the
month of June, American travelers are extremely numerous, it may be
said, indeed, that Vevey assumes at this period some of the characteristics of an American watering place. There are sights and sounds which
evoke a vision, an echo, of Newport and Saratoga. There is a flitting[4]
hither and thither of "stylish" young girls, a rustling[5] of muslin

flounces[6], a rattle of dance music in the morning hours, a sound of high-pitched voices at all times. You receive an impression of these things at the excellent inn of the "Trois Couronnes" and are transported in fancy to the Ocean House or to Congress Hall. But at the "Trois Couronnes", it must be added, there are other features that are much at variance with these suggestions: neat German waiters, who look like secretaries of legation; Russian princesses sitting in the garden; little Polish boys walking about held by the hand, with their governors; a view of the sunny crest[7] of the Dent du Midi and the picturesque towers of the Castle of Chillon. I hardly know whether it was the analogies[8] or the differences that were uppermost in the mind of a young American, who, two or three years ago, sat in the garden of the "Trois Couronnes", looking about him, rather idly, at some of the graceful objects I have mentioned. It was a beautiful summer morning, and in whatever fashion the young American looked at things, they must have seemed to him charming. He had come from Geneva the day before by the little steamer[9], to see his aunt, who was staying at the hotel—Geneva having been for a long time his place of residence. But his aunt had a headache— his aunt had almost always a headache—and now she was shut up in her room, smelling camphor[10], so that he was at liberty to wander about. He was some seven-and-twenty years of age; when his friends spoke of him, they usually said that he was at Geneva "studying". When his enemies spoke of him, they said—but, after all, he had no enemies; he was an extremely amiable[11] fellow, and universally liked. What I should say is, simply, that when certain persons spoke of him they affirmed that the reason of his spending so much time at Geneva was that he was extremely devoted to a lady who lived there—a foreign lady—a person older than himself. Very few Americans—indeed, I think none—had ever seen this lady, about whom there were some singular stories. But Winterbourne had an old attachment for the little metropolis[12] of Calvinism; he had been put to school there as a boy, and he had afterward gone to college there—circumstances which had led to his forming a great many youthful friendships. Many of these he had kept, and they were a source of great satisfaction to him.

After knocking at his aunt's door and learning that she was indisposed[13], he had taken a walk about the town, and then he had come in to his breakfast. He had now finished his breakfast, but he was drinking a small cup of coffee, which had been served to him on a little table in the garden by one of the waiters who looked like an attache[14]. At last he finished his coffee and lit a cigarette. Presently a small boy came walking along the path—an urchin[15] of nine or ten. The child, who was diminutive[16] for his years, had an aged expression of countenance[17], a pale complexion, and sharp little features. He was dressed in knickerbockers[18], with red stockings, which displayed his poor little spindleshanks[19], he also wore a brilliant red cravat[20]. He carried in his hand a long alpenstock[21], the sharp point of which he thrust into everything that he approached—the flowerbeds, the garden benches, the trains of the ladies' dresses. In front of Winterbourne he paused, looking at him with a pair of bright, penetrating little eyes.

"Will you give me a lump[22] of sugar?" he asked in a sharp, hard little voice— a voice immature and yet, somehow, not young.

Winterbourne glanced at the small table near him, on which his coffee service rested, and saw that several morsels[23] of sugar remained. "Yes, you may take one," he answered, "but I don't think sugar is good for little boys. "

This little boy stepped forward and carefully selected three of the coveted[24] fragments, two of which he buried in the pocket of his knickerbockers, depositing the other as promptly in another place. He poked his alpenstock, lance[25]-fashion, into Winterbourne's bench and tried to crack the lump of sugar with his teeth.

"Oh, blazes; it's har-r-d!" he exclaimed, pronouncing the adjective in a peculiar manner.

Winterbourne had immediately perceived that he might have the honor of claiming him as a fellow countryman. "Take care you don't hurt your teeth," he said, paternally.

"I haven't got any teeth to hurt. They have all come out. I have only got seven teeth. My mother counted them last night, and one came out right afterward. She said she'd slap me if any more came out. I can't help it. It's this old Europe. It's the climate that makes them come out. In America they didn't come out. It's these hotels. "

Winterbourne was much amused. "If you eat three lumps of sugar, your mother will certainly slap you," he said.

"She's got to give me some candy, then," rejoined his young interlocutor. "I can't get any candy here—any American candy. American candy's the best candy. "

"And are American little boys the best little boys?" asked Winterbourne.

"I don't know. I'm an American boy," said the child.

"I see you are one of the best!" laughed Winterbourne.

"Are you an American man?" pursued this vivacious[26] infant. And then, on Winterbourne's affirmative reply—"American men are the best. " he declared.

His companion thanked him for the compliment, and the child, who had now got astride of his alpenstock, stood looking about him, while he attacked a second lump of sugar. Winterbourne wondered if he himself had been like this in his infancy, for he had been brought to Europe at about this age.

"Here comes my sister!" cried the child in a moment. "She's an American girl. "

Winterbourne looked along the path and saw a beautiful young lady advancing. "American girls are the best girls," he said cheerfully to his young companion.

"My sister ain't the best!" the child declared. "She's always blowing at me. "

"I imagine that is your fault, not hers," said Winterbourne. The young lady meanwhile had drawn near. She was dressed in white muslin, with a hundred frills[27] and flounces, and knots of pale-colored ribbon. She was bareheaded, but she balanced in her hand a large parasol[28], with a deep border of embroidery; and she was strikingly, admirably pretty. "How pretty they are!" thought Winterbourne, straightening himself in his seat, as if he were prepared to rise.

The young lady paused in front of his bench, near the parapet[29] of the garden, which overlooked the lake. The little boy had now converted his alpenstock into a vaulting pole, by the aid of which he was springing about in the gravel[30] and kicking it up not a little.

"Randolph," said the young lady, "what ARE you doing?"

"I'm going up the Alps," replied Randolph. "This is the way!" And he gave another little jump, scattering the pebbles about Winterbourne's ears.

"That's the way they come down," said Winterbourne.

"He's an American man!" cried Randolph, in his little hard voice.

The young lady gave no heed[31] to this announcement, but looked straight at her brother. "Well, I guess you had better be quiet," she simply observed. It seemed to Winterbourne that he had been in a manner presented. He got up and stepped slowly toward the young girl, throwing away his cigarette. "This little boy and I have made acquaintance," he said, with great civility. In Geneva, as he had been perfectly aware, a young man was not at liberty to speak to a young unmarried lady except under certain rarely occurring conditions; but here at Vevey, what conditions could be better than these? — a pretty American girl coming and standing in front of you in a garden. This pretty American girl, however, on hearing Winterbourne's observation, simply glanced at him, she then turned her head and looked over the parapet[32], at the lake and the opposite mountains. He wondered whether he had gone too far, but he decided that he must advance farther, rather than retreat. While he was thinking of something else to say, the young lady turned to the little boy again.

"I should like to know where you got that pole," she said.

"I bought it," responded Randolph.

"You don't mean to say you're going to take it to Italy?"

"Yes, I am going to take it to Italy," the child declared.

The young girl glanced over the front of her dress and smoothed out a knot or two of ribbon. Then she rested her eyes upon the prospect again. "Well, I guess you had better leave it somewhere," she said after a moment.

"Are you going to Italy?" Winterbourne inquired in a tone of great respect.

The young lady glanced at him again. "Yes, sir," she replied. And she said nothing more.

"Are you—a— going over the Simplon?" Winterbourne pursued, a little embarrassed.

"I don't know," she said. "I suppose it's some mountain. Randolph, what mountain are we going over?"

"Going where?" the child demanded.

"To Italy," Winterbourne explained.

"I don't know," said Randolph. "I don't want to go to Italy. I want to go to America."

"Oh, Italy is a beautiful place!" rejoined the young man.

"Can you get candy there?" Randolph loudly inquired.

"I hope not," said his sister. "I guess you have had enough candy, and mother thinks so too."

"I haven't had any for ever so long—for a hundred weeks!" cried the boy, still jumping about.

The young lady inspected her flounces and smoothed her ribbons again, and Winterbourne presently risked an observation upon the beauty of the view. He was ceasing to be embarrassed, for he had begun to perceive that she was not in the least embarrassed herself. There had not been the slightest alteration in her charming complexion; she was evidently neither offended nor flattered. If she looked another way when he spoke to her, and seemed not particularly to hear him, this was simply her habit, her manner. Yet, as he talked a little more and pointed out some of the objects of interest in the view, with which she appeared quite unacquainted, she gradually gave him more of the benefit of her glance, and then he saw that this glance was perfectly direct and un-shrinking. It was not, however, what would have been called an immo-dest glance, for the young girl's eyes were singularly honest and fresh. They were wonderfully pretty eyes, and, indeed, Winterbourne had not seen for a long time anything prettier than his fair countrywoman's vari-ous features—her complexion, her nose, her ears, her teeth. He had a great relish for feminine beauty; he was addicted to observing and analy-zing it; and as regards this young lady's face he made several observa-tions. It was not at all insipid[33], but it was not exactly expressive; and though it was eminently delicate, Winterbourne mentally accused it—very forgivingly—of a want of finish. He thought it very possible that Master Randolph's sister was a coquette[34]; he was sure she had a spirit of her own; but in her bright, sweet, superficial little visage there was no mockery, no irony. Before long it became obvious that she was much disposed toward conversation. She told him that they were going to Rome for the winter—she and her mother and Randolph. She asked him if he was a " real American "; she shouldn't have taken him for one; he seemed more like a German—this was said after a little hesitation— es-pecially when he spoke. Winterbourne, laughing, answered that he had met Germans who spoke like Americans, but that he had not, so far as he remembered, met an American who spoke like a German. Then he asked her if she should not be more comfortable in sitting upon the bench which he had just quitted. She answered that she liked standing up and walking about; but she presently sat down. She told him she was from New York State—" if you know where that is. " Winterbourne learned more about her by catching hold of her small, slippery brother and making him stand a few minutes by his side.

"Tell me your name, my boy," he said.

"Randolph C. Miller," said the boy sharply. "And I'll tell you her name", and he leveled[35] his alpenstock at his sister.

"You had better wait till you are asked!" said this young lady calmly.

"I should like very much to know your name," said Winterbourne.

"Her name is Daisy Miller!" cried the child. "But that isn't her real name; that isn't her name on her cards."

"It's a pity you haven't got one of my cards!" said Miss Miller.

"Her real name is Annie P. Miller," the boy went on.

"Ask him HIS name," said his sister, indicating Winterbourne.

But on this point Randolph seemed perfectly indifferent; he continued to supply information with regard to his own family. "My father's name is Ezra B. Miller," he announced. "My father ain't in Europe; my father's in a better place than Europe."

Winterbourne imagined for a moment that this was the manner in which the child had been taught to intimate that Mr. Miller had been removed to the sphere of celestial[36] reward. But Randolph immediately added, "My father's in Schenectady. He's got a big business. My father's rich, you bet!"

"Well!" ejaculated[37] Miss Miller, lowering her parasol[38] and looking at the embroidered[39] border. Winterbourne presently released the child, who departed, dragging his alpenstock[a]long the path. "He doesn't like Europe," said the young girl. "He wants to go back."

"To Schenectady, you mean?"

"Yes; he wants to go right home. He hasn't got any boys here. There is one boy here, but he always goes round with a teacher, they won't let him play."

"And your brother hasn't any teacher?" Winterbourne inquired.

"Mother thought of getting him one, to travel round with us. There was a lady told her of a very good teacher; an American lady—perhaps you know her—Mrs. Sanders. I think she came from Boston. She told her of this teacher, and we thought of getting him to travel round with us. But Randolph said he didn't want a teacher traveling round with us. He said he wouldn't have lessons when he was in the cars. And we ARE in the cars about half the time. There was an English lady we met in the cars—I think her name was Miss Featherstone; perhaps you know her. She wanted to know why I didn't give Randolph lessons—give him 'instruction', she called it. I guess he could give me more instruction than I could give him. He's very smart.

"Yes," said Winterbourne; "he seems very smart."

Notes：

1. behoove *vt.* 理应；对……有此必要

    E. g. New account book and old debt behoove are apart.

    It would behoove you to consider this among the most important management laws.

2. pension *n.* 退休金, 抚恤金

    E. g. The firm granted him a pension.

    Since then he has been drawing a pension.

3. upstart *adj.* 暴富的；自命不凡的

    E. g. He tried to pass for a gentleman; but everyone knew he was upstart.

    Advertisers have been waiting for years for the upstart to settle on a formula for ads.

4. flitting *v.* 翩翩飞起；高速移动

    E. g. His name flitted through my mind, only to be forgotten again.

    A humming-bird flitted by.

5. rustling *adj.* 沙沙作响的

    E. g. I heard someone rustling the papers in my office.

    As he was walking along the river, he heard a rustling in the bushes behind him.

6. flounce *n.* 衣裙上的荷边装饰

7. crest *n.* 冠；顶饰

8. analogy *n.* 类比；类推

 E. g. The analogy is rather farfetched.

9. steamer *n.* 轮船；蒸汽机

10. camphor *n.* 莰酮，樟脑

11. amiable *adj.* 和蔼可亲的，亲切的

 E. g. The leader did the amiable.

 In the flesh, however, he's more like an amiable professor.

12. metropolis *n.* 大都市；首府

 E. g. But the desert is encroaching on this metropolis.

 He was dazzled by the gaiety and splendour of the metropolis.

13. indisposed *adj.* 不舒服的；不合适的

 E. g. When a woman was heavily pregnant or otherwise indisposed, she and her children were dependent on other women in the group.

 The report stated that the firm has identified three outstanding internal candidates who could replace Mr Buffett as CEO if he becomes permanently indisposed.

14. attache *n.* 专员，公使

15. urchin *n.* 顽童，淘气鬼

16. diminutive *adj.* 小的，小型的

 E. g. All fifteen boys pick up their textbooks and thump their diminutive desks.

 The lapels link them together, the tight boots call to order, the diminutive clutch is a symbol of power.

17. countenance *n.* 面容，表情

 E. g. He possesses a mild and benevolent countenance.

 Catherine heard all this, and quite out of countenance, could listen no longer.

18. knickerbockers *n.* 灯笼裤

19. spindle-shank *n.* 细长腿；细长腿的人

20. cravat *n.* 领带；领巾

21. alpenstock *n.* 铁头登山杖

22. lump *n.* 块，肿块

    E. g. You are the one with a lump.

    One day, I noticed a lump in her skin.

23. morsel *n.* 一口；(食物)少量

    E. g. As part of his life extension program, he monitors every morsel of food that passes through his system.

    Rather than writing down every morsel, take a picture of it, and file the photos on your phone or computer by date.

24. coveted *adj.* 垂涎的；梦寐以求的

    E. g. He won the prize they all coveted.

    Coveted her and me.

25. lance *n.* 长矛；柳叶刀

26. vivacious *adj.* 活泼的；快活的

    E. g. Ms. Prose's vivacious prose initially made the road there fairly scenic.

    You're an extroverted, vivacious type who loves to be the center of the social scene.

27. frill *n.* 装饰；褶边

28. parasol *n.* 阳伞

29. parapet *n.* 栏杆；扶手；矮护墙

30. gravel *n.* 碎石；沙砾

    E. g. His old car bumped down the gravel road.

    The truck dumped two loads of gravel on the driveway.

31. heed *n.* 注意到；留心到

    E. g. You should heed this lesson well.

    He didn't heed my advice.

32. parapet *n.* 栏杆；扶手；矮护墙

33. insipid *adj.* 清淡的；无趣的

E. g. Ornament is not in itself bad, only when it's camouflage on insipid form.

Sadly Knightley ends up in one of the more insipid segments.

34. coquette *n.* 卖弄风情的女人

E. g. Of course she had a perfect right to suit herself about the kind of a man she took for a husband, but he certainly had not thought she was such an utter coquette.

The moment she met a man she would play the coquette.

35. level *vt.* 使同等; 对准

E. g. The economic slide has now leveled off, although a swift return to growth looks less likely than a month ago.

The giant earthquake in Chile that struck Friday—one of the most powerful ever recorded—killed more than 700 people and leveled cities.

36. celestial *adj.* 天上的, 天空的

E. g. He would hear and sing those songs to others inapprehensible, the celestial music.

The souls of gods reach the summit, go outside and stand upon the surface of heaven, and enjoy celestial bliss.

37. ejaculate *vt.* 突然说出; 射出

E. g. You need to remember that semen can pass to your partner even before you fully ejaculate.

The difficulty with pulling out is that, to do it perfectly, the guy must be really in tune with when he is going to ejaculate.

38. embroidered *adj.* 绣花的; 刺绣的

E. g. She embroidered silver stars on her blue dress.

He embroidered on the story to hold his listener's interest.

Questions:

1. Why do you think James chose to call his heroine "Daisy Miller"?

2. Why do people say Daisy represents America?

3. What does Daisy's brother Randolph symbolize?

4. What kind of character is Winterbourne?

5. Why did James choose the setting in Rome and Geneva?

Analysis of Part 1

The narrator of Daisy Miller presents the events as "true"—that is, the narrator tells us the events took place "three or four years ago" to a young man, named Winterbourne, with whom the narrator does not claim to be intimately associated but about whom there are many stories. The device of the distant, first-person narrator who knows but is not knowledgeable, who is interested but not involved, has the effect of setting the whole story up within the framework of a piece of gossip. This strategy is iro-nic, since the story itself is about gossip: the things one hears about people, the assumptions one makes about them based on the things one hears, and the difficulty of judging character based on the stories one hears.

As often happens in the work of Henry James, a number of the novel's primary themes are established in the opening paragraph, which offers contrasts between old and young, history and novelty, movement and stillness, and American vibrancy and European dignity. The narrator tells us that the selection of hotels that line the lakefront include many different kinds of establishments, from the "grand" hotels "of the newest fashion" to the older boardinghouse-style pensions. The narrator tells us that the Trois Couronnes, the particular hotel in whose garden Winterbourne is sitting, is one of the "classical" variety, distinguished from its "upstart neighbors" by an air of "maturity". Vevey is filled with American tourists, "stylish young girls" who flit to and fro bringing with them "a rustle of muslin flounces, a rattle of dance music" in the stillness of morning. Set against these vivid images are the European elements, the quiet German waiters who have the bearing and gravity of state officials; the sedate Russian princesses; and the well-behaved little Polish boys whose "governors", nannies and tutors, accompany them wherever they go. These observations set the stage for the conflicts Daisy and Winterbourne will encounter between American and European values and social expectations.

中文译文：

在瑞士小镇韦维，有个特别舒适的旅馆。其实那里有很多旅馆，因为这个地方的主要业务就是招待旅游者。就像许多旅客记得的那样，它们坐落在一个非常蓝的湖边——一个每一个旅游者理应一观风景的湖。一连串各式各样的旅馆呈现在湖岸边，从最新式的"大饭店"——前面用白粉刷的，有许多阳台和屋顶上飘着的旗子，到旧式一点的小小的瑞士式膳宿公寓——它粉红色或黄色的墙上有看起来像是德国字母写着的公寓名称，以及在花园的一隅占地的不美观的凉亭。然而，在沃韦的一家著名甚至可以说是古典式的旅馆，以其奢华和成熟的气氛将其与许多自命不凡的邻居区别开。这个地区到了六月，美国旅客特别多简直可以说这一段时间的韦维有着某些美国滨水地区的特色。有些景色和声音令人想到纽波特和萨拉托加。这里那里时常有"时髦"的少女轻盈地走过，滚着细薄荷叶边的长裙发出呗呗的声音：在上午的那几个小时里嗒嗒响着舞蹈音乐随时都听得到尖声尖气说话的声音。在"三顶皇冠"这个十分出色的旅馆里你就可以得到这种印象，你会感到你已移居到了大洋旅馆或国会厅。但是必须附带一句：在"三顶皇冠"那里还有些和上述印象不尽相同的特征——使馆秘书式的衣冠楚楚的德籍侍者；花园里坐着的俄罗斯公主男教师用于挽着走来走去的波兰小男孩阳光笼罩着的米迫峰景色，和美丽如画的锡庸城堡的塔状建筑。

我不大清楚一个年轻的美国人，他首先想到的是那些共同点还是不同点。这个人两三年前正坐在"三顶皇冠"的花园里，没有目的地东看看西看看，望着那些我已经提到过的柔美多姿的人物。这是一个美丽的夏天早晨，不管这个年轻的美国人观点如何，他一定觉得当前的一切相当可喜。他前一天才乘小火轮从日内瓦来，看望住在这里旅馆里的姑母——他在日内瓦已住了很长时间但是他姑母在犯头痛病——他姑母几乎老是头痛——现在她正将自己关在屋子里闻樟脑油，所以他可以自由随意走动。他大约二十七岁。他的朋友在谈到他时总是说他在日内瓦"学习"；他的敌人谈到他时——可是，他毕竟并无敌人；他为人非常和蔼可亲，大家都喜欢他。我应该指出的只是：某些人在说到他时，都肯定他是因为十分倾倒于一位住在那里的小姐，所以才在自内瓦消磨了如许光阴。这是一个外国小姐，一个比他年纪稍大的人。没有多少美国人——其实我认为并无其人——见过这位小姐，关于她还传闻着一些奇特的故事。但是温特伯恩对这个小小的加尔文主义都市怀着深厚感情，他幼年时曾在那里上过学，又在那里上大学，后来又在那里交上了许多青年时代的朋友。其中他一直保持着与许多人的友谊。他们给予了他极大的满足。

他敲了敲姑母的房门。知道她不舒服时，就到镇里转一圈，然后回来吃早饭。此时他已吃罢早饭；正在喝一小杯咖啡，是一个像使馆专员一样的侍者给他放在花园里的一张小桌上的。他终于喝完了咖啡，点上了一支烟。不多时一个小男孩沿着小径走过来——一个十岁左右的孩童。这孩子长得个子小，脸上的表情颇老气：苍白的肤色，尖小的五官。他穿着灯笼裤、红袜子，露出他那瘦得可怜的长腿，还打着一条鲜红的大领带。他手里拿着一根长长的铁头登山杖，一路走，一路遇到什么就用杖尖捅一捅——像花圃、园里的长凳、太太小姐们的长裙等。他在温特伯恩面前站住了脚，用一对亮晶晶、逼人的小眼睛望着他。

"给我一块白糖，好吗？"他要求，声音尖细而又绷硬——是一种尚未成熟，但不知怎么又并非年轻的声音。

温特伯恩望一望身边的小桌子，上面的咖啡用具还在那里，还有几块剩下来的白糖。"好，你拿一块吧"，他回答说，"可是白糖对小男孩可没有什么好处。"

这个小男孩走上前仔细挑了三块他心怡的白糖，把其中两块藏在一边的裤兜里，又马上把剩下的一块放进另一边口袋。他像使长矛那样用他那登山杖戳了戳温特伯恩的长凳，又试着用牙齿咬碎那块白糖。

"啊哟，该死的；真——硬！他叫道，用古怪的声音用力说着那个形容词。

温特伯恩立刻意识到他很可能应该把他认作同胞。"小心别伤了牙，"他慈祥地说道。

"我没有可伤的牙。已经出齐了。我只有七颗牙。昨晚我母亲还数了数，后来还掉了一颗。她说再掉的话就打我耳光。没办法。怪只怪这个古老的欧洲。是受这里气候的影响才掉的。在美国就不掉。是这儿的旅馆缘故。"

温特伯恩觉得可笑。"如果你吃三块白糖的话，你母亲一定会掴你"，他说。

"那她就该给我点糖果吃"，他那年轻的对话者回答说。

"我在这里吃不到糖果——什么美国糖果都吃不到。美国糖果是最好吃的糖果。"

"美国小男孩是最好的小男孩吗？"温特伯恩问道。

"我不知道。我是个美国男孩，"孩子说。

"我看你是好样的！"温特伯恩笑道。

"你是个美国男人吗？"这个活泼的娃娃紧跟着说。在听了温特伯恩肯定的答复后——"美国男人是最好的"他断言。

他的同伴谢了谢他的称赞：这个孩子现在已骑在他的登山杖上，站在那里东张西望，一边开始吃第二块白糖。温特伯恩思忖他自己还是娃娃的时候是否也这个样子，因为像这样年纪的时候他也已经到了欧洲。

"我姐姐来了！"孩子过不久叫道。"她是个美国女孩。"

温特伯恩沿着小径望去，看见一个年轻美丽的姑娘在朝前走来。"美国女孩是最好的女孩！"他乐呵呵地对他的小伴说。

"我姐姐不是最好的！"孩子宣告。"她总是跟我发脾气。"

"准是你不对，不是她，"温特伯恩说。这时那位年轻小姐已经走近。她穿的是白色细纱衣服，足有百十来个皱褶和荷叶边，还有浅色的缎带结。她没有戴帽子；但手里摆弄着一把大阳伞，镶着很宽的一道绣花边；她的美貌引人注目。"这些女孩子真漂亮！"温特伯恩一边想，一边坐直了身躯，好像准备站起来的样子。

年轻小姐在他的长凳面前站住了脚，那地方靠近花园的护墙，下面就是湖。小男孩这时候正把他的登山杖转变为撑竿跳的竿子，正在借助于它在石子路上跳来蹦去，把石子也踢了些起来。

"冉道尔夫，"年轻小姐说，"你在干什么？"

"我在登阿尔卑斯山，"冉道尔夫回答说。"就这样往上登！"他又轻轻跳了一下，把石子溅到温特伯恩的耳朵边。

"下山就是这么下的"，温特伯恩说。

"他是个美国男人！"冉道尔夫叫道，嗓音小而坚挺。

年轻小组没理会他的宣告，只是直望着她的弟弟。"我看你最好安静点，"她说了这样一句。

据特伯恩认为他已经算是被介绍过了。他站了起来，丢掉香烟，朝着年轻姑娘缓缓走去。"我和这个小男孩已经认识了"，他非常有礼貌地说道。他完全意识到，在日内瓦，除了在某些罕凡的场合下，一个青年男子是不能随便和一个还没有结婚的年轻小姐说话的，可是在韦维这个地方，还有什么比目前条件更好的呢？——花园里一个漂亮的美国姑娘走来站在你面前。但是这个漂亮的美国姑娘听了温特伯恩的话后，只是对他看了一看，然后回过头去向护墙那边望着，望望湖和对面的峰恋。他不知道他是否越了轨；但是他决心必须更进一步而不是后退。他正想再说点什么时，年轻小姐又回过头来对着小男孩。

"我想知道你这根棍子是哪里来的"她说。

"我买的"，冉道尔夫回答。

"你不会想把它带到意大利去吧？"

"要的，我要把它带到意大利去"，孩子宣告。

年轻姑娘看了看她衣服的前襟，理了理一两个缎带结。然后眼睛又望着眼前的景物。"我看你最好把它留在这里"，过了一会儿她说。"你是打算去意大利吗？"温特伯恩问道，声音非常恭敬。

年轻小姐又瞧了瞧他。"是的，先生"，她回答。然后也就没有再说什么。

"你们——呃——会经过辛普龙吗？"温特伯恩又问，略有点窘。

"我不知道，"她说。"是座山吧。冉道尔夫，我们会经过哪座山?"

　　"上哪儿去?"孩子想要知道。

　　"去意大利",温特伯恩解释道。

　　"我不知道",冉道尔夫说,"我不想去意大利。我要去美国。"

　　"噢,意大利是个美丽的地方",年轻人回答说。

　　"那儿买得到糖果吗?"冉道尔夫大声问道。

　　"我希望买不到",他姐姐说,"我看你糖果已经吃得够了,母亲也这么说。"

　　"我已经好久没有吃了——有一百个星期了!"男孩叫道,依然跳来蹦去。

　　年轻小姐又检查了她的荷叶边,理了理缎带;温特伯恩又斗胆说了说当前景色如何如何美好。他已经不感到窘了,因为他意识到她本人丝毫都不感到窘。她那可爱的肤色分毫未变;她显然既未恼怒也未觉得不安。假如说在他和她说话时她眼望着别处,似乎没有怎么听见他说的话,那也只是她的风度与习惯如此。不过他又稍讲了几句,指出某些景色特别引人入胜的地方;这些她似乎并不熟悉,于是她逐渐对他多看了几眼。他也看到这种目光是非常直率、毫不畏缩的,绝谈不上任何轻佻之处,因为年轻姑娘的眼睛非常诚实,非常明亮。这是一双非常漂亮的眼睛;说实在的,温特伯恩已经很久没有见过比这位美丽的女同胞更漂亮的相貌特征了——她的肤色、她的鼻子、她的耳朵、她的牙齿。他非常赏识女性美;他素喜观察它、分析它。至于这位年轻小姐的脸,他已观察良久。它绝非毫无生气,但也说不上表情丰富,虽然它十分姣好,温特伯恩心目中却感到它是有所不足的——但也是可谅解的——认为它绝非十分完美。他认为冉道尔夫少爷的姐姐很可能有些轻浮;他肯定她有她自己的主见;可是在她那明亮、甜蜜、浮浅的小脸上并无嗤笑或嘲弄的神态。过不久,事情就清楚了,她很喜欢和人交谈。她告诉他要到罗马去过冬——她、她母亲和冉道尔夫。她问他是不是一个"真正的美国人";她认为他不大像;他比较像个德国人——这话是经过犹疑才说的——特别在他说话的时候。温特伯恩笑着回答说,他遇见过说话像美国人的德国人;可是就他记忆所及,还没有遇见过一个说话像德国人的美国人。接着他又问她:坐在他刚让出的那个长凳上是否舒适一些。她回答说她喜欢站着，喜欢走动；但是不久她还是坐了下来。她告诉他，她是纽约州来的——"不知你是否知道这地方。"温特伯恩抓住了她抓不大住的小弟，让他在自己身旁站几分钟，并且从他那里多知道了一些她的情况。

"告诉我，你叫什么名字，孩子，"他说。

"冉道尔夫·C 密勒"，孩子尖声尖气地说。"我来告诉你她叫什么。"他把登山杖对准了姐姐。

"等人家问了你再说不迟！"这位年轻小姐安详地说。

"我很想知道你的名字"，温特伯恩说。

"她的名字是黛西·密勒"，孩子叫道，"可这不是她的真名字；不是她名片上的名字。"

"可惜你没有我的名片"密勒小姐说。

"她真正的名字是安妮·P 密勒"，男孩接下去说。

"问问他叫什么名字"，他的姐姐说，指指温特伯恩。

可是冉道尔夫对此似毫无兴趣；他继续提供他自己家里的情况。"我父亲名叫埃士勒·B·密勒"，他宣布。"我父亲不在欧洲；我父亲在一个比欧洲更好的地方。"

温特伯恩以为这是教给孩子说话的一种方法，暗示密勒先生已经移居到一个上天赐福的地方去了。可是冉道尔夫立刻加上一句，"我父亲在斯克内克塔迪。他做的是大买卖，我父亲很有钱，没错儿！"

"可了不得！"密勒小姐叫了一声，放下阳伞，看着那道绣花的边。温特伯恩不久放开了孩子，孩子走了，沿路拖着他那根登山杖。"他不喜欢欧洲"，年轻姑娘说道，"他要回去。"

"是回斯克内克塔迪吗？"

"是的，他想马上就回家。这里没有别的小男孩。有是有一个，可是总有个教师跟着他；他们不让他玩。"

"你弟弟没有教师吗？"植特伯恩问道。

"母亲想给他找一个，陪着我们旅行。有位太太告诉她有个很好的教师；一位美国太太——你也许认识——杉德士太太。我想她是波士顿人。她介绍了这个教师，我们想请他和我们一块儿旅行。可是冉道尔夫说他不想找个教师和我们一块儿旅行。他说他不愿意在车厢里上课。而我们一半时间确实是在车厢里。我们在车上遇到一位英国小姐——她的名字好像是费瑟斯东小姐；也许你认识。她问我为什么不给冉道尔夫上课——给他以'指导'。我看与其说我指导他不如说他更能指导我。他很聪明。"

"是的"，温特伯恩说，"他看来很聪明。"

❧ Answers for questions

1. Daisy is a flower in full bloom, without inhibitions and in the springtime of her life. Daisy contrasts sharply with Winterbourne. Flowers die in winter and this is precisely what happens to Daisy after catching the Roman Fever.

2. Because Daisy is young, fresh, ingenuous, clueless, naive, innocent, well meaning, self-centered, untaught, scornful of convention, unaware of social distinctions, utterly lacking in any sense of propriety, and unwilling to adapt to the mores and standards of others. These traits have no fixed moral content, and nearly all of them can be regarded as either virtues or faults. Her ambiguity correlates with that of the future of a young America, still carving out its own values and traditions.

3. Randolph symbolizes the type of the "ugly American" tourist: boorish, boastful and stridently nationalistic.

4. At first glance, Winterbourne seems the ideal type of romantic hero, but the more we get to know him, the more shallow and unimpressive he seems. This change is largely a function of the way in which he responds to his aunt's views about Daisy. He defends Daisy feebly and takes his aunt's opinion very much to heart. Winterbourne accepts his aunt's judgment as fact. Winterbourne is a rather shabby protagonist, a young man who is completely a product of his environment and of the values of the society that has produced him.

5. Daisy Miller's setting in the capitals of Italy and Switzerland is significant on a number of levels. These two countries represent oppo-

sing values embodied by their capital cities, Rome and Geneva. Geneva was the birthplace of Calvinism, the fanatical protestant sect that influenced so much of American culture, New England in particular. Geneva is referred to as "the dark old city at the other end of the lake. " It is also Winterbourne's chosen place of residence. Rome had many associations for cultivated people like Winterbourne and Mrs. Costello. It was a city of contrasts. As a cradle of ancient civilization and the birthplace of the Renaissance, it represented both glory and corruption, a society whose greatness had brought about its own destruction. Rome is a city of ruins, which suggest death and decay. Rome is also a city of sophistication, the Machiavellian mind-set. In a sense, Rome represents the antithesis of everything Daisy stands for—freshness, youth, ingenuousness, candor, innocence, and naive.

References

[1] http://en. wikipedia. org/wiki/Henry_James (图片来源)

[2] http://en. wikipedia. org/wiki/Daisy_Miller(图片来源)

[3] http://www. pagebypagebooks. com/Henry_James/Daisy_Miller/

[4] http://www. sparknotes. com/lit/daisy/

[5] http://www. cliffsnotes. com/literature/d/daisy − miller/character − list

[6] http://www. 123helpme. com/a − character − analysis − of − daisy − miller − view. asp? id = 195686

[7] 亨利·詹姆斯. 外国文艺丛书黛西·密勒[M]. 赵萝蕤,巫宁坤,译. 上海: 上海译文出版社, 1985.

Unit 10
Jack London (1876 – 1916)

✴ Bibliography

John Griffith "Jack" London (born John Griffith Chaney) was an American author, journalist,
and social activist. He was a pioneer in the then-
burgeoning world of commercial magazine fiction
and was one of the first fiction writers to obtain
worldwide celebrity and a large fortune from his
fiction alone. Some of his most famous works in-

clude *The Call of the Wild* and *White Fang*, both set in the Klondike
Gold Rush, as well as the short stories "To Build a Fire" "An Odyssey
of the North", and "Love of Life". He also wrote of the South Pacific in
such stories as *The Pearls of Parlay* and *The Heathen*, and of the San
Francisco Bay area in *The Sea Wolf.*

London was a passionate advocate of unionization, socialism, and
the rights of workers. He wrote several powerful works dealing with these
topics, such as his dystopian novel *The Iron Heel*, his non-fiction expose
The People of the Abyss, and *The War of the Classes.*

✴ The Call of the Wild

The Call of the Wild is a novel by Jack London published in 1903.
The story is set in the Yukon during the 1890s Klondike Gold Rush—a
period in which strong sled dogs were in high demand. The novel's cen-

tral character is a dog named Buck, a domesticated
dog living at a ranch in the Santa Clara Valley of
California as the story opens. Stolen from his home
and sold into service as sled dog in Alaska, he re-
verts to a wild state. Buck is forced to fight in order to dominate other dogs in a harsh climate.
Eventually he sheds the veneer of civilization, re-
lying on primordial instincts and learned experience to emerge as a leader in the wild.

London lived for most of a year in the Yukon collecting material for
the book. The story was serialized in the *Saturday Evening Post* in the
summer of 1903, a month later it was released in book form. The novel's
great popularity and success made a reputation for London. Much of its
appeal derives from the simplicity of this tale of survival.

Characters in *The Call of the Wild*

1. Buck—A powerful dog, half St. Bernard and half sheepdog, who is
   stolen from a California estate and sold as a sled dog in the Arctic.
   Buck gradually evolves from a pampered pet into a fierce, masterful
   animal, able to hold his own in the cruel, kill-or-be-killed world of
   the North. Though he loves his final master, John Thornton, he feels
   the wild calling him away from civilization and longs to reconnect
   with the primitive roots of his species.

2. John Thornton—Buck's final master, a gold hunter experienced in
   the ways of the Klondike. Thornton saves Buck from death at the
   hands of Hal, and Buck rewards Thornton with fierce loyalty.
   Thornton's relationship to Buck is the ideal man-dog relationship:
   each guards the other's back and is completely devoted to the other.
   The strength of their bond is enough to keep Buck from acting on the
   forces he feels are calling him into the wild.

3. Spitz—Buck's archival and the original leader of Francois' dog team.
   Spitz is a fierce animal who is used to fighting with other dogs and

winning. He meets his match in Buck, however, who is as strong as Spitz and possesses more cunning. Spitz is an amoral being who fights for survival with all of his might, disregarding what is right and wrong.

4. Francois—A French Canadian mail driver who buys Buck and adds him to his team. Francois is an experienced man, accustomed to life in the North, and he impresses Buck with his fairness and good sense.

5. Perrault—A French Canadian who, together with Francois, turns Buck into a sled dog for the Canadian government. Both Perrault and Francois speak in heavily accented English, which London distinguishes from the rest of the novel's dialogue.

6. Hal—Mercedes's brother; he carries a whip, a gun, and a knife, and he is cruel to Buck.

7. Mercedes—Charles's wife; she attempts to live in the North as if she were on an "extended social camping trip".

Summary

The Call of the Wild is one of Jack London's most popular novels. The story follows a dog named Buck, a Saint Bernard and Scotch Shepard mix. Buck is abducted from a comfortable life as a pet and tossed into the chaos of the Klondike Gold Rush and the brutal realities of frontier life. Buck changes hands a number of times before landing in the kindly hands of John Thornton.

Thornton takes ownership of Buck from a trio of ignorant stampeders, intent upon making a dangerous river crossing. Buck refuses to cross, despite a vicious beating. Thornton recognizes the dog's intelligence and strength. He steps in to claim the dog and nurses Buck back to health. But Buck is forever changed by the treatment he has received at the hands of other men.

Jack London spent a year living in the Yukon and drew heavily upon his experiences there while writing the book. He later said, "It was in the Klondike that I found myself."

Comments on *The Call of the Wild*

The Call of the Wild was enormously popular from the moment it was published. H. L. Menken wrote of London's story: "No other popular writer of his time did any better writing than you will find in *Call of the Wild.* " A reviewer for *The New York Times* wrote of it in 1903: "If nothing else makes Mr. London's book popular, it ought to be rendered so by the complete way in which it will satisfy the love of dog fights apparently inherent in every man. " The reviewer for *The Atlantic Monthly* wrote that it was a book: "untouched by bookishness... making and the achievement of such a hero constitute, not a pretty story at all, but a very powerful one. "

The book secured London a place in the canon of American literature. The first printing of 10,000 copies sold out immediately, it is still one of the best known stories written by an American author, and continues to be read and taught in schools. It has been published in 47 languages. London's first success, the book secured his prospects as a writer and gained him a readership that stayed with him throughout his career.

After the success of *The Call of the Wild*, London wrote to Macmillan in 1904 proposing a second book (*White Fang*) in which he wanted to describe the opposite of Buck: a dog that transforms from wild to tame: "I'm going to reverse the process... Instead of devolution of decivilization ... I'm going to give the evolution, the civilization of a dog. "

Introduction to Chapter 1

By 1897, California native Jack London had traveled around the United States as a hobo, returned to California to finish high school, and spent a year in college at Berkeley. He then traveled to the Klondike by way of Alaska during the height of the Klondike Gold Rush, later saying of the experience: "It was in the Klondike I found myself. " London stayed in the Klondike for almost a year.

In the spring of 1898, as the annual gold stampedes began to stream into the area, London left. He had contracted scurvy, common in the Arctic winters, where fresh produce was unavailable. When London's gums began to swell he decided to return to California. With his compa nions, he rafted 2,000 miles down the Yukon River, through portions of the wildest territory in the region, until they reached St. Michael, where he hired himself out on a boat and returned to San Francisco.

In Alaska, London found material that inspired him to write the no- vella *The Call of the Wild*. Dyea Beach was the primary point of arrival for miners at the time London visited, but without a harbor access was treacherous, so Skagway became the new arrival point. From there, to reach the Klondike prospectors had to navigate the White Pass, which be- came known as "Dead Horse Pass", with horse carcasses littering the route, it was too steep and harsh for them to survive the ascent. Dogs be- gan to replace horses to transport material over the pass, and at this time strong dogs with thick fur were "much desired, scarce and high in price".

London would have seen many dogs, especially prized Husky sled dogs, in Dawson City and in winter camps close to the main sled route. He became friends with Marshall Latham Bond and his brother Louis Whitford Bond, who owned a mixed St. Bernard-Scotch Collie dog; in a letter to his friend London later wrote: "Yes, Buck is based on your dog at Dawson." Beinecke Library at Yale University holds a photograph of Bond's dog, taken during London's stay in the Klondike in 1897. The depiction of the California ranch in the beginning of the story was based on the Bond family ranch.

From   *The Call of the Wild*

Chapter 1 Into The Primitive

Old longings nomadic leap,
Chafing at custom's chain;
Again from its brumal sleep

Wakens the ferine[1] strain.

Buck did not read the newspapers, or he would have known that trouble was brewing[2], not alone for himself, but for every tidewater dog, strong of muscle and with warm, long hair, from Puget Sound to San Diego. Because men, groping in the Arctic darkness, had found a yellow metal, and because steamship and transportation companies were booming the find, thousands of men were rushing into the Northland. These men wanted dogs, and the dogs they wanted were heavy dogs, with strong muscles by which to toil, and furry coats to protect them from the frost.

Buck lived at a big house in the sun-kissed Santa Clara Valley. Judge Miller's place, it was called. It stood back from the road, half-hidden among the trees, through which glimpses could be caught of the wide cool veranda that ran around its four sides. The house was approached by graveled driveways which wound about through wide-spreading lawns and under the interlacing boughs of tall poplars. At the rear things were on even a more spacious scale than at the front. There were great stables, where a dozen grooms and boys held forth, rows of vine-clad servants' cottages, an endless and orderly array of outhouses, long grape arbors, green pastures, orchards, and berry patches. Then there was the pumping plant for the artesian well, and the big cement tank where Judge Miler's boys took their morning plunge and kept cool in the hot afternoon.

And over this great demesne Buck ruled. Here he was born, and here he had lived the four years of his life. It was true, there were other dogs. There could not but be other dogs on so vast a place, but they did not count. They came and went, resided in the populous[3] kennels[4], or lived obscurely in the recesses of the house after the fashion of Toots, the Japanese pug, or Ysabel, the Mexican hairless, strange creatures that rarely put nose out of doors or set foot to ground. On the other hand, there were the fox terriers, a score of them at least, who yelped fearful promises at Toots and Ysabel looking out of the windows at them and protected by a legion of housemaids armed with brooms and mops.

But Buck was neither house dog nor kennel dog. The whole realm was his. He plunged into the swimming tank or went hunting with the Judge's sons; he escorted Mollie and Alice, the Judge's daughters, on long twilight or early morning rambles; on wintry nights he lay at the Judge's feet before the roaring library fire; he carried the Judge's grandsons on his back, or rolled them in the grass, and guarded their footsteps through wild adventures down to the fountain in the stable yard, and even beyond, where the paddocks were, and the berry patches. Among the terriers he stalked imperiously[5], and Toots and Ysabel he utterly ignored, for he was king—king over all creeping, crawling, flying things of Judge Miller's place, humans included.

His father, Elmo, a huge St. Bernard, had been the Judge's inseparable companion, and Buck bid fair to follow in the way of his father. He was not so large—he weighed only one hundred and forty pounds—for his mother, She, had been a Scotch shepherd dog. Nevertheless, one hundred and forty pounds, to which was added the dignity that comes of good living and universal respect, enabled him to carry himself in right royal fashion. During the four years since his puppyhood he had lived the life of a sated aristocrat; he had a fine pride in himself, was even a trifle egotistical, as country gentlemen sometimes become because of their insular[6] situation. But he had saved himself by not becoming a mere pampered house dog. Hunting and kindred outdoor delights had kept down the fat and hardened his muscles; and to him, as to the cold-tubbing races, the love of water had been a tonic and a health preserver.

And this was the manner of dog Buck was in the fall of 1897, when the Klondike strike dragged men from all the world into the frozen North. But Buck did not read the newspapers, and he did not know that Manuel, one of the gardener's helpers, was an undesirable acquaintance. Manuel had one besetting sin. He loved to play Chinese lottery. Also, in his gambling, he had one besetting weakness—faith in a system; and this made his damnation certain. For to play a system requires money, while the wages of a gardener's helper do not lap over the needs of a wife and numerous progeny[7].

The Judge was at a meeting of the Raisin Growers' Association, and the boys were busy organizing an athletic club, on the memorable night of Manuel's treachery[8]. No one saw him and Buck go off through the orchard on what Buck imagined was merely a stroll. And with the exception of a solitary man, no one saw them arrive at the little flag station known as College Park. This man talked with Manuel, and money chinked between them.

"You might wrap up the goods before you deliver them," the stranger said gruffly[9], and Manuel doubled a piece of stout rope around Buck's neck under the collar.

"Twist it, and you'll choke him plenty," said Manuel, and the stranger grunted a ready affirmative[10].

Buck had accepted the rope with quiet dignity. To be sure, it was an unwonted performance but he had learned to trust in men he knew, and to give them credit for a wisdom that outreached his own. But when the ends of the rope were placed in the stranger's hands, he growled menacingly[11]. He had merely intimated his displeasure, in his pride believing that to intimate was to command. But to his surprise the rope tightened around his neck, shutting off his breath. In a quick rage he sprang at the man, who met him halfway, grappled[12] him close by the throat, and with a deft twist threw him over on his back. Then the rope tightened mercilessly, while Buck struggled in a fury, his tongue lolling out of his mouth and his great chest panting futilely. Never in all his life had he been so vilely treated, and never in all his life had he been so angry. But his strength ebbed, his eyes glazed, and he knew nothing when the train was flagged and the two men threw him into the baggage car.

The next he knew, he was dimly aware that his tongue was hurting and that he was being jolted along in some kind of a conveyance. The hoarse shriek of a locomotive whistling a crossing told him where he was. He had traveled too often with the Judge not to know the sensation of riding in a baggage car. He opened his eyes, and into them came the unbridled anger of a kidnapped king. The man sprang for his throat, but Buck was too quick for him. His jaws closed on the hand, nor did they relax till his senses were choked out of him once more.

"Yep, has fits," the man said, hiding his mangled hand from the baggage man, who had been attracted by the sounds of struggle. "I'm taking him up for the boss to 'Frisco. A crack dog doctor there thinks that he can cure him."

Concerning that night's ride, the man spoke most eloquently[13] for himself, in a little shed back of a saloon on the San Francisco water front.

"All I get is fifty for it," he grumbled[14], "and I wouldn't do it over for a thousand, cold cash."

His hand was wrapped in a bloody handkerchief, and the right trouser leg was ripped from knee to ankle.

"How much did the other mug get?" the saloon-keeper demanded.

"A hundred," was the reply. "Wouldn't take a sou less, so help me."

"That makes a hundred and fifty," the saloon-keeper calculated, "and he's worth it, or I'm a squarehead."

The kidnaper undid the bloody wrappings and looked at his lacerated hand. "If I don't get hydrophobia—"

"It'll be because you was born to hang," laughed the saloon-keeper. "Here, lend me a hand before you pull your freight," he added.

Dazed, suffering intolerable pain from throat and tongue, with the life half throttled[15] out of him, Buck attempted to face his tormentors[16]. But he was thrown down and choked repeatedly, till they succeeded in filing the heavy brass collar from off his neck. Then the rope was removed, and he was flung into a cage-like crate.

There he lay for the remainder of the weary night, nursing his wrath and wounded pride. He could not understand what it all meant. What did they want with him, these strange men? Why were they keeping him pent up in this narrow crate? He did not know why, but he felt oppressed by the vague sense of impending[17] calamity[18]. Several times during the night he sprang to his feet when the shed door rattled open, expecting to see the Judge, or the boys at least. But each time it was the bulging face of the saloon-keeper that peered in at him by the sickly light of a tallow candle. And each time the joyful bark that trembled in Buck's throat was twisted into a savage growl.

But the saloon-keeper let him alone, and in the morning four men entered and picked up the crate. More tormentors, Buck decided, for they were evil-looking creatures, ragged[19] and unkempt[20]; and he stormed and raged at them through the bars. They only laughed and poked sticks at him, which he promptly assailed with his teeth till he realized that was what they wanted. Whereupon he lay down sullenly[21] and allowed the crate to be lifted into a wagon. Then he, and the crate in which he was imprisoned, began a passage through many hands. Clerks in the express office took charge of him; he was carted about in another wagon; a truck carried him, with an assortment of boxes and parcels, upon a ferry steamer; he was trucked off the steamer into a great railway depot, and finally he was deposited in an express car.

For two days and nights this express car was dragged along at the tail of shrieking locomotives; and for two days and nights Buck neither ate nor drank. In his anger he had met the first advances of the express messengers with growls, and they had retaliated[22] by teasing him. When he flung himself against the bars, quivering and frothing[23], they laughed at him and taunted[24] him. They growled and barked like detestable[25] dogs, mewed, and flapped their arms and crowed. It was all very silly, he knew; but therefore the more outrage to his dignity, and his anger waxed and waxed. He did not mind the hunger so much, but the lack of water caused him severe suffering and fanned his wrath to fever-pitch. For that matter, high-strung and finely sensitive, the ill treatment had flung him into a fever, which was fed by the inflammation of his parched and swollen throat and tongue.

He was glad for one thing: the rope was off his neck. That had given them an unfair advantage; but now that it was off, he would show them. They would never get another rope around his neck. Upon that he was resolved. For two days and nights he neither ate nor drank, and during those two days and nights of torment, he accumulated a fund of wrath that boded ill for whoever first fell foul of him. His eyes turned bloodshot, and he was metamorphosed[26] into a raging fiend[27]. So changed was he that the Judge himself would not have recognized him; and the express messengers breathed with relief when they bundled him off the train at Seattle.

Four men gingerly carried the crate from the wagon into a small, high-walled back yard. A stout man, with a red sweater that sagged generously at the neck, came out and signed the book for the driver. That was the man, Buck divined, the next tormentor, and he hurled himself savagely[28] against the bars. The man smiled grimly, and brought a hatchet and a club.

"You ain't going to take him out now?" the driver asked.

"Sure," the man replied, driving the hatchet into the crate for a pry.

There was an instantaneous scattering of the four men who had carried it in, and from safe perches on top the wall they prepared to watch the performance.

Buck rushed at the splintering wood, sinking his teeth into it, surging and wrestling with it. Wherever the hatchet fell on the outside, he was there on the inside, snarling and growling, as furiously anxious to get out as the man in the red sweater was calmly intent on getting him out.

"Now, you red-eyed devil," he said, when he had made an opening sufficient for the passage of Buck's body. At the same time he dropped the hatchet and shifted the club[29] to his right hand.

And Buck was truly a red-eyed devil, as he drew himself together for the spring, hair bristling, mouth foaming, a mad glitter in his blood-shot eyes. Straight at the man he launched his one hundred and forty pounds of fury, surcharged[30] with the pent passion of two days and nights. In mid-air, just as his jaws were about to close on the man, he received a shock that checked his body and brought his teeth together with an agonizing clip. He whirled over, fetching the ground on his back and side. He had never been struck by a club in his life, and did not understand. With a snarl that was part bark and more scream he was again on his feet and launched into the air. And again the shock came and he was brought crushingly to the ground. This time he was aware that it was the club, but His madness knew no caution. A dozen times he charged, and as often the club broke the charge and smashed him down.

Notes:

1. ferine *adj.* 野生的；凶猛的

2. brew *vt.* 酿造；酝酿

   E. g. The boy just wants to brew mischief.

   At home a crisis was brewing.

3. populous *adj.* 人口稠密的

   E. g. Indonesia, with 216 million people, is the fourth most populous country in the world.

   Tahiti is the most populous of the islands.

4. kennel *n.* 狗舍

5. imperiously *adv.* 专制地；妄自尊大地

   E. g. But there was also another duty which bound him and impelled him imperiously in the opposite direction.

   It is important to resolve and answer imperiously how to understand the importance of the station under the social market economy.

6. insular *adj.* 与世隔绝的；海岛的

E. g. It was very insular, a walled garden.

It is a nationalism that is cosmopolitan rather than insular and xenophobic.

7. progeny *n.* 子孙; 后裔

E. g. Anyway there is no record that he ever married or had any progeny.

From ostrich to orangutan, egg sac to live birth, infanticide to matricide, the diversity of behaviors between parent and progeny is as great as the diversity of life on our planet.

8. treachery *n.* 背叛; 背叛行为

E. g. For these views we have been labelled traitors; and if this be treachery, we wear that label proudly.

A network of hate, treachery, and fanaticism was closing around him.

9. gruffly *adv.* 粗暴地; 粗声地

E. g. "Now, don't ask me anymore," said Hagrid gruffly

"Of course," said the man gruffly, as if he'd never heard a more ridiculous question.

10. affirmative *n.* 肯定语; *adj.* 肯定的; 积极的

E. g. Her answer is in the affirmative.

But ask me if I think aliens exist, somewhere, anywhere, and I answer with a loud and affirmative yes.

11. menacingly *adv.* 胁迫地; 险恶地

E. g. "Be careful," he said menacingly, before sliding away.

Outside, by the riverbank, vultures hovered menacingly in a cobalt sky.

12. grapple *vt. & vi.* 抓住; 与格斗

E. g. The thug grappled him around the neck.

The police warned the public that it would be dangerous to grapple with the wanted man, as he was armed

13. eloquently *adv.* 善辩地; 富有表现力地

E. g. But as Hoffman details so eloquently in his book, this is how most of the world's population travels.

As Samuel Johnson so eloquently said, "The chains of habit are generally too small to be felt until they are too strong to be broken."

14. grumble *vi.* 抱怨；嘟囔

E. g. She is always grumbling!

Taxpayers are grumbling about the waste of government money.

15. throttle *vi.* 节流，减速

16. tormentor *n.* 使苦恼的东西；使苦痛的人

E. g. Realize that the tormentor has a problem.

Don't tell this to the tormentor directly.

17. impending *adj.* 即将发生的；迫切的

E. g. She decathected from him in order to cope with his impending bankruptcy.

If you find yourself in this predicament, I encourage you to take the blue pill and wake up from your impending nightmare.

18. calamity *n.* 灾难；不幸事件

E. g. Even a greater natural calamity cannot daunt us.

"If not checked, this could lead to a national calamity," he said.

19. ragged *adj.* 衣衫褴褛的；粗糙的

E. g. A ragged man emerged from behind the tree.

Do you have ragged, unkempt cuticles or nails?

20. unkempt *adj.* 蓬乱的，不整洁的

E. g. The move was based on the so-called, "broken windows theory," that disorderly, unkempt neighborhoods attract crime.

If you're constantly arguing about the unkempt lawn, or the moldering laundry, see if you can throw some money at the problem.

21. sullenly *adv.* 阴沉地，不高兴地

    E. g. "You won't give me a chance of life", she said sullenly.

    As Archer before dinner sat smoking sullenly in his study, Janey wandered in on him.

22. retaliate *vi.* 报复；回敬 *vt.* 报复

    E. g. If you are rude to me, I shall retaliate with equal rudeness.

    If we raise our import duties on their goods, they may retaliate against us.

23. froth *vi.* 吐白沫；起泡沫

    E. g. Giant waves froth the sand.

24. taunt *n.* 嘲弄；讥讽 vt. 奚落；逗弄 *adj.* 很高的

    E. g. They taunted Frank with being poor.

    He taunted me into taking the dare.

25. detestable *adj.* 可憎的，可恶的

    E. g. Keep my requirements and do not follow any of the detestable custom.

    If anyone turns a deaf ear to the law, even his prayers are detestable.

26. metamorphose *vt.* 变质；变形

    E. g. The magician metamorphosed the frog into a prince.

    The fox was perceived as a spectral animal able to metamorphose and to bewitch people.

27. fiend *n.* 魔鬼；能手

    E. g. This wretched and wronged old man is opposing it with all his might! —with all his own might, and the fiend's!

    It was a face fiend-like, full of smiling malice.

28. savagely *adv.* 野蛮地；残忍地

    E. g. "Get it ready, will you?" was the answer, uttered so savagely that I started.

    "Drag her away!" he cried savagely.

29. club *n.* 棍棒

　　E. g.　We affiliated ourselves with their club.

　　Men armed with knives and clubs attacked his home.

30. surcharge *vt.* 追加罚款；使……装载过多；使……负担过重

　　E. g.　The overdue fines shall be surcharged through separate calculation.

　　The street now is surcharged with cars.

Questions：

1. What's Buck's life like at Judge Miller's place?

2. Why does Buck think he is simply out for a stroll with Manuel?

3. What does the man in the red sweater teach Buck?

4. Why is the first chapter called "Into the Primitive"?

5. How does *The Call of the Wild*? present the human-dog relationship?

Analysis of Chapter 1

The meaning of chapter titles in *The Call of the Wild* extends beyond a simple description of the plot. The first chapter "Into the Primitive" is concerned not only with Buck's departure from civilization and his entrance into a more savage, primitive world, but also with the contrast between civilized life and primitive life. This contrast is strong throughout the novel, and the story of Buck's adventures in the Klondike is largely the story of how he gradually sheds all the customs that define his earlier life in human society to become a creature of the wild, primal world of the north. Here, in the first days after his kidnapping, he takes the first steps away from his old life and toward a new one.

中文译文：

第一章　回归原始

原古的渴望，

流动地跳越在习俗的链条上，

一阵阵地焦急躁动；

在冬天的睡梦中，

又醒来了那野性的情愫。

巴克没有读报，否则它就会知道麻烦事正在向它走来。这麻烦不单单是它自己的，而是所有从普格特桑德地区到圣迪戈地区——这些水位受潮汐影响的沿海低洼地区里的狗都会有的麻烦。这些地区里的狗肌肉强键，全身毛发又长又暖。麻烦的形成是因为这个地区里的人们在北极圈的隐秘地区一直在探寻，他们已经发现了一种黄色的金属。还因为蒸汽轮船公司和运输公司也正轰鸣着在寻找。而成千上万的人们正在冲进北极圈，这些人需要大量的狗，他们还都要大狗。这些狗要肌肉发达、能干苦役、厚厚的皮毛要能给它们自己防寒。

巴克住在太阳能亲吻到的桑塔克拉拉山谷的一所大房子里。这房子是一位磨坊主兼法官的。门前有条大道，树荫遮住了房子的一半，透过树荫往里看去，能看到围着房子有一条凉凉的走廊。房子紧靠着沙石铺就的大车道，大车道从纵横交错的白杨树下穿过宽广的草地。房后的北杨树要比房前的繁茂得多。这里有个巨大的马厩，有十几个马夫和男仆管理着。一排排爬满葡萄树的雇工住屋，无边无际有秩序地排列开来。长长的葡萄林下是绿色的牧场、果园和种干果的小块土地。还有一座自流水井的泵房，泵房前有个很大的水泥槽。磨坊主兼法官的伙计们早上将水管子插入井里，凉水就一直流到下午天热的时候。

这一大片领域都是由巴克统治的。它出生在这里，它在这里已经生活四年了。是的，这里还有别的狗，但是别的狗没有这么大的地盘，它们根本"说话"就不能算数。它们只是来来去去地行走着，成群结队地住在狗窝里：它们不是在观看了日本哈巴狗"图茨"的时兴表演后躲在屋子的阴凉处休息休息；就是如墨西哥狗"伊斯拜儿"（这是只无毛的奇怪生物）那样，罕见地将鼻子伸出屋外；再不干脆就支起前腿坐在地上。另外，还有一些像狐狸似的小型矮腿家犬，加起来至少有二十多只，"图茨"和"伊斯拜儿"只要在窗口上向它们看上一眼，它们就害怕地、许诺似地大叫起来，于是一大群拿着扫帚和拖把的女仆就过来保护它们。

但是巴克既不是家犬也不是窝里的狗，这整个领域都是它的。

它不是一头扎进游泳池去找法官的儿子们，就是保护着法官的女儿莫丽和艾丽斯在漫长的黄昏中和早早的黎明里散步。在寒冷的冬夜里，它躺在法官的脚下，在熊熊的大火前吼叫，它把法官的孙子们驮在背上在草地上打滚；它护着他们穿过荒芜的旷野走到马厩边的泉水旁，甚至越过泉水来到那一小块一小块的小牧场里，还走到种干果的小块土地里。在那些矮腿狗群中，它专横而骄傲地走着，而对"图茨"和"伊斯拜儿"，它根本就不睬不问。——因为它是王——它在磨坊主兼法官的地盘上统治着一切爬着的和飞着的东西，就连某些人也包括在内。

它的父亲"艾尔莫"是一条巨大的圣·伯纳犬，一直是老法官分不开的伙伴。巴克现在正走着它父亲的老路，只是它没有它父亲那么重——它只有 140 磅——它母亲是一条苏格兰牧羊犬。140磅的体重得益于优裕的生活和普遍受尊敬的结果，这使得它浑身上下洋溢着一种王者之气。在它幼犬期的这四年里，它一直都过着一种心满意足的生活，它自我感觉非常高傲。它曾经是一个为琐事而操心的利己主义者，有时就像那些狭隘保守的乡村绅士一样。可是它已经挽救了它自己，不至于变成一条纵容娇惯的家犬。打猎和类似户外的那些嗜好使脂肪积聚了下来，使它的肌肉变得更结实。对它来说，那些冷水浴、那种对水的热爱，一直都是一种使身心愉快的、有益健康的东西。

这就是巴克 1897 年的生活方式和精神状态。当时克朗代克人的罢工把全世界的人都吸引到了寒冷的北极。可是巴克没有读报。它不知道曼纽儿要对它做点事儿了。这个曼纽儿是个护院人的助手，一个不怎么对它心思的熟人。他有一个讨厌的毛病，爱玩中国式的赌钱游戏，但他却又太老实、太守规矩，这就使得他必然要受到各方面的责备。因为要玩赢钱的把戏，一个护院人助手的工资是远远不够的，况且他还有老婆和那么一大群孩子要养活呢。

那时法官正在葡萄协会里开会，仆人们也忙着在组织一个运动俱乐部。那个曼纽儿，他太不中厚了。就在那个难忘的晚上，没人看见他和巴克穿过了果园，而巴克自己也把这看成是一次散步。没人看见他们到了一个被称作"大学公园"的小旗站，只有一个孤独的男子例外。这个人和曼纽儿谈了几句话，金币在他们中间叮当作响。

"你可以把这些东西拿走了，在你移交前就行。"那个陌生人粗鲁地说。曼纽儿拿了条粗绳把它绕在巴克衣领下的脖子上。

"用劲拧，你要把它弄窒息才行。"曼纽儿说，于是陌生人就哼哼地准备下手。巴克十分威严地接受了绳子。确定无疑的是，这是一个不怎么习惯的动作。但它已经习惯了要信任它所认识的人，它对他们的信任超出了对它自己的信任。可是当绳子的两端捏在陌生人手里的时候，它就有点恐怖地叫了起来。它只是暗示了它的不愉快，在它骄傲的对人的信任中，这种暗示就是一种命令。可是使它奇怪的是，这条绳子紧紧地绕在它的脖子上使它的呼吸都快憋住了。在迅速的狂怒中，它扑向这个人。那人在中途迎击了它。那人紧紧地抓住了它的喉咙，灵巧地一拧，将它翻了个个儿，然后用绳子残忍地捆住了它。当巴克在凶残的狂怒中挣扎时，它的舌头懒洋洋地从嘴里伸了出来，它巨大的胸脯无用地喘着气。在它有生以来，从没有人这么卑贱地对待过它，它也从来没有如此这般地愤怒过。但是它的力气逐渐地衰弱了，它只能双目怒视着。

当火车沿着铁路开过来，两个人把它扔进行李车厢时，它知道一切都没用了。

接下来它矇矇眬眬地知道它的舌头受伤了。它被装进一节车厢里，又震、又晃、又摇。火车头沙哑的呼啸声告诉它，它已经走了很远很远。它随法官旅行得太多了，行李车上的轰动已经不怎么觉得了。它睁开双眼，扑入眼帘的是绑架它的那家伙无拘无束的愤怒。那家伙正反撬着它的喉咙，它使劲地甩起了头，爪子紧紧地抓住那个人的手，一直到它的感官又一次被窒息了才松开了它们。

"你……你有种！"那人说着把被它抓烂的手藏在身后。押运员已被这边挣扎的响声吸引了过来："我把它带上去交给费兰西克老板，那里有一流的狗大夫，能把它的舌头治好。"

由于要关注那天的行程，那人坐在行李车后小屋子里的旧金山热水器上，嘴里一直都在滔滔不绝地自言自语着。

"我这次才弄了 50 只，"他愤愤不平地："还赚不到 1000 元钱。"

他的手包着一块露血的手帕，右边的裤腿从膝盖以下全被撕破了。

"别的那些笨蛋们都弄了多少?"看大厅的人问。

"100 只。都是最低的价格。来,这么帮帮我。"

"这只能值 150"看大门的人大声地说:"它值,要不我就是个鳖。"

那人拆去了血崩带,看着划破了的手:"我不会得狂犬病吧?"

"都因为你爹是绞刑犯的刽子手!"看大门的人大笑着:"来,过来再帮我一把。"他又追加了一句。

巴克眼花缭乱,喉咙和舌头无法忍受地疼痛,生命有一半都被勒死了。它试图勇敢地反抗折磨它的人,但它又被摔倒了,又被重新勒住了,直到他们成功地将一个厚厚的黄铜领圈套在它的脖子上,然后绳索才被拿走。巴克被猛地扔进了一个像笼子的条板箱里。

它躺在剩下的货堆上,度着难熬的夜,护理着它的愤怒和自尊。它不理解,这到底是为什么? 他们要它干什么? 这些奇怪的人! 为什么他们一直把它关在这么个狭窄的条板箱里? 它不知道为什么,但它感觉得到有种灾难正在向它走来,这种感觉一直压迫着它。

那天晚上,每当那小屋的门"咔嗒咔嗒"开了的时候,它都努力地蹬着腿,期望着能看到法官,或者至少也应该能看到那些孩子们。可是每一次都是大厅把门人那张膨胀的脸在微弱的灯光下凝视着它,并且每一次巴克从颤抖的喉咙里发出的愉快的吠叫声,都是在那看门人野蛮的呻吟声中回旋缭绕。

大厅把门人一直让它独自待在一处。

早晨,来了四个人,他们抬起了条板箱。巴克认定他们都是些更多的来折磨它的人,因为他们看上去都像魔鬼似的,穿着又破又烂。它愤怒地在条板箱里向他们狂叫,咬着他们伸过来的棍子。他们只是笑笑,用棍子戳着它。它敏捷地用牙咬着戳过来的棍子,直到意识到这正是他们所需要的。因此,最后,它只好邋里邋遢地躺下来允许条板箱被抬到货车上,然后它和那个装它的条板箱就开始从人们的手上传过来传过去。快车办公室的职员们负责看管它,它被装进了另一节货车里。这是一辆卡车,箱子和包裹混装在

223

一起。这辆卡车开上了一艘小轮船，又从小轮船上开了下来，开到了一个大的铁路车站。最后，它又被装上了一辆邮政快车。

两天两夜里，这辆邮政快车迎着沿途尖声高叫的机车声向前开着。在这两天两夜里，巴克既没吃又没喝。一怒之下，它第一次遇见邮车的送信人就咆哮了一阵，而那些送信人就把逗引它作为对它的报复。它猛得冲向条板箱，哆嗦着、狂叫着。他们就嘲笑它，他们就像对待那些讨人嫌的狗一样对它大喊着、呜呜地向它叫着。他们跳着，轻轻地拍着他们的胸脯，互相挤来挤去。它知道，它太愚蠢了。他们对它的体面和威严极尽嘲弄、侮辱之能事。于是它就越来越愤怒，它一点儿都不在乎它是那么饥饿，但水的缺少却使它遭受到很大的痛苦，这就更增大了它狂暴的愤怒。因此，高度的冲动和极端的敏感，使它猛地一下子陷进了一种热病之中，而这种热病又加重了它喉咙和舌头发烧似的疼痛。

它高兴的是，它的脖子上不再有绳索了。那玩意儿曾不公平地给了那些人一个好处，但现在那玩意儿不在了。它要显示给他们看，他们将再也不能给它的脖子系什么绳索了。脖子上一有那玩意儿，它马上就被解决了。

两天两夜了，它既没吃又没喝。但在这痛苦的两天两夜里，它积累了所有的愤怒，不管是谁第一个侮辱了它，它都要狠狠地报复他。它的双眼里充满了要迸发出来的血，它愤怒得都要变态了，它要变成一个魔鬼，这样的变化将使法官本人都不一定能认出它来。

邮车的邮差们平静而又安稳地呼吸着，他们在西雅图把它绑着离开了火车。

四个人小心谨慎地把木板箱从货车上抬了下来，抬进了一所四周都是高墙的小院子的后面。一个穿着红毛衣，毛衣上有着又宽又松领子的壮汉走了出来，他给司机在本子上签了字。这个人巴克一眼就看清了他，他就是下一个要折磨它的人。就是这个人猛地把它扔到了酒店的柜台前，这人残忍地笑着，手里拿着一把斧子和一根棍子。

"你现在就要把它放出来?"司机问。

"对!"这人答道，一下把斧子劈在条板箱上，向里面张望着。

把它抬进来的那四个人一下子散开了，为了安全他们爬到了墙上,他们准备看巴克有什么表演。

巴克一下子咬住了那快裂开了的木头,和木头滚在了一起。不管斧子落在了箱子的哪里,它都在箱子的哪里咆哮着,它狂怒焦虑地想早点出来。一开始那个红毛衣还想平静地让它出来,这时也焦急地想让它早点出来。

"你这个红眼的魔鬼!"当他把木箱弄得足够巴克的身子出来的时候,他说。与此同时,他把斧子扔到了一边顺手抄起了棍子。

巴克确实是个红眼睛的魔鬼了。它浑身充满力气跳了出来,毛发竖起,嘴里吐着白沫,充血的眼睛里闪着疯狂的光。它用它140磅重的狂怒向这个红毛衣进攻,渲泄着两天两夜来被监禁起来的情欲。半空中,就在它的爪子要扑在这个人身上的时候,它受到了猛猛的一击,这一击阻止了它的身体向前。它的所有牙齿就像被一只令人苦恼的夹子夹住了似的挤在了一起。它在空中转了一圈,背落在了地上。在它的一生中,它从没遇到过棒子的攻击,它也不理解棒子。随着一声咆哮、一声尖叫,它又重新站了起来,跃起到空中。又一次,那种打击来了,它又被击溃到地上。这次它明白了,原来是那根棒子。但它的疯狂使它失去了理智,它一次又一次地进攻着,那根棒子一次又一次地粉碎了它的进攻,把它击落到地上。

🎋 **Answers for questions**

1. Buck is the king of Judge Miller's place and can roam as he pleases. He is petted, fed, groomed, and treated like the loved and cherished dog that he is. He has the life of a pampered dog who can hunt, eat, sleep, or play as he wishes. He had everything he could possibly want until he was stolen from his home and sold into captivity.

2. Buck is a kind-hearted dog. His life at the Judge's house is carefree. He wanders everywhere, unhindered and unbothered by anyone else. His time is spent playing and not having to worry about anything. He knows neither anger nor hunger nor pain nor treachery. So Buck, unaware of Manuel's plan, naively accompanies Manuel to the flag station.

3. The law of club and fang actually. The man in the red sweater teaches Buck that whoever has a weapon is to be obeyed. A weapon signifies dominance, authority and the ultimate power.

4. The first chapter is given this title because it follows Buck as he goes from civilization to a life that is much more primitive than what he is used to. At the start of the book, Buck is a beloved pet dog. He is completely pampered. But then he gets kidnapped and sent to Alaska. Along the way, he meets the man in the red sweater. Now, for the first time in his life, he's getting beaten—much more savage and primitive life. At the end of the chapter, he's in Alaska and is going to have to start adapting to primitive life.

5. London's novel is the story of Buck's transformation from a pampered pet to a fierce, masterful wild animal. Nevertheless, *The Call of the Wild* ultimately offers an ambiguous, rather than negative, portrait of Buck's relationship to humanity. It suggests that while some human-dog relationships can be disastrous to the dog's welfare, others are mutually beneficial, and a natural love can develop between dogs and their masters. It is Thornton who embodies the better way in which humans and dogs can be partners. Buck's visions of primitive man and his faithful dog suggest that this relationship is ultimately more primitive than civilized, and that there may be a natural bond between men and their dogs that predates modern society.

References

[1] http://www. lrb. co. uk/v36/n18/james – camp/in – a – boat – of – his – own – making (图片来源)

[2] http://en. wikipedia. org/wiki/The_Call_of_the_Wild (图片来源)

[3] http://en. wikipedia. org/wiki/Jack_London

[4] http://www. sparknotes. com/lit/call/study. html

[5] http://blog. sina. com. cn/s/blog_6ca315710100mcz7. html

[6] http://london. sonoma. edu/writings/CallOfTheWild/chapter1. html

Unit 11
Theodore Dreiser (1871 – 1945)

Bibliography

Theodore Dreiser(1871 – 1945), the son of a German immigrant, was the ninth of 10 children and grew up in poverty. He spent a year at Indiana University before becoming a newspaper reporter in 1892. His reading (especially of T. H. Huxley, John Tyndall, and Herbert Spencer) and personal experiences led him to a pessimistic view of human helplessness in the face of instinct and social forces.

The initial failure of his first novel, *Sister Carrie* (1900), the story of a kept woman whose behavior goes unpunished, plunged him into depression, but he recovered and achieved financial success as the editor in chief of several women's magazines until he was forced to resign in 1910 because of his involvement with an assistant's daughter.

In 1911, his second novel *Jennie Gerhardt* was published. It was followed in 1912 by *The Financier*, and in 1914 by *The Titan*, two volumes in a projected trilogy based on the life of the transportation magnate Charles T. Yerkes. *The "Genius"* (1915), a sprawling semiautobiographical chronicle of Dreiser's numerous love affairs, was censured by the New York Society for the Suppression of Vice. Its sequel *The Bulwark* appeared posthumously in 1946.

In 1925, he published his first novel in a decade, *An American Tragedy*. Based on a celebrated murder case, it brought him a degree of critical and commercial success he had never before attained. Its highly critical view of the American legal system made him the adopted champion of social reformers. Though a visit to the Soviet Union had left him skeptical about communism, *the Great Depression* caused him to reconsider his opposition. His autobiographical *Dawn* (1931) is one of the most candid self-revelations by any major writer. He completed most of *The Stoic*, the long-postponed third volume of his trilogy on Yerkes, in the weeks before his death. His other works include short stories, plays, and essays.

Sister Carrie

Sister Carrie shocked the public when Doubleday, Page and Company published it in 1900. In fact, it was so controversial that it almost missed being printed at all. Harpers refused the first copy, and the book went to Frank Doubleday. After the Doubleday printers typeset the book, one of the partners' wives read it and so strongly opposed its sexual nature that the publisher produced only a few editions.

In addition to the book's theme of sexual impropriety, the public disliked the fact that Theodore Dreiser presented a side of life that proper Americans did not care to acknowledge. Even worse, Dreiser made no moral judgments on his characters' actions. He wrote about infidelity and prostitution as natural occurrences in the course of human relationships. Dreiser wrote about his characters with pity, compassion, and a sense of awe.

While the book appalled Americans, the English appreciated it. William Heinemann published an English version of the book in 1901. While the book sold well in England, *Sister Carrie* did not enjoy much success in the United States, even though B. W. Dodge & Co. had reprinted it. In order to make ends meet Dreiser worked at other literary jobs. In 1911, when the magazine where he was employed stopped publication and he was out of work, he began to write nonstop to complete his next novel *Jennie Gerhardt*. Critics liked *Jennie Gerhardt* so much that they began to reconsider the merits of *Sister Carrie*. A new edition of *Sister Carrie* was published, and it became Dreiser's most successful novel.

Characters in *Sister Carrie*

1. Caroline (Carrie) Meeber—A young woman from rural Wisconsin; the protagonist.
2. Minnie Hanson—Carrie's dour elder sister who lives in Chicago and puts up Carrie on her arrival.
3. Sven Hanson—Minnie's husband, of Swedish extraction and taciturn temperament.
4. Charles H. Drouet—A buoyant traveling salesman Carrie meets on the train to Chicago.
5. George W. Hurstwood—A well-to-do, sophisticated man who manages Fitzgerald and Moy's resort.
6. Julia Hurstwood—George's strong-willed, social-climbing wife.
7. Jessica Hurstwood—George and Julia's daughter, who shares her mother's aspirations to social status.
8. George Hurstwood, Jr. —George and Julia's son.
9. Mr. and Mrs. Vance—A wealthy merchant and his wife, who live in the same building as Hurstwood and Carrie in New York City.
10. Robert Ames—Mrs. Vance's cousin from Indiana, a handsome young scholar whom Carrie regards as a male ideal.
11. Lola Osborne—a chorus girl Carrie meets during a theatre production in New York, who encourages Carrie to become her roommate.

Summary

In August, 1889, Caroline Meeber boards the train at her family home in Columbia City and travels to Chicago. Filled with fears, tears, and regrets, she is nonetheless determined to make her way in the big city.

On the long train ride she meets a handsome young traveling salesman named Charles Drouet. Shy at first, she is warmed and made confident by Drouet's easy manner and flashy clothes. He seems to her the epitome of wealth and influence. When the train arrives in Chicago, she and Drouet make plans to meet again the following week so that he can show her the sights of the city.

Carrie is met at the station by her sister Minnie Hanson. The two girls travel to the flat where Minnie lives with her husband Sven and their baby. The couple plan to have Carrie live with them while she works in the city. It is thought that Carrie will pay for her room and board in order to help the Hansons reduce expenses.

Carrie is thrilled by the prospect of finding work in Chicago. She imagines herself part of the great swirl of activity in the city. Her hopes are somewhat dampened when she finally obtains a job in a shoe factory at four and a half dollars a week.

Carrie realizes that she must abandon some of her more ambitious and fantastic plans. The Hansons disapprove of her wish to go to the theater. Minnie points out to Carrie that after paying four dollars for room and board, she will hardly have enough money left for carfare. Because the flat is so small, Carrie is unable to invite Drouet to visit.

As the cold winter sets in, Carrie finds that it is impossible to keep up the hard work at the factory. Finally, the combination of long hours, hard work, and inadequate clothing causes Carrie to become ill and she loses her job. The Hansons talk of sending her back to Columbia City, but she is determined to remain in Chicago.

One day as she wanders about downtown looking for a new job, she meets Drouet on the street. He buys her a splendid meal and "lends" her twenty dollars to buy decent clothes. Eventually he persuades Carrie to leave the Hansons and take a room of her own, offering to support her until she is settled. Soon Carrie and Drouet are living together in a cozy apartment. As time passes, Carrie perceives that Drouet is not nearly such an ideal figure as she had first imagined. He is egotistical and insensitive, but he is also kind and generous, and so she accepts her lot graciously. Drouet takes it upon himself to "educate" the untutored girl in the ways of society, teaching her to Aress and behave according to fashion.

One evening the young couple are visited by George Hurstwood, a friend of Drouet's, the manager of a "way up, truly swell saloon". He is mature and attractive; he finds Carrie naive and pretty. The two are struck by an instantaneous fascination for each other and meet together frequently whenever the salesman is out of town.

Without Carrie's knowledge, Drouet enlists her talents as an actress in an amateur performance. To the surprise of Carrie, as well as her two admirers, the girl is a brilliant success. The next day Hurstwood confesses his love to Carrie and she responds favorably.

Eventually Drouet discovers that Carrie and Hurstwood have been seeing a great deal of each other and he moves out of the flat in order to frighten her. Hurstwood's wife, meanwhile, a shrewd and selfish woman, accuses Hurstwood of having an affair and initiates a divorce action against him.

One night when he stays late in his office to finish some paperwork, Hurstwood discovers that the safe has been left unlocked with over ten thousand dollars in it. While he is debating with himself whether to take the money, the door of the safe slams shut as he holds the entire amount in his hands. He is frightened and decides to flee. He rushes to Carrie's flat, tells her that Drouet has been injured and wishes to see her and whisks her away with him on a train to Canada.

Carrie is repelled by Hurstwood now, for she has learned from Drouet that he is married. Hurstwood argues that he has left his wife in order to be with Carrie. She believes him and agrees to remain with him if he will marry her.

In Canada, Hurstwood is tracked down by a private detective and returns most of the stolen money on the promise that his employers will not prosecute. The couple are married in a hasty ceremony, although the marriage is not valid.

The couple continue on to New York, where they find a comfortable apartment. Hurstwood is forced to invest the little money he has retained in a second-rate saloon. He and Carrie settle down to a routine existence in New York, never going out or meeting anyone.

Carrie strikes up a friendship with her neighbor, Mrs. Vance, a young lady of fine manners and expensive taste. Through the influence of Mrs. Vance and her cousin Bob Ames, Carrie begins to feel dissatisfied with being an ordinary housewife.

Hurstwood's business venture terminates and he finds himself unable to find employment. After a while he gives up searching and simply settles back to watch his meager savings dwindle. He loses his pride and dignity. He hardly ever leaves the house. Conditions become so difficult that Carrie decides to find work. She eventually finds a part as a chorus girl in a Broadway opera. Her fortunes rise steadily after that. Carrie decides to leave Hurstwood on his own, for he has become a deadweight to her.

In a few years Carrie gains fame and fortune as a stage comedienne. Hurstwood continues to decline until he becomes a Bowery tramp and finally commits suicide.

At the time of Hurstwood's suicide, Carrie has gained all that she had originally hoped for: wealth, finery, and prestige. Nevertheless she remains unsatisfied, always pondering the vagaries of fortune that make her desire something new and indefinable. It is clear that she will never gain the happiness she dreams of.

Comments on *Sister Carrie*

Sister Carrie is frequently regarded as a turning point in American fiction. Firmly embedded in the realist tradition, the book's simple yet serious naturalistic outlook emphasizes that human behavior results from instinct, self-interest, and social pressure and not from any real understanding or sense of ethical responsibility. Dreiser's experiences in Chicago and New York keenly observing the details of city life are rendered in the novel with detached, emotionless objectivity. The author is equally silent about the unconventionality and amorality of his characters.

1. Carrie's rise to success as a chorus girl and stage actress as well as the questionable motives and actions of Drouet and Hurstwood, her two worldly patrons and lovers, are presented against a backdrop of urban glitter and decay, an enticing but cold world evocative of an equally remote and uncaring cosmos.

2. Naive and passive, casually accepting favors and their consequences, Carrie nevertheless slowly learns the ways of the world as well as the need to free herself from the emotional and sexual domination of the men in her life who see her merely as extensions of their own egos.

3. In a world where destiny seems to be controlled by forces beyond one's reach, Carrie is not only a survivor but a victor. Yet her success can be regarded as dubious: ever restless, good but shallow, optimistic but uncertain of who she really is, Carrie may represent the typical American morally adrift in the brutal, unprincipled, materialistic world of our culture's own creation. If Carrie is seen as triumphant, then the false values of that culture endure.

4. Although loosely based on the experiences of his sister Emma, in many ways Carrie is suggestive of Dreiser himself, notably his search for artistic identity and acceptance in a world bound by outmoded conventions.

Introduction to Chapter 18

The evening of the performance Carrie is escorted to the lodge in a carriage, accompanied by Drouet. She is nervous but looking forward to the show. Hurstwood arrives and sees that his influence has packed the theater with respectable citizens of the local middle classes. He greets many of his friends, all of them members of the lodge with him. They are not there for the show, but mostly because he asked them to come, and as a result they all surround Hurstwood and make him seem quite important.

From　　　　　　　　*Sister Carrie*

Chapter 18

Just Over the Border—A Hall and Farewell

By the evening of the 16th the subtle hand of Hurstwood had made itself apparent. He had given the word among his friends—and they were many and influential—that here was something which they ought to attend, and, as a consequence, the sale of tickets by Mr. Quincel, acting for the lodge, had been large. Small four-line notes had appeared in all of the daily newspapers. These he had arranged for by the aid of one of his newspaper friends on the "Times", Mr. Harry McGarren, the managing editor.

"Say, Harry," Hurstwood said to him one evening, as the latter stood at the bar drinking before wending[1] his belated way homeward, "you can help the boys out, I guess. "

"What is it?" said McGarren, pleased to be consulted by the opulent[2] manager.

"The Custer Lodge is getting up a little entertainment for their own good, and they'd like a little newspaper notice. You know what I mean—a squib or two saying that it's going to take place. "

"Certainly," said McGarren, "I can fix that for you, George. "

At the same time Hurstwood kept himself wholly in the background. The members of Custer Lodge could scarcely understand why their little affair was taking so well. Mr. Harry Quincel was looked upon as quite a star for this sort of work.

By the time the 16th had arrived Hurstwood's friends had rallied[3] like Romans to a senator's call. A well-dressed, good-natured, flatteringly-inclined audience was assured from the moment he thought of assisting Carrie.

That little student had mastered her part to her own satisfaction, much as she trembled for her fate when she should once face the gath-

ered throng[4], behind the glare of the footlights. She tried to console herself with the thought that a score of other persons, men and women,
were equally tremulous[5] concerning the outcome of their efforts, but she
could not disassociate the general danger from her own individual liabil-
ity. She feared that she would forget her lines, that she might be unable
to master the feeling which she now felt concerning her own movements
in the play. At times she wished that she had never gone into the affair;
at others, she trembled lest she should be paralysed with fear and stand
white and gasping, not knowing what to say and spoiling the entire performance.

　　In the matter of the company, Mr. Bamberger had disappeared.
That hopeless example had fallen under the lance of the director's criticism. Mrs. Morgan was still present, but envious and determined, if for
nothing more than spite, to do as well as Carrie at least. A loafing professional had been called in to assume the role of Ray, and, while he
was a poor stick of his kind, he was not troubled by any of those qualms
which attack the spirit of those who have never faced an audience. He
swashed about (cautioned though he was to maintain silence concerning
his past theatrical relationships) in such a self-confident manner that he
was like to convince every one of his identity by mere matter of circum-
stantial evidence.

　　" It is so easy, " he said to Mrs. Morgan, in the usual affected stage
voice. "An audience would be the last thing to trouble me. It's the spirit
of the part, you know, that is difficult. "

　　Carrie disliked his appearance, but she was too much the actress
not to swallow his qualities with complaisance[6], seeing that she must
suffer his fictitious[7] love for the evening.

　　At six she was ready to go. Theatrical paraphernalia had been provided over and above her care. She had practised her make-up in the
morning, had rehearsed and arranged her material for the evening by one
o'clock, and had gone home to have a final look at her part, waiting for
the evening to come.

On this occasion the lodge sent a carriage. Drouet rode with her as far as the door, and then went about the neighbouring stores, looking for some good cigars. The little actress marched nervously into her dressing-room and began that painfully anticipated matter of make-up which was to transform her, a simple maiden, to Laura, the Belle of Society.

The flare of the gas-jets, the open trunks, suggestive of travel and display, the scattered contents of the make-up box—rouge, pearl powder, whiting, burnt cork, India ink, pencils for the eye-lids, wigs, scissors, looking-glasses, drapery—in short, all the nameless paraphernalia of disguise, have a remarkable atmosphere of their own. Since her arrival in the city many things had influenced her, but always in a far-removed manner. This new atmosphere was more friendly. It was wholly unlike the great brilliant mansions which waved her coldly away, permitting her only awe and distant wonder. This took her by the hand kindly, as one who says, "My dear, come in." It opened for her as if for its own. She had wondered at the greatness of the names upon the billboards, the marvel of the long notices in the papers, the beauty of the dresses upon the stage, the atmosphere of carriages, flowers, refinement. Here was no illusion. Here was an open door to see all of that. She had come upon it as one who stumbles upon a secret passage and, behold, she was in the chamber of diamonds and delight!

As she dressed with a flutter, in her little stage room, hearing the voices outside, seeing Mr. Quincel hurrying here and there, noting Mrs. Morgan and Mrs. Hoagland at their nervous work of preparation, seeing all the twenty members of the cast moving about and worrying o-ver what the result would be, she could not help thinking what a delight this would be if it would endure; how perfect a state, if she could only do well now, and then some time get a place as a real actress. The thought had taken a mighty hold upon her. It hummed in her ears as the melody of an old song.

Outside in the little lobby another scene was begin enacted. With-out the interest of Hurstwood, the little hall would probably have been

236

comfortably filled, for the members of the lodge were moderately interested in its welfare. Hurstwood's word, however, had gone the
rounds. It was to be a full-dress affair. The four boxes had been taken.
Dr. Norman McNeill Hale and his wife were to occupy one. This was
quite a card. C. R. Walker, dry-goods merchant and possessor of at
least two hundred thousand dollars, had taken another; a well-known
coal merchant had been induced to take the third, and Hurstwood and
his friends the fourth. Among the latter was Drouet. The people who
were now pouring here were not celebrities, nor even local notabilities,
in a general sense. They were the lights of a certain circle—the circle of
small fortunes and secret order distinctions. These gentlemen Elks knew
the standing of one another. They had regard for the ability which could
amass[8] a small fortune, own a nice home, keep a barouche[9] or carriage,
perhaps, wear fine clothes, and maintain a good mercantile position.
Naturally, Hurstwood, who was a little above the order of mind which
accepted this standard as perfect, who had shrewdness and much as-
sumption of dignity, who held an imposing and authoritative position,
and commanded friendship by intuitive tact in handling people, was
quite a figure. He was more generally known than most others in the
same circle, and was looked upon as someone whose reserve covered a
mine of influence and solid financial prosperity.

Tonight he was in his element. He came with several friends directly from Rector's in a carriage. In the lobby he met Drouet, who was just
returning from a trip for more cigars. All five now joined in an animated
conversation concerning the company present and the general drift of
lodge affairs.

"Who's here?" said Hurstwood, passing into the theatre proper,
where the lights were turned up and a company of gentlemen were laughing and talking in the open space back of the seats.

"Why, how do you do, Mr. Hurstwood?" came from the first individual recognised.

"Glad to see you," said the latter, grasping his hand lightly.

"Looks quite an affair, doesn't it?"

"Yes, indeed," said the manager.

"Custer seems to have the backing of its members," observed the friend.

"So it should," said the knowing manager. "I'm glad to see it."

"Well, George," said another rotund citizen, whose avoirdupois made necessary an almost alarming display of starched shirt bosom, "how goes it with you?"

"Excellent," said the manager.

"What brings you over here? You're not a member of Custer."

"Good-nature," returned the manager. "Like to see the boys, you know."

"Wife here?"

"She couldn't come tonight. She's not well."

"Sorry to hear it—nothing serious, I hope."

"No, just feeling a little ill."

"I remember Mrs. Hurstwood when she was travelling once with you over to St. Joe—" and here the newcomer launched off in a trivial recollection, which was terminated by the arrival of more friends.

"Why, George, how are you?" said another genial West Side politician and lodge member. "My, but I'm glad to see you again; how are things, anyhow?"

"Very well; I see you got that nomination for alderman."

"Yes, we whipped them out over there without much trouble."

"What do you suppose Hennessy will do now?"

"Oh, he'll go back to his brick business. He has a brick-yard, you know."

"I didn't know that," said the manager. "Felt pretty sore, I suppose, over his defeat." "Perhaps," said the other, winking shrewdly.

Some of the more favoured of his friends whom he had invited began to roll up in carriages now. They came shuffling in with a great show of finery and much evident feeling of content and importance.

"Here we are," said Hurstwood, turning to one from a group with whom he was talking.

"That's right," returned the newcomer, a gentleman of about forty-five.

"And say," he whispered, jovially, pulling Hurstwood over by the shoulder so that he might whisper in his ear, "if this isn't a good show, I'll punch your head. "

"You ought to pay for seeing your old friends. Bother the show!"

To another who inquired, "Is it something really good?" the manager replied:

"I don't know. I don't suppose so. " Then, lifting his hand graciously, "For the lodge. "

"Lots of boys out, eh?"

"Yes, look up Shanahan. He was just asking for you a moment ago. "

It was thus that the little theatre resounded[10] to a babble of successful voices, the creak of fine clothes, the commonplace of good-nature, and all largely because of this man's bidding. Look at him any time within the half hour before the curtain was up, he was a member of an eminent group—a rounded company of five or more whose stout figures, large white bosoms, and shining pins bespoke the character of their success. The gentlemen who brought their wives called him out to shake hands. Seats clicked, ushers bowed while he looked blandly on. He was evidently a light among them, reflecting in his personality the ambitions of those who greeted him. He was acknowledged, fawned upon, in a way lionised. Through it all one could see the standing of the man. It was greatness in a way, small as it was.

Notes:

    1. wend v. 走, 行

        E. g. Sleepy-eyed commuters were wending their way to work.

2. opulent *adj.* 富裕的；豪华的

E. g. Most of the cash went on supporting his opulent lifestyle.

3. rally *v.* 召集，集合

E. g. His supporters have rallied to his defence.

4. throng *n.* 人群

E. g. An official pushed through the throng.

5. tremulous *adj.* 颤抖的

E. g. She fidgeted in her chair as she took a deep, tremulous breath.

6. complaisance *n.* 殷勤；柔顺

E. g. Anne had always felt that she would pretend what was proper on her arrival, but the complaisance of the others was unlooked for.

7. fictitious *adj.* 虚假的，假装的

E. g. We're interested in the source of these fictitious rumours.

8. amass *vt.* 积累，积聚

E. g. How had he amassed his fortune?

9. barouche *n.* 四轮大马车

10. resound *vi.* 回响

E. g. A roar of approval resounded through the hall.

Questions:

1. How had Hurstwood helped spread the word about the play?
2. How did Carrie feel the day of the play?
3. What did Carrie fear before the performance?
4. Once Carrie arrived at the theater, how did she feel?
5. How did Hurstwood explain her wife's absence?

Analysis of Chapter Eighteen

Dreiser uses this chapter to critique the middle classes and their petty behavior. He describes Hurstwood as surrounded by other wealthy men, part of an eminent elite. However, he then belittles this situation, saying, "It was greatness in a way, small as it was". Dreiser is effectively downplaying the scene, showing that this perceived greatness is a facade. He is implying that Hurstwood has done nothing great here, yet he is surrounded as if he were important. In reality, the entire audience is contrived for Carrie, not Hurstwood.

中文译文：

到了16日晚上，赫斯渥已经巧妙地大显神通。他在他的朋友们中间散布消息说这场演出很值得一看——而他的朋友不仅人数众多，而且很有势力——结果支部干事昆塞尔先生卖出了大量的戏票。所有的日报都为这事发了一条四行的消息。这一点是靠他新闻界的朋友哈莱·麦格伦先生办到的。麦格伦先生是芝加哥《时报》的主编。

"喂，哈莱，"一天夜里麦格伦回家前先在酒馆柜台边喝上两杯时，赫斯渥对他说，"我看你能给支部的那些孩子们帮个忙"。"什么事啊？"麦格伦先生问道。这个富有的经理这么看得起他，着实让他高兴。

"寇斯特支部为了筹款要举办一场小小的演出，他们很希望报纸能发条消息。你明白我的意思——来上两三句说明何时何地有这么场演出就行了。""没问题，"麦格伦说，"这事我能替你办到，乔治。"这期间，赫斯渥自己一直躲在幕后。寇斯特支部的人几乎无法理解他们的小玩意儿为什么这么受欢迎。于是昆塞尔先生被看作是主办这类事的天才。

到了16日这天，赫斯渥的朋友们纷纷去捧场，就好像罗马人听到了他们元老的召唤一样。从赫斯渥决定帮嘉莉那一刻起，就可以肯定，去看演出的将都是些衣冠楚楚、满怀善意、一心想捧场的人士。

那个戏剧界的小学生这时已经掌握了她那个角色的表演，自己还相当满意。尽管她一想到自己要在舞台强烈的灯光下，在满堂观众面前演戏，不禁吓得发抖，为自己的命运担心。

她竭力安慰自己说，还有二十来个别的人，有男有女，也在为演出的结果紧张得发抖。可是这没有用。她想到总体失败的可能性就不能不想到她个人失败的可能性。她担心自己会临时忘词，又担心在舞台上她不能把她对角色的情感变化的理解表现出来。

有时候她真希望自己当初没有参与这件事就好了。有时候她又担心自己到了台上会吓呆了，只会脸色苍白气喘吁吁地站在台上，不知道说什么好，使整个演出都砸在她手里，这种可能性让她吓得发抖。

在演员阵容方面，班贝格先生已经去掉了。这个不可救药的先生在导演唇枪舌剑的指责下只好退出。莫根太太还在班子里，但是妒忌得要命，不为别的，光为这份怨恨，她也决心要演得至少像嘉莉一样好。一个失业的演员被请来演雷埃这个角色。尽管他只是个蹩脚演员，他不像那些没有在观众前亮过相的演员那样提心吊胆，焦虑不安。尽管他已被警告过不要提起他以前和戏剧界的联系，可是他那么神气活现地走来走去，一副信心十足的样子，单凭这些间接证据，就足以让别人知道他吃的是哪一行饭了。

"演戏是很容易的"，他用舞台上念道白的口气拿腔拿调地对莫根太太说，"我一点也不为观众操心，你要知道，难的是把握角色的气质。"嘉莉不喜欢他的样子。但她是一个好演员，所以温顺地容忍了他这些气质。她知道这一晚上她必须忍受他那装模作样的谈情说爱。

6点钟，她已一切准备就绪可以出发了。演戏用的行头是主办单位提供的，不用她操心。上午她已试过化妆，1点钟时彩排完毕，晚上演戏用的东西也都准备好了。然后她回家最后看了一遍她的台词，就等晚上到来了。

为了当晚的演出，支部派了马车来接她。杜洛埃和她一起坐马车到了剧场门口，就下车到附近店里去买几支上等雪茄。

这小女演员一个人惴惴不安地走进她的化妆间，开始焦虑痛苦地期待着化妆，这化妆要把一个单纯的姑娘变成罗拉——社交皇后。

耀眼的煤气灯，打开的箱子(令人想起旅行和排场)，散乱的化妆用品——胭脂、珍珠粉、白垩粉、软木炭、墨汁、眼睑笔、假发、剪刀、镜子、戏装——总之，各种叫不上名来的化妆用的行头，应有尽有，各有自己独特的气息。自从她来到芝加哥，城里的许多东西深深吸引了她，但那些东西对她来说总是高不可攀。这新的气氛要友好得多。它完全不像那些豪门府第令她望而生畏，不准她走近，只准她远远地惊叹。这里的气氛却像一个老朋友，亲热地拉着她的手，对她说："请进吧，亲爱的。"它把她当自己人向她敞开大门。戏院广告牌上那些大名鼎鼎的明星名字，报上长长的剧目，舞台上的华丽服装，还有马车，鲜花和高雅服饰带来的剧场气氛—这一切一直令她赞叹和好奇。如今这已不是幻想了。这扇门敞开着让她看着这一切。她就像一个偶然发现秘密通道的人一样，瞎碰瞎撞来到这里。睁眼一看，自己来到了一个堆满钻石和奇珍的宝库！

　　她在自己的小化妆间激动不安地穿戏装时，可以听到外面的说话声，看到昆塞尔先生在东奔西忙，莫根太太和霍格兰太太在忐忑不安地做准备工作，全团二十个演员都在走来走去，担心着戏不知会演得怎么样，这使她不禁暗想，如果这一切能永远地延续下去，那将多么令人愉快。如果她这次能够演成功，以后某个时候再谋到一个当女演员的位子，那事情就太理想了。这个念头让她非常动心，就像一首古老民歌的旋律在她耳边不断地回响。

　　外面的小休息室里又是一番景象。即使赫斯渥不施加影响，这个小剧场也许仍然会客满的，因为支部的人对支部的事情还是比较关心的。但是赫斯渥的话一传开，这场演出就成了必须穿晚礼服的社交盛会。四个包厢都让人包下了。诺曼·麦克尼·海尔医生和太太包了一个，这是张王牌。至少拥有二十万财产的呢绒商西·阿·华尔格也包了一个。一个有名的煤炭商听了劝说，订了第三个包厢。赫斯渥和他的朋友们订了第四个包厢。杜洛埃也在这群人中间。涌入这剧场来看戏的，总的来说，并不是名流们，甚至算不上当地的要人们，但他们是某一阶层的头面人物——那个颇有点资产的阶层加上帮会的要人们。这些兄弟会的先生们相互都知道各人的地位，对于彼此的能力表示敬意，因为他们都是凭自己的本事，创起一份小家业。他们都拥有一幢漂亮的住宅，置起了四轮大马车或者二轮马车，也许还穿得衣冠楚楚地在商界出人头地。在这群人中，赫斯渥自然是个重要人物。他比那些满足于目前地位的人在精神上要高出一筹。他为人精明，举止庄重，地位显要有权势，在待人接物上天生的灵活机敏，容易博得人们的友谊。

　　在这个圈子里，他比大多数人出名，被看作是一个势力很大、财力殷实的人物。

今晚他在自己的圈子里活动，如鱼得水。他是和一些朋友直接从雷克脱饭店坐马车来戏院的。在休息室里他遇到杜洛埃买雪茄回来。五个人都兴高采烈地聊了起来，他们聊的是即将演出的班子和支部事务的一般情况。

"谁在这里啊?"赫斯渥从休息室走进演出大厅。大厅里灯都点起来了，一群先生正聚在座位后面的空地上高声谈笑着。

"喂，你好吗，赫斯渥先生?"他认出的第一个人向他打招呼。

"很高兴见到你"，赫斯渥和他轻轻地握了手说道。

"这看上去很像一回事，是不是?"

"是啊，真不错"，经理先生说。

"寇斯特支部的人看来很齐心"，他的朋友议论说。

"应该这样"，世故的经理说道，"看到他们这样真让人高兴。"

"喂，乔治"，另一个胖子说。他胖得把礼服领口都绷开了，露出了好大一片浆过的衬衫前胸，"你怎么样啊?""很好"，经理说。

"你怎么会来? 你不是寇斯特支部的人嘛。""我是好心好意来的"，经理回答说，"想看看这里的朋友，你知道。""太太也来了?""她今天来不了，她身体不太好。""真遗憾——我希望不是什么大病""不是，只是小有不适。""我还记得赫斯渥太太和你一起到圣乔旅行——"话题说到这里，这个新来的人开始回忆一些琐碎的小事。又来了一群朋友把这回忆打断了。

"喂，乔治，你好吗?"另一个人和颜悦色地问道。他是西区的政客又是支部的成员，"哇，我真高兴又见到你。你的情况怎么样?""很不错。我得知你被提名当市议员了。""是啊，我们没费多少事，就把他们打败了。""依你看汉纳赛先生现在会做些什么?""还是回去做他的砖瓦生意嘛。你知道他有一座砖厂。""这一点我倒不知道"，经理说。"我猜想他这次竞选失败心里一定很不是滋味。""也许吧"，对方精明地眨了一下眼睛说道。

他邀请来的那些和他交情更深一些的朋友现在也坐着马车陆陆续续来了，他们大摇大摆地进来，炫耀地穿着考究、精美的服装，一副明显地志得意满的要人气派。

"我们都来了"，赫斯渥离开正在谈话的这些人，朝新来的一个人说道。

"是啊",新来的人说道,他是个大约四十五岁的绅士。

"喂",他快活地拉着赫斯渥的肩膀,把他拉过来说句悄悄话,"要是戏不好,我可要敲你的头。""为了看看老朋友,也该掏腰包才对。这戏嘛,管它好不好!"另一个问他:"是不是有点看头?"经理回答:"我也不知道。我想不会有什么看头的。"然后他大度地扬扬手说,"为支部捧个场嘛。""来了不少的人,是吧。""是啊,你去找找珊纳汉先生吧,他刚才还在问起你。"就这样,这小小的剧场里回响着这些春风得意人物的交谈声,考究的服装发出的窸窣声,还有一般的表示善意的寒暄声。一大部分人是赫斯渥招来的。在戏开场前的半个小时里,你随时可以看到他和一群大人物在一起——五六个人围成一圈,一个个身子肥胖,西服领露出一大片白衬衫前胸,身上别着闪亮的饰针,处处显示他们是些成功的人物。那些携带太太同来的先生们都把他招呼过去和他握手。座位发出啪啦啪啦的声响,领座员朝客人们鞠躬,而他在一边温和殷勤地看着。

很显然,他是这群人中的佼佼者,在他身上反映着那些和他打招呼的人们的野心。他为他们所承认,受到他们的奉承,甚至有一点儿被当作大人物看待,从中可以看出这个人的地位。尽管他不属于最上层的社会,他在自己的圈子里可以算得上了不起了。

❧ Answers for questions

1. He had given the word among his friends that there was something which they ought to attend, and his friends were many and influential. As a consequence, the sale of tickets by Mr. Quincel, acting for the lodge, had been large. He had arranged for small four-line notes to appear in all of the daily newspapers by the aid of one of his newspaper friends on the "Times", Mr. Harry McGarren, the managing editor.

2. She was very nervous the day of the play, despite Hurstwood's assurances at the rehearsal. That night while the theater filled with people, Carrie prepared for the play, growing more nervous by the minute.

3. She feared that she would forget her lines, that she might be

unable to master the feeling which she now felt concerning her own movements in the play. At times she wished that she had never gone into the affair; at others, she trembled lest she should be paralysed with fear and stand white and gasping, not knowing what to say and spoiling the entire performance.

4. Once she arrived at the theater, however, all the "nameless paraphernalia of disguise" transport her into a new and friendly atmosphere. Here she is part of the world of beautiful clothes, flowers, and elegant carriages. "She had come upon it as one who stumbles upon a secret passage, and, behold, she was in the chamber of diamonds and delight!" The gaslights, the makeup, and the costume transform Carrie into "Laura, the Belle of Society".

5. He told one gentleman that his wife could not attend because she was ill.

References

[1] http://upload. wikimedia. org/wikipedia/commons/0/0e/Theodore_Dreiser_1. jpg（图片来源）

[2] http://www. americanwriters. org/writers/dreiser. asp

[3] http://xroads. virginia. edu/ ~ hyper/DREISER/carrie. html（图片来源）

[4] http://www. bookrags. com/studyguide – sistercarrie/

[5] http://en. wikipedia. org/wiki/Sister_Carrie#Characters

[6] http://www. cliffsnotes. com/literature/s/sister – carrie/book – summary

[7] http://wenku. baidu. com/view/036af228915f804d2b16c1ac. html

[8] http://xroads. virginia. edu/ ~ hyper/DREISER/ch18. html

[9] http://t. icesmall. cn/book/2/350/18. html

[10] http://www. gradesaver. com/sister – carrie/study – guide/summary – chapters – 17 – 24

Unit 12
F. Scott Fitzgerald (1896 – 1940)

🔖 Bibliography

F. Scott Fitzgerald, (1896 – 1940), was the leading writer of America's Jazz Age, the Roaring Twenties, and one of its glittering heroes. The chief quality of Fitzgerald's talent was his ability to be both a leading participant in the high life he described, and a detached observer of it. Few readers saw the serious side of Fitzgerald, and he was not generally recognized as a gifted writer during his lifetime. While he lived, most readers considered his stories a chronicle and even a celebration of moral decline. But later readers realized that Fitzgerald's works have a deeper moral theme.

Francis Scott Key Fitzgerald was born in St. Paul, Minnesota, on Sept. 24, 1896. He attended Princeton University, where he wrote amateur musical comedies. He left Princeton in 1917 without a degree. Years later, Fitzgerald remarked that perhaps he should have continued writing musicals, but he said, "I am too much a moralist at heart, and really want to preach at people in some acceptable form, rather than entertain them."

Fitzgerald won fame and fortune for his first novel, *This Side of Paradise* (1920). It is an immature work but was the first novel to anticipate the pleasure-seeking generation of the Roaring Twenties. A similar novel, *The Beautiful and Damned* (1921), and two collections of short stories, *Flappers and Philosophers* (1920) and *Tales of the Jazz Age* (1922), increased his popularity.

The *Great Gatsby* (1925) was less popular than Fitzgerald's early works, but it was his masterpiece and the first of three successive novels that give him lasting literary importance. The lively yet deeply moral novel centers around Jay Gatsby, a wealthy bootlegger. It presents a penetrating criticism of the moral emptiness Fitzgerald saw in wealthy American society of the 1920's.

Fitzgerald's next novel, *Tender is the Night* (1934, revised edition by Malcolm Cowley, 1951), is a beautifully written but disjointed account of the general decline of a few glamorous Americans in Europe. The book failed because readers during the Great Depression of the 1930s were not interested in Jazz Age "parties." Fitzgerald died before he completed *The Last Tycoon* (1941), a novel about Hollywood life.

Critics generally agree that Fitzgerald's early success damaged his personal life and marred his literary production. This success led to extravagant living and a need for a large income. It probably contributed to Fitzgerald's alcoholism and the mental breakdown of his wife, Zelda. The success also probably led to his physical and spiritual collapse, which he described frankly in the long essay "The Crack-Up" (1936). Fitzgerald spent his last years as a scriptwriter in Hollywood and died there on Dec. 21, 1940. A few years after his death, his books won him the recognition he had desired while alive.

The Great Gatsby

The *Great Gatsby*, follows Jay Gatsby, a man who orders his life around one desire: to be reunited with Daisy Buchanan, the love he lost five years earlier. Gatsby's quest leads him from poverty to wealth, into the arms of his beloved, and eventually to death. Published in 1925, *The Great Gatsby* is a classic piece of American fiction. It is

a novel of triumph and tragedy, noted for the remarkable way Fitzgerald captured a cross-section of American society.

In *The Great Gatsby* Fitzgerald, known for his imagistic and poetic prose, holds a mirror up to the society of which he was a part. The initial success of the book was limited, although in the more than 75 years since it has come to be regarded as a classic piece of American short fiction. In 1925, however, the novel served as a snapshot of the frenzied post-war society known as the Jazz Age, while today it provides readers with, among other things, a portal through which to observe life in the 1920s. Part of Fitzgerald's charm in *The Great Gatsby*, in fact, is his ability to encapsulate the mood of a generation during a politically and socially crucial and chaotic period of American history.

Characters in *The Great Gatsby*

1. Jay Gatsby—The protagonist who gives his name to the story. Gatsby is a newly wealthy Midwesterner-turned-Easterner who orders his life around one desire: to be reunited with Daisy Buchanan, the love he lost five years earlier. His quest for the American dream leads him from poverty to wealth, into the arms of his beloved and, eventually, to death.

2. Nick Carraway—The story's narrator. Nick rents the small house next to Gatsby's mansion in West Egg and, over the course of events, helps Gatsby reunite with Daisy.

3. Daisy Buchanan—Beautiful and mesmerizing, Daisy is the apex of sociability. Her privileged upbringing in Louisville has conditioned her to a particular lifestyle, which Tom, her husband, is able to provide her.

4. Tom Buchanan—Daisy's hulking brute of a husband. Tom comes from an old, wealthy Chicago family and takes pride in his rough ways.

5. Pammy Buchanan—Toddler daughter of Tom and Daisy Buchanan. She represents the children of the Jazz Agers.

6. Jordan Baker—Professional golfer of questionable integrity. Friend of Daisy's who, like Daisy, represents women of a particular class. Jordan is the young, single woman of wealth, admired by men wherever she goes.

7. Myrtle Wilson—Married lover of Tom Buchanan. Myrtle serves as a representative of the lower class. Through her affair with Tom she gains entrée into the world of the elite, and the change in her personality is remarkable.

8. George Wilson—Myrtle's unassuming husband. He runs a garage and gas station in the valley of ashes and seems trapped by his position in life.

9. Catherine—Sister of Myrtle Wilson who is aware of her sister's secret life and willing to partake of its benefits.

10. Meyer Wolfshiem—Gatsby's business associate and link to organized crime.

Summary

Nick Carraway, a young man from Minnesota, moves to New York in the summer of 1922 to learn about the bond business. He rents a house in the West Egg district of Long Island, a wealthy but unfashionable area populated by the new rich, a group who have made their fortunes too recently to have established social connections and who are prone to garish displays of wealth. Nick's next-door neighbor in West Egg is a mysterious man named Jay Gatsby, who lives in a gigantic Gothic mansion and throws extravagant parties every Saturday night.

Nick is unlike the other inhabitants of West Egg—he was educated at Yale and has social connections in East Egg, a fashionable area of Long Island home to the established upper class. Nick drives out to East Egg one evening for dinner with his cousin, Daisy Buchanan, and her husband, Tom, an erstwhile classmate of Nick's at Yale. Daisy and Tom introduce Nick to Jordan Baker, a beautiful, cynical young woman with whom Nick begins a romantic relationship. Nick also learns a bit about

Daisy and Tom's marriage: Jordan tells him that Tom has a lover, Myrtle Wilson, who lives in the valley of ashes, a gray industrial dumping ground between West Egg and New York City. Not long after this revelation, Nick travels to New York City with Tom and Myrtle. At a vulgar, gaudy party in the apartment that Tom keeps for the affair, Myrtle begins to taunt Tom about Daisy, and Tom responds by breaking her nose.

As the summer progresses, Nick eventually garners an invitation to one of Gatsby's legendary parties. He encounters Jordan Baker at the party, and they meet Gatsby himself, a surprisingly young man who affects an English accent, has a remarkable smile, and calls everyone "old sport." Gatsby asks to speak to Jordan alone, and, through Jordan, Nick later learns more about his mysterious neighbor. Gatsby tells Jordan that he knew Daisy in Louisville in 1917 and is deeply in love with her. He spends many nights staring at the green light at the end of her dock, across the bay from his mansion. Gatsby's extravagant lifestyle and wild parties are simply an attempt to impress Daisy. Gatsby now wants Nick to arrange a reunion between himself and Daisy, but he is afraid that Daisy will refuse to see him if she knows that he still loves her. Nick invites Daisy to have tea at his house, without telling her that Gatsby will also be there. After an initially awkward reunion, Gatsby and Daisy reestablish their connection. Their love rekindled, they begin an affair.

After a short time, Tom grows increasingly suspicious of his wife's relationship with Gatsby. At a luncheon at the Buchanans' house, Gatsby stares at Daisy with such undisguised passion that Tom realizes Gatsby is in love with her. Though Tom is himself involved in an extramarital affair, he is deeply outraged by the thought that his wife could be unfaithful to him. He forces the group to drive into New York City, where he confronts Gatsby in a suite at the Plaza Hotel. Tom asserts that he and Daisy have a history that Gatsby could never understand, and he announces to his wife that Gatsby is a criminal—his fortune comes from bootlegging alcohol and other illegal activities. Daisy realizes that her allegiance is to Tom, and Tom contemptuously sends her back to East Egg with Gatsby, attempting to prove that Gatsby cannot hurt him.

When Nick, Jordan, and Tom drive through the valley of ashes, however, they discover that Gatsby's car has struck and killed Myrtle, Tom's lover. They rush back to Long Island, where Nick learns from Gatsby that Daisy was driving the car when it struck Myrtle, but that Gatsby intends to take the blame. The next day, Tom tells Myrtle's husband, George, that Gatsby was the driver of the car. George, who has leapt to the conclusion that the driver of the car that killed Myrtle must have been her lover, finds Gatsby in the pool at his mansion and shoots him dead. He then fatally shoots himself.

Nick stages a small funeral for Gatsby, ends his relationship with Jordan, and moves back to the Midwest to escape the disgust he feels for the people surrounding Gatsby's life and for the emptiness and moral decay of life among the wealthy on the East Coast. Nick reflects that just as Gatsby's dream of Daisy was corrupted by money and dishonesty, the American dream of happiness and individualism has disintegrated into the mere pursuit of wealth. Though Gatsby's power to transform his dreams into reality is what makes him "great," Nick reflects that the era of dreaming—both Gatsby's dream and the American dream—is over.

Comments on *The Great Gatsby*

The three most important aspects of *The Great Gatsby*:

Nick Carraway is the narrator, or storyteller, of The Great Gatsby, but he is not the story's protagonist, or main character. Instead, Jay Gatsby is the protagonist of the novel that bears his name. Tom Buchanan is the book's antagonist, opposing Gatsby's attempts to get what he wants: Tom's wife Daisy.

From the gold hat mentioned in the novel's epigram to the green light at the end of Daisy's dock, The Great Gatsby is filled with things that are gold and green: the colors of money.

There are two kinds of wealth in *The Great Gatsby*: the inherited wealth of Daisy and Tom Buchanan, and the newly acquired wealth of Gatsby. The first kind comes with social standing and protects the Buchanans from punishment, as Daisy literally gets away with murder. Gatsby's kind of wealth, though considerable, leaves its owner vulnerable.

Introduction to Chapter Six

The rumors about Gatsby continue to circulate in New York—a reporter even travels to Gatsby's mansion hoping to interview him. Having learned the truth about Gatsby's early life sometime before writing his account, Nick now interrupts the story to relate Gatsby's personal history— not as it is rumored to have occurred, nor as Gatsby claimed it occurred, but as it really happened.

Gatsby was born James Gatz on a North Dakota farm, and though he attended college at St. Olaf's in Minnesota, he dropped out after two weeks, loathing the humiliating janitorial work by means of which he paid his tuition. He worked on Lake Superior the next summer fishing for salmon and digging for clams. One day, he saw a yacht owned by Dan Cody, a wealthy copper mogul, and rowed out to warn him about an impending storm. The grateful Cody took young Gatz, who gave his name as Jay Gatsby, on board his yacht as his personal assistant. Traveling with Cody to the Barbary Coast and the West Indies, Gatsby fell in love with wealth and luxury. Cody was a heavy drinker, and one of Gatsby's jobs was to look after him during his drunken binges. This gave Gatsby a healthy respect for the dangers of alcohol and convinced him not to become a drinker himself. When Cody died, he left Gatsby MYM25,000, but Cody's mistress prevented him from claiming his inheritance. Gatsby then dedicated himself to becoming a wealthy and successful man.

Nick sees neither Gatsby nor Daisy for several weeks after their reunion at Nick's house. Stopping by Gatsby's house one afternoon, he is alarmed to find Tom Buchanan there. Tom has stopped for a drink at

Gatsby's house with Mr. and Mrs. Sloane, with whom he has been out riding. Gatsby seems nervous and agitated, and tells Tom awkwardly that he knows Daisy. Gatsby invites Tom and the Sloanes to stay for dinner, but they refuse. To be polite, they invite Gatsby to dine with them, and he accepts, not realizing the insincerity of the invitation. Tom is contemptuous of Gatsby's lack of social grace and highly critical of Daisy's habit of visiting Gatsby's house alone. He is suspicious, but he has not yet discovered Gatsby and Daisy's love.

The following Saturday night, Tom and Daisy go to a party at Gatsby's house. Though Tom has no interest in the party, his dislike for Gatsby causes him to want to keep an eye on Daisy. Gatsby's party strikes Nick much more unfavorably this time around—he finds the revelry oppressive and notices that even Daisy has a bad time. Tom upsets her by telling her that Gatsby's fortune comes from bootlegging. She angrily replies that Gatsby's wealth comes from a chain of drugstores that he owns.

Gatsby seeks out Nick after Tom and Daisy leave the party; he is unhappy because Daisy has had such an unpleasant time. Gatsby wants things to be exactly the same as they were before he left Louisville; he wants Daisy to leave Tom so that he can be with her. Nick reminds Gatsby that he cannot re-create the past. Gatsby, distraught, protests that he can. He believes that his money can accomplish anything as far as Daisy is concerned. As he walks amid the debris from the party, Nick thinks about the first time Gatsby kissed Daisy, the moment when his dream of Daisy became the dominant force in his life. Now that he has her, Nick reflects, his dream is effectively over.

From   *The Great Gatsby*
Chapter Six

He told me all this very much later, but I've put it down here with the idea of exploding those first wild rumors about his antecedents[1], which weren't even faintly true. Moreover he told it to me at a time of confusion, when I had reached the point of believing everything and nothing about him. So I take advantage of this short halt, while Gatsby, so to speak, caught his breath, to clear this set of misconceptions away.

It was a halt, too, in my association with his affairs. For several weeks I didn't see him or hear his voice on the phone — mostly I was in New York, trotting[2] around with Jordan and trying to ingratiate myself with her senile[3] aunt — but finally I went over to his house one Sunday afternoon. I hadn't been there two minutes when somebody brought Tom Buchanan in for a drink. I was startled, naturally, but the really surprising thing was that it hadn't happened before.

They were a party of three on horseback — Tom and a man named Sloane and a pretty woman in a brown riding-habit, who had been there previously.

"I'm delighted to see you," said Gatsby, standing on his porch. "I'm delighted that you dropped in. "

As though they cared!

"Sit right down. Have a cigarette or a cigar. " He walked around the room quickly, ringing bells. "I'll have something to drink for you in just a minute. "

He was profoundly affected by the fact that Tom was there. But he would be uneasy anyhow until he had given them something, realizing in a vague way that that was all they came for. Mr. Sloane wanted nothing. A lemonade? No, thanks. A little champagne? Nothing at all, thanks⋯ . I'm sorry —

"Did you have a nice ride?"

"Very good roads around here. "

"I suppose the automobiles —"

"Yeah. "

Moved by an irresistible impulse, Gatsby turned to Tom, who had accepted the introduction as a stranger.

"I believe we've met somewhere before, Mr. Buchanan. "

"Oh, yes," said Tom, gruffly[4] polite, but obviously not remembering. "So we did. I remember very well. "

"About two weeks ago. "

"That's right. You were with Nick here. "

"I know your wife," continued Gatsby, almost aggressively.

"That so?"

Tom turned to me.

"You live near here, Nick?"

"Next door. "

"That so?"

Mr. Sloane didn't enter into the conversation, but lounged back haughtily[5] in his chair; the woman said nothing either — until unexpectedly, after two highballs, she became cordial.

"We'll all come over to your next party, Mr. Gatsby," she suggested. "What do you say?"

"Certainly; I'd be delighted to have you. "

"Be ver' nice," said Mr. Sloane, without gratitude. "Well — think ought to be starting home. "

"Please don't hurry," Gatsby urged them. He had control of himself now, and he wanted to see more of Tom. "Why don't you — why don't you stay for supper? I wouldn't be surprised if some other people dropped in from New York. "

"You come to supper with me," said the lady enthusiastically. "Both of you. "

This included me. Mr. Sloane got to his feet.

"Come along," he said — but to her only.

"I mean it," she insisted. "I'd love to have you. Lots of room. "

Gatsby looked at me questioningly. He wanted to go, and he didn't see that Mr. Sloane had determined he shouldn't.

"I'm afraid I won't be able to," I said.

"Well, you come," she urged, concentrating on Gatsby.

Mr. Sloane murmured something close to her ear.

"We won't be late if we start now," she insisted aloud.

"I haven't got a horse," said Gatsby. "I used to ride in the army, but I've never bought a horse. I'll have to follow you in my car. Excuse me for just a minute. "

The rest of us walked out on the porch, where Sloane and the lady began an impassioned conversation aside.

"My God, I believe the man's coming," said Tom. "Doesn't he know she doesn't want him?"

"She says she does want him. "

"She has a big dinner party and he won't know a soul there. " He frowned. "I wonder where in the devil he met Daisy. By God, I may be old-fashioned in my ideas, but women run around too much these days to suit me. They meet all kinds of crazy fish. "

Suddenly Mr. Sloane and the lady walked down the steps and mounted their horses.

"Come on," said Mr. Sloane to Tom, "we're late. We've got to go. " And then to me: "Tell him we couldn't wait, will you?"

Tom and I shook hands, the rest of us exchanged a cool nod, and they trotted quickly down the drive, disappearing under the August foliage[6] just as Gatsby, with hat and light overcoat in hand, came out the front door.

Tom was evidently perturbed[7] at Daisy's running around alone, for on the following Saturday night he came with her to Gatsby's party. Perhaps his presence gave the evening its peculiar quality of oppressiveness — it stands out in my memory from Gatsby's other parties that summer. There were the same people, or at least the same sort of people, the same profusion of champagne, the same many-colored, many-keyed commotion, but I felt an unpleasantness in the air, a pervading harshness that hadn't been there before. Or perhaps I had merely grown used to it, grown to accept West Egg as a world complete in itself, with its own standards and its own great figures, second to nothing because it had no consciousness of being so, and now I was looking at it again, through Daisy's eyes. It is invariably saddening to look through new eyes at things upon which you have expended your own powers of adjustment.

They arrived at twilight, and, as we strolled out among the sparkling hundreds, Daisy's voice was playing murmurous tricks in her throat.

"These things excite me so," she whispered.

"If you want to kiss me any time during the evening, Nick, just let me know and I'll be glad to arrange it for you. Just mention my name. Or present a green card. I'm giving out green —"

"Look around," suggested Gatsby.

"I'm looking around. I'm having a marvelous —"

"You must see the faces of many people you've heard about. "

Tom's arrogant eyes roamed the crowd.

"We don't go around very much," he said. "In fact, I was just thinking I don't know a soul here. "

"Perhaps you know that lady. " Gatsby indicated a gorgeous, scarcely human orchid of a woman who sat in state under a white plum tree. Tom and Daisy stared, with that peculiarly unreal feeling that accompanies the recognition of a hitherto ghostly celebrity of the movies.

"She's lovely," said Daisy.

"The man bending over her is her director. "

He took them ceremoniously from group to group:

"Mrs. Buchanan··· and Mr. Buchanan —" After an instant's hesitation he added: "the polo player. "

"Oh no," objected Tom quickly, "not me. "

But evidently the sound of it pleased Gatsby, for Tom remained "the polo player" for the rest of the evening.

"I've never met so many celebrities!" Daisy exclaimed. "I liked that man — what was his name? — with the sort of blue nose. "

Gatsby identified him, adding that he was a small producer.

"Well, I liked him anyhow. "

"I'd a little rather not be the polo player," said Tom pleasantly, "I'd rather look at all these famous people in — in oblivion[8]. "

Daisy and Gatsby danced. I remember being surprised by his graceful, conservative fox-trot — I had never seen him dance before. Then they sauntered over to my house and sat on the steps for half an hour, while at her request I remained watchfully in the garden. "In case there's a fire or a flood," she explained, "or any act of God. "

Tom appeared from his oblivion as we were sitting down to supper together. "Do you mind if I eat with some people over here?" he said. "A fellow's getting off some funny stuff. "

"Go ahead," answered Daisy genially, "and if you want to take down any addresses here's my little gold pencil. " ... she looked around after a moment and told me the girl was "common but pretty," and I knew that except for the half-hour she'd been alone with Gatsby she wasn't having a good time.

We were at a particularly tipsy table. That was my fault — Gatsby had been called to the phone, and I'd enjoyed these same people only two weeks before. But what had amused me then turned septic on the air now.

"How do you feel, Miss Baedeker?"

The girl addressed was trying, unsuccessfully, to slump against my shoulder. At this inquiry she sat up and opened her eyes.

"Wha'?"

A massive and lethargic woman, who had been urging Daisy to play golf with her at the local club to-morrow, spoke in Miss Baedeker's defence:

"Oh, she's all right now. When she's had five or six cocktails she always starts screaming like that. I tell her she ought to leave it alone. "

"I do leave it alone," affirmed the accused hollowly.

"We heard you yelling, so I said to Doc Civet here: ' There's somebody that needs your help, Doc. '"

"She's much obliged, I'm sure," said another friend, without gratitude. "But you got her dress all wet when you stuck her head in the pool. "

"Anything I hate is to get my head stuck in a pool," mumbled Miss Baedeker. "They almost drowned me once over in New Jersey."

"Then you ought to leave it alone," countered Doctor Civet.

"Speak for yourself!" cried Miss Baedeker violently. "Your hand shakes. I wouldn't let you operate on me!"

It was like that. Almost the last thing I remember was standing with Daisy and watching the moving-picture director and his Star. They were still under the white plum tree and their faces were touching except for a pale, thin ray of moonlight between. It occurred to me that he had been very slowly bending toward her all evening to attain this proximity, and even while I watched I saw him stoop one ultimate degree and kiss at her cheek.

"I like her," said Daisy, "I think she's lovely."

But the rest offended her — and inarguably, because it wasn't a gesture but an emotion. She was appalled by West Egg, this unprecedented "place" that Broadway had begotten upon a Long Island fishing village — appalled by its raw vigor that chafed under the old euphemisms and by the too obtrusive[9] fate that herded its inhabitants along a short-cut from nothing to nothing. She saw something awful in the very simplicity she failed to understand.

I sat on the front steps with them while they waited for their car. It was dark here in front; only the bright door sent ten square feet of light volleying out into the soft black morning. Sometimes a shadow moved against a dressing-room blind above, gave way to another shadow, an indefinite procession of shadows, who rouged and powdered in an invisible glass.

"Who is this Gatsby anyhow?" demanded Tom suddenly. "Some big bootlegger?"

"Where'd you hear that?" I inquired.

"I didn't hear it. I imagined it. A lot of these newly rich people are just big bootleggers, you know."

"Not Gatsby," I said shortly.

He was silent for a moment. The pebbles of the drive crunched under his feet.

"Well, he certainly must have strained himself to get this menagerie together. "

A breeze stirred the gray haze of Daisy's fur collar.

"At least they're more interesting than the people we know," she said with an effort.

"You didn't look so interested. "

"Well, I was. "

Tom laughed and turned to me.

"Did you notice Daisy's face when that girl asked her to put her under a cold shower?"

Daisy began to sing with the music in a husky[10], rhythmic whisper, bringing out a meaning in each word that it had never had before and would never have again. When the melody rose, her voice broke up sweetly, following it, in a way contralto voices have, and each change tipped out a little of her warm human magic upon the air.

"Lots of people come who haven't been invited," she said suddenly. "That girl hadn't been invited. They simply force their way in and he's too polite to object. "

"I'd like to know who he is and what he does," insisted Tom. "And I think I'll make a point of finding out. "

"I can tell you right now," she answered. "He owned some drugstores, a lot of drug-stores. He built them up himself. "

The dilatory limousine came rolling up the drive.

"Good night, Nick," said Daisy.

Her glance left me and sought the lighted top of the steps, where Three O'clock in the Morning, a neat, sad little waltz of that year, was drifting out the open door. After all, in the very casualness of Gatsby's party there were romantic possibilities totally absent from her world. What was it up there in the song that seemed to be calling her back inside? What would happen now in the dim, incalculable hours? Perhaps some unbelievable guest would arrive, a person infinitely rare and to be marvelled at, some authentically radiant young girl who with one fresh glance at Gatsby, one moment of magical encounter, would blot out those five years of unwavering devotion.

I stayed late that night, Gatsby asked me to wait until he was free, and I lingered in the garden until the inevitable swimming party had run up, chilled and exalted, from the black beach, until the lights were extinguished in the guest-rooms overhead. When he came down the steps at last the tanned skin was drawn unusually tight on his face, and his eyes were bright and tired.

"She didn't like it," he said immediately.

"Of course she did."

"She didn't like it," he insisted. "She didn't have a good time."

He was silent, and I guessed at his unutterable depression.

"I feel far away from her," he said. "It's hard to make her understand."

"You mean about the dance?"

"The dance?" He dismissed all the dances he had given with a snap of his fingers. "Old sport, the dance is unimportant."

He wanted nothing less of Daisy than that she should go to Tom and say: "I never loved you." After she had obliterated four years with that sentence they could decide upon the more practical measures to be taken. One of them was that, after she was free, they were to go back to Louisville and be married from her house — just as if it were five years ago.

"And she doesn't understand," he said. "She used to be able to understand. We'd sit for hours —"

He broke off and began to walk up and down a desolate path of fruit rinds and discarded favors and crushed flowers.

"I wouldn't ask too much of her," I ventured. "You can't repeat the past."

"Can't repeat the past?" he cried incredulously. "Why of course you can !"

He looked around him wildly, as if the past were lurking here in the shadow of his house, just out of reach of his hand.

"I'm going to fix everything just the way it was before," he said, nodding determinedly. "She'll see. "

He talked a lot about the past, and I gathered that he wanted to recover something, some idea of himself perhaps, that had gone into loving Daisy. His life had been confused and disordered since then, but if he could once return to a certain starting place and go over it all slowly, he could find out what that thing was. . .

One autumn night, five years before, they had been walking down the street when the leaves were falling, and they came to a place where there were no trees and the sidewalk was white with moonlight. They stopped here and turned toward each other. Now it was a cool night with that mysterious excitement in it which comes at the two changes of the year. The quiet lights in the houses were humming out into the darkness and there was a stir and bustle among the stars. Out of the corner of his eye Gatsby saw that the blocks of the sidewalks really formed a ladder and mounted to a secret place above the trees — he could climb to it, if he climbed alone, and once there he could suck on the pap of life, gulp down the incomparable milk of wonder.

His heart beat faster and faster as Daisy's white face came up to his own. He knew that when he kissed this girl, and forever wed his unutterable visions to her perishable breath, his mind would never romp again like the mind of God. So he waited, listening for a moment longer to the tuning-fork that had been struck upon a star. Then he kissed her. At his lips' touch she blossomed for him like a flower and the incarnation was complete.

Through all he said, even through his appalling sentimentality, I was reminded of something — an elusive rhythm, a fragment of lost words, that I had heard somewhere a long time ago. For a moment a phrase tried to take shape in my mouth and my lips parted like a dumb man's, as though there was more struggling upon them than a wisp of startled air. But they made no sound, and what I had almost remembered was uncommunicable forever.

Notes:

1. antecedent *n.* 前事，前身

   E. g. We shall first look briefly at the historical antecedents of this theory.

2. trot *vt.* 快步走

   E. g. I trotted down the steps and out to the shed.

3. senile *adj.* 衰老的，年老的

   E. g. All his movements were those of a senile man.

4. gruffly *adv.* 粗暴地，粗声地

   E. g. When he left he cut short the father's nervous thanks gruffly.

5. haughtily *adv.* 傲慢地

   E. g. You became to act haughtily since we last met.

6. foliage *n.* 树叶

   E. g. The path was completely covered by the dense foliage.

7. perturb *vt.* 使烦恼，使不安

   E. g. Her sudden appearance did not seem to perturb him in the least.

8. oblivion *n.* 遗忘

   E. g. It seems that the so-called new theory is likely to sink into oblivion.

9. obtrusive *adj.* 显眼的，过分突出的

   E. g. The sofa would be less obtrusive in a paler colour.

10. husky *adj.* 沙哑的，深沉的

    E. g. His voice was husky with grief.

Questions:

1. How is the theme of class distinctions explored in the episode

when three riders (Tom, Mr. Sloane, and Mrs. Sloane) stopped at Gatsby's for a drink?

2. Why did the three riders ride away without waiting for Gatsby?

3. How did Tom and Daisy feel about the party?

4. Why did Gatsby ask Nick to stay late after the party?

5. What can be inferred from the conversation between Gatsby and Nick?

Analysis of Chapter Six

Chapter Six further explores the topic of social class as it relates to Gatsby. Nick's description of Gatsby's early life reveals the sensitivity to status that spurs Gatsby on. His humiliation at having to work as a janitor in college contrasts with the promise that he experiences when he meets Dan Cody, who represents the attainment of everything that Gatsby wants. Acutely aware of his poverty, the young Gatsby develops a powerful obsession with amassing wealth and status. Gatsby's act of re-christening himself symbolizes his desire to jettison his lower-class identity and recast himself as the wealthy man he envisions.

It is easy to see how a man who has gone to such great lengths to a-chieve wealth and luxury would find Daisy so alluring: for her, the aura of wealth and luxury comes effortlessly. She is able to take her position for granted, and she becomes, for Gatsby, the epitome of everything that he invented "Jay Gatsby" to achieve. As is true throughout the book, Gatsby's power to make his dreams real is what makes him "great." In this chapter, it becomes clear that his most powerfully realized dream is his own identity, his sense of self. It is important to realize, in addition, that Gatsby's conception of Daisy is itself a dream. He thinks of her as the sweet girl who loved him in Louisville, blinding himself to the reality that she would never desert her own class and background to be with him.

Fitzgerald continues to explore the theme of social class by illustrating the contempt with which the aristocratic East Eggers, Tom and the Sloanes, regard Gatsby. Even though Gatsby seems to have as much money as they do, he lacks their sense of social nuance and easy, aristocratic grace. As a result, they mock and despise him for being "new money." As the division between East Egg and West Egg shows, even among the very rich there are class distinctions.

中文译文：

这一切都是他好久以后才告诉我的，但是我在这里写了下来，为的是驳斥早先那些关于他的来历的荒唐谣言，那些都是连一点儿影子也没有的事。再有，他是在一个十分混乱的时刻告诉我的，那时关于他的种种传闻使我已经到了将信将疑的地步。所以我现在利用这个短暂的停顿，仿佛趁盖茨比喘口气的机会，把这些误解清除一下。

在我和他的交往之中，这也是一个停顿。有好几个星期我既没和他见面，也没在电话里听到过他的声音——大部分时间我是在纽约跟乔丹四处跑，同时极力讨她那老朽的姑妈的欢心——但是我终于在一个星期日下午到他家去了。我待了还没两分钟就有一个人把汤姆·布坎农带进来喝杯酒。我自然吃了一惊，但是真正令人惊奇的却是以前竟然还没发生过这样的事。

他们一行三人是骑马来的——汤姆和一个姓斯隆的男人，还有一个身穿棕色骑装的漂亮女人，是以前来过的。

"我很高兴见到你们，"盖茨比站在阳台上说，"我很高兴你们光临。"

仿佛承他们的情似的！

"请坐，请坐。抽支香烟或者抽支雪茄。"他在屋子里跑来跑去，忙着打铃喊人，"我马上就让人给你们送点什么喝的来。"

汤姆的到来使他受到很大震动。但是他反正会感到局促不安，直到他招待了他们一点什么才行，因为他也隐约知道他们就是为了这个才来的。斯隆先生什么都不要。来杯柠檬水？不要，谢谢。来点香槟吧？什么都不要，谢谢……对不起……

"你们骑马骑得很痛快吧？"

"这一带的路很好。"

"大概来往的汽车……"

"是嘛。"

　　刚才介绍的时候汤姆只当彼此是初次见面，此刻盖茨比突然情不自禁地掉脸朝着他。

　　"我相信我们以前在哪儿见过面，布坎农先生。"

　　"噢，是的，"汤姆生硬而有礼貌地说，他显然并不记得，"我们是见过的，我记得很清楚。"

　　"大概两个星期以前。"

　　"对啦。你是跟尼克在一起的。"

　　"我认识你太太。"盖茨比接下去说，几乎有一点挑衅的意味。

　　"是吗？"

　　汤姆掉脸朝着我。

　　"你住在这附近吗，尼克？"

　　"就在隔壁。"

　　"是吗？"

　　斯隆光生没有参加谈话，而是大模大样地仰靠在他的椅子上。那个女的也没说什么—直到两杯姜汁威士忌下肚之后，她忽然变得有说有笑了。

　　"我们都来参加你下次的晚会，盖茨比先生，"她提议说，"你看好不好？"

　　"当然好了。你们能来，我太高兴了。"

　　"那很好吧，"斯隆先生毫不承情地说，"呃——我看该回家了。"

　　"请不要忙着走。"盖茨比劝他们。他现在已经能控制自己，并且他要多看看汤姆。"你们何不——你们何不就在这儿吃晚饭呢？说不定纽约还有一些别的人会来。"

　　"你到我家来吃晚饭，"那位太太热烈地说，"你们俩都来。"

　　这也包括了我。斯隆先生站起身来。

　　"我是当真的，"她坚持说，"我真希望你们来。都坐得下。"

　　盖茨比疑惑地看着我。他想去，他也看不出斯隆先生打定了主意不让他去。

　　"我恐怕去不了。"我说。

　　"那么你来。"她极力怂恿盖茨比一个人。

　　斯隆先生凑着她耳边咕哝了一下。

267

"我们如果马上就走，一点都不会晚的。"她固执地大声说。

"我没有马，"盖茨比说，"我在军队里骑过马的，但是我自己从来没买过马。我只好开车跟你们走。对不起，等一下我就来。"

我们其余几个人走到外面阳台上，斯隆和那位太太站在一边。开始气冲冲地交谈。

"我的天，我相信这家伙真的要来，"汤姆说，"难道他不知道她并不要他来吗？"

"她说她要他来的嘛。"

"她要举行盛大的宴会，他在那儿一个人都不会认得的。"他皱皱眉头，"我真纳闷他到底在哪儿认识黛西的。天晓得，也许我的思想太古板，但是这年头女人家到处乱跑，我可看不惯。她们遇上各式各样的怪物。"

忽然间斯隆先生和那位太太走下台阶，随即上了马。

"来吧，"斯隆先生对汤姆说，"我们已经晚了。我们一定得走了。"然后对我说，"请你告诉他我们不能等了，行吗？"

汤姆跟我握握手，我们其余几个人彼此冷冷地点了点头，他们就骑着马沿着车道小跑起来，很快消失在八月的树荫里，这时，盖茨比手里拿着帽子和薄大衣，正从大门里走出来。

汤姆对于黛西单独四处乱跑显然放不下心，因为下一个星期六晚上他和她要一道来参加盖茨比的晚会。也许是由于他的在场，那次晚会有一种特殊的沉闷气氛——它鲜明地留在我记忆里，与那个夏天盖茨比的其他晚会迥然不同。还是那些同样的人，或者至少是同一类的人，同样的源源不绝的香槟，同样的五颜六色、七嘴八舌的喧闹，可是我觉得无形中有一种不愉快的感觉，弥漫着一种以前从没有过的恶感。要不然，或许是我本来已经逐渐习惯于这一套，逐渐认为西卵是一个独立完整的世界，自有它独特的标准和大人物，首屈一指因为它并不感到相形见绌，而此刻我却通过黛西的眼睛重新去看这一切。要通过新的眼睛去看那些你已经花了很多气力才适应的事物，那总是令人难受的。

他们在黄昏时刻到达，然后当我们几人漫步走到几百名珠光宝气的客人当中时，黛西的声音在她喉咙里玩着呢呢喃喃的花样。

"这些东西真叫我兴奋，"她低声说，"如果你今晚上任何时候想吻我，尼克，你让我知道好了，我一定高兴为你安排。只要提我的名字就行，或者出示一张绿色的请帖。我正在散发绿色的……"

"四面看看。"盖茨比敦促她。

"我正在四面看啊。我真开心……"

"你一定看到许多你听见过的人物的面孔。"

汤姆傲慢的眼睛向人群一扫。

"我们平时不大外出，"他说，"实际上，我刚才正在想我这里一个人都不认识。"

"也许你认得那位小姐。"盖茨比指出一位如花似玉的美人，端庄地坐在一棵白梅树下。汤姆和黛西目不转睛地看着，认出来这是一位一向只在银幕上见到的大明星，几乎不敢相信是真的。

"她真美啊。"黛西说。

"站在她身边弯着腰的是她的导演。"

盖茨比礼貌周全地领着他们向一群又一群的客人介绍。

"布坎农夫人……布坎农先生，"踌躇片刻之后，他又补充说，"马球健将。"

"不是的，"汤姆连忙否认，"我可不是。"

但是盖茨比显然喜欢这个名称的含意，因为以后整个晚上汤姆就一直是"马球健将"。

"我从来没见过这么多名人，"黛西兴奋地说，"我喜欢那个人……他叫什么名字来着？就是鼻子有点发青的那个。"

盖茨比报了那人的姓名，并说他是一个小制片商。

"哦，我反正喜欢他。"

"我宁愿不做马球健将，"汤姆愉快地说，"我倒宁愿以……以一个默默无闻的人的身份看看这么多有名的人。"

黛西和盖茨比跳了舞。我记得我当时正在为看到他跳着优雅的老式狐步舞感到很诧异——我以前从未见过他跳舞。后来他俩溜到我家，在我的台阶上坐了半个小时，她让我待在园子里把风。"万一着火或是发大水。"她解释道，"或是什么天灾啦。"

我们正在一起坐下来吃晚饭时，汤姆又从默默无闻中出现了。"我跟那边几个人一起吃饭，行吗？"他说，"有一个家伙正在大讲笑话。"

"去吧,"黛西和颜悦色地回答,"如果你要留几个住址下来,这里是我的小金铅笔。"……过了一会她四面张望了一下,对我说那个女孩"俗气可是漂亮",于是我明白除了她单独跟盖茨比待在一起的半小时之外,她玩得并不开心。

我们这一桌的人喝得特别醉。这得怪我不好——盖茨比被叫去听电话,又碰巧两星期前我还觉得这些人挺有意思,但是当时我觉得好玩的晚上变得索然无味了。

"你感觉怎么样,贝达克小姐?"

我同她说话的这个姑娘正在想慢慢倒在我的肩上,可是并没成功。听到这个问题,她坐起身来,睁开了眼睛。

"什么?"

一个大块头、懒洋洋的女人,本来一直在怂恿黛西明天到本地俱乐部去和她一起打高尔夫球的,现在来为贝达克小姐辩白了:

"噢,她现在什么事也没有了。她每次五六杯鸡尾酒下肚,总是这样大喊大叫。我跟她说她不应当喝酒。"

"我是不喝酒。"受到指责的那个人随口说道。

"我们听到你嚷嚷,于是我跟这位希维特大夫说:'那里有人需要您帮忙,大夫。'"

"她非常感激,我相信,"另一位朋友用并不感激的口气说,"可是你把她的头接到游泳池里去,把她的衣服全搞湿了。"

"我最恨的就是把我的头接到游泳池里,"贝达克小姐咕哝着说,"有一回在新泽西州他们差一点没把我淹死。"

"那你就不应当喝酒嘛。"希维特大夫堵她的嘴说。

"说你自己吧!"贝达克小姐激烈地大喊道,"你的手发抖。我才不会让你给我开刀哩!"

情况就是这样。我记得的差不多是最后的一件事是我和黛西站在一起望着那位电影导演和他的"大明星"。他们仍然在那棵白梅树下,他们的脸快要贴到一起了,中间只隔着一线淡淡的月光。我忽然想到他整个晚上大概一直在非常非常慢地弯下腰来,才终于和她靠得这么近,然后正在我望着的这一刻,我看见他弯下最后一点距离,亲吻了她的面颊。

"我喜欢她,"黛西说,"我觉得她美极了。"

但是其他的一切她都讨厌——而且是不容置辩的，因为这并不是一种姿态，而是一种感情。她十分厌恶西卵，这个由百老汇强加在一个长岛渔村上的没有先例的"胜地"——厌恶它那不安于陈旧的委婉辞令的粗犷活力，厌恶那种驱使它的居民沿着一条捷径从零跑到零的过分突兀的命运。她正是在这种她不了解的单纯之中看到了什么可怕的东西。

他们在等车子开过来的时候，我和他们一同坐在大门前的台阶上。这里很暗，只有敞开的门向幽暗的黎明射出十平方英尺的亮光。有时楼上化妆室的遮帘上有一个人影掠过，然后又出现一个人影，络绎不绝的女客对着一面看不见的镜子涂脂抹粉。

"这个姓盖茨比的究竟是谁？"汤姆突然质问我，"一个大私酒贩子？"

"你从哪儿听来的？"我问他。

"我不是听来的。我猜的。有很多这样的暴发户都是大私酒贩子，你要知道。"

"盖茨比可不是。"我简单地说。

他沉默了一会。汽车道上的小石子在他脚底下咔嚓作响。

"我说，他一定花了很大的气力才搜罗到这么一大帮牛头马面。"

一阵微风吹动了黛西的毛茸茸的灰皮领子。

"至少他们比我们认得的人有趣。"她有点勉强地说。

"看上去你并不怎么感兴趣嘛。"

"噢，我很感兴趣。"

汤姆哈哈一笑，把脸转向我。

"当那个女孩让她给她来个冷水淋浴的时候，你有没有注意到黛西的脸？"

黛西跟着音乐沙哑而有节奏地低声唱了起来，把每个字都唱出一种以前从未有过，以后也决不会再有的意义。当曲调升高的时候，她的嗓音也跟着改变，悠扬婉转，正是女低音的本色，而且每一点变化都在空气中散发出一点她那温暖的人情味很浓的魔力。

"来的人有好多并不是邀请来的，"她忽然说，"那个女孩子就没有接到邀请。他们干脆闯上门来，而他又太客气，不好意思

271

谢绝。"

"我很想知道他是什么人，又是干什么的，"汤姆固执地说，"并且我一定要去打听清楚。"

"我马上就可以告诉你，"她答道，"他是开药房的，好多家药房。都是他一手创办起来的。"

那辆姗姗来迟的大型轿车沿着汽车道开了上来。

"晚安，尼克。"黛西说。

她的目光离开了我，朝着灯光照亮的最上一层台阶看去，在那里一支当年流行的哀婉动人的小华尔兹舞曲《凌晨三点钟》正从敞开的大门传出来。话说回来，正是在盖茨比的晚会上随随便便的气氛之中，才有她自己的世界中完全没有的种种浪漫的可能性。那支歌曲里面有什么东西仿佛在呼唤她回到里面去呢？现在在这幽暗的、难以预测的时辰里会发生什么事情呢？也许会光临一位令人难以置信的客人，一位世上少有的、令人惊异不已的佳人，一位真正艳丽夺目的少女，只要对盖茨比看上一眼，只要一刹那魔术般的相逢，她就可以把五年来坚贞不移的爱情一笔勾销。

✿ Answers for questions

1. Gatsby, ever the good host, receives them warmly. The three drop by to drink his liquor and little else. Their concern for him is minimal and their purposes mercenary. Gatsby invites the group to supper, but Mrs. Sloane hastily refuses; perhaps ashamed of her own rudeness, she then half-heartedly offers Gatsby and Nick an invitation to dine at her home.

2. Under the pretense of sociability, Mrs. Sloane invites Gatsby to join them for dinner. The three riders know the invitation is rhetorical — just a formality that is not meant to be accepted. Gatsby, however, is unable to sense the invitation's hollowness and agrees to attend. The group, appalled at his behavior, sneaks out without him, marveling at his poor taste.

3. At the party, Gatsby tries his best to impress the Buchanans by pointing out all the famous guests. Tom and Daisy, however, are re-

markably unimpressed, although Tom does seem to be having a better time after he finds a woman to pursue and Daisy, not surprisingly, is drawn to the luminescent quality of the movie star. By and large, though, Tom and especially Daisy are unimpressed by the West Eggers. The "raw vigor" of the party disgusts them, offending their "old money" sensibilities, providing another example of how the Buchanans and the people they represent discriminate on the basis of social class.

    4. After Tom and Daisy head home, Nick and Gatsby debrief the evening's events. Gatsby, worried that Daisy didn't have a good time, shares his concern with Nick.

    5. Gatsby is living in the past. He has his dream of reuniting with Daisy. Although it would be going too far to say Gatsby is weak in character, he is unable to function in the present. He must continually return to the past, revising it and modifying it until it takes on epic qualities which, sadly, can never be realized in the everyday world. Gatsby, just as he is at his parties and with the social elite, is once again marginalized, forced to the fringes by the vivacity of his dream.

References

[1] http://www. brunswick. k12. me. us/hdwyer/files/2012/07/portrait. jpg（图片来源）

[2] http://www. pbs. org/wnet/americannovel/timeline/fitzgerald. html

[3] http://media. npr. org/assets/bakertaylor/covers/t/the – great – gatsby/9780 743273565_custom – s6 – c30. jpg? t = 1340884943（图片来源）

[4] http://www. cliffsnotes. com/literature/g/the – great – gatsby/the – great – gatsby – at – a – glance

[5] http://www. cliffsnotes. com/literature/g/the – great – gatsby/character – list

[6] http://www. sparknotes. com/lit/gatsby/summary. html

[7] https://ebooks. adelaide. edu. au/f/fitzgerald/f_scott/gatsby/chapter6. html

[8] http://www. sparknotes. com/lit/gatsby/section6. rhtml

[9] http://www. kanunu8. com/book/3836/39279. html

Unit 13
Ernest Hemingway (1899 – 1961)

🎇 Bibliography

Ernest Hemingway (1899 – 1961), born in Oak Park, Illinois, started his career as a writer in a newspaper office in Kansas City at the age of seventeen. After the United States entered the First World War, he joined a volunteer ambulance unit in the Italian army. Serving at the front, he was wounded, was decorated by the Italian Government, and spent considerable time in hospitals. After his return to the United States, he became a reporter for Canadian and American newspapers and was soon sent back to Europe to cover such events as the Greek Revolution.

During the twenties, Hemingway became a member of the group of expatriate Americans in Paris, which he described in his first important work, *The Sun Also Rises* (1926). Equally successful was *A Farewell to Arms* (1929), the study of an American ambulance officer's disillusionment in the war and his role as a deserter. Hemingway used his experiences as a reporter during the civil war in Spain as the background for his most ambitious novel, *For Whom the Bell Tolls* (1940). Among his later works, the most outstanding is the short novel, *The Old Man and the Sea* (1952), the story of an old fisherman's journey, his long and lonely struggle with a fish and the sea, and his victory in defeat.

Hemingway – himself a great sportsman – liked to portray soldiers, hunters, bullfighters: tough, at times primitive people whose courage and honesty are set against the brutal ways of modern society, and who in this confrontation lose hope and faith. His straightforward prose, his spare dialogue, and his predilection for understatement are particularly effective in his short stories, some of which are collected in *Men Without Women* (1927) and *The Fifth Column and the First Forty-Nine Stories* (1938). Hemingway died in Idaho in 1961.

The Old Man and the Sea

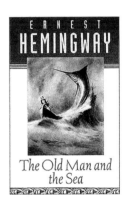

The Old Man and the Sea was published 1952 after the bleakest ten years in Hemingway's literary career. His last major work, *Across the River and into the Trees*, was condemned as unintentional self-parody, and people began to think that Hemingway had exhausted his store of ideas.

The Old Man and the Sea, published in its entirety in one edition of Life magazine, was an instant success. In two days the September 1st edition of Life sold 5,300,000 copies and the book version sold 153,000. The novella soared to the top of the best-seller list and remained there for six months. The Old Man and the Sea was awarded the 1953 Pulitizer Prize and American Academy of Arts and Letters' Award of Merit Medal for the Novel and played a significant role in Hemingway's selection for the Nobel Prize for Literature in 1954.

Characters in *The Old Man and the Sea*

1. Santiago—The novella's central character. A dedicated fisherman who taught Manolin everything he knows about fishing, Santiago is now old and poor and has gone 84 days without a catch.
2. Manolin—A young man from the fishing village who has fished with Santiago since the age of five and now cares for the old man. Manolin recently began fishing with another fisherman whom his parents con-

sider luckier than Santiago.

3. Martin—The owner of the Terrace (his name is Spanish for St. Martin), he sends food and drink to Santiago through Manolin.

4. Rogelio—A man of the village who on occasion helps Santiago with the fishing net.

5. Perico—A man at the bodega (his name is Spanish for St. Peter, an apostle and fisherman) who gives Santiago newspapers to read.

6. Marlin—An eighteen-foot bluish billfish and a catch of legendary proportions.

7. Mako—A mackerel shark (dentuso in Spanish) that is a voracious and frightening killer known for its rows of large, sharp teeth.

8. Shovel-nosed sharks—The scavenger sharks (galanos in Spanish) that destroy the marlin.

9. Pedrico—A fisherman in the village who looks after Santiago's skiff and gear and receives the marlin's head to use in fish traps.

10. Tourists—A man and woman at the Terrace who see the marlin's skeleton and, misunderstanding a waiter's explanation of what happened, think the skeleton is that of a shark.

Summary

For 84 days, the old fisherman Santiago has caught nothing. Alone, impoverished, and facing his own mortality, Santiago is now considered unlucky. So Manolin (Santiago's fishing partner until recently and the young man Santiago has taught since the age of five) has been constrained by his parents to fish in another, more productive boat. Every evening, though, when Santiago again returns empty-handed, Manolin helps carry home the old man's equipment, keeps him company, and brings him food.

On the morning of the 85th day, Santiago sets out before dawn on a three-day odyssey that takes him far out to sea. In search of an epic catch, he eventually does snag a marlin of epic proportions, enduring tremendous hardship to land the great fish. He straps the marlin along the length of his skiff and heads for home, hardly believing his own victory. Within an hour, a mako shark attacks the marlin, tearing away a great hunk of its flesh and mutilating Santiago's prize. Santiago fights the mako, enduring great suffering, and eventually kills it with his harpoon, which he loses in the struggle.

The great tear in the marlin's flesh releases the fish's blood and scent into the water, attracting packs of shovel-nosed sharks. With whatever equipment remains on board, Santiago repeatedly fights off the packs of these scavengers, enduring exhaustion and great physical pain, even tearing something in his chest. Eventually, the sharks pick the marlin clean. Defeated, Santiago reaches shore and beaches the skiff. Alone in the dark, he looks back at the marlin's skeleton in the reflection from a street light and then stumbles home to his shack, falling face down onto his cot in exhaustion.

The next morning, Manolin finds Santiago in his hut and cries over the old man's injuries. Manolin fetches coffee and hears from the other fisherman what he had already seen — that the marlin's skeleton lashed to the skiff is eighteen feet long, the greatest fish the village has known. Manolin sits with Santiago until he awakes and then gives the old man some coffee. The old man tells Manolin that he was beaten. But Manolin reassures him that the great fish didn't beat him and that they will fish together again, that luck doesn't matter, and that the old man still has much to teach him.

That afternoon, some tourists see the marlin's skeleton waiting to go out with the tide and ask a waiter what it is. Trying to explain what happened to the marlin, the waiter replies, "Eshark. " But the tourists misunderstand and assume that's what the skeleton is.

Back in his shack, with Manolin sitting beside him, Santiago sleeps again and dreams of the young lions he had seen along the coast of Africa when he was a young man.

Comments on *The Old Man and the Sea*

The Old Man and the Sea was an enormous success for Ernest Hemingway. At first glance, the story appears to be an extremely simple story of an old Cuban fisherman (Santiago), who catches an enormously large fish then loses it again. But, there's much more to the story than that.

In the novella, Hemingway has stripped down the basic story of human life to its basic elements. A single human being, represented by the fisherman Santiago, is blessed with the intelligence to do big things and to dream of even grander things. Santiago shows great skill in devising ways to tire out the huge fish he has hooked and ways to conserve his strength in order to land it. Yet in the struggle to survive, this human must often suffer and even destroy the very thing he dreams of. Thus Santiago cuts his hands badly and loses the fish to sharks in the process of trying to get his catch back to shore. Yet the struggle to achieve one's dreams is still worthwhile, for without dreams, a human remains a mere physical presence in the universe, with no creative or spiritual dimension. And so at the end of the story, Santiago, in spite of his great loss, physical pain, and exhaustion, is still "dreaming about the lions"—the same ones he saw in Africa when he was younger and would like to see again.

Against the seeming indifference of the universe, love is often the only force that endures. This force is best seen in the relationship of Santiago and Manolin, which has endured since Manolin's early childhood. Over the years, Santiago has taught Manolin to fish and given him companionship and a sense of self-worth that Manolin failed to get from his own father. Manolin in return shows his love for Santiago by bringing him food and by weeping for him when he sees how much he suffered in fighting the marlin. Manolin also plans to take care of Santiago during the coming winter by bringing him clothing and water for washing.

Santiago's love, of course, extends to other people as well. He loved his wife when they were married, though when she died he had to take down her portrait because it made him feel lonely. Similarly, even in his suffering he thinks of others, remembering his promise to send the fish head to his friend Pederico to use as bait. Santiago's love also extends to include nature itself, even though he has often suffered at its hands. His love for all living creatures, whether fish, birds, or turtles, is often described, as is his love for the sea, which he sees as a woman who gives or withholds favors. Some of the younger fishermen, in contrast, often spoke of the sea as a "contestant" or even an "enemy. "

Introduction to Part One

For 84 days, the old fisherman Santiago has caught nothing, returning empty-handed in his skiff to the small Cuban fishing village where he lives. After 40 days without a catch, Manolin's father has insisted that Manolin, the young man Santiago taught to fish from the age of five, fish in another boat.

This evening, as every evening, Manolin meets the old man to help carry the coiled line, gaff, harpoon, and sail back to his shack. Along the way, Manolin tries to cheer Santiago by reminding him of the time, when they were fishing together, that the old man went 87 days without a fish and then they caught big fish for three weeks.

On their way home, Manolin buys Santiago a beer at the Terrace. Some of the other fishermen make fun of Santiago; others look at him and are sad, speaking politely about the current and the depths at which they had fished and what they had seen at sea. The fishermen who were successful this day have taken their marlin to the fish house or their sharks to the shark factory. Manolin asks if he can get sardines for Santiago tomorrow. Santiago at first tells him to go play baseball but eventually relents. They reminisce a while, talk of Santiago's plans for going out the next day, and then go to Santiago's shack. Because Santiago has nothing to eat, Manolin fetches Santiago the dinner that the Terrace owner, Martin, sends for free, as he has many times before. As Santiago eats, he and the boy talk of baseball, the great Joe DiMaggio, and other topics of mutual interest.

The next morning, Santiago picks up the boy at his house. They have coffee (which is all that Santiago will have all day) at an early morning spot that serves fishermen. The boy fetches sardines and fresh bait and helps the old man ease his skiff into the water. They wish each other good luck, and the old man rows away.

From　　　　*The Old Man and the Sea*
Part One

He was an old man who fished alone in a skiff[1] in the Gulf Stream and he had gone eighty-four days now without taking a fish. In the first forty days a boy had been with him. But after forty days without a fish the boy's parents had told him that the old man was now definitely and finally salao, which is the worst form of unlucky, and the boy had gone at their orders in another boat which caught three good fish the first week. It made the boy sad to see the old man come in each day with his skiff empty and he always went down to help him carry either the coiled lines or the gaff[2] and harpoon[3] and the sail that was furled[4] around the mast. The sail was patched with flour sacks and, furled, it looked like the flag of permanent defeat.

The old man was thin and gaunt[5] with deep wrinkles in the back of his neck. The brown blotches[6] of the benevolent skin cancer the sun brings from its reflection on the tropic sea were on his cheeks. The blotches ran well down the sides of his face and his hands had the deep-creased scars from handling heavy fish on the cords. But none of these scars were fresh. They were as old as erosions in a fishless desert.

Everything about him was old except his eyes and they were the same color as the sea and were cheerful and undefeated.

"Santiago," the boy said to him as they climbed the bank from where the skiff was hauled up. "I could go with you again. We've made some money."

The old man had taught the boy to fish and the boy loved him.

"No," the old man said. "You're with a lucky boat. Stay with them. "

"But remember how you went eighty-seven days without fish and then we caught big ones every day for three weeks. "

"I remember," the old man said. "I know you did not leave me because you doubted. "

"It was papa made me leave. I am a boy and I must obey him. "

"I know," the old man said. "It is quite normal. "

"He hasn't much faith. "

"No," the old man said. "But we have. Haven't we?"

"Yes," the boy said. "Can I offer you a beer on the Terrace and then we'll take the stuff home. "

"Why not?" the old man said. "Between fishermen. "

They sat on the Terrace and many of the fishermen made fun of the old man and he was not angry. Others, of the older fishermen, looked at him and were sad. But they did not show it and they spoke politely about the current and the depths they had drifted their lines at and the steady good weather and of what they had seen. The successful fishermen of that day were already in and had butchered their marlin out and carried them laid full length across two planks[7], with two men staggering at the end of each plank, to the fish house where they waited for the ice truck to carry them to the market in Havana. Those who had caught sharks had taken them to the shark factory on the other side of the cove where they were hoisted on a block and tackle, their livers removed, their fins cut off and their hides skinned out and their flesh cut into strips for salting.

When the wind was in the east a smell came across the harbour from the shark factory; but today there was only the faint edge of the odour because the wind had backed into the north and then dropped off and it was pleasant and sunny on the Terrace.

"Santiago," the boy said.

"Yes," the old man said. He was holding his glass and thinking of many years ago.

"Can I go out to get sardines for you for tomorrow?"

"No. Go and play baseball. I can still row and Rogelio will throw the net. "

"I would like to go. If I cannot fish with you. I would like to serve in some way. "

"You bought me a beer," the old man said. "You are already a man. "

"How old was I when you first took me in a boat?"

"Five and you nearly were killed when I brought the fish in too green and he nearly tore the boat to pieces. Can you remember?"

"I can remember the tail slapping and banging and the thwart[8] breaking and the noise of the clubbing. I can remember you throwing me into the bow where the wet coiled lines were and feeling the whole boat shiver and the noise of you clubbing him like chopping a tree down and the sweet blood smell all over me. "

"Can you really remember that or did I just tell it to you?"

"I remember everything from when we first went together. "

The old man looked at him with his sun-burned, confident loving eyes.

"If you were my boy I'd take you out and gamble," he said. "But you are your father's and your mother's and you are in a lucky boat. "

"May I get the sardines? I know where I can get four baits too. "

"I have mine left from today. I put them in salt in the box. "

"Let me get four fresh ones. "

"One," the old man said. His hope and his confidence had never gone. But now they

were freshening as when the breeze rises.

"Two," the boy said.

"Two," the old man agreed. "You didn't steal them?"

"I would," the boy said. "But I bought these. "

"Thank you," the old man said. He was too simple to wonder

when he had attained humility. But he knew he had attained it and he knew it was not disgraceful and it carried no loss of true pride.

"Tomorrow is going to be a good day with this current," he said.

"Where are you going?" the boy asked.

"Far out to come in when the wind shifts. I want to be out before it is light. "

"I'll try to get him to work far out," the boy said. "Then if you hook something truly big we can come to your aid. "

"He does not like to work too far out. "

"No," the boy said. "But I will see something that he cannot see such as a bird working and get him to come out after dolphin. " "Are his eyes that bad?" "He is almost blind. " "It is strange," the old man said. "He never went turtle-ing. That is what kills the eyes. " "But you went turtle-ing for years off the Mosquito Coast and your eyes are good. "

"I am a strange old man"

"But are you strong enough now for a truly big fish?"

"I think so. And there are many tricks. "

"Let us take the stuff home," the boy said. "So I can get the cast net and go after the sardines. "

They picked up the gear from the boat. The old man carried the mast on his shoulder and the boy carried the wooden boat with the coiled, hard-braided brown lines, the gaff and the harpoon with its shaft. The box with the baits was under the stern of the skiff along with the club that was used to subdue the big fish when they were brought a-longside. No one would steal from the old man but it was better to take the sail and the heavy lines home as the dew was bad for them and, though he was quite sure no local people would steal from him, the old man thought that a gaff and a harpoon were needless temptations to leave in a boat.

They walked up the road together to the old man's shack and went in through its open door. The old man leaned the mast with its wrapped sail against the wall and the boy put the box and the other gear beside it. The mast was nearly as long as the one room of the shack. The shack was made of the tough budshields of the royal palm which are called guano and in it there was a bed, a table, one chair, and a place on the dirt floor to cook with charcoal. On the brown walls of the flattened, overlapping leaves of the sturdy fibered guano there was a picture in color of the Sacred Heart of Jesus and another of the Virgin of Cobre. These were relics[9] of his wife. Once there had been a tinted photograph of his wife on the wall but he had taken it down because it made him too lonely to see it and it was on the shelf in the corner under his clean shirt.

"What do you have to eat?" the boy asked.

"A pot of yellow rice with fish. Do you want some?"

"No. I will eat at home. Do you want me to make the fire?"

"No. I will make it later on. Or I may eat the rice cold. "

"May I take the cast net?"

"Of course. "

There was no cast net and the boy remembered when they had sold it. But they went through this fiction every day. There was no pot of yellow rice and fish and the boy knew this too. "Eighty-five is a lucky number," the old man said. "How would you like to see me bring one in that dressed out over a thousand pounds?" "I'll get the cast net and go for sardines. Will you sit in the sun in the doorway?"

"Yes. I have yesterday's paper and I will read the baseball. " The boy did not know whether yesterday's paper was a fiction too. But the old man brought it out from under the bed.

"Perico gave it to me at the bodega[10]," he explained. "I'll be back when I have the sardines. I'll keep yours and mine together on ice and we can share them in the morning. When I come back you can tell me about the baseball. "

"The Yankees cannot lose. "

"But I fear the Indians of Cleveland. "

"Have faith in the Yankees my son. Think of the great DiMaggio. "

"I fear both the Tigers of Detroit and the Indians of Cleveland. "

"Be careful or you will fear even the Reds of Cincinnati and the White Sax of Chicago. "

"You study it and tell me when I come back. "

"Do you think we should buy a terminal of the lottery with an eighty-five? Tomorrow is the eighty-fifth day. " "We can do that," the boy said. "But what about the eighty-seven of your great record?"

"It could not happen twice. Do you think you can find an eighty-five?"

"I can order one. One sheet. That's two dollars and a half. Who can we borrow that from?"

"That's easy. I can always borrow two dollars and a half. "

"I think perhaps I can too. But I try not to borrow. First you borrow. Then you beg. "

"Keep warm old man," the boy said. "Remember we are in September. "

"The month when the great fish come," the old man said. "Anyone can be a fisherman in May. "

"I go now for the sardines," the boy said.

When the boy came back the old man was asleep in the chair and the sun was down. The boy took the old army blanket off the bed and spread it over the back of the chair and over the old man's shoulders. They were strange shoulders, still powerful although very old, and the neck was still strong too and the creases did not show so much when the old man was asleep and his head fallen forward. His shirt had been patched so many times that it was like the sail and the patches were faded to many different shades by the sun. The old man's head was very old though and with his eyes closed there was no life in his face. The newspaper lay across his knees and the weight of his arm held it there in the evening breeze. He was barefooted.

The boy left him there and when he came back the old man was still asleep.

"Wake up old man," the boy said and put his hand on one of the old man's knees.

The old man opened his eyes and for a moment he was coming back from a long way away. Then he smiled.

"What have you got?" he asked.

"Supper," said the boy. "We're going to have supper."

"I'm not very hungry."

"Come on and eat. You can't fish and not eat."

"I have," the old man said getting up and taking the newspaper and folding it. Then he started to fold the blanket.

"Keep the blanket around you," the boy said. "You'll not fish without eating while I'm alive."

"Then live a long time and take care of yourself," the old man said. "What are we eating?"

"Black beans and rice, fried bananas, and some stew."

The boy had brought them in a two-decker metal container from the Terrace. The two sets of knives and forks and spoons were in his pocket with a paper napkin wrapped around each set.

"Who gave this to you?"

"Martin. The owner."

"I must thank him."

"I thanked him already," the boy said. "You don't need to thank him."

"I'll give him the belly meat of a big fish," the old man said. "Has he done this for us more than once?"

"I think so."

"I must give him something more than the belly meat then. He is very thoughtful for us."

"He sent two beers."

"I like the beer in cans best."

"I know. But this is in bottles, Hatuey beer, and I take back the bottles."

"That's very kind of you," the old man said. "Should we eat?"

"I've been asking you to," the boy told him gently. "I have not wished to open the container until you were ready."

"I'm ready now," the old man said. "I only needed time to wash."

Where did you wash? the boy thought. The village water supply was two streets down the road. I must have water here for him, the boy thought, and soap and a good towel. Why am I so thoughtless? I must get him another shirt and a jacket for the winter and some sort of shoes and another blanket.

"Your stew is excellent," the old man said.

Notes:

1. skiff *n.* 小艇

   E. g. All lights were out when he sailed into the little harbor and beached his skiff.

2. gaff *n.* (钓大鱼的)手钩, 挽钩

   E. g. The fisherman used the gaff to hook a fish.

3. harpoon *n.* 鱼叉

   E. g. The harpoon drove deep into the body of the whale.

4. furl *v.* 卷起, 卷收

   E. g. An attempt was made to furl the headsail.

5. gaunt *adj.* 憔悴的, 消瘦的

   E. g. Looking gaunt and tired, he denied there was anything to worry about.

6. blotch *n.* 斑点

   E. g. His face was covered in red blotches, seemingly a nasty case of acne.

7. plank *n.* (厚)木板

   E. g. It was very strong, made of three solid planks of wood.

8. thwart *n.* (船)横座板

   E. g. He sat down and, clinging to the thwart, began to sob

quietly.

9. relic *n.* 遗物

E. g. The tower is a relic of grim days when big houses had to be fortified against invaders.

10. bodega *n.* 杂货铺

E. g. Do you think I can just come home and run the bodega?

Questions:

1. Why did Manolin leave Santiago to fish in another boat?

2. Does the novella have a set stance on the concept of luck? How might you describe the way that the novel presents luck?

3. Even though the boy can no longer fish with Santiago, how does he show his loyalty?

4. From Hemingway's descriptions, what do you know about the character of Santiago?

5. Santiago is considered to be a tragic hero, in that his greatest strength—his pride—leads to his eventual downfall. Discuss the role of pride in Santiago's plight.

Analysis of Part 1

The opening pages of the book establish Santiago's character and set the scene for the action to follow. Even though he loves Manolin and is loved dearly by the boy, the old man lives as an outsider. The greeting he receives from the fishermen, most of whom mock him for his fruitless voyages to sea, shows Santiago to be an alienated, almost ostracized figure. Such an alienated position is characteristic of Hemingway's heroes, whose greatest achievements depend, in large part, upon their isolation. Yet, although Hemingway's message in *The Old Man and the Sea* is tragic in many respects, the story of Santiago and the destruction of his greatest catch is far from dismal. Santiago is not defeated by his enlightenment. The narrator emphasizes Santiago's perseverance in the opening pages, mentioning that the old man's eyes are still "cheerful and undefeated" after suffering nearly three months without a single catch. And, although Santiago's struggle will bring about defeat—the great marlin will be devoured by sharks—Santiago will emerge as a victor. As he tells the boy, in order for this to happen, he must venture far out, farther than the other fishermen are willing to go.

中文译文：

他是个独自在湾流中一条小船上钓鱼的老人，至今已去了八十四天，一条鱼也没逮住。头四十天里，有个男孩子跟他在一起。可是，过了四十天还没捉到一条鱼，孩子的父母对他说，老人如今准是十足地"倒了血霉"，这就是说，倒霉到了极点，于是孩子听从了他们的吩咐，上了另外一条船，头一个礼拜就捕到了三条好鱼。孩子看见老人每天回来时船总是空的，感到很难受，他总是走下岸去，帮老人拿卷起的钓索，或者鱼钩和鱼叉，还有绕在桅杆上的帆。帆上用面粉袋片打了些补丁，收拢后看上去像是一面标志着永远失败的旗子。

老人消瘦而憔悴，脖颈上有些很深的皱纹。腮帮上有些褐斑，那是太阳在热带海面上反射的光线引起的良性皮肤癌变。褐斑从他脸的两侧一直蔓延下去，他的双手常用绳索拉大鱼，留下了刻得很深的伤疤。但是这些伤疤中没有一块是新的。它们像无鱼可打的沙漠中被侵蚀的地方一般古老。他身上的一切都显得古老，除了那双眼睛，它们像海水一般蓝，是愉快而不肯认输的。

"圣地亚哥"，他们俩从小船停泊的地方爬上岸时，孩子对他说。"我又能陪你出海了。我家挣到了一点儿钱。"

老人教会了这孩子捕鱼，孩子爱他。

"不，"老人说。"你遇上了一条交好运的船。跟他们待下去吧。"

"不过你该记得，你有一回八十七天钓不到一条鱼，跟着有三个礼拜，我们每天都逮住了大鱼。"

"我记得，"老人说。"我知道你不是因为没把握才离开我的。"

"是爸爸叫我走的。我是孩子，不能不听从他。"

"我明白，"老人说。"这是理该如此的。"

"他没多大的信心。"

"是啊，"老人说。"可是我们有。可不是吗？"

"对，"孩子说。"我请你到露台饭店去喝杯啤酒，然后一起把打鱼的家什带回去。"

"那敢情好，"老人说。"都是打鱼人嘛。"

他们坐在饭店的露台上，不少渔夫拿老人开玩笑，老人并不生气。另外一些上了些年纪的渔夫望着他，感到难受。不过他们并不流露出来，只是斯文地谈起海流，谈起他们把钓索送到海面下有多深，天气一贯多么好，谈起他们的见闻。当天打鱼得手的渔夫都已回来，把大马林鱼剖开，整片儿排在两块木板上，每块木板的一端由两个人抬着，摇摇晃晃地送到收鱼站，在那里等冷藏车来把它们运往哈瓦那的市场。逮到鲨鱼的人们已把它们送到海湾另一边的鲨鱼加工厂去，吊在复合滑车上，除去肝脏，割掉鱼鳍，剥去外皮，把鱼肉切成一条条，以备腌制。

刮东风的时候，鲨鱼加工厂隔着海湾送来一股气味；但今天只有淡淡的一丝，因为风转向了北方，后来逐渐平息了，饭店露台上可人心意、阳光明媚。

"圣地亚哥，"孩子说。

"哦，"老人说。他正握着酒杯，思量好多年前的事儿。

"要我去弄点沙丁鱼来给你明天用吗？"

"不。打棒球去吧。我划船还行，罗赫略会给我撒网的。"

"我很想去。即使不能陪你钓鱼，我也很想给你多少做点事。"

"你请我喝了杯啤酒，"老人说。"你已经是个大人啦。"

"你头一回带我上船，我有多大？"

"五岁，那天我把一条活蹦乱跳的鱼拖上船去，它差一点把船撞得粉碎，你也差一点给送了命。还记得吗？"

"我记得鱼尾巴砰砰地拍打着，船上的座板给打断了，还有棍子打鱼的声音。我记得你把我朝船头猛推，那儿搁着湿漉漉的钓索卷儿，我感到整条船在颤抖，听到你啪啪地用棍子打鱼的声音，像砍一棵树，还记得我浑身上下都是甜丝丝的血腥味儿。"

"你当真记得那回事儿，还是我不久前刚跟你说过？""打从我们头一回一起出海时起，什么事儿我都记得清清楚楚。"

老人用他那双常遭日晒而目光坚定的眼睛爱怜地望着他。

"如果你是我自己的小子，我准会带你出去闯一下，"他说。

"可你是你爸爸和你妈妈的小子，你搭的又是一条交上了好运的船。"

"我去弄沙丁鱼来好吗？我还知道上哪儿去弄四条鱼饵来。"

"我今天还有自个儿剩下的。我把它们放在匣子里腌了。"

"让我给你弄四条新鲜的来吧。"

"一条，"老人说。他的希望和信心从没消失过。现在可又像微风初起时那么清新了。

"两条，"孩子说。

"就两条吧，"老人同意了。"你不是去偷的吧？"

"我愿意去偷，"孩子说。"不过这些是买来的。"

"谢谢你了，"老人说。他心地单纯，不去捉摸自己什么时候达到这样谦卑的地步。可是他知道这时正达到了这地步，知道这并不丢脸，所以也无损于真正的自尊心。

"看这海流，明儿会是个好日子，"他说。

"你打算上哪儿？"孩子问。

"驶到远方，等转了风才回来。我想天亮前就出发。"

"我要想法叫船主人也驶到远方，"孩子说。"这样，如果你确实钓到了大鱼，我们可以赶去帮你的忙。"

"他可不会愿意驶到很远的地方。"

"是啊，"孩子说。"不过我会看见一些他看不见的东西，比如说有只鸟儿在空中盘旋，我就会叫他赶去追鲯鳅的。"

"他眼睛这么不行吗？"

"简直是个瞎子。"

"这可怪了，"老人说。"他从没捕过海龟。这玩意儿才伤眼睛哪。"

"你可在莫斯基托海岸外捕了好多年海龟，你的眼力还是挺好的嘛。""我是个不同寻常的老头儿。"

"不过你现在还有力气对付一条真正大的鱼吗？"

"我想还有。再说有不少窍门可用呢。"

"我们把家什拿回家去吧，"孩子说。"这样我可以拿了渔网去逮沙丁鱼。"

他们从船上拿起打鱼的家什。老人把桅杆扛上肩头，孩子拿着里子编得很紧密的褐色钓索卷儿的木箱、鱼钩和带杆子的鱼叉。盛鱼饵的匣子给藏在小船的船艄下面，那儿还有那根在大鱼被拖到船边时用来收服它们的棍子，谁也不会来偷老人的东西，不过还是把桅杆和那些粗钓索带回家去的好，因为露水对这些东西不利，再说，尽管老人深信当地不会有人来偷他的东西，但他认为，把一把鱼钩和一支鱼叉留在船上实在是不必要的引诱。

他们顺着大路一起走到老人的窝棚，从敞开的门走进去。老人把绕着帆的桅杆靠在墙上，孩子把木箱和其他家什搁在它的旁边。桅杆跟这窝棚内的单间屋子差不多一般长。窝棚用大椰子树的叫作"海鸟粪"的坚韧的苞壳做成，里面有一张床、一张桌子、一把椅子和泥地上一处用木炭烧饭的地方。

在用纤维结实的"海鸟粪"展平了叠盖而成的褐色墙壁上，有一幅彩色的耶稣圣心图和另一幅科布莱圣母图。这是他妻子的遗物。墙上一度挂着幅他妻子的着色照，但他把它取下了，因为看了觉得自己太孤单了，它如今在屋角搁板上，在他的一件干净衬衫下面。

"有什么吃的东西？"

"有锅鱼煮黄米饭。要吃点吗？"

"不。我回家去吃。要我给你生火吗？"

"不用。过一会儿我自己来生。也许就吃冷饭算了。"

"我把渔网拿去好吗？"

"当然好。"

实在并没有渔网，孩子还记得他们是什么时候把它卖掉的。然而他们每天要扯一套这种谎话。也没有什么鱼煮黄米饭，这一点孩子也知道。

"八十五是个吉利的数目，"老人说。"你可想看到我逮住一条去掉了下鳍有一千多磅重的鱼？"

"我拿渔网捞沙丁鱼去。你坐在门口晒晒太阳可好？"

"好吧。我有张昨天的报纸，我来看看棒球消息。"孩子不知道昨天的报纸是不是也是乌有的。但是老人把它从床下取出来了。

"佩里科在杂货铺里给我的，"他解释说。

"我弄到了沙丁鱼就回来。我要把你的鱼跟我的一起用冰镇着，明儿早上就可以分着用了。等我回来了，你告诉我棒球消息。"

"扬基队不会输。"

"可是我怕克利夫兰印第安人队会赢。"

"相信扬基队吧，好孩子。别忘了那了不起的迪马吉奥。"

"我担心底特律老虎队，也担心克利夫兰印第安人队。"

"当心点，要不然连辛辛那提红队和芝加哥白短袜队，你都要担心啦。"

"你好好儿看报，等我回来了给我讲讲。"

"你看我们该去买张末尾数是八五的彩票吗？明儿是第八十五天。"

"这样做行啊，"孩子说。"不过你上次创纪录的是八十七天，这怎么说？"

"这种事儿不会再发生。你看能弄到一张末尾是八五的吗？"

"我可以去订一张。"

"订一张。这要两块半。我们向谁去借这笔钱呢？"

"这个容易。我总能借到两块半的。"

"我看没准儿我也借得到。不过我不想借钱。第一步是借钱。下一步就要讨饭啰。"

"穿得暖和点，老大爷，"孩子说。"别忘了，我们这是在九月里。"

"正是大鱼露面的月份，"老人说，"在五月里，人人都能当个好渔夫。"

"我现在去捞沙丁鱼，"孩子说。

等孩子回来的时候，老人在椅子上熟睡着，太阳已经下去了。孩子从床上捡起一条旧军毯，铺在椅背上，盖住了老人的双肩。这两个肩膀挺怪，人非常老迈了，肩膀却依然很强健，脖子也依然很壮实，而且当老人睡着了，脑袋向前耷拉着的时候，皱纹也不大明显了。他的衬衫上不知打了多少次补丁，弄得像他那张帆一样，这些补丁被阳光晒得褪成了许多深浅不同的颜色。老人的头非常苍老，眼睛闭上了，脸上就一点生气也没有。报纸摊在他膝盖上，在晚风中，靠他一条胳臂压着才没被吹走。他光着脚。

孩子撇下老人走了，等他回来时，老人还是熟睡着。

"醒来吧，老大爷，"孩子说，一手搭上老人的膝盖。老人张开眼睛，他的神志一时仿佛正在从老远的地方回来。随后他微笑了。

"你拿来了什么?"他问。

"晚饭，"孩子说。"我们就来吃吧。"

"我肚子不大饿。"

"得了，吃吧。你不能只打鱼不吃饭。"

"我这样干过。"老人说着，站起身来，拿起报纸，把它折好。跟着他动手折叠毯子。

"把毯子披在身上吧，"孩子说。"只要我活着，你就决不会不吃饭就去打鱼。"

"这么说，祝你长寿，多保重自己吧，"老人说。"我们吃什么?"

"黑豆饭、油炸香蕉，还有些炖菜。"孩子是把这些饭菜放在双层饭匣里从露台饭店拿来的。他口袋里有两副刀叉和汤匙，每一副都用纸餐巾包着。

"这是谁给你的。"

"马丁。那老板。"

"我得去谢谢他。"

"我已经谢过啦，"孩子说。"你用不着去谢他了。"

"我要给他一块大鱼肚子上的肉，"老人说。"他这样帮助我们不止一次了?"

"我想是这样吧。"

"这样的话，我该在鱼肚子肉以外，再送他一些东西。他对我们真关心。"

"他还送了两瓶啤酒。"

"我喜欢罐装的啤酒。"

"我知道。不过这是瓶装的，阿图埃牌啤酒，我还得把瓶子送回去。"

"你真周到，"老人说。"我们就吃好吗?"

"我已经问过你啦，"孩子温和地对他说。"不等你准备好，我是不愿打开饭匣子的。"

"我准备好啦，"老人说。"我只消洗洗手脸就行。"

你上哪儿去洗呢？孩子想。村里的水龙头在大路上第二条横路的转角上。我该把水带到这儿让他用的，孩子想，还带块肥皂和一条干净毛巾来。我为什么这样粗心大意？我该再弄件衬衫和一件夹克衫来让他过冬，还要一双什么鞋子，并且再给他弄条毯子来。

"这炖菜呱呱叫。"老人说。

🔖 Answers for questions

1. After 40 days without a catch in Santiago's boat, Manolin's parents have sent him out with another fisherman because they believe that Santiago is unlucky.

2. The fishermen are superstitious and believe it is bad luck that brings Santiago home empty handed for eighty-four days. Santiago thinks luck has more to do with the choices he makes. Then when good luck comes, he is ready.

3. The boy continues to visit Santiago and help him load and unload his boat every day. Along the way, Manolin tries to cheer Santiago by reminding him of the time, when they were fishing together, that the old man went 87 days without a fish and then they caught big fish for three weeks. On their way home, Manolin buys Santiago a beer at the Terrace. Because Santiago has nothing to eat, Manolin fetches Santiago the dinner that the Terrace owner, Martin, sends for free, as he has many times before.

4. Santiago is an impoverished old man who has endured many ordeals, whose best days are behind him, whose wife has died, and who never had children. For 84 days, he has gone without catching the fish upon which his meager existence, the community's respect, and his sense of identity as an accomplished fisherman all depend.

5. At first, Santiago's plight seems rather hopeless. He has gone eighty-four days without catching a fish, and he is the laughingstock of his small village. Regardless of his past, the old man determines to change his luck and sail out farther than he or the other fishermen ever

have before. His commitment to sailing out to where the big fish are testifies to the depth of his pride.

References

［1］http：//www. thepursuitofsassiness. com/wp － content/uploads/2012/12/hway
8. jpg（图片来源）

［2］http：//www. nobelprize. org/nobel＿prizes/literature/laureates/1954/heming-
way － bio. html

［3］https：//sp. yimg. com/ib/th？ id ＝ JN. tPfIP21MiHgNnpnnXFMk％2fw&pid ＝
15. 1&P ＝0（图片来源）

［4］http：//www. gradesaver. com/the － old － man － and － the － sea/

［5］http：//www. cliffsnotes. com/literature/o/the － old － man － and － the － sea/
character － list

［6］http：//www. cliffsnotes. com/literature/o/the － old － man － and － the － sea/
book － summary

［7］http：//www. enotes. com/topics/old － man － and － the － sea/themes

［8］http：//www. cliffsnotes. com/literature/o/the － old － man － and － the － sea/
summary － and － analysis/part － 1

［9］https：//la. utexas. edu/users/jmciver/Honors/Fiction％202013/Hemmingway＿
The％20Old％20Man％20and％20the％20Sea_1952. pdf

［10］http：//www. sparknotes. com/lit/oldman/section1. rhtml

［11］http：//www. kanunu8. com/book/3829/39322. html

Unit 14
William Cuthbert Faulkner (1897 – 1962)

✂ Bibliography

William Cuthbert Faulkner (1897 – 1962) was born in New Albany, Mississippi, but his family soon moved to Oxford, Mississippi. Almost all of his novels take place in and around Oxford, which he renames Jefferson, Mississippi. Even though Faulkner is a contemporary American author, he is already considered to be one of the world's greatest novelists. In 1949, he was awar-ded the Nobel Prize for literature, the highest prize that can be awarded to a writer.

Faulkner came from a rather distinguished Mississippi family. His great-grandfather, Colonel William Cuthbert Falkner (the "u" was added to Faulkner's name by mistake when his first novel was published and Faulkner retained this spelling), came to Mississippi from South Carolina during the first part of the nineteenth century. The Colonel appears in many of Faulkner's novels under the name of Colonel John Sartoris. Colonel William Falkner had a fairly notable career as a soldier both in the Mexican War and in the American Civil War. During the Civil War, Falkner's hot temper was responsible for his demotion from full colonel to lieutenant colonel. After the Civil War, Colonel Falkner was deeply involved in the problems of the reconstruction period. He killed several men during this time and became a rather notorious figure. He also built a railroad and ran for public office. During all of these fascinating activities, he took out time to write one of the nation's bestsellers, *The White Rose of Memphis*, which appeared in 1880. He also wrote two other books, but only his first was an outstanding success. He was finally killed by one of his rivals. The later members of the Falkner family were not quite so distinguished as was the great-grandfather.

With the publication of his third novel, *Sartoris*, William Faulkner placed his novels in a mythological county that he called Yoknapatawpha County. Most of the rest of his novels and short stories are set in this county. The Compsons, who are the central characters in this novel, also appear in later works. One of Faulkner's great achievements is the creation of this imaginary county. He worked out his plan so carefully that many characters who are minor characters in one novel become central characters in a later work. He also drew a map of this county to show where certain events take place; it appears at the end of a later novel, *Absalom, Absalom*!

In all of his work, Faulkner has used new techniques to express his views of man's position in the modern world. In his earlier works, Faulkner viewed man's position in the universe with despair. He saw man as a weak creature incapable of rising above his selfish needs. Later, Faulkner's view changed. In his more recent works, he sees man as potentially great, or, in Faulkner's own words, "Man will not merely endure: he will prevail." In almost all of his novels, Faulkner penetrates deeply into the psychological motivations for man's actions and investigates man's dilemma in the modern world. Of all his achievements, *The Sound and the Fury* is considered to be one of his greatest novels.

🕮 The Sound and the Fury

The Sound and the Fury, the first major novel of William Faulkner, was published in 1929. Set in Faulkner's Yoknapatawpha County, Miss., in the

early 20th century, the novel describes the decay and fall of the aristocratic Compson family, and, implicitly, of an entire social order, from
four different points of view. The first three sections are presented from
the perspectives of the three Compson sons: Benjy, an "idiot"; Quentin,
a suicidal Harvard freshman; and Jason, the eldest. Each section focuses
primarily on a sister who has married and left home. The fourth section
comments on the other three as the Compsons's black servants, whose
chief virtue is their endurance, reveal the family's moral decline.

In this novel, Faulkner for the first time incorporated such challenging stylistic techniques as interior monologues and stream-of-con-
sciousness narrative.

Characters in The Sound and the Fury

1. Jason Compson III—The cynical and detached father.
2. Caroline Compson—The whining, selfish, neurotic mother.
3. Quentin Compson—The oldest son who is overly sensitive of his sister's
   sin; he commits suicide by drowning on June 2, 1910.
4. Candace (Caddy) Compson—The only Compson daughter; her
   promiscuity is one of the central narrative concerns of the novel.
5. Jason Compson IV—The last male Compson since he will probably
   never marry.
6. Benjy (Benjamin — previously Maury)—The youngest of the Compson children, whose name is changed when it is discovered that he is
   severely retarded.
7. Miss Quentin—Caddy's daughter, who was born too soon after her
   mother's wedding and who is reared by the Compsons.
8. Uncle Maury Bascomb—Mrs. Compson's worthless brother, who sponges
   off her.
9. Damuddy—The children's (maternal) grandmother, who dies in 1898.
10. Dilsey Gibson—The black cook whose task it is to bring order out of
    the sound and fury created by the Compsons.
11. Roskus—Dilsey's husband, who also works for the Compsons.

12. Versh and T. P. —Dilsey's sons, who are Benjy's keepers during the earlier parts of Benjy's life.

13. Frony—Dilsey's daughter, who helps out in the kitchen.

14. Luster—Frony's son (probably), who is Benjy's attendant in the present action.

15. Dalton Ames—He is one of Caddy's lovers and is probably the father of Caddy's child.

16. Gerald Bland—A fellow student at Harvard who reminds Quentin of Dalton Ames.

17. Mrs. Bland—Gerald's mother, who brags about her son's conquests with women.

18. Charlie—Caddy's earliest boyfriend; Benjy discovers him in the swing with Caddy.

19. Deacon—An old black character at Harvard whom Quentin entrusts with his suicide letters.

20. Earl—Owner of the hardware store where Jason Compson IV works.

21. (Sydney) Herbert Head—The man whom Caddy marries when she discovers that she is pregnant and has to marry someone.

22. Uncle Job—An old black man who also works for Earl, Jason's employer.

23. Julio—The brother of the little Italian girl who attaches herself to Quentin.

24. Lorraine—The mistress Jason keeps in Memphis.

25. Shreve MacKenzie—QuentinCompson's Canadian roommate at Harvard. (Shreve MacKenzie becomes Shreve McCannon in Absalom, Absalom!)

26. Mrs. Patterson—The woman with whom Uncle Maury is having an affair.

27. Mr. Patterson—Her husband, who discovers the affair and assaults Uncle Maury.

28. Reverend Shegog—A wise black preacher who delivers an effective sermon on Easter Sunday.

Summary

April Seventh, 1928: Benjy accompanies Luster as he searches for a quarter to go to the circus that night. At the same time he relives memories of his youth, most of which have to do with Caddy. He remembers, for example, the night his grandmother（Damuddy）died, when Caddy climbed a tree to look in the parlor windows, showing her siblings her muddy drawers. He also remembers her precocious sexuality, which led to her pregnancy and marriage, taking her out of his life. He can smell the change in Caddy; when she is young and pure she smells like trees to him, and when she begins to have sex she no longer smells like trees. He has a specific order to the day's events, and when Luster interrupts this order, he howls.

June Second, 1910: this section follows the events of the last day of Quentin's life, as he makes meticulous preparations for his suicide. He puts on clean clothes and packs all his belongings, then buys two flat irons to weight himself down with and heads out of town（he is attending Harvard at the time）. He arrives in a little riverside town and meets up with a small immigrant girl, who follows him around until her brother finds them and accuses him of kidnapping her. He also runs into his friends, who are in town for a picnic. He ends up getting into a fight with one of them when he confuses his rantings on women with those of Dalton Ames, the boy who got his sister pregnant. He returns to Cambridge to clean his clothes, then heads back out to the same town to drown himself in the river. Throughout the day he is haunted by memories of Caddy, especially of her affair with Dalton Ames, her pregnancy, and her marriage to Herbert Head.

April Sixth, 1928: this section follows Jason through his day as he deals with Quentin, Caddy's illegitimate daughter, who skips school and sleeps around. He takes her to school but then sees her skipping later with one of the musicians who is in town for the circus. Furious, he chases the two of them out of town but loses them when they let the air out of his tires. At the same time he is dealing with the finances of his life. He loses MYM200 in the stock market, and also receives a MYM200 check from Caddy for Quentin's upkeep. He cashes this check, then makes out a fake check for his mother to burn. He resents Quentin as the symbol of the job he was deprived of when Caddy divorced Herbert Head. We discover that he has embezzled thousands of dollars from Caddy, money that should have been Quentin's.

April Eighth, 1928: This section continues to follow Jason while also following Dilsey through her day. It is Easter Sunday, and Dilsey takes her family and Benjy to church and is powerfully affected by Reverend Shegog's sermon. She proclaims that she has seen the beginning and the end, the first and the last. At the same time, Jason wakes to discover that Quentin has run away and has taken the money he was saving in a strongbox in his room, MYM7,000 in total. Caroline is sure that Quentin has committed suicide like her namesake, but Jason drives out of town trying to find her. He meets up with the traveling circus in the next town, but is forcibly driven away by some circus workers. The owner of the circus tells him that Quentin and her boyfriend have left town. He returns to Jackson. At the end of the section, Luster is taking Benjy to the graveyard. When Luster takes a wrong turn, Benjy starts to howl, and Jason, who has just returned to town, stops the carriage and turns it the right way.

Comments on *The Sound and the Fury*

The first three sections are narrated in a technique known as stream of consciousness, in which the writer takes down the character's thoughts as they occur to him, paying little attention to chronology of events or continuity of story line. The technique is the most marked in the first section, wherein Benjy's mind skips backward and forward in time as he relives events from the past while simultaneously conducting himself in the present. Quentin's section is slightly more ordered, although his agitated state of mind causes him to experience similar skips in time.

Jason's section is almost totally chronological, much more structured than the first two. In order to make reading this difficult novel easier, Faulkner at one time suggested printing it in colored ink in order to mark the different time periods, but this was too expensive. Instead, in the first section, he writes some sentences in italics in order to signal a shift in time. Even with these italics, however, the story is difficult to read.

Not much happens in the three days in which the novel is mainly set; instead the stream of consciousness narration allows the reader to experience the history of the Compson family and step into the lives of this dwindling Southern family. The troubled relationships of the family are at once mundane and sweepingly tragic, pulling the reader into its downward spiral.

Introduction to Section One

On the day before Easter, 1928, a teenaged "Negro" boy named Luster is watching after Benjy, the severely retarded youngest son of the aristocratic Compson family of Jefferson, Mississippi. It is Benjy's thirty-third birthday, and Dilsey, the Compsons' cook and Luster's grandmother, has baked him a cake. Luster takes Benjy around the Compson property to search for a quarter he has lost. Luster had intended to use the quarter to buy a ticket to the minstrel show in Jefferson that weekend.

Luster leads Benjy to a nearby golf course, hoping to earn back his lost quarter by fetching lost golf balls from the rough. The golf course lies on a stretch of what used to be the Compson pasture, which Mr. Compson sold to developers to pay for his son Quentin's education at Harvard. When Benjy hears one of the golfers calling out to his caddie, he moans because the sound of the word "caddie" reminds him of his sister.

Luster helps Benjy climb through a fence. Benjy catches his clothes on a nail, which brings back a memory of a time when Caddy helped Benjy free himself from that same nail twenty-six years before.

This event occurred around Christmas, 1902, when Benjy was seven years old. In this memory, Mrs. Compson and her brother, Uncle Maury, are arguing inside the Compson house. Uncle Maury lives off of the Compsons' money and hospitality, and he is also having an affair with Mrs. Patterson, the Compsons' next-door neighbor. Uncle Maury uses young Benjy and Caddy as messengers to deliver his love letters to Mrs. Patterson. Mrs. Compson worries that Benjy will get sick from the cold, but she seems more concerned about the prospect of Benjy's sickness ruining her Christmas party than about his actual welfare. These memories of Caddy make Benjy moan again, which annoys Luster.

Returning to 1928, Benjy and Luster walk past the carriage house on the Compson property, which reminds Benjy of a time he saw the carriage house long ago during a trip to the family cemetery. In this memory, from approximately 1912 or 1913, Benjy and his mother are riding in the Compsons' carriage to visit the graveyard where Quentin and Mr. Compson were laid to rest. Dilsey mentions that Jason should buy the family a new carriage, as the current one is getting old. Jason mentions that Uncle Maury has been asking for money from Mrs. Compson. Luster chides Benjy for his crying once again.

From _The Sound and the fury_
Section One: April Seventh, 1928

Through the fence, between the curling flower spaces, I could see them hitting. They were coming toward where the flag was and I went along the fence. Luster was hunting in the grass by the flower tree. They took the flag out, and they were hitting. Then they put the flag back and they went to the table, and he hit and the other hit. Then they went on, and I went along the fence. Luster came away from the flower tree and we went along the fence and they stopped and we stopped and I looked through the fence while Luster was hunting in the grass.

"Here, caddie." He hit. They went away across the pasture. I held to the fence and watched them going away.

"Listen at you, now. " Luster said. "Aren't you something, thirty three years old, going on that way. After I done went all the way to town to buy you that cake. Hush up that moaning. Aren't you going to help me find that quarter so I can go to the show tonight. "

They were hitting little, across the pasture. I went back along the fence to where the flag was. It flapped[1] on the bright grass and the trees.

"Come on. " Luster said. "We done looked there. They aren't no more coming right now. Les go down to the branch and find that quarter before them niggers finds it. "

It was red, flapping on the pasture. Then there was a bird slanting[2] and tilting[3] on it. Luster threw. The flag flapped on the bright grass and the trees. I held to the fence.

"Shut up that moaning. " Luster said. "I cant make them come if they aint coming, can I. If you don't hush up, mammy aren't going to have no birthday for you. If you don't hush, you know what I going to do. I going to eat that cake all up. Eat them candles, too. Eat all them thirty three candles. Come on, les go down to the branch. I got to find my quarter. Maybe we can find one of they balls. Here. Here they is. Way over yonder. See. " He came to the fence and pointed his arm. "See them. They aren't coming back here no more. Come on. "

We went along the fence and came to the garden fence, where our shadows were. My shadow was higher than Luster's on the fence. We came to the broken place and went through it.

"Wait a minute. " Luster said. "You snagged[4] on that nail again. Cant you never crawl through here without snagging on that nail. "

Caddy uncaught me and we crawled through. Uncle Maury said to not let anybody see us, so we better stoop[5] over, Caddy said. Stoop o- ver, Benjy. Like this, see. We stooped over and crossed the garden, where the flowers rasped and rattled[6] against us. The ground was hard. We climbed the fence, where the pigs were grunting[7] and snuffing. I ex- pect they're sorry because one of them got killed today, Caddy said. The ground was hard, churned[8] and knotted.

Keep your hands in your pockets, Caddy said. Or they'll get froze. You don't want your hands froze on Christmas, do you.

"It's too cold out there. " Versh said. "You don't want to go outdoors. "

"What is it now. " Mother said.

"He want to go outdoors. " Versh said.

"Let him go. " Uncle Maury said.

"It's too cold. " Mother said. "He'd better stay in. Benjamin. Stop that, now. "

"It wont hurt him. " Uncle Maury said.

"You, Benjamin. " Mother said. "If you don't be good, you'll have to go to the kitchen. "

"Mammy say keep him out the kitchen today. " Versh said. "She say she got all that cooking to get done. "

"Let him go, Caroline. " Uncle Maury said. "You'll worry yourself sick over him. "

"I know it. " Mother said. "It's a judgment on me. I sometimes wonder. "

"I know, I know. " Uncle Maury said. "You must keep your strength up. I'll make you a toddy⁹. "

"It just upsets me that much more. " Mother said. "Don't you know it does. "

"You'll feel better. " Uncle Maury said. "Wrap him up good, boy, and take him out for a while. "

Uncle Maury went away. Versh went away.

"Please hush. " Mother said. "We're trying to get you out as fast as we can. I don't want you to get sick. "

Versh put my overshoes and overcoat on and we took my cap and went out. Uncle Maury was putting the bottle away in the sideboard in the dining room.

"Keep him out about half an hour, boy. " Uncle Maury said. "Keep him in the yard, now. "

"Yes, sir. " Versh said. "We don't never let him get off the place. "

We went out doors. The sun was cold and bright.

"Where you heading for. " Versh said. "You don't think you going to town, does you. " We went through the rattling leaves. The gate was cold. "You better keep them hands in your pockets. " Versh said. "You get them froze onto that gate, then what you do. Whyn't you wait for them in the house. " He put my hands into my pockets. I could hear him rattling in the leaves. I could smell the cold. The gate was cold.

"Here some hickeynuts. Whooey. Git up that tree. Look here at this squirl, Benjy. "

I couldn't feel the gate at all, but I could smell the bright cold.

"You better put them hands back in your pockets. "

Caddy was walking. Then she was running, her book-satchel swinging and jouncing behind her.

"Hello, Benjy. " Caddy said. She opened the gate and came in and stooped down. Caddy smelled like leaves. "Did you come to meet me. " she said. "Did you come to meet Caddy. What did you let him get his hands so cold for, Versh. "

"I told him to keep them in his pockets. " Versh said. "Holding on to that gate. "

"Did you come to meet Caddy," she said, rubbing my hands. "What is it. What are you trying to tell Caddy. " Caddy smelled like trees and like when she says we were asleep.

What are you moaning about, Luster said. You can watch them a-gain when we get to the branch. Here. Here's you a jimson weed. He gave me the flower. We went through the fence, into the lot.

"What is it. " Caddy said. "What are you trying to tell Caddy. Did they send him out, Versh. "

"Couldn't keep him in. " Versh said. "He kept on until they let him go and he come right straight down here, looking through the gate. "

"What is it. " Caddy said. "Did you think it would be Christmas

307

when I came home from school. Is that what you thought. Christmas is the day after tomorrow. Santy Claus, Benjy. Santy Claus. Come on, let's run to the house and get warm. " She took my hand and we ran through the bright rustling leaves. We ran up the steps and out of the bright cold, into the dark cold. Uncle Maury was putting the bottle back in the sideboard. He called Caddy. Caddy said,

"Take him in to the fire, Versh. Go with Versh. " she said. "I'll come in a minute. "

We went to the fire. Mother said,

"Is he cold, Versh. "

"Nome. " Versh said.

"Take his overcoat and overshoes off. " Mother said. "How many times do I have to tell you not to bring him into the house with his overshoes on. "

"Yessum. " Versh said. "Hold still, now. " He took my overshoes off and unbuttoned my coat. Caddy said,

"Wait, Versh. Cant he go out again, Mother. I want him to go with me. "

"You'd better leave him here. " Uncle Maury said. "He's been out enough today. "

"I think you'd both better stay in. " Mother said. "It's getting colder, Dilsey says. "

"Oh, Mother. " Caddy said.

"Nonsense. " Uncle Maury said. "She's been in school all day. She needs the fresh air. Run along, Candace. "

"Let him go, Mother. " Caddy said. "Please. You know he'll cry. "

"Then why did you mention it before him. " Mother said. "Why did you come in here. To give him some excuse to worry me again. You've been out enough today. I think you'd better sit down here and play with him. "

"Let them go, Caroline. " Uncle Maury said. "A little cold wont hurt them. Remember, you've got to keep your strength up. "

"I know. " Mother said. "Nobody knows how I dread Christmas. Nobody knows. I am not one of those women who can stand things. I wish for Jason's and the children's sakes I was stronger. "

"You must do the best you can and not let them worry you. " Uncle Maury said. "Run along, you two. But don't stay out long, now. Your mother will worry. "

"Yes, sir. " Caddy said. "Come on, Benjy. We're going out doors again. " She buttoned my coat and we went toward the door.

"Are you going to take that baby out without his overshoes. " Mother said. "Do you want to make him sick, with the house full of company. "

"I forgot. " Caddy said. "I thought he had them on. "

We went back. "You must think. " Mother said. Hold still now Versh said. He put my overshoes on. "Someday I'll be gone, and you'll have to think for him. " Now stomp Versh said. "Come here and kiss Mother, Benjamin. "

Caddy took me to Mother's chair and Mother took my face in her hands and then she held me against her.

"My poor baby. " she said. She let me go. "You and Versh take good care of him, honey. "

"Yessum. " Caddy said. We went out. Caddy said,

"You needn't go, Versh. I'll keep him for a while. "

"All right. " Versh said. "I amnot going out in that cold for no fun. " He went on and we stopped in the hall and Caddy knelt and put her arms around me and her cold bright face against mine. She smelled like trees.

"You're not a poor baby. Are you. Are you. You've got your Caddy. Haven't you got your Caddy. "

Cant you shut up that moaning and slobbering, Luster said. Are not you shamed of yourself, making all this racket[10]. We passed the carriage house, where the carriage was. It had a new wheel.

"Git in, now, and set still until your maw come." Dilsey said. She shoved me into the carriage. T. P. held the reins. "Clare I dont see how come Jason wont get a new surrey." Dilsey said. "This thing going to fall to pieces under you all some day. Look at them wheels."

Mother came out, pulling her veil down. She had some flowers. "Where's Roskus." she said.

"Roskus cant lift his arms, today." Dilsey said. "T. P. can drive all right."

Notes：

1. flap *v.* 飘动，摆动

   E. g. Grey sheets flapped on the clothes line.

2. slant *v.* 倾斜，歪斜

   E. g. The morning sun slanted through the glass roof.

3. tilt *v.* 倾斜，歪斜

   E. g. She tilted the mirror and began to comb her hair.

4. snag *v.* 钩破，绊住

   E. g. She snagged a heel on a root and tumbled to the ground.

5. stoop *v.* 弯腰，俯身

   E. g. He stooped to pick up the carrier bag of groceries.

6. rattle *v.* 发出碰撞声

   E. g. The truck pulled away, and she listened to the rattling noises fade down the lane.

7. grunt *v.* 咕噜，嘟囔着说

   E. g. The driver grunted, convinced that Michael was crazy.

8. churn *v.* 搅动，搅拌

   E. g. The tractor churned up the soil.

9. toddy *n.* 热甜酒

   E. g. When it storms outside, it's time for steamy hot chocolate or even a soothing toddy.

10. racket *n.* 吵闹

E. g.　My dream was interrupted by the most awful racket coming through the walls.

Questions:

1. The opening section of The Sound and the Fury is considered one of the most challenging narratives in modern American literature. What makes this section so challenging?

2. Benjy remarks several times throughout this section that Caddy smells like trees or leaves. Why does Benjy have this feeling?

3. Stream of consciousness is a technique in which the writer takes down the character's thoughts as they occur to him, paying little attention to chronology of events or continuity of story line. How is this technique used in this section?

4. Benjy is mentally slow and incapable of logical thinking. Why does Faulkner narrate this section through the eyes of a retarded man?

5. "We went along the fence and came to the garden fence, where our shadows were. My shadow was higher than Luster's on the fence. " What do shadowes symbolize in this quotation?

Analysis of Section One

This section of the book is commonly referred to as "Benjy's section" because it is narrated by the retarded youngest son of the Compson family, Benjamin Compson. At this point in the story, Benjy is 33 years old—in fact, today is his birthday—but the story skips back and forth in time as various events trigger memories. When the reader first plunges into this narrative, the jumps in time are difficult to navigate or understand, although many scenes are marked by recurring images, sounds, or words. In addition, a sort of chronology can be established depending on who is Benjy's caretaker: first Versh when Benjy is a child, then T. P. when he is an adolescent, then Luster when he is an adult.

Benjy recalls three important events: the evening of his grandmother "Damuddy's" death in 1898, his name change in 1900, and Caddy's sexual promiscuity and wedding in 1910, although these events are punctuated by other memories, including the delivery of a letter to his uncle's mistress in 1902 or 1903, Caddy's wearing perfume in 1906, a sequence of events at the gate of the house in 1910 and 1911 that culminates in his castration, Quentin's death in 1910, his father's death and funeral in 1912, and Roskus's death some time after this.

中文译文：

透过栅栏，穿过攀绕的花枝的空当，我看见他们在打球。他们朝插着小旗的地方走过来，我顺着栅栏朝前走。勒斯特在那棵开花的树旁草地里找东西。他们把小旗拔出来，打球了。接着他们又把小旗插回去，来到高地上，这人打了一下，另外那人也打了一下。他们接着朝前走，我也顺着栅栏朝前走。勒斯特离开了那棵开花的树，我们沿着栅栏一起走，这时候他们站住了，我们也站住了。我透过栅栏张望，勒斯特在草丛里找东西。

"球在这儿，开弟。"那人打了一下。他们穿过草地往远处走去。我贴紧栅栏，瞧着他们走开。

"听听，你哼哼得多难听。"勒斯特说。"也真有你的，都三十三了，还这副样子。我还老远到镇上去给你买来了生日蛋糕呢。别哼哼唧唧了。你就不能帮我找找那只两毛五的镚子儿，好让我今儿晚上去看演出。"

他们过好半天才打一下球，球在草场上飞过去。我顺着栅栏走回到小旗附近去。小旗在耀眼的绿草和树木间飘荡。

"过来呀。"勒斯特说，"那边咱们找过了。他们一时半刻不会再过来的。咱们上小河沟那边去找，再晚就要让那帮黑小子捡去了。"

小旗红红的，在草地上呼呼地飘着。这时有一只小鸟斜飞下来停歇在上面。勒斯特扔了块过去。小旗在耀眼的绿草和树木间飘荡。我紧紧地贴着栅栏。

"快别哼哼了。"勒斯特说。"他们不上这边来，我也没法让他们过来呀，是不是。你要是还不住口，姥姥就不给你过生日了。你还不住口，知道我会怎么样。我要把那只蛋糕全都吃掉。连蜡烛也吃掉。把三十三根蜡烛全都吃下去。来呀，咱们上小河沟那边去。我得找到那只镚子儿。没准还能找到一只掉在那儿的球呢。

哟。他们在那儿。挺远的。瞧见没有。"他来到栅栏边，伸直了胳膊指着。"看见他们了吧。他们不会再回来了。来吧。"

　　我们沿着栅栏，走到花园的栅栏旁，我们的影子落在栅栏上，在栅栏上；我的影子比勒斯特的高。我们来到缺口那儿，从那里钻了过去。

　　"等一等。"勒斯特说。"你又挂在钉子上了。你就不能好好地钻过去不让衣服挂在钉子上吗。"

　　凯蒂把我的衣服从钉子上解下来，我们钻了过去。凯蒂说，毛莱舅舅关照了，不要让任何人看见我们，咱们还是猫着腰。猫着腰，班吉。像这样，懂吗。我们猫下了腰，穿过花园，花儿刮着我们，沙沙直响。地蹦蹦硬。我们又从栅栏上翻过去，几只猪在那儿嗅着闻着，发出了哼哼声。凯蒂说，我猜它们准是在伤心，因为它们的一个伙伴今儿个给宰了。地蹦蹦硬，是给翻掘过的，有一大块一大块土疙瘩。把手插在兜里，凯蒂说。不然会冻坏的。快过圣诞节了，你不想让你的手冻坏吧，是吗。

　　"外面太冷了。"威尔许说。"你不要出去了吧。"

　　"这又怎么的啦。"母亲说。

　　"他想到外面去呢。"威尔许说。

　　"让他出去吧。"毛莱舅舅说。

　　"天气太冷了。"母亲说。"他还是待在家里得了。班吉明。好了，别哼哼了。"

　　"对他不会有害处的。"毛莱舅舅说。

　　"喂，班吉明。"母亲说。"你要是不乖，那只好让你到厨房去了。"

　　"妈咪说今儿个别让他上厨房去。"威尔许说。"她说她要把那么些过节吃的东西都做出来。"

　　"让他出去吧，卡罗琳。"毛莱舅舅说。"你为他操心太多了，自己会生病的。"

　　"我知道。"母亲说。"有时候我想，这准是老天对我的一种惩罚。"

　　"我明白，我明白。"毛莱舅舅说。"你得好好保重。我给你调一杯热酒吧。"

"喝了只会让我觉得更加难受。"母亲说。"这你不知道吗。"

"你会觉得好一些的。"毛莱舅舅说。"给他穿戴得严实些,小子,出去的时间可别太长了。"

毛莱舅舅走开了。威尔许也走开了。

"别吵了好不好。"母亲说。"我们还巴不得你快点出去呢,我只是不想让你害病。"

威尔许给我穿上套鞋和大衣,我们拿了我的帽子就出去了。毛莱舅舅在饭厅里,正在把酒瓶放回到酒柜里去。

"让他在外面待半个小时,小子。"毛莱舅舅说。"就让他在院子里玩得了。"

"是的,您哪。"威尔许说。"我们从来不让他到外面街上去。"

我们走出门口。阳光很冷,也很耀眼。

"你上哪儿去啊。"威尔许说。"你不见得是到镇上去吧,是不是啊。"我们走在沙沙响的落叶上。铁院门冰冰冷的。"你最好把手插在兜里。"威尔许说。"你的手捏在门上会冻坏的,那你怎么办。你干吗不待在屋子里等他们呢。"他把我的手塞到我口袋里去。我能听见他踩在落叶上的沙沙声。我能闻到冷的气味。铁门是冰冰冷的。

"这儿有几个山核桃。好哎。窜到那棵树上去了,瞧呀,这儿有一只松鼠,班吉。"

我已经一点也不觉得铁门冷了,不过我还能闻到耀眼的冷的气味。

"你还是把手插回到兜里去吧。"

凯蒂走来了。接着她跑起来了,她的书包在背后一跳一跳,晃到这边又晃到那边。

"嗨,班吉。"凯蒂说。她打开铁门走进来,就弯下身子。凯蒂身上有一股树叶的香气。"你是来接我的吧。"她说。"你是来等凯蒂的吧。威尔许,你怎么让他两只手冻成这样。"

"我是叫他把手放在兜里的。"威尔许说,"他喜欢抓住铁门。"

"你是来接凯蒂的吧。"她说,一边搓着我的手。"什么事。你想告诉凯蒂什么呀。"凯蒂有一股树的香味,当她说我们这就要睡着了的时候,她也有这种香味。

你哼哼唧唧的干什么呀，勒斯特说。等我们到小河沟你还可以看他们的嘛。哪。给你一根吉姆生草。他把花递给我。我们穿过栅栏，来到空地上。

"什么呀。"凯蒂说。"你想跟凯蒂说什么呀。是他们叫他出来的吗，威尔许？"

"没法把他圈在屋里。"威尔许说。"他老是闹个没完，他们只好让他出来。他一出来就直奔这儿，朝院门外面张望。"

"你要说什么呀。"凯蒂说。"你以为我放学回来就是过圣诞节了吗。你是这样想的吧。圣诞节是后天。圣诞老公公，班吉。圣诞老公公。来吧，咱们跑回家去暖和暖和。"她拉住我的手；我们穿过了亮晃晃、沙沙响的树叶。我们跑上台阶，离开亮亮的寒冷，走进黑黑的寒冷。毛莱舅舅正把瓶子放回到酒柜里去，他喊凯蒂。凯蒂说，

"把他带到炉火跟前去，威尔许。跟威尔许去吧。"他说。"我一会儿就来。"

我们来到炉火那儿。母亲说，

"他冷不冷，威尔许。"

"一点不冷，太太。"威尔许说。

"给他把大衣和套鞋脱了。"母亲说。"我还得跟你说多少遍，别让他穿着套鞋走到房间里来。"

"是的，太太。"威尔许说。"好，别动了。"他给我脱下套鞋，又来解我的大衣纽扣。凯蒂说，

"等一等，威尔许。妈妈，能让他再出去一趟吗。我想让他陪我去。"

"你还是让他留在这儿得了。"毛莱舅舅说。"他今天出去得够多的了。"

"依我说，你们俩最好都待在家里。"母亲说。"迪尔西说，天越来越冷了。"

"哦，妈妈。"凯蒂说。

"瞎说八道。"毛莱舅舅说。"她在学校里关了一整天了。她需要新鲜空气。快走吧，凯丹斯。"

"让他也去吧，妈妈。"凯蒂说。"求求您。您知道他会哭的。"

"那你干吗当他的面提这件事呢。"母亲说。"你干吗进这屋里来呢。就是要给他个理由，让他再来跟我纠缠不清。你今天在外面待的时间够多的了。我看你最好还是坐下来陪他玩一会儿吧。"

"让他们去吧，卡罗琳。"毛莱舅舅说。"挨点儿冷对他们也没什么害处。记住了，你自己可别累倒了。"

"我知道。"母亲说。"没有人知道我多么怕过圣诞节。没有人知道。我可不是那种精力旺盛能吃苦耐劳的女人。"为了杰生和孩子们，我真希望我身体能结实些。"

"你一定要多加保重，别为他们的事操劳过度。"毛莱舅舅说。"快走吧，你们俩。只是别在外面待太久了，听见了吗。你妈要担心的。"

"是咧，您哪。"凯蒂说。"来吧，班吉。咱们又要出去喽。"她给我把大衣扣子扣好，我们朝门口走去。

"你不给小宝贝穿上套鞋就带他出去吗。"母亲说。"家里乱哄哄人正多的时候，你还想让他得病吗。"

"我忘了。"凯蒂说。"我以为他是穿着的呢。"

我们又走回来。"你得多动动脑子。"母亲说。别动了，威尔许说。他给我穿上套鞋。"不定哪一天我就要离开人世了，就得由你们来替他操心了。"现在顿顿脚，威尔许说。"过来跟妈妈亲一亲，班吉明。"

凯蒂把我拉到母亲的椅子前面去，母亲双手捧住我的脸，把我搂进怀里。

"我可怜的宝贝儿。"她说。她放开我。"你和威尔许好好照顾他，乖妞儿。"

"是的，您哪。"凯蒂说。我们走出去。凯蒂说，

"你不用去了，威尔许。我来管他一会儿吧。"

"好咧。"威尔许说。"这么冷，出去是没啥意思。"他走开去了，我们在门厅里停住脚步，凯蒂跪下来，用两只胳膊搂住我，把她那张发亮的冻脸贴在我的脸颊上。她有一股树的香味。

"你不是可怜的宝贝儿。是不是啊。你有你的凯蒂呢。你不是有你的凯蒂姐吗。"

你又是嘟哝，又是哼哼，就不能停一会儿吗，勒斯特说。你吵

个没完，害不害臊。我们经过车房，马车停在那里。马车新换了一只车轱辘。

"现在，你坐到车上去吧，安安静静地坐着，等你妈出来。"迪尔西说。她把我推上车去。T. P. 拉着缰绳。"我说，我真不明白杰生干吗不去买一辆新的轻便马车。"迪尔西说，"这辆破车迟早会让你们坐着坐着就散了架。瞧瞧这些破轱辘。"

母亲走出来了，她边走边把面纱放下来。她拿着几枝花儿。

"罗斯库司在哪儿啦。"她说。

"罗斯库司今儿个胳膊举不起来了。"迪尔西说，"T. P. 也能赶车，没事儿。"

❧ Answers for questions

1. Benjy narrates the first section of the novel. Due to his severe mental retardation, he has no concept of time. This makes his narrative incoherent and frustrating at times because he cannot separate events in the past from those in the present. Benjy can only associate the images of his daily existence, such as the golf course and fencepost, with other occurrences of those images in the past. Benjy's fusion of past and present explains why he still haunts the front yard waiting for Caddy to come home from school—he does not understand that Caddy has grown up, moved away, and will never return.

Benjy's distorted perspective conveys Faulkner's idea that the past lives on to haunt the present. Benjy's condition allows Faulkner to introduce the Compsons' struggle to reconcile their present with a past they cannot escape. This unique narrative voice provides an unbiased introduction to Quentin's equally difficult section, in which Quentin struggles with his own distorted vision of a past that eventually overwhelms and destroys him.

2. Caddy is Benjy's only mother figure and source of affection when he is young, and she provides the cornerstone of comfort and order in Benjy's mind. Benjy has relied heavily on his sister, and her absence plunges him into chaos. In his earliest memories of Caddy, Benjy pleas-

antly associates her youthful innocence with the smell of the trees in which they used to play. When Caddy becomes sexually active, Benjy notices the change she has undergone. The troubling realization corrupts his sense of order. Caddy knows Benjy is upset and begins to avoid him. Benjy laments this new distance between himself and his sister by saying that Caddy suddenly does not smell like trees. Trees are a pleasant memory associated with the affection and repose that Caddy has brought to Benjy's life, and when that order disappears, Benjy ceases to associate Caddy with that memory.

3. The technique is the most marked in the first section, wherein Benjy's mind skips backward and forward in time as he relives events from the past while simultaneously conducting himself in the present. For example, when he hears the golfers call for their caddie, the word reminds him of his sister, Caddy, whom Benjy loves more than any other person. The mention of her name causes him to start moaning. Likewise, the golf course at one time belonged to the Compsons. It was generally referred to as " Benjy" s pasture. " In 1909, Mr. Compson sold this pasture in order to send Quentin to Harvard and to buy more liquor for himself. Thus, in one sense, Benjy misses both his sister, Caddy, and his pasture. Furthermore, in 1910, Benjy was castrated after people thought he was trying to attack some young girls. Consequently, when Benjy sees the golf balls, he is perhaps reminded of his castration.

4. Benjy has no concept of time and cannot distinguish between past and present. His disability enables him to draw connections between the past and present that others might not see, and it allows him to escape the other Compsons' obsessions with the past greatness of their name.

5. Shadows imply that the present state of the Compson family is merely a shadow of its past greatness. Shadows serve as a subtle reminder of the passage of time, as they slowly shift with the sun through the course of a day.

References

[1] http://www. rudata. ru/w/images/9/9a/William_Faulkner_01_KMJ. jpg（图片来源）

[2] http://www. cliffsnotes. com/literature/s/the − sound − and − the − fury/william − faulkner − biography

[3] http://onehundredonebooks. files. wordpress. com/2011/09/sound_and_the_fury − cover. jpg（图片来源）

[4] http://www. americanwriters. org/works/sound. asp

[5] http://www. gradesaver. com/the − sound − and − the − fury/study − guide/summary

[6] http://www. gradesaver. com/the − sound − and − the − fury

[7] http://www. sparknotes. com/lit/soundfury/section1. rhtml

[8] http://www. americanwriters. org/works/first_faulkner. asp

[9] http://www. gradesaver. com/the − sound − and − the − fury/study − guide/summary − april − 7th − 1928

[10] http://www. kanunu8. com/book3/8197/181465. html

Unit 15
O. Henry (1862 – 1910)

🌿 Bibliography

O. Henry (1862 – 1910), the American short story writer, was born under the name William Sydney Porter. His short stories are well known throughout the world; noted for their witticism, clever wordplay, and unexpected "twist" endings.

William Sidney Porter was born 11 September, 1862 in Greensboro, North Carolina, to physician Algernon Sidney Porter (1825 – 1888) and Mary Jane Virginia Swaim (1833 – 1865). Mary was a graduate of Greensboro Female College (founded in 1838) now Greensboro College. She wrote poetry and had a promising artistic temperament with a natural eye for drawing and painting, surely a talent which young Will inherited. She ran her household with a firm but loving hand. Unfortunately she died of tuberculosis at the age of thirty when Will was only three years old. After Mary's death, widower Sidney and his son moved to his mother's farm, that of Will's paternal grandmother Ruth Coffyn Worth Porter (1805 – 1890). Also living at the farm was Will's aunt, Evalina Maria Porter who would become the most influential person in the first 20 years of Will's life. She became teacher, parent, and mentor to him. She had established a school on the Porter property. Will studied the basics there. As a child, Porter was always reading, everything from classics to dime novels; his favorite works were Lane's translation of *One Thousand and One Nights*, and Burton's *Anatomy of Melancholy.*

Porter graduated from his aunt Evelina Maria Porter's elementary school in 1876. He then enrolled at the Lindsey Street High School. At the age of fifteen Porter began working as a clerk in his uncle Clark Porter's store. The combination store was a local gathering spot in the small town, where Porter met different kinds of people and became immersed in the social scene, entertaining the customers with stories and drawing caricatures of them for which he became well known. He saw the humor in the everyday, and made notes of all the colorful characters he encountered, fodder for his future stories. He also obtained a pharmacist license in 1881.

Hoping that a change of environment would help alleviate a persistent cough he had developed, Porter traveled with Dr. James K. Hall to Texas in March 1882 and took up residence on the sheep ranch of Richard Hall, James' son, in La Salle County and helped out as a shepherd, ranch hand, cook and baby-sitter. While there, he took up residence on a sheep ranch, learned shepherding, cooking, babysitting, and bits of Spanish and German from the many migrant farmhands. He also spent time reading classic literature. Porter's health did improve and he traveled with Richard to Austin in 1884. He had an active social life in Austin and was a fine musician, skilled with the guitar and mandolin. He became a member of the "Hill City Quartet," a group of young men who sang at gatherings and serenaded young women of the town. Porter met and began courting Athol Estes, then seventeen years old and from a wealthy family. Her mother objected to the match because Athol was ill, suffering from tuberculosis. On July 1, 1887, Porter eloped with Athol to the home of Reverend R. K. Smoot, where they were married.

The young couple continued to participate in musical and theater groups, and Athol encouraged her husband to pursue his writing. Porter started as a draftsman at the Texas General Land Office (GLO) in 1887 at a salary of MYM100 a month. The salary was enough to support his family, but he continued his contributions to magazines and newspapers. In the GLO building, he began developing characters and plots for such stories as "Georgia's Ruling" (1900), and "Buried Treasure" (1908). The castle-like building he worked in was even woven into some of his tales such as "Bexar Scrip No. 2692" (1894).

In 1890, Porter began working as a bank teller with the First National Bank and bookkeeper at the same salary he had made at the GLO. But banking in particular was not to be O. Henry's calling; he was quite careless with his bookkeeping and may have crossed some ethical and legal boundaries. In 1894, the bank accused him of embezzlement. He lost his job but was not indicted. He was always a lover of classic literature, and while pursuing these other ventures, O. Henry had begun writing as a hobby. When he lost his banking job he moved to Houston in 1895 and started writing for the *The Post*, earning MYM25 per month (an average salary at this time in American history was probably about MYM300 a year, less than a dollar a day). O. Henry collected ideas for his column by loitering in hotel lobbies and observing and talking to people there. He relied on this technique to gain creative inspiration throughout his writing career; which is a fun fact to keep in mind while reading a story like "Transients in Arcadia".

When he was in Houston, he was arrested on charges of embezzlement. Before he was due to stand trial, he fled on impulse. He escaped first to New Orleans and later to Latin America. While holed up in a Trujillo hotel for several months, he wrote Cabbages and Kings, in which he coined the term "banana republic" to describe the country, a phrase subsequently used widely to describe a small, unstable tropical nation in Latin America with a narrowly focused, agrarian economy. When he learned that his wife was dying, Porter returned to Austin in February 1897 and surrendered to the court. After his wife died of tuberculosis, Porter, having little to say in his own defense, was found guilty of embezzlement in February 1898, sentenced to five years in prison. As a pharmacist, Porter worked in the prison hospital as the night druggist. Instead of spending time in the in the cell block of the prison, Porter was given his own room in the hospital wing. With the help of a friend in New Orleans, who forwarded his stories to publishers, Porter had fourteen stories published under various pseudonyms, but was becoming best known as "O. Henry", which first appeared over the story "Whistling Dick's Christmas Stocking" in the December 1899 issue of *McClure's Magazine*.

For good behavior after serving three years, Porter was released on July 24, 1901. He started his most prolific writing period in 1902, when he moved to New York City to be near his publishers. He wrote 381 short stories. He wrote one story a week for *The New York World Sunday Magazine* for over a year. Some of his best and least known work is contained in *Cabbages and Kings*, his first collection of published stories, set in a central American town, in which sub-plots and larger plots are interwoven in an engaging manner. His second collection of stories, The Four Million, was released in 1906. The stories are set in New York City and the title is based on the population of the city at that time. The collection contained several short story masterpieces, including The Gift of the Magi, The Cop and the Anthem, and many others. Henry had an obvious affection for New York City, a reverence that rises up through some of these stories.

Unfortunately, O. Henry's personal tragedy was heavy drinking and by 1908 his health had deteriorated and his writing dropped off accordingly. He died in 1910 of cirrhosis of the liver, complications of diabetes, and an enlarged heart. The funeral was held in New York City, but he was buried in North Carolina, the state where he was born.

The Gift of the Magi

The Gift of the Magi is one of the best known short stories written by O Henry. It is a popular Christmas story about love and sacrifice. The newlyweds — Jim and Della approach their first Christmas together, although they struggle to meet the rent, they could not be happier. Each wants to give the other a special Christmas gift as a symbol of love. For this, they sacrifice their most valuable possessions. Jim sells his gold watch to buy combs for Della's beautiful long hair. And she sold her long hair to a wig-maker to buy a chain for the heirloom which her husband no longer owns. Shock and disappointment quickly give way to the joyful understanding: They have already given each other with life's most cherished gifts. The plot and its "twist ending" are well-known, and the ending is generally considered an example of comic irony. The story was initially published in *The New York Sunday World* under the title "Gifts of the Magi" on December 10, 1905. It was first published in book form in the O. Henry Anthology *The Four Million* in April 1906.

Characters in the *The Gift of the Magi*

1. Della. Della is the loving, considerate, selfless, and occasionally hysterical heroine of the story. Della's financially poor. As a "mistress of the home", she spends all her days in housekeeping. Della basically lives for one person: Jim, her husband. She's spent a lot of the time leading up to Christmas just thinking of what to get him.

It could not be difficult to gather from that, Della throws just about every bit of energy she has into being good to Jim. She's been saving for months just to round up money for a Christmas present. She has even endured the humiliation of pinching pennies at stores.

Although Jim, Della's husband may not be bringing in much money, Jim is the most important person for Della. He deserves the Della's selfless love, which is why she's so set on getting him the perfect present: "Something fine and rare and sterling-something just a little bit near to being worthy of the honor of being owned by Jim". Della is willing to go to any length to achieve this goal, and ends up selling her one prized possession-her hair-to do it. Although she sheds a tear or two over the hair, really it doesn't seem to affect her that much. She doesn't even think it's much of a choice. She has to get Jim a present: "I had my hair cut off and sold because I couldn't have lived through Christmas without giving you a present. It'll grow out a-gain-you won't mind, will you? I just had to do it".

In fact, the thing that seems to bother Della most about losing her hair is that Jim likes it so much. She's worried he won't find her pret-ty anymore (though she doesn't really have anything to worry about). She barely seems to think of herself at all. That's devotion.

2. Jim. Jim's job is not satisfying. It seems he works long hours, but his salary is low. Recently the things went from bad to worse: whereas he used to make MYM30 a week he's now down to just MYM20. He and Della are struggling just to pay the expenses of their small flat. So if Jim happens to seem a little tired, serious, overworked, and perhaps a tad underweight, there's a good reason for it.

The one thing that keeps Jim going is his love for Della. We don't ob-tain half as much exposure to his feelings as we do for Della's, but all evidence points to him being just as devoted to her as she is to him. Just like Della, Jim gives up his most precious possession to find a perfect gift for the person he loves. And it's not just because of her looks, even though she worries about them.

It might be easy to notice that Jim is definitely the more levelheaded one in the relationship while Della is a little jumpy. When Della re-acts to his present with shrieks and wails, he just reacts to hers by rolling onto the couch and smiling.

3. Madame Sofronie. Madame Sofronie is the owner of a hair shop, who sells "hair goods of all kinds". She is "large," "white," and "chil-ly". Her manner is direct and to-the-point: she doesn't give off any signs of being impressed by Della's gorgeous hair, and casually offers to buy it for MYM20.

Madame Sofronie's attitude creates a sharp contrast to that of Della and Jim. For both of them, Della's hair is a prized possession-her on-ly prized possession-and Della's sale of it amounts to an enormous sacrifice. None of this matters to Madame Sofronie, for whom it's just another business transaction, which will perhaps fetch a bit more profit. To some extent, she represents "the cold, uncaring world" which exists outside the haven of love Della and Jim have built for themselves. She also represents a very different way of valuing things-purely for the money they fetch.

The Gift of the Magi[1]

One dollar and eighty-seven cents. That was all. And sixty cents of it was in pennies. Pennies saved one and two at a time by bulldozing the grocer and the vegetable man and the butcher until one's cheeks burned with the silent imputation of parsimony[2] that such close dealing implied. Three times Della counted it. One dollar and eighty-seven cents. And the next day would be Christmas.

There was clearly nothing left to do but flop down on the shabby little couch and howl. So Della did it. Which instigates the moral reflection that life is made up of sobs, sniffles, and smiles, with sniffles predominating[3].

While the mistress of the home is gradually subsiding from the first stage to the second, take a look at the home. A furnished flat at MYM8 per week. It did not exactly beggar description, but it certainly had that word on the look-out for the mendicancy squad.

In the vestibule below was a letter-box into which no letter would go, and an electric button from which no mortal finger could coax a ring. Also appertaining[4] thereunto was a card bearing the name "Mr. James Dillingham Young."

The "Dillingham" had been flung to the breeze during a former period of prosperity when its possessor was being paid MYM30 per week. Now, when the income was shrunk to MYM20, the letters of "Dillingham" looked blurred, as though they were thinking seriously of contracting to a modest and unassuming D. But whenever Mr. James Dillingham Young came home and reached his flat above he was called "Jim" and greatly hugged by Mrs. James Dillingham Young, already introduced to you as Della. Which is all very good.

Della finished her cry and attended to her cheeks with the powder rag. She stood by the window and looked out dully at a grey cat walking a grey fence in a grey backyard. To-morrow would be Christmas Day, and she had only MYM1. 87 with which to buy Jim a present. She had been saving every penny she could for months, with this result. Twenty dollars a week doesn't go far. Expenses had been greater than she had calculated. They always are. Only MYM1. 87 to buy a present for Jim. Her Jim. Many a happy hour she had spent planning for something nice for him. Something fine and rare and sterling—something just a little bit near to being worthy of the honour of being owned by Jim.

There was a pier-glass between the windows of the room. Perhaps you have seen a pier-glass in an MYM8 Bat. A very thin and very agile person may, by observing his reflection in a rapid sequence of longitudinal strips, obtain a fairly accurate conception of his looks. Della, being slender, had mastered the art.

Suddenly she whirled from the window and stood before the glass. Her eyes were shining brilliantly, but her face had lost its colour within twenty seconds. Rapidly she pulled down her hair and let it fall to its full length.

Now, there were two possessions of the James Dillingham Youngs in which they both took a mighty pride. One was Jim's gold watch that had been his father's and his grandfather's. The other was Della's hair. Had the Queen of Sheba[5] lived in the flat across the airshaft, Della would have let her hair hang out of the window some day to dry just to depreciate Her Majesty's jewels and gifts. Had King Solomon been the janitor, with all his treasures piled up in the basement, Jim would have pulled out his watch every time he passed, just to see him pluck at his beard from envy.

So now Della's beautiful hair fell about her, rippling and shining like a cascade of brown waters. It reached below her knee and made itself almost a garment for her. And then she did it up again nervously and quickly. Once she faltered for a minute and stood still while a tear or two splashed on the worn red carpet.

On went her old brown jacket; on went her old brown hat. With a whirl of skirts and with the brilliant sparkle still in her eyes, she cluttered out of the door and down the stairs to the street.

Where she stopped the sign read: "Mme Sofronie. Hair Goods of All Kinds." One Eight up Della ran, and collected herself, panting. Madame, large, too white, chilly, hardly looked the "Sofronie."

"Will you buy my hair?" asked Della.

"I buy hair," said Madame. "Take yer hat off and let's have a sight at the looks of it."

Down rippled the brown cascade.

"Twenty dollars," said Madame, lifting the mass with a practised hand.

"Give it to me quick" said Della.

Oh, and the next two hours tripped by on rosy wings. Forget the hashed metaphor. She was ransacking the stores for Jim's present.

She found it at last. It surely had been made for Jim and no one else. There was no other like it in any of the stores, and she had turned all of them inside out. It was a platinum fob chain simple and chaste in design, properly proclaiming its value by substance alone and not by meretricious[6] ornamentation[7]—as all good things should do. It was even worthy of The Watch. As soon as she saw it she knew that it must be Jim's. It was like him. Quietness and value—the description applied to both. Twenty-one dollars they took from her for it, and she hurried home with the 78 cents. With that chain on his watch Jim might be properly anxious about the time in any company. Grand as the watch was, he sometimes looked at it on the sly on account of the old leather strap that he used in place of a chain.

When Della reached home her intoxication[8] gave way a little to prudence[9] and reason. She got out her curling irons and lighted the gas and went to work repairing the ravages made by generosity added to love.

Which is always a tremendous task dear friends—a mammoth task.

Within forty minutes her head was covered with tiny, close-lying curls that made her look wonderfully like a truant schoolboy. She looked at her reflection in the mirror long, carefully, and critically.

"If Jim doesn't kill me," she said to herself, "before he takes a second look at me, he'll say I look like a Coney Island chorus girl. But what could I do—oh! what could I do with a dollar and eighty-seven cents?"

At 7 o'clock the coffee was made and the frying-pan was on the back of the stove hot and ready to cook the chops.

Jim was never late. Della doubled the fob chain in her hand and sat on the corner of the table near the door that he always entered. Then she heard his step on the stair away down on the first flight, and she turned white for just a moment. She had a habit of saying little silent prayers about the simplest everyday things, and now she whispered: "Please, God, make him think I am still pretty. "

The door opened and Jim stepped in and closed it. He looked thin and very serious. Poor fellow, he was only twenty-two—and to be burdened with a family! He needed a new overcoat and he was with out gloves.

Jim stepped inside the door, as immovable as a setter at the scent of quail. His eyes were fixed upon Della, and there was an expression in them that she could not read, and it terrified her. It was not anger, nor surprise, nor disapproval, nor horror, nor any of the sentiments that she had been prepared for. He simply stared at her fixedly with that peculiar expression on his face.

Della wriggled off the table and went for him.

"Jim, darling," she cried, "don't look at me that way. I had my hair cut off and sold it because I couldn't have lived through Christmas without giving you a present. It'll grow out again—you won't mind, will you? I just had to do it. My hair grows awfully fast. Say' Merry Christmas! ' Jim, and let's be happy. You don't know what a nice-what a beautiful, nice gift I've got for you. "

"You've cut off your hair?" asked Jim, laboriously[10], as if he had not arrived at that patent fact yet, even after the hardest mental labour.

"Cut it off and sold it," said Della. "Don't you like me just as well, anyhow? I'm me without my hair, ain't I?"

Jim looked about the room curiously.

"You say your hair is gone?" he said, with an air almost of idiocy.

"You needn't look for it," said Della. "It's sold, I tell you—sold and gone, too. It's Christmas Eve, boy. Be good to me, for it went for you. Maybe the hairs of my head were numbered," she went on with a sudden serious sweetness, "but nobody could ever count my love for you. Shall I put the chops on, Jim?"

Out of his trance Jim seemed quickly to wake. He enfolded his Della. For ten seconds let us regard with discreet scrutiny some inconsequential object in the other direction. Eight dollars a week or a million a year—what is the difference? A mathematician or a wit would give you the wrong answer. The magi brought valuable gifts, but that was not among them. I his dark assertion will be illuminated later on.

Jim drew a package from his overcoat pocket and threw it upon the table.

"Don't make any mistake, Dell," he said, "about me. I don't think there's anything in the way of a haircut or a shave or a shampoo that could make me like my girl any less. But if you'll unwrap that package you may see why you had me going a while at first."

White fingers and nimble tore at the string and paper. And then an ecstatic scream of joy; and then, alas! a quick feminine change to hysterical[11] tears and wails, necessitating the immediate employment of all the comforting powers of the lord of the flat.

For there lay The Combs—the set of combs, side and back, that Della had worshipped for long in a Broadway window. Beautiful combs, pure tortoise-shell, with jewelled rims—just the shade to wear in the beautiful vanished hair. They were expensive combs, she knew, and her heart had simply craved and yearned over them without the least hope of possession. And now, they were hers, but the tresses that should have adorned the coveted adornments were gone.

But she hugged them to her bosom, and at length she was able to look up with dim eyes and a smile and say: "My hair grows so fast, Jim!"

And then Della leaped up like a little singed cat and cried, "Oh, oh!"

Jim had not yet seen his beautiful present. She held it out to him eagerly upon her open palm. The dull precious metal seemed to flash with a reflection of her bright and ardent spirit.

"Isn't it a dandy, Jim? I hunted all over town to find it. You'll have to look at the time a hundred times a day now. Give me your watch. I want to see how it looks on it."

Instead of obeying, Jim tumbled down on the couch and put his hands under the back of his head and smiled.

"Dell," said he, "let's put our Christmas presents away and keep ' em a while. They're too nice to use just at present. I sold the watch to get the money to buy your combs. And now suppose you put the chops on."

The magi, as you know, were wise men—wonderfully wise men-who brought gifts to the Babe in the manger. They invented the art of giving Christmas presents. Being wise, their gifts were no doubt wise ones, possibly bearing the privilege of exchange in case of duplication. And here I have lamely related to you the uneventful chronicle of two foolish children in a flat who most unwisely sacrificed for each other the greatest treasures of their house. But in a last word to the wise of these days let it be said that of all who give gifts these two were the wisest. Of all who give and receive gifts, such as they are wisest. Everywhere they are wisest. They are the magi.

Notes:

1. Magi Magus 的复数形式 指圣婴基督出生时来自东方送礼的三贤人，载于圣经马太福音第二章第一节和第七至第十三节

2. parsimony *n.* 过分吝啬，过度节俭

   E. g. They offer every inducement to foreign businesses to invest in their states. javascript:;

   Over the years, even as he drove his wife nuts with his parsimony, he harbored a deep secret.

3. predominate *v.* 支配，占主导地位

   E. g. All colors are lost in the predominating grey. javascript:;

   In aspect of the relation of the government and market, adopt the principle of government predominating based on the market mechanism. javascript:;

4. appertain *v.* 属于

   E. g. Have put forward the rational supplying mode of the appertaining parking.

   The responsibilities that appertain to parenthood were discussed at the meeting.

5. Queen of Sheba 示巴女王，基督教《圣经》中朝觐所罗门王，以测其智慧的示巴女王，她以美貌著称

6. meretricious *a.* 俗气的，华丽而庸俗的，华而不实的

   E. g. Google-generated kadosh is meretricious, offering a desiccated kind of choice. javascript:;

   Most of the other issues swirling in the lawyer-soldier tornado are either trivial or meretricious.

7. ornamentation *n.* 装饰物

   E. g. The chairs were comfortable, functional, and free of ornamentation. javascript:;

   The architects who designed facade ornamentation often relied on popular handbooks for traditional styles, like the classical or Gothic.

8. intoxication *n.* 陶醉, 喝醉, 中毒

   E. g. Caffeine intoxication can occur if more than 400 milli-grams of caffeine is ingested in a short period.

   The liberation that accompanied the end of the Cold War often produced a dangerous intoxication.

9. prudence *n.* 谨慎, 审慎

   E. g. Western businessmen are showing remarkable prudence in investing in the region.

   It's an understandable reaction but we need to balance it with prudence in dealing with the economy.

10. laboriously *adv.* 辛苦地; 费力地; 不流畅地

    E. g. The oldman traced his name laboriously. javascript: ;

    Slowly and laboriously, she let us know that she was thirsty and they would not allow her to drink anything.

11. hysterical *adj.* 歇斯底里的; 异常兴奋的

    E. g. All he can to calm myself down, he seems some hysteri-cal, he wants to tell the person of whole world, I finally have the news magazine sent him manuscripts culverts. javascript: ;

    So he publicly opposed the hysterical warnings from financial eminences, similar to those we hear today.

Questions:

1. What is the setting of the story?
2. What genre does The Gift of the Magi belongs to?
3. How do you describe O Henry's style?
4. Which point of view does O Henry adopt in this story?
5. What do you think of the ending?

Plot Analysis

The story's opening sentences confront us right away with situation: Della only has MYM1. 87 to buy a Christmas present, and it's Christmas Eve. Later, the narrator gives us a bit more fleshing out of the situation.

Della's in a meager flat, she and her husband Jim are poor, she loves her husband more than anything else in the whole world. Plus, she positively needs to buy him the perfect Christmas present. With MYM1. 87. When Della lets down her hair, we also learn the other most important fact for the story: her hair and Jim's gold watch are the only prized possessions the couple has. Everything is now set up for the rest of the story to unfold.

The conflict is supposedly the moment where the "problem" in the story appears, but in "Gift of the Magi" the point of conflict actually solves the first problem and replaces it with a second. By selling her hair, Della gets the money to buy Jim a great present, eliminating the first problem through decisive action. Shortly thereafter she finds the perfect present, so neither the money nor the present is the issue any longer. But now there's a new problem: will Jim be pleased by Della's action and appreciate her gift, or will he be angry with her for parting with the hair he loved so much?

The complication happens when Jim arrives, he doesn't seem to react well: he stares at Della and can't seem to process that her hair is gone. But it doesn't look like he's angry, so much as simply shocked. Della can't quite understand what kind of reaction he's having, nor can we. This creates suspense; we want to know what it is he's actually feeling. We also want to know how he'll react to Della's gift. When Jim snaps out of his shock, he tells Della (and us) that his reaction will make sense when Della opens the present he bought her.

Then the climax comes. When Della opens Jim's present to find the combs, we understand why Jim was so shocked. It also becomes clear now that he's not angry with Della, and he assures her he'll love her no matter how she looks. Although the climax doesn't fully "predict" the ending, it is the first half of the twist. And if we do get to thinking about where Jim got the money to buy those combs, we might be able to guess what happens next.

Now the narrator gives all of the readers this suspense: We're still waiting to know how Jim will react to Della's gift, and we might also be wondering just how he got the money to buy those expensive combs. Della gives Jim the watch chain, and... a lot of questions attract the readers.

The twist ending appears: Presented with his gift, Jim calmly reveals (with a smile) that he sold his watch to buy Della her combs. So her present is useless too. Well, that does it for the Christmas presents.

In the narrator's conclusion, which is definitely an epitome of epic proportions, the narrator tells us that it doesn't really matter that Jim and Della's presents turned out to be useless. They are the wisest givers of all-in fact, they're the magi. We leave feeling satisfied and happy.

中文译文:

麦琪的礼物

一元八角七。全都在这儿了,其中六角是一分一分的铜板。这些分分钱是在杂货店老板、菜贩子和肉店老板那儿软硬兼施地一分两分地扣下来,直弄得自己羞愧难当,深感这种掂斤播两的交易实在丢人现眼。德拉反复数了三次,还是一元八角七,而第二天就是圣诞节了。

除了扑倒在那破旧的小睡椅上哭嚎之外,显然别无他途。德拉这样做了,可精神上的感慨油然而生,生活就是哭泣、抽噎和微笑,尤以抽噎占统治地位。

当这位家庭主妇逐渐平静下来之际,让我们看看这个家吧。一套带家具的公寓房子,每周房租八美元。尽管难以用笔墨形容,可它真真够得上乞丐帮这个词儿。

楼下的门道里有个信箱,可从来没有装过信,还有一个电钮,也从没有人的手指按响过电铃。而且,那儿还有一张名片,上写着"詹姆斯·迪林厄姆·杨先生"。

"迪林厄姆"这个名号是主人先前春风得意之际,一时兴起加上去的,那时候他每星期挣三十美元。现在,他的收入缩减到二十美元,"迪林厄姆"的字母也显得模糊不清,似乎它们正严肃地思忖着是否缩写成谦逊而又讲求实际的字母D。不过,每当詹姆斯·

迪林厄姆·杨回家，走进楼上的房间时，詹姆斯·迪林厄姆·杨太太，就是刚介绍给诸位的德拉，总是把他称作"吉姆"，而且热烈地拥抱他。这当然是再好不过的了。

德拉哭完之后，往面颊上抹了抹粉，她站在窗前，痴痴地瞅着灰蒙蒙的后院里一只灰白色的猫正行走在灰白色的篱笆上。明天就是圣诞节，她只有一元八角七分给吉姆买一份礼物。她花去好几个月的时间，用了最大的努力一分一分地攒积下来，才得了这样一个结果。一周二十美元实在经不起花，支出大于预算，总是如此。只有一元八角七分给吉姆买礼物，她的吉姆啊。她花费了多少幸福的时日筹划着要送他一件可心的礼物，一件精致、珍奇、贵重的礼物——至少应有点儿配得上吉姆所有的东西才成啊。

房间的两扇窗子之间有一面壁镜。也许你见过每周房租八美元的公寓壁镜吧。一个非常瘦小而灵巧的人，从观察自己在一连串的纵条影像中，可能会对自己的容貌得到一个大致精确的概念。德拉身材苗条，已精通了这门子艺术。

突然，她从窗口旋风般地转过身来，站在壁镜前面。她两眼晶莹透亮，但二十秒钟之内她的面色失去了光彩。她急速地拆散头发，使之完全泼洒开来。

现在，詹姆斯·迪林厄姆·杨夫妇俩各有一件特别引以为豪的东西。一件是吉姆的金表，是他祖父传给父亲，父亲又传给他的传家宝；另一件则是德拉的秀发。如果示巴女王也住在天井对面的公寓里，总有一天德拉会把头发披散下来，露出窗外晾干，使那女王的珍珠宝贝黯然失色；如果地下室堆满金银财宝、所罗门王又是守门人的话，每当吉姆路过那儿，准会摸出金表，好让那所罗门王忌妒得吹胡子瞪眼睛。

此时此刻，德拉的秀发泼洒在她的周围，微波起伏，闪耀光芒，有如那褐色的瀑布。她的美发长及膝下，仿佛是她的一件长袍。接着，她又神经质地赶紧把头发梳好。踌躇了一分钟，一动不动地立在那儿，破旧的红地毯上溅落了一两滴眼泪。

她穿上那件褐色的旧外衣，戴上褐色的旧帽子，眼睛里残留着晶莹的泪花，裙子一摆，便飘出房门，下楼来到街上。

她走到一块招牌前停下来，上写着"索弗罗妮夫人——专营各式头发"。德拉奔上楼梯，气喘吁吁地定了定神。那位夫人身躯肥大，过于苍白，冷若冰霜，同"索弗罗妮"的雅号简直牛头不对马嘴。

"你要买我的头发吗?"德拉问。

"我买头发，"夫人说。"揭掉帽子，让我看看头发什么样。"

那褐色的瀑布泼散了下来。

"二十美元，"夫人一边说，一边内行似地抓起头发。

"快给我钱，"德拉说。

呵，接踵而至的两个小时犹如长了翅膀，愉快地飞掠而过。请不用理会这胡诌的比喻。她正在彻底搜寻各家店铺，为吉姆买礼物。

她终于找到了，那准是专为吉姆特制的，决非为别人。她找遍了各家商店，哪儿也没有这样的东西，一条朴素的白金表链，镂刻着花纹。正如一切优质东西那样，它只以货色论长短，不以装潢来炫耀。而且它正配得上那只金表。她一见这条表链，就知道一定属于吉姆所有。它就像吉姆本人，文静而有价值——这一形容对两者都恰如其分。她花去二十一美元买下了，匆匆赶回家，只剩下八角七分钱。金表匹配这条链子，无论在任何场合，吉姆都可以毫无愧色地看时间了。尽管这只表华丽珍贵，因为用的是旧皮带取代表链，他有时只偷偷地瞥上一眼。

德拉回家之后，她的狂喜有点儿变得审慎和理智了。她找出烫发铁钳，点燃煤气，着手修补因爱情加慷慨造成的破坏，这永远是件极其艰巨的任务——简直是件了不起的任务，亲爱的朋友们。

不出四十分钟，她的头上布满了紧贴头皮的一绺绺小卷发，使她活像个逃学的小男孩。她在镜子里老盯着自己瞧，小心地、苛刻地照来照去。

"假如吉姆看我一眼不把我宰掉的话，"她自言自语，"他定会说我像个科尼岛上合唱队的卖唱姑娘。但是我能怎么办呢——唉，只有一元八角七，我能干什么呢?"

七点钟，她煮好了咖啡，把煎锅置于热炉上，随时都可做肉排。

吉姆一贯准时回家。德拉将表链对叠握在手心，坐在离他一贯进门最近的桌子角上。接着，她听见下面楼梯上响起了他的脚步声，她紧张得脸色失去了一会儿血色。她习惯于为了最简单的日常事务而默默祈祷，此刻，她悄声道："求求上帝，让他觉得我还是漂亮的吧。"

门开了，吉姆步入，随手关上了门。他显得瘦削而又非常严肃。可怜的人儿，他才二十二岁，就挑起了家庭重担！他需要买件新大衣，连手套也没有呀。

吉姆站在屋里的门口边，纹丝不动地好像猎犬嗅到了鹌鹑的气味似的。他的两眼固定在德拉身上，其神情使她无法理解，令她毛骨悚然。既不是愤怒，也不是惊讶，又不是不满，更不是嫌恶，根本不是她预料的任何一种神情。他仅仅是面带这种神情死死地盯着德拉。

德拉一扭腰，从桌上跳了下来，向他走过去。

"吉姆，亲爱的，"她喊道，"别那样盯着我。我把头发剪掉卖了，因为不送你一件礼物，我无法过圣诞节。头发会再长起来——你不会介意，是吗？我非这么做不可。我的头发长得快极了。说'恭贺圣诞'吧！吉姆，让我们快快乐乐的。你肯定猜不着我给你买了一件多么好多么美丽精致的礼物啊！"

"你已经把头发剪掉了？"吉姆吃力地问道，似乎他绞尽脑汁也没弄明白这明摆着的事实。

"剪掉卖了，"德拉说。"不管怎么说，你不也同样喜欢我吗？没了长发，我还是我嘛，对吗？"

吉姆古怪地四下望望这房间。

"你说你的头发没有了吗？"他差不多是白痴似地问道。

"别找啦，"德拉说。"告诉你，我已经卖了——卖掉了，没有啦。这是圣诞前夜，好人儿。好好待我，这是为了你呀。也许我的头发数得清，"突然她特别温柔地接下去，"可谁也数不清我对你的恩爱啊。我可以做肉排了吗，吉姆？"

吉姆好像从恍惚之中醒来，把德拉紧紧地搂在怀里。现在，别着急，先让我们花个十秒钟从另一个角度审慎地思索一下某些无关紧要的事。房租每周八美元，或者一百万美元——那有什么差别呢？数学家或才子会给你错误的答案。麦琪带来了宝贵的礼物，但就是缺少了那件东西。这句晦涩的话，下文将有所交代。

吉姆从大衣口袋里掏出一个小包，扔在桌上。

"别对我产生误会，德尔，"他说道，"无论剪发、修面还是洗头，我以为世上没有什么东西能减低一点点我对我妻子的爱情。不过，你只消打开那包东西，就会明白刚才为什么使我楞头楞脑了。"

白皙的手指灵巧地解开绳子，打开纸包。紧接着是欣喜若狂的尖叫，哎呀！突然变成了女性神经质的泪水和哭泣，急需男主人千方百计地慰藉。

因为摆在桌上的梳子——全套梳子，包括两鬓用的，后面的，样样俱全。那是很久以前德拉在百老汇的一个橱窗里见过并羡慕得要死的东西。这些美妙的发梳，纯玳瑁做的，边上镶着珠宝——其色彩正好同她失去的美发相匹配。她明白，这套梳子实在太昂贵，对此，她仅仅是羡慕渴望，但从未想到过据为己有。现在，这一切居然属于她了，可惜那有资格佩戴这垂涎已久的装饰品的美丽长发已无影无踪了。

不过，她依然把发梳搂在胸前，过了好一阵子才抬起泪水迷蒙的双眼，微笑着说："我的头发长得飞快，吉姆！"

随后，德拉活像一只被烫伤的小猫跳了起来，叫道，"喔！喔！"

吉姆还没有瞧见他的美丽的礼物哩。她急不可耐地把手掌摊开，伸到他面前，那没有知觉的贵重金属似乎闪现着她的欢快和热忱。

"漂亮吗，吉姆？我搜遍了全城才找到了它。现在，你每天可以看一百次时间了。把表给我，我要看看它配在表上的样子。"

吉姆非但不按她的吩咐行事，反而倒在睡椅上，两手枕在头下，微微发笑。

"德尔，"他说，"让我们把圣诞礼物放在一边，保存一会儿吧。它们实在太好了，目前尚不宜用。我卖掉金表，换钱为你买了发梳。现在，你去做肉排吧。"

正如诸位所知，麦琪是聪明人，聪明绝顶的人，他们把礼物带来送给出生在马槽里的耶稣。他们发明送圣诞礼物这玩意儿。由于他们是聪明人，毫无疑问，他们的礼物也是聪明的礼物，如果碰上两样东西完全一样，可能还具有交换的权利。在这儿，我已经笨拙地给你们介绍了住公寓套间的两个傻孩子不足为奇的平淡故事，他们极不明智地为了对方而牺牲了他们家最最宝贵的东西。不过，让我们对现今的聪明人说最后一句话，在一切馈赠礼品的人当中，那两个人是最聪明的。在一切馈赠又接收礼品的人当中，像他们两个这样的人也是最聪明的。无论在任何地方，他们都是最聪明的人。他们就是麦琪。

Answers for questions

1. The narrator draws our attention almost immediately to the two most important details of the story's setting: it takes place on a Christmas Eve, and its two main characters live in a very unassuming flat. O. Henry sketches the flat with just enough detail to convey an image of its squalor: it's cheap, sparsely furnished, and has a broken mailbox and a broken doorbell. The drabness of the physical setting in which Jim and Della live creates a contrast with the warmth and richness of their love for each other. The fact that everything outside the flat is "grey"-Della watches a "gray cat walking a gray fence in a gray backyard"-develops the contrast even further. Inside, we get the sense, Jim and Della's affection creates a welcoming love nest, in spite of the flat's humble nature. Outside, it's a cold, gray world, and one that is about as uncaring as Madame Sofronie.

2. The Gift of the Magi belongs to a parable. The key feature of a parable is that it uses a situation, which feels very simple to make a more complex or general point, often a moral one. (Also, unlike a fable, a parable does this with people, not animals.) This classification defines "The Gift of the Magi," which is a remarkably simple story. It boils down to a few bare essentials: Della and Jim are poor, but love each other very much; they each want to buy the perfect Christmas gift for each other; they each have one prized possession which they give up to buy the other a present, and the presents they buy are meant for the

prized possessions they've sacrificed. You don't need to know almost anything else about the story to "get it," and there's very little in the story itself that doesn't serve to develop one of those elements. That there is actually something specific to get is the other reason "The Gift of the Magi" is a parable: it has a point, and it is a moral one. This story is about what it means to give a gift. All of the elements of the story serve to bring that point across. The slightly "preachy" tone of the story is part of the parable. That last paragraph especially, which is just a slightly more stylish version of the "moral" that predictably comes at the end of an Aesop fable.

　　3. The story is narrated as if someone were telling it to you aloud. O Henry achieve this effect through his breaking basic grammar rules. There are lots of sentences that aren't really sentences, like the first one: "One dollar and eighty-seven cents". There's no verb or action in that sentence; it just states a sum of money. We need more information about what that sum of money "means" or "does" in order to understand the sentence. We get that information in the next sentence: "That was all". Although the second sentence at least has a verb, it's also technically not a complete sentence: the subject "that," is unspecified, and only makes sense given the previous sentence. Likewise, the narrator is fond of starting sentences with words that grammar sticklers would say you're not supposed to start with, like "And" or "Which. " This also has the effect of making one sentence hinge on the sentence before. Looking at those first two sentences clues us in on how the story's style tends to operate as a whole: lots of short sentences that often depend on other sentences in order to work. This technique has a way of weaving together the story across individual sentences and gives it a flow that would be broken apart by writing in more complete, self-contained sentences. It's typical of the ways we tell stories when we speak. This style keeps listeners hanging on from one sentence to the next. It also prevents them from getting lost in overly long sentences. Since when you're listening to a story you can't go back and read a sentence again, it's im-

portant that you don't get lost. If you get caught on a particular sentence it might make you lose the thread of the whole story. Of course, as O. Henry is trying to capture that feel of telling a story orally, he also throws in plenty of addresses to his audience of listeners, as in, "Which is always a tremendous task, dear friends-a mammoth task". This further creates the feeling that he is talking directly to us.

4. Technically, the story seems to be third person limited omniscient. It's told in the third-person, and only follows Della. We don't see what Jim is doing during the story, and once he does show up, he remains closed to us: we don't know what his reaction to Della's hair is any more than Della does. We can't be entirely satisfied with this classification, though, because the narrator has such an independent personality and seems to know a lot more than Della does at times. He's "The Storyteller." It's as if he sees everything, but usually limits himself to Della's point of view by choice for storytelling purposes. If the narrator described everything that were going on, he'd ruin the surprise ending. We know the narrator is really more like an omniscient being, though, because every so often he "zooms out" to make much more general pronouncements that fly way above the action of the story's characters. The most obvious of these is at the end, when he mentions "the magi" (to which Della and Jim are totally oblivious). But there are other places too, like when he zooms out from the weeping Della to describe the flat. There are also all those moments when he makes a more universal remark about "the way life is," such as, "Life is made up of sobs, sniffles, and smiles, with sniffles predominating".

5. O. Henry is famous for his "twist endings," and the ending of "The Gift of the Magi" is probably the most famous of them all. At the end of the story Della cuts and sells her hair to buy Jim a chain for his watch, and Jim sells his watch to buy Della combs for her hair. Here we have a classic case of irony. The determination to find the perfect gift leads each character to make a sacrifice; that sacrifice makes each gift useless. The result is the exact opposite of what Jim and Della intended.

What makes this ending so bittersweet is that it only comes about because they acted on their intentions: their gifts wouldn't have been useless if they hadn't given up their prize possessions. And since we follow only Della in the story, we don't know what has happened until the very end, during the exchange itself. It's the sudden, unexpected irony, which only strikes at the very end that makes the ending a twist.

References

［1］ http://americanliterature. com/author/o − henry/bio − books − stories（图片来源）

［2］ http://www. online − literature. com/o_henry/

［3］ http://www. en8848. com. cn/soft/

［4］ http://en. wikipedia. org/wiki/O. _Henry

［5］ http://www. shmoop. com/